"ENCHANTING."—*People*

"Weaves a spell that will enchant you."
—Meg Cabot, #1 *New York Times* bestselling author of the Princess Diaries series and the Heather Wells mystery series

"Magical...imaginative, evocative, full of surprises."
—M. J. Rose, international bestselling author of *Seduction*

"Like no version of the Sleeping Beauty story that you've read before."—Alma Katsu, author of the Taker trilogy

"Unexpected and heartrending . . . [A] beautiful, original reinterpretation of a classic story."
—*Library Journal* (starred review)

"[An] engrossing historical fantasy...Elise is an appealing narrator, and Blackwell's narrative style invites the reader to sink into the story... a clever twist at the end."
—*The Historical Novel Review*

"Fans of novels like *Wicked* and lovers of fairy tales will no doubt find something new to love in *While Beauty Slept*, as will anyone who enjoys a layered drama rich with juicy palace intrigue."
—*BookPage*

PRAISE FOR

While Beauty Slept

"Old-fashioned storytelling and historical fiction create a charming alchemy in this clever reimagining of *Sleeping Beauty*."
—People

"Elizabeth Blackwell's writing is magical in this complex, dark, and sensual retelling of *Sleeping Beauty*. Imaginative, evocative, full of surprises, this is a captivating debut. And like all great fairy tales, this one has the kind of happy ending that requires tissues to wipe away the tears." —M. J. Rose, international bestselling author of *Seduction*

"Intelligent escapism that should please Brothers Grimm lovers."
—*Kirkus Reviews*

"A gripping tale full of romance, secrets, and promises made and broken. This beautiful, original reinterpretation of a classic story is engrossing and often surprising." —*Library Journal*

"Not your *grand-mère*'s *Sleeping Beauty*. Do you love fairy tales? Elizabeth Blackwell's enchanting *While Beauty Slept* is like no version of the Sleeping Beauty story that you've read before. Told from the perspective of Elise, a peasant girl who sets out to make her fortune while hiding a secret past, *While Beauty Slept* is a rich and immensely satisfying reimagining of the classic fairy tale, one that looks at the ageless struggle between love and duty, and asks whether it's possible to be true to both." —Alma Katsu, author of *The Taker* trilogy

"Blackwell is faithful to the original while offering a fresh interpretation. . . . [T]he twists that resolve the women's stories are both convincing and moving." —*Publishers Weekly*

"Blackwell treats readers to a retelling that makes historical fiction of the fantasy. . . . Following in the inspired footsteps of Gregory Maguire's fairy-tale twists, this debut novel puts a spellbinding new spin on a classic yarn."

—*Booklist*

While Beauty Slept

Elizabeth Blackwell

BERKLEY BOOKS
New York

THE BERKLEY PUBLISHING GROUP
Published by the Penguin Group
Penguin Group (USA) LLC
375 Hudson Street, New York, New York 10014

USA • Canada • UK • Ireland • Australia • New Zealand • India • South Africa • China

penguin.com

A Penguin Random House Company

Berkley trade paperback ISBN: 978-0-425-27384-5

The Library of Congress has cataloged the Amy Einhorn Books / G. P. Putnam's Sons hardcover edition as follows:

Blackwell, Elizabeth Canning.
While beauty slept / Elizabeth Blackwell.
p. cm.
ISBN 978-0-399-16623-5
1. Women—Fiction. I. Sleeping Beauty. English. II. Title.
PS3602.L32575W48 2014 2013030337
813'.6—dc23

PUBLISHING HISTORY
Amy Einhorn Books / G. P. Putnam's Sons hardcover edition / February 2014
Berkley trade paperback edition / November 2014

PRINTED IN THE UNITED STATES OF AMERICA

10 9 8 7 6 5 4 3 2 1

Cover photograph © Maurizio Blasetti / Trevillion Images.
Cover design by Lisa Amoroso.

For Mom, Dad, and Rachel,

my first readers

PROLOGUE

She has already become a legend. The beautiful, headstrong girl I knew is gone forever, her life transformed into myth. The princess who pricked her finger on a spinning wheel and fell asleep for a hundred years, only to be awakened by true love's kiss.

I heard the tale last night, as I shuffled past the children's room on my way to bed. My hearing's not what it was, but Raimy's voice carried clearly enough through the door. No doubt she was prancing about as she recounted it, for I heard the telltale creaks of the floorboards. My great-granddaughter is rarely content to recount a story; she must enact it, as if her whole body has a part in the telling.

I heard her cackle as she embodied the witch who cast the spell, then gasp as the princess touched the fatal needle. Most of it was nonsense, of course, yet I remained rooted in the hallway, despite the dull ache in my knees and ankles. Raimy's brother and sister must have been equally enthralled, for they made no sound as the story continued.

"On the first day of the hundredth year, a prince came to the land, a prince more handsome and brave than any before him," I heard Raimy say. "He could not rest till he had seen the sleeping princess of legend. As he rode up toward the wall of thorny trees, the branches parted. He rode through and saw the castle before him, its stone and marble gleaming in the sunlight.

"He entered the grand hall and was confronted with a miraculous sight: the whole court, lying in a sleep that looked like death. He raced through the castle until he came to the highest tower. There, on a bed in the center of the room, lay Sleeping Beauty, her golden hair spread on the pillow, her cheeks still flushed pink. He could not resist. He bent his head and kissed her.

"The spell was broken. Sleeping Beauty awakened, and around her the castle came to life once again. The king and queen wept with joy to be reunited with their daughter, and happiness was restored to the realm. The prince married the princess, and they lived happily ever after."

Ha! It would be a fine trick indeed to fell a royal daughter with a needle, then see her revived by a single kiss. If such magic exists, I have yet to witness it. The horror of what really happened has been lost, and no wonder. The truth is hardly a story for children.

The next day I asked Raimy where she had heard the tale.

"A minstrel sang it, at the fair." Her eyes gleamed at the memory, and I could picture her in the village square, pushing herself to the front of the crowd. "Can you imagine the princess all alone in her tower, waiting for her true love? It gives me a chill to think of it."

It chilled me as well, though Raimy could never guess the reason. Does anyone believe that a woman can survive a sleeping death and emerge unscathed? How we tried to heal her, those who loved her most. But some damage is too deep to reach.

"Better to fill your mind with Bible verses than such nonsense," her father grumbled.

I have never liked him. Raimy's mother, my granddaughter Thelyn, treats me kindly and carefully, as one would a decrepit family pet not long for this world, but her husband complains of how much I eat—as if my withered body should be denied food!—and calls me an old crone when he thinks I'm out of earshot.

Raimy pouted at him. "It's only a story," she said.

Approaching fourteen, already beautiful, she chafes at her life on this farm. Looking at her then, I was struck with a vision of Rose at the same age: lips curved in a mischievous smile, the flicker of her long eyelashes. I felt a pang of adoration, for both Raimy and the princess I had once known. Though I often struggle to match names to my other great-grandchildren, Raimy has always been my favorite. Self-assured and intensely curious, she seems more fully alive than those around her.

She is also perceptive enough to notice when her prattling provokes an unexpected reaction. Over the following days, she returned often to her story of the sleeping princess, glancing my way expectantly as I attempted to maintain an expression of blank disinterest. One evening, irritated when she failed to reappear with a cap I had asked her to fetch, I hobbled to the bedroom that Thelyn and her husband had given over to me—another cause, no doubt, of the man's continual grumbling at my presence. As I walked in, I saw that the small trunk holding my possessions had been flung open, my clothes tossed haphazardly over the sides. Raimy, kneeling before it, jolted her head upward, her gasp matching my own as I saw what she clutched in her hand.

Even in that dimly lit space, the emeralds and rubies embedded in the dagger's handle sparkled. The sharp, cruel blade retained its silvery luster, and I felt a wave of revulsion as I remembered that same surface coated in blood. Could minuscule drops still cling to those jewels, within reach of Raimy's tender skin?

Any other child caught trespassing among an adult's private possessions would have made a show of embarrassment or contrition. Not Raimy.

"What is this?" she asked, her voice awed. Such an object, so costly and so deadly, had no place among the things of a simple tradesman's widow.

I could have put Raimy off with a falsehood and shooed her away. But I looked at my beloved great-granddaughter and found I could not lie. In the fifty years since those terrible days in the tower, I have never spoken of what happened there. But with my body failing and death in my sights, I have been plagued by memories, rushing in unbidden, provoking waves of longing for what once was. Perhaps that is why I remain on this earth, the only person who knew Rose when she was young and untouched by tragedy. The only one who watched it all unfold, from the curse to the final kiss.

Gently, I took the dagger from Raimy's hand and slid it back into the leather pouch where it had been concealed. I looked at the jumble of objects she had pulled from the bottom of my trunk: a braided leather bracelet that was more precious to me than any diamond-encrusted ornament, intricate lace trim salvaged from dresses that had long since disintegrated, a verse written in elegant script on a cracking piece of parchment. A golden three-tiered necklace adorned with miniature flowers that Raimy gazed at in covetous wonder while my heart grieved anew for the woman who had once worn it. Remnants of a life, meaningless to anyone but myself.

Easing myself slowly onto the bed, I gestured to Raimy to join me. The household was settling down to sleep; we would not be missed if we kept to ourselves for a few hours.

And so I began. "I will tell you a tale. . . ."

Part I

Once upon a Time

One

A DESTINY REVEALED

I am not the sort of person about whom stories are told. Those of humble birth suffer their heartbreaks and celebrate their triumphs unnoticed by the bards, leaving no trace in the fables of their time. Raised on a meager farm with five brothers, I knew that the expected course of my life was to be married off at sixteen, to work a similarly poor piece of property with my own brood of underfed children. It was a path I would have followed without question, had it not been for my mother.

I must start my tale with her, for all the events that followed, all the wonders and horrors I have witnessed in my many years upon this earth, began with a seed she planted in my soul almost from birth: a deep-rooted, unshakable certainty that I was meant to be more than a peasant's wife. Every time Mother corrected my grammar or admonished me to stand up straight, it was with an eye to my future, a reminder that despite my ragtag clothes I must comport myself with the manners of my betters. For she herself was proof that great changes in fortune were possible: Born into a poor servant family and orphaned at a young age, she had risen to a position as seamstress at the castle of St. Elsip, seat of the king who ruled our lands.

The castle! How I used to dream of it, envisioning an edifice of soaring turrets and polished marble that bore little resemblance to the hulking fortress I would later know so well. My girlish fascination extended into imagined conversations with elegant ladies and gallant knights, fantasies my mother did her best to suppress, for she knew all too well the dangers that came from putting on airs above one's station. My mother rarely spoke of her youth, but I hoarded the few stories she told me like a ragman collecting scraps, wondering why she had given up her position as a cosseted royal servant for a life of crushing drudgery. Once her slim fingers had caressed silk threads and rich velvets; now her hands were chapped and reddened from years of scrubbing, her face set most often in an expression of weary resignation. The only times I remember her smiling were during the private moments we stole together, in between the baby feedings and the planting and the harvesting, those precious hours when she taught me to read and write. Most of my practice was done in the dirt at the side of the house, using a stick to form the lines and swirls of the words. If I spotted my father approaching, I would hastily rub out the scribbles with my feet and scramble to find a chore to occupy myself. To him an idle child was a wicked one, and a daughter had no cause to learn her letters.

Mert Dalriss was known in our parts as a hard man, and the description was apt. His eyes were the cold gray-blue of stone, and his hands had been gnarled and roughened by a lifetime of physical labor; when he slapped me, it felt like a blow from a shovel. His voice was gruff and harsh, and he used his words sparingly, as if uttering each one caused great physical effort. Though I felt no affection for my father, I did not hate him either; he was simply an unpleasant feature of my existence, much like the mud that clung to my feet each spring or the hungry ache that filled my stomach instead of food. I took his harshness as nothing more than the usual resentment of a poor man toward a daughter who will cost him a dowry.

It was not until I was ten years old that I learned the true reason he had never loved me and never would.

It was a Saturday morning, and I had accompanied my mother to the weekly market at our local village, a gathering of some dozen houses a half hour's walk from our ramshackle one-room cottage. Farmers and townspeople would meet to haggle over a meager range of scraps: a few turnips or onions, small sacks of salt or sugar, perhaps a pig or a lamb. Rarely did coins change hands; more often meat or eggs were exchanged for pieces of cloth or barrels of ale. The luckiest sellers claimed a spot in front of the church, where they could stand on the clean, dry flagstones; the rest simply stopped their carts in the middle of the muddy road that passed through town. A few of the more prosperous farmers would tap into their ale barrels and remain there most of the morning, laughing and slapping one another's backs as their faces grew redder. My father was never among these men, drunkenness being one of the many weaknesses he despised in others.

The market was a place to exchange gossip as much as goods, for which reason most women lingered longer than it took them to stock up on supplies. My mother never paused after her business was conducted; it seemed she had taken my father's disparagement of the villagers' idleness to heart. I would move slowly from cart to cart, hoping to drag out the visit, but she passed me by with brisk efficiency, nodding at neighbors but rarely stopping to talk. Usually I hurried to follow her, ignored. Until one day when I froze in front of the baker's cart. The smell of fresh rolls was so tempting; I thought I could satisfy my cramping stomach by drinking in the aroma. Perhaps, if I smelled it long enough, I might fool my appetite into thinking it had been sated.

I turned around to find my mother gone. Not wishing to be left behind, I pushed my way through the huddle of people gathered before the baker's wares, stepping on a boy's foot in the process. No one there was a stranger, for we all worshipped at the same church, but I could not remember his name, only that his family worked a farm substantially larger than ours on the other side of the village, where the land was more fertile. He had the ruddy, round cheeks of someone well fed.

"Watch it!" he scolded, then rolled his eyes toward a friend standing at his side.

Intent on finding my mother, I paid him no mind. And that would have been the end of it, had the boy not said one thing more.

"Bastard."

I do not think he intended me to hear. The word was whispered rather than shouted, but it had slipped from his mouth like a dangerous, powerful incantation. When I found my mother a few moments later, searching for me from the church steps, I asked her what it meant.

She caught her breath, then glanced around to make certain I had not been overheard. "That's a nasty word, and I won't have you utter it again!" she whispered vehemently.

"A boy said it to me," I protested. "Why did he call me that?"

Mother pursed her lips. She pulled me by the wrist with one hand, clutching her basket under her other arm. We walked away from the church, along the road leading back to the farm, without saying anything for some time. When we could no longer see the village behind a hill in the distance, she turned to me.

"That word," she said. "It is used for children who are born out of wedlock."

"Are you not wed, Mother?" I asked.

She sighed. I can still remember the look of defeat that settled over her, and my own apprehension at seeing my strong, determined mother reduced almost to tears.

"I had hoped you would never know," she said quietly, looking away, over the fields. Then, collecting herself, she continued in her usual brisk, no-nonsense tone. "If my life remains village gossip after all this time, I suppose it's best you hear the truth. I gave birth to you before I met Mr. Dalriss."

I knew enough by then to understand how a man and woman beget a child; farm girls who see animals rutting in the fields do not stay innocent for long. Shock mixed with exhilaration as I realized that my mother had lain with someone other than the man I called Father. Who? And why had he not claimed me? My mind reeled, each question leading to another as I tried to piece together what little I knew of my mother's youth in the light of this revelation.

"Is that why you left the castle?" I asked. "Because of me?"

"Yes." There was no bitterness in her voice, no reproach. Simply a weary acceptance.

She turned away and started back on the road, as if nothing had changed. Yet, for me, everything had. It was that moment, I realize now, that started me on the fateful path toward the castle, toward the king and queen and Rose, toward Millicent's dark powers. I could have accepted my mother's wish to wall off her past and followed her home in silence. I could have made what would have been considered a good marriage, to a prosperous farmer's son or a village shopkeeper, and lived out the rest of my life within a few miles of the place where I had been raised.

Instead I galloped to my mother's side, eager to extend the brief glimpse she had granted into her life before the farm.

"Did you not wish to raise me there?" I asked.

Mother did not slow her pace, but she glanced at me, mouth tightened disapprovingly. I braced myself for a telling-off, but instead she answered my question with unexpected directness.

"It was not my choice," she said. "The castle was the most wondrous place I have ever seen. I would have stayed forever if I could. But the man who fathered you would not make an honest woman of me, and I was turned out in disgrace. I was deceived, as many foolish women are, and I paid a heavy price."

I did not completely understand; the nature of relations between men and women was unclear to a girl of my age. But I can still hear the harshness in her words. She blamed herself for what had happened, perhaps even more than the man who had cast her aside. How I wish I could reach back in time and release the burden of guilt that weighed so heavily upon her! Had I been older, more compassionate, she might have told me everything and found some measure of peace in the confession. But perhaps it was for the best that the secret of my parentage remained hidden. What would a girl of my age have done with such dangerous knowledge?

"So I was not born at the castle?" I asked, a child still, and concerned above all with my place in the story.

Mother shook her head. "No, you were born in town, in St. Elsip."

"At your sister's?"

My aunt Agna was the wife of a cloth merchant, a mysterious figure who sent rolls of wool each Christmas, allowing us to make new clothes when our old ones were shredded with wear. But I had never met her. Having come up in the world, she preferred to keep her distance from our family's poverty.

"Agna did her best," Mother said. "She gave me money and some swaddling clothes. But she would not have me in her home. She was a respectable married woman with children of her own. I did not want her reputation to suffer for my mistake."

"What did you do?" I asked.

"I found a rooming house, run by a woman who had once been in the same state," Mother said. "She was kind, in her way, and helped you come into the world. Without her you might never have lived past a few days. It was there that I met your father."

"You mean Mr. Dalriss?"

"Father," she hissed. "You will call him Father, miss. He saved us from starvation, never forget that. Every time you bite into a crust of bread, you should be thanking him."

"Yes, Mother."

I feared she was angry enough to walk the rest of the way home in silence, so it was a relief when she continued her story.

"You were two years old. I had sewn a few dresses for my landlady to pay my keep, but after a time there was nothing more I could barter. She allowed us to sleep in her kitchen, provided I help with the cooking. Mr. Dalriss came to town to buy a new horse and heard that my landlady ran a clean house. He saw me serving at dinner, inquired about me, and I suppose he thought he might as well come home with a wife. The first time he spoke to me was to ask if I would marry him. I said yes immediately, and gratefully. Not many men would take a penniless girl with a bastard child. And here was a man who owned his own farm, his own land. I had prepared myself to accept far less promising offers."

Perhaps he had been kinder then, less worn down by disappointment. But I could not imagine that Mr. Dalriss was ever an appealing prospect. Mother must have been desperate indeed for her to have accepted him.

"I worked so hard to show him he had made the right choice," Mother said. "When I told him I was with child not four months after our marriage, it was the first time I saw him smile. He told me, 'I knew you were good breeding stock.' I will always remember that, because it was the closest to a kind word I've ever gotten from him."

He had chosen my mother as he would a cow. She had already proved she could bear a healthy child, so he felt confident she would produce a pack of children to work the farm. And Mother had kept her side of the bargain. Did she ever regret the choice she'd made?

"The man, my true father . . ." I began.

Mother twisted around and slapped me hard on the cheek. "You are never to speak of him," she said. "He would not call you daughter. He would spit on you."

The cruelty of her words brought tears to my eyes, more than the blow. Father would have beaten me again for crying, but my mother softened at the sight of my misery. She wrapped her arms around my body, pressing my face against her chest, something she had not done since I was a small child.

"There, there," she murmured. "You must hold your head high. I will see you make something of yourself, no matter what the circumstances of your birth."

"Do you think I might be accepted in service? At the castle?"

I could imagine no greater accomplishment, so I was surprised to see my mother hesitate, her face tense with concern. *She does not want me to go,* I thought, seeing her reaction as a mother's natural inclination to keep her child close to home. Now, so many years later, I wonder if she was planning to warn me away. Given her own sad history, she knew only too well the malevolent intrigues that hide behind courtly manners. Had a cart not come rattling up behind us, causing Mother to extract herself from our embrace and offer a curt nod of greeting to the farmer who passed us by, what might she have said?

"Come along," she urged, self-consciously straightening her sleeves as the cart rumbled off. "Your father will be expecting his dinner."

My heart sank as I imagined his harsh complaints if we were late. Mother ran a finger gently along my cheek.

"Your face is so browned from the harvesting," she said. "Time your brothers took on more of the field work. I won't have you grow up with the skin of a country bumpkin."

"Then you agree?" I asked hesitantly. "That I might find a place at court one day?" My stomach fluttered with expectation.

"Now is hardly the time for such a discussion," she said. "We shall see, when you are older."

At ten years old, I felt my future stretch before me as an unending horizon, with the years of my adulthood impossibly distant.

There was time enough to ponder my prospects, to plot the course of my life. But whenever I tried to discuss going into service, Mother changed the subject, and in time I stopped asking.

We did not speak of the castle again until the day she died.

The spring I turned fourteen, fierce rainstorms turned our fields into rivers of mud, delaying the planting even as our winter food stores dwindled. Father had begun to speak of marrying me off early, saying that it would be one less mouth to feed, and such was my hunger that I might have said "I do" to any man who offered me a warm meal. While some trade on their looks to improve their marriage prospects, I did not think such a tactic could work in my favor. When I gazed at my reflection in the river, I saw no signs of the beauty that was remarked upon in certain other girls of the village. While their hair was golden blond and their eyes blue or green, my thick, wavy hair was a deep chestnut brown. My dark eyes, while large and pleasingly framed by long lashes, were incapable of mimicking the flirtatious glances other women had perfected; I looked upon the world with a direct, forthright gaze. I did note a few marks in my favor: My complexion was clear and even, and the curves of my hips and chest gave my body a healthy solidity. With the right clothes, I might make a fitting shopkeeper's wife, a fate that had become the height of my ambition.

In the end, another village wedding allowed me to delay my own. A wealthy landowner's wife hired Mother to embroider linens for her soon-to-be-married daughter, saving us from starvation. I shouldered as much of the burden as I could, sitting by the fireside well into the night with a needle in hand, squinting at the flowers I created with colored thread. Life in our one-room cottage revolved around the fireplace, the only place one could be assured of warmth. My mother spent hours there, cooking and heating water for washing; when it was too cool to dry laundry outside, damp underclothes hung on a line in front of the hearth, and we had to fight with the swaying fabric to claim a spot for ourselves. The flour, salt, and oats we were paid for the needlework allowed our family to survive another month, and we thought the worst behind us.

Then the cows fell sick.

We had three, an ancient bull that Father used in the fields and two milk cows. I was the first to notice the red scabs on their teats as I milked the cows early one morning. They felt scaly but showed no signs of blood, and I gave them no further thought. It wasn't until the next day, when one of the cows stared at me with dazed eyes, leaning against the side of the barn, that I realized something was terribly wrong.

As I went outside to tell my father, I saw him coming toward me, muttering with frustration. He used to hang his head low when he was angry, hurling curses to the ground as he walked, and he did so now.

"Father . . ." I began.

"Hush!" he spat at me. "Sukey's dead."

My heart dropped. Sukey was the name we used for the biggest of our pigs; whenever one Sukey died, the next largest took the name, and so the cycle progressed. This latest Sukey had given birth to a litter of pigs not a week before. If she were not alive to suckle them, they might all die, and with them went our meat for the rest of the year.

"What happened?" I asked, trailing after him on the way to the house.

"The pox."

It was all that needed to be said. The pox was an ailment that swept through farms with no warning, sickening livestock and people with alarming fickleness. It might be mild and merely weaken creatures for a few days, but it also could prove devastating. It was reputed to have killed entire families in the village once, years before I was born.

It was my mother who first noticed the spots on my face the following day. I had woken with a dry, raspy cough and a fever, but that in itself was no reason for me to be excused from my daily labors. Only complete infirmity merited a rest in my parents' bed, with its feather-stuffed mattress. Usually we children slept packed together in a loft under the eaves, a bleak expanse of wood topped with a pile of straw and worn blankets. It was tolerable when I had to share it with only Nairn, the brother closest to me in age, but as a new sibling appeared almost every year, it grew steadily more crowded. I was often startled awake in the middle of the night by a foot kicking my stomach or an arm flung across my face.

"What is this?" Mother asked, peering at my cheek.

"What?" I asked.

"These spots." She pushed the hair away from my face and put her palm against my forehead. "You're burning up."

I was ready to protest that I felt well enough, until I saw the fear in her face. She was holding my youngest brother in one arm, and she pulled him closer to her body, away from the threat of my illness. The heat I had tried to ignore flashed through my body, leaving a chill in its wake. My skin prickled as if the pox were about to burst through in angry red eruptions.

Mother laid the baby down in the cradle by the fireplace and pulled my wool dress off, leaving me in my chemise.

"You must rest," she urged, pushing me toward her bed. "If you take care, I have heard that the pox can pass without lasting harm."

I chose to believe her. What girl, at fourteen, ever thought she was mortal?

The following days passed in an eternal hazy twilight, for the illness tormented its sufferers with a wakefulness that allowed no respite from its horrors. My body blazed with pain as the pox erupted across my skin, yet I was unable to escape into the oblivion of sleep. Delirious, I saw visions of the castle and imagined myself walking along its wide corridors. It was warm, always warm, as I passed one fireplace after another. I gawked at the flames, amazed by the extravagance that allowed hearths to burn day and night. I have dim memories of my mother sitting on the edge of the bed, leaning over to wipe my forehead with a wet cloth. Then leaning forward to do the same to my brother Nairn beside me and another brother beside him. Mother watched us without expression, staring as if the heat of our fevers had scorched her eyes to blindness. The baby lay in her lap, ominously still. I closed my eyes, resigned to death.

Yet that was not to be my fate. After what might have been hours or years, I became aware of the sweat-stained pillow against my cheek, felt the weight of the blanket spread across my chest. My eyes burned with exhaustion, yet the fever that had so tormented me had subsided. I saw Nairn lying next to me, his face red and distorted with swelling. I heard his breath laboriously draw inward, then wheeze out. The rest of the bed was empty. Across the room faint embers glowed in the fireplace. Our house, usually bustling and crowded, was silent.

I sat up too quickly, for my head pounded with the effort and I had to shut my eyes to block out the swimming images before me. After the rushing sensation quieted, I looked again. By the dim light of the dying fire, I saw a pile of clothes thrown on the floor. Again Nairn took a shuddering breath and seemed as if he might expire from the effort. I looked at the heap of clothes and saw a movement.

A rat, I thought. They made their way into the house from time to time but rarely lingered, as we ate every crumb we had. I pulled myself from the bed, willing myself the strength to stand and shoo the intruder away. It was not until I had walked unsteadily across the room that I realized the pile of clothes was my mother.

I collapsed next to her. She was wrapped in her cloak, with the hood pulled over her head. Her legs were pressed up against her chest, her hands hidden in the folds of her skirt. I plucked the hood away and was confronted with a terrible sight: my mother's face, drawn and tired in all the time I had known her but with faint traces of loveliness still, had been transformed to that of a monster. Red sores that oozed pus and blood had erupted from her skin. Her neck was disfigured by a massive swelling, and her lips, stained with blood, were frozen in a rigor of pain. Her eyes slowly opened. They had once been blue and kind; now they were pink and empty of all feeling.

"Mother." It was all I could think to say. I was not sure she knew me.

Her body did not move, but one hand emerged from the fabric and reached toward me. Her lips parted slightly, and a sound escaped. It could have been my name, it could have been a moan of pain; I could not tell.

"Please, come to the bed," I urged. I could not think of any way to tend to her, but it sickened me to see her there, lying on the floor like an animal. She deserved better than such a fate.

"Elise."

This time I recognized my name, and I smiled. If she still knew me, there might be hope yet.

"Come." I pulled at her shoulders. She lifted them slightly and reached toward me with her arms, but she was not strong enough to stand. I dragged her as best I could across the room, hoping her skirt would lessen the impact to her legs, but she did not complain. I draped her head and arms against the side of the bed, then leaned over to lift her lower body upward. My head ached with the effort, and by the time I had laid her next to Nairn, I was afraid I might faint. I crawled into the bed beside her and began stroking her arm.

"Mother, the others . . ." I began, then stopped. Her watery eyes stared into mine, confirming what I could not put into words. They were dead. In the time I'd been lost to fever, my family had vanished. I remembered seeing the baby in her lap, so small and so still. I hoped it had been quick for him at least.

Yet I lived. Which meant this pox, this terrible scourge that had laid waste to my family, could be conquered. Weak as I was, I could feel my head clearing, my body gathering strength. I wrapped my arms around her body—so very thin, little more than bones—willing the life to return to her.

"Please," I begged, "do not leave me. I cannot bear it here without you."

"Agna." She said it so slowly and quietly, barely even a whisper.

The swelling in her neck must have made speaking unbearably painful, and I could feel her suffering with every word. "You must go."

I leaned my head closer to hers, so she would not have to make an effort to be heard. A thin stream of blood trickled from her nose, and I wiped it gently with the edge of my sleeve.

"Yes, I will go to St. Elsip," I agreed, "but not till you are well. We can go together."

Her hands fumbled laboriously in the folds of her skirt. I clutched them in my own, as if my touch could prevent her from leaving me. Her fingers pulled away from my grasp and plucked at her ragged dress. Following her gaze, I looked toward the hem. She nodded, moaning with the effort, and I ran my fingers along the bottom of her dress until I found a hard lump. I could make out the shape of a metal coin, then another and another. Money she had hidden away, unbeknownst to my father. Money that would allow my escape.

The thought of starting a new life alone, without her, brought tears streaming down my cheeks. A low moan, hardly louder than a whisper, rumbled from Mother's throat, and I realized she was trying to comfort me, that witnessing my sorrow brought more pain than the torments of her body. Determined not to add to her suffering, I suppressed my sobs and forced a smile.

"Do not worry," I said. "I will find a place at the castle. I will do you proud."

Her hands suddenly gripped my forearms, and I flinched at the sharp pressure of her fingernails. My fever had not yet fully subsided, but her skin felt like fire against mine. She could no longer speak, only breathe quickly and shallowly, as one does when climbing a steep hill. I can hardly bear to think upon the memory: my beloved mother, so close to death yet so desperate to protect me. A single word escaped her parched lips. It sounded like "pell," though it might just have easily been "bell." Was she warning me away? Urging me to go? Frantic, I asked her what it meant, but she could emit no more than a hoarse rasp.

"I will fetch water," I said, frantic to do something, anything, to ease her distress.

I struggled up from the bed. One of my brothers' first duties in the morning had been to fetch water from the well, but when had that last been done? The pail stood between the doorway and the fireplace, as if it had been dropped in a rush. I peered inside and saw a shallow pool of water barely covering the bottom. It was enough to wet a corner of my chemise, and I carried it, dripping, to the bed.

But I was too late. My mother's eyes were closed, and she lay motionless, her face horribly altered by the ravages of disease but free of the rigor of pain. She was at peace. I crumpled by the side of the bed, surrendering to despair. Grief and shock weighed down my weakened body, and I might have been a newborn again, unable to speak or stand. Without my mother, my protector, I had nothing. I sat slumped on hands and knees for what felt like hours, so drained by the ordeal of her death that I could not even cry.

The only sound in the room came from Nairn's shuddering breaths. One after the other they came, slow but increasingly steady. Grimly, I forced myself to rise from the floor. My brother's face was flushed, but his skin did not blaze with heat as my mother's had. I might yet salvage one life.

I picked up the pail and stumbled toward the door, intent on fetching fresh water from the well. When I walked outside, it was a surprise to be greeted by daylight. The closed-up house had seemed to exist in an eternal night. I heard sounds coming from the barn;

the horse at least might have survived. As I approached the building, the door was flung open, and I stood face-to-face with my father.

"Elise!" He froze in place, astonished. I must have presented quite a sight in my chemise, flushed and filthy, but his appearance was even more shocking. For the father I had taken for dead looked the same as ever. Weathered, as always, with bent shoulders and a suspicious frown. But healthy.

"I thought . . . I thought you were dead," I said.

"I thought the same of you." We stood staring at each other, two ghosts.

"Mother," I mumbled, "she said . . ."

"She lives?" Father asked, surprised.

I shook my head, and my voice trembled. "She is gone."

"Aye, it's as I expected. I thought she might have passed on yesterday, but I couldn't be sure."

How could he not know if his wife lived or died? "Were you not tending to her?" I asked.

His face settled into the dark cast it took before I got a beating. "I did my best, missy. I watched my livestock die off, one by one, till I was left with but a few chickens and a horse. I buried my boys, four of them, while you lay abed!"

It did not escape me that he spoke of the livestock before his children.

"Should I have stayed in that house and risked dying myself?" he asked. "Who do you think left water and food at the door each morning? How dare you say I did not look to my family!"

He might have helped us live. But I would not bow in gratitude for his feeble offerings.

"I bedded down here in the straw," he continued, "but now you're better, you can get the house sorted. Just as well that I sleep in my own bed for a change."

"You forgot to ask after Nairn."

Father watched me, neither mournful nor hopeful. Simply waiting.

"I think he will live."

"Good," Father said. "He's a strong one. I'll need his help clearing the fields."

"He's in no state to plow," I said sharply. "He cannot even stand."

"He'll be well soon enough. You can see to him until then. A few other farms lost animals, but none as bad as us, and those who were spared have sent meat and pies, enough to keep us from starvation. I'll show you what I've got stocked away in the barn, and you can take on the cooking for this evening. Start by cleaning yourself; find something of your mother's to wear."

She was not yet in her grave, and already he was urging me to rifle through her things. The anger I had kept tamped down for so many years swelled up, a river overflowing its banks.

"I will set the house in order for my brother's sake, not yours."

He stared, caught short by my defiance.

"As soon as the funeral is held, I will leave for St. Elsip. Mother arranged a place at court for me." The lie slipped so easily from my lips that I almost believed it the truth.

"Court?" He came the closest I ever saw to laughing—his eyes widened and his mouth hung open. "They'll slam the door in your face."

"I'll find a better living there than here," I said.

To this he had no reply. I spent the rest of that endless day cleaning until my hands were raw and stinging, stopping only when my head spun with fatigue and I feared I would faint. Father wrapped

Mother's body in a sheet, grumbling about the cost of replacing it, and said she could lie in the barn until a funeral service could be arranged with the village priest. Before Father did his grim duty, I asked for a moment alone with her to pray. As he paced outside the door, I knelt alongside Mother and whispered what was in my heart: how much I loved her, my vow to do her proud. All the while my fingers crept along the hem of her underskirt, my nails cutting through the thread that held it together, until I felt the smooth metal disks slip into my hand. Five silver coins. All that my mother had to show for a lifetime of labor. I slid them into my shoe and rushed from the house before Father could see my red eyes and wet cheeks.

During the following days, as my strength gradually returned, I saw Father only for meals. I ate more from determination than hunger, but I was heartened to see Nairn regain his usual vigor, and I sometimes set an extra portion aside for him to eat after Father had returned to the fields. I never saw my brother cry. As soon as he was able to walk, he spent most hours in the animal paddocks or helping Father clear out weeds. I did not begrudge him the wish to escape a house that had seen so much death.

Mother was laid to rest on a bright, clear day, her body buried beside those of her sons in the village churchyard. I had never attended a funeral before, and only in hindsight did I realize that the priest performed the quickest rite possible, most likely because my father had skimped on the fee. Rushed as the ceremony might have been, I felt the weight of my grief lighten for a moment, as if God himself were urging me to lay it down. Mother and the boys had been welcomed into heaven. Their suffering had ended.

The next morning, as dawn started to push aside the darkness, I climbed down from the sleeping loft, past Father snoring in the bed.

I gathered the small bundle that held my few possessions: a chemise, a pair of winter stockings, a few needles and some thread, and a small loaf of bread. I carefully opened the chest that held my parents' clothing and took out Mother's best dress, the one she had saved for Sundays. With the years it had become worn and stained, marked forever as a peasant's garment. Still, the fabric was of better quality than that of my tattered clothes, and I pulled it on.

I heard a rustle of straw behind me and turned to see Nairn peering down from the loft. I offered a smile, but he only nodded somberly before turning away. Perhaps, given the losses he had already suffered, he could not summon the will to grieve my absence. Such was my leave-taking from the only home I had ever known.

I headed for the cart path that led toward the village, the lure of what lay before me overpowering my fear. Where did I find the strength to take step after step into the unknown, alone and unprotected? To this day I cannot explain why I set my sights so single-mindedly on the castle. All I can say is that I felt called, whether by devilish temptation or God's will I'll never know.

Or do I?

Is it possible that Millicent, on the hunt for an acolyte, sent out a call that only I was capable of hearing, a call I was powerless to resist? It would be madness to believe such a thing. Yet what else could explain the unshakable certainty that drew me forward? Every great legend is at its heart a tale of innocence lost, and perhaps that was the role I was destined to play. I was ignorant indeed of the choices that lay ahead, choices that would raise me to heights I never imagined and others that pierce my heart with anguish to this day.

Two

TO THE CASTLE

Two days later, squeezed in the back of a jostling cart with an assortment of hogs and sheep, I arrived in St. Elsip. Good fortune had hastened my journey, for I had not walked more than a mile when I was offered a ride by a passing farmer and his wife who were traveling in the same direction. My anticipation rose so high that the first sight of our destination came as a crushing disappointment: The ramshackle buildings on the outskirts of town were not much different from the humble country shacks I had left behind. But then the cart turned a corner and I saw it: a soaring fortress of stone encircling the top of a rugged hill. The castle. From that distance only the outer walls were clearly visible, yet my heart leaped all the same. I could hear Mother's words, as clearly as if she sat beside me: *It was the most wondrous place I have ever seen.*

How I ached for her in that moment! It is only now I realize that my hunger to enter those gates was fueled by grief. Deep down I hoped that some trace of my mother's spirit would linger in those grand halls.

On we drove, as modest dwellings gave way to solidly built homes that pressed up against one another. Taverns began to outnumber churches. Our wagon's progress slowed considerably as we fought for passage with other carriages and riders, and I felt the unsettling sensation of the world closing in around me. People swarmed the streets, wending their way amid the hooves and wheels. The buildings grew ever higher, crowding out the sky. I craned my neck and still could not see the roofs.

"Here we are," announced the farmer, Mr. Fitz, who had acted as my protector during our travels. We pulled into a large square, where roads from every direction converged in a wide, open space surrounded by shops and a large stone church. The center, laid with bricks, had been given over to animals of every size and shape: cows on one side, pigs on another, smaller varieties such as chickens and songbirds in the middle. The noise, both human and animal, was overpowering. Disoriented and overwhelmed, I hung against the side of the cart. Mrs. Fitz placed a hand on my shoulder, but I could barely hear what she was saying.

"I'll go ask after your aunt. We won't leave till you're sorted out."

I nodded dumbly and remained where I was while Mr. Fitz unloaded his animals. All around me people jostled against one another, their voices assaulting my ears in a cacophony of shouts. How would I ever navigate such a place on my own?

"You're in luck, my girl," Mrs. Fitz said, reappearing by my side. "The ribbon maker told me how to find your uncle's house. Come, I'll take you."

I was grateful for the press of her hand against my back as we elbowed our way through the square, past jittery horses and impatient shoppers. We had just turned down a dark, narrow side street when suddenly she threw her arm across my chest, pushing me aside and slamming my body flat against a wall. Liquid splattered on the ground next to us, and I looked up and saw a jug being pulled into a window above my head.

"Can you believe that?" Mrs. Fitz exclaimed indignantly. "They put on airs in town, but you never see country folk empty chamber pots out the window." I stepped around the filthy puddle with a grimace.

As we turned from one crooked road to another, the streets and houses grew wider. Instead of passing mud-spattered workmen or scowling mothers tugging along their grubby children, we now walked past finely dressed ladies and gentlemen who strolled with the poise of good breeding.

"This must be it, brick with a red door." Mrs. Fitz nodded toward the building in front of us. To the right side of where I stood, a carving of a shoe hung over a simple wooden door; on the other side were two windows covered with iron bars. I looked up and saw that the house rose three stories. Cowed by her home's size, I wondered if it had been a mistake to arrive on my aunt's doorstep without warning. This was a woman who had not offered her own sister shelter when she needed it most desperately.

Mrs. Fitz knocked, and the door was opened almost immediately by a middle-aged man wearing a short black tunic and black stockings. He stared at us, his expression unchanging. I wondered if this could be my uncle.

Mrs. Fitz, more skilled in reading status from clothing, addressed him as a servant.

"Is this the home of Agna Diepper? This girl is her niece."

The man looked me over as he might any other delivery from the market, then pulled the door open wider.

"Madam is at home. I will announce you."

Cautiously, I took a step inside, then glanced back at Mrs. Fitz.

"Good luck to you," she said, patting me quickly on the back before taking her leave.

The man who answered the door was already halfway down the hall, and I hurried to catch up. I glanced into the room we passed: a formal reception area, with carved wooden chairs arrayed before a grand stone mantelpiece; to the other side, I glimpsed a gleaming table surrounded by more chairs than I could count. Such a place would not intimidate me now, with all the riches I have seen, but at the time it seemed astounding that a person related to me by blood should live in such luxury.

Ahead, at the end of the hall, I heard voices coming from behind a pair of closed doors.

"Wait here," the man ordered, opening the doors enough to allow his passage.

I stood motionless, my hands clutching each other for reassurance, as the man shut the doors behind him. I heard muffled sounds but could not make out the words. Was it possible my aunt would refuse to receive me? What would I do then? Sick with worry, I waited to discover my fate.

The doors opened, and the man waved me inside. The kitchen I entered was unlike any I had ever seen. It extended the entire width of the house, a space that could easily have accommodated twice over the hovel where I had grown up. To my right was an enormous fireplace, big enough to house two massive kettles and a spit for meat. The walls were hung with a mouth-watering abundance of food: onions, baskets of carrots and leeks, bundles of dried herbs, slabs of cured meat. To my left, a girl stood at a basin, washing a stack of pans. I had never seen so many plates in one place; there were enough to set a meal for my whole village. Against the wall at my side were barrels filled with oats and flour, any one of which could have fed my family for months.

The center of the room was dominated by a wide worktable. At one end a young woman was flattening out a pile of dough, twisting and turning her rolling pin with practiced ease. At the center stood two women, both looking directly at me. The first, dressed all in black except for a white apron and cap, was the widest person I had ever seen; her ample belly was proof that in this house no one went hungry. The other woman's air of authority and elegant yellow dress signaled her as the mistress of the house. I was surprised to see she held a quill in her hand; I had never known a woman other than my mother who could write.

"Aunt Agna?" I asked nervously.

"Elise, is it?" She looked me over suspiciously. She had the sort of features referred to as handsome rather than beautiful, with a strong brow and a sharp chin. Her lips were drawn together in a tight, thin line. "What brings you here?"

"My mother . . ." I began, then found myself without words.

"How does she?"

The despair that washed over my face conveyed the message I could not utter aloud, shaken as I was by silent sobs. Aunt Agna nodded slowly, her wary expression unchanged.

"What happened?" she asked.

I sniffled and got hold of myself. "The pox. It took four of my brothers as well."

She walked around the table and halfheartedly patted my shoulder. "Poor Mayren. She deserved a better fate." She spoke briskly, without sentiment. Still keeping her thoughts in reserve, as if she had not yet made up her mind what to do with me.

"I had hoped to find a place at the castle, as my mother once did," I said nervously. "If I could impose upon your hospitality for this evening, perhaps tomorrow you could tell me the best way to proceed."

Agna shook her head quickly. "Nonsense. They'd never accept you, looking like that. Stay with us for a spell, and I'll see you're properly prepared."

"Thank you." The relief was so intense that I came close to relapsing into tears.

"Was it your mother's wish that you seek me out?" Agna asked.

"Your name was one of the last words she uttered," I said. The revelation momentarily broke through Agna's reserve, and she sighed deeply. In her eyes I saw the pain that comes from regrets that will never be lifted.

"She said one other thing before she died," I added. "Perhaps you might know what it means. A word that sounded like 'pell,' although that makes no sense—"

"Pelleg," Agna interrupted. "She was a friend of Mayren's, at the castle, though she's improved her lot since then. She's known as Mrs. Tewkes now, the head housekeeper."

Now I understood why my mother had so labored to utter that one final word. With her dying breath, she had given me permission to go, directing me toward a person who could guide my way at court. A person who could protect me, after she was gone.

Or so I thought. Now, with the wisdom of my years, I cannot help seeing my mother's actions in another light, one more in keeping with her character. All her life she had dissuaded me from imagining a life at the castle, switching the subject whenever I spoke of it. Is it likely she changed her mind on the point of death? Or had she invoked her friend's name as a last desperate attempt to save me, hoping Pelleg Tewkes might be the one person who could dissuade me from entering that treacherous world?

I will never know.

"The first thing we must do is clean you up," Agna said, looking disapprovingly at my clothes. "If you expect to be hired at the castle, you must look the part, as well as understand how things are done there. I will tell you all you need to know, in good time."

Relieved, yet still uncertain as to my place in the household, I waited for further instructions. Was I to stay in the family quarters upstairs? Or in one of the small servants' rooms I glimpsed off the kitchen, as befitting a penniless orphan?

"Come, I will introduce you to your cousins," Agna said, taking me by the arm. Her mouth curved into a wry smile. "Don't look so worried. I'm not heartless, no matter what your mother might have said."

In fact, my mother had spoken very little of her sister. There were fleeting similarities between them: Agna had the same curly hair that bobbed in tendrils around her face, and her eyes turned downward in a way that gave her a melancholy air, as had my mother's.

But, seen side by side, the two women would never have been taken for sisters. My mother, married to a poor, belligerent farmer, hid her strength beneath a cowering posture and cautious utterances. Agna, the wife of a wealthy cloth merchant, carried herself with the assurance that her words would be obeyed. She kept order among a staff of bustling servants, three children, and a husband without ever raising her voice. My uncle may have been head of the household in name, but my aunt wielded the power within those walls.

During the two weeks I lived under her roof, I learned that kindness lurked beneath my aunt's brusque manner. She bade me sleep in the same bed as her daughter Damilla, a few years older than me and already engaged to be married, and insisted I take a bath with heated water each Sunday, just as her own children did. My cousins, accustomed to such indulgences, were polite but indifferent to my presence, and I suspected that my lack of polish made me a figure of fun behind closed doors. Had they known the heights to which I would rise, would they have treated me differently? It is tempting to envision a comeuppance for those who have slighted you. And yet, knowing what their family was to suffer in the years to come, I cannot nurse a grudge. It is truly a blessing we are spared foreknowledge of our ultimate ends.

Agna, who had worked at the castle alongside my mother before her marriage, instructed me in courtly etiquette and the servant hierarchies. She had one of Damilla's old dresses altered to fit me and clucked in disapproval at my shoes. I owned only a single pair, made from wood and bark by my father. At home I went barefoot most of the year.

"You can't be seen in those," she declared. "Hannolt will make you a pair."

Hannolt, I soon learned, was the shoemaker whose shop stood on the ground floor of my aunt's house; it was common for homeowners to rent out their lower levels, since no decent family would want passersby staring into their windows. The top of Hannolt's head barely reached my shoulder, but he made up for his lack of size by creating a storm of activity around himself and speaking in a loud yammer.

"My niece should have a good, stout pair," Agna told him as we stood in his shop. "Leather, of course, but not extravagant."

"Yes, yes, I understand," Hannolt said, nodding. "Something that will withstand hard wear. Still, a young lady deserves a touch of beauty, does she not? Some embroidery, perhaps?"

Agna shook her head firmly. "There's no need for such frippery."

"Well then, we shall take her measurements. Marcus!"

A young man pushed through the curtains that hung across the back of the room. I wish I could tell you exactly how he struck me on first sight; were this a different sort of tale, I might recall his soulful eyes or the crush of longing that weakened me upon seeing his face or some other foolishness. But I have vowed to tell the truth. On that day I noted only that he was a young man of about my own age, considerably taller than his father but far less effusive. He said nothing as he knelt before me and reached his hands toward my legs. I was so surprised by the gesture that I flinched backward and almost lost my balance.

"Let the girl be seated first!" Hannolt laughed.

He ushered me to a bench along the wall, then motioned Marcus forward. The boy cautiously pulled one of my feet out from under my skirt and slid off the slipper I had borrowed from Aunt Agna. I could barely feel the weight of his hands through my stockings as he placed my foot on a flat piece of wood, engraved with foot tracings of various sizes. He looked at his father and pointed to the line where my foot matched up, then took a thin leather strap from around his neck and wrapped it around my foot from bottom to top, then around my ankle. He removed the strap and nodded toward his father. Still he said nothing. I wondered if he was dumb. Or perhaps he had given up hope of being heard above his father's prattling.

"Done?" Hannolt asked. "Good. Now, about the color." He waved his hand toward samples of leather hanging from hooks above my head.

Agna scanned the choices and pointed to a dark brown piece. "That one."

I reached into the pocket of my apron and drew out one of the coins my mother had given me. "Will this do?"

Agna took hold of my fingers and wrapped them around the coin. "This is my gift to you. A fine aunt I'd be, sending you off to the castle in those wooden shoes."

"The castle?" Hannolt's eyes lit up with surprise. "Are you paying a visit, miss?"

"She's to be in service," Agna said.

"We'll be going there ourselves in a few days," Hannolt said. "One of the finest ladies at court buys her shoes from us, ten pairs at a time. Would that all my customers were so free-spending!"

"Perhaps you could escort Elise when you go?"

"It would be a pleasure. She'll arrive safe and sound, you have my word."

I had thought my aunt would bring me to the castle herself, and I felt a stab of disappointment when she pawned me off on the shoemaker. How would I navigate my way through those massive fortifications without her guidance? Self-centered, as girls of that age can be, I never considered that Agna might have had a good reason for avoiding the place. Those who have once been servants can be sensitive about their formerly low rank, as I would one day know only too well.

"Send word of your departure, and I'll see she is ready," Agna said.

"You'll arrive at the castle a lady," Hannolt assured me. "Your shoes will be as finely made as any, though the queen, they say, has hers encrusted with diamonds. . . ."

Following a loving description of the queen's footwear, Hannolt continued on to a detailed examination of court fashion, ignoring Agna's attempts to take her leave. I momentarily turned toward Marcus, and he smiled almost imperceptibly, just enough to make me notice his dark eyes, crinkled with amusement at his father's chattering. Enough to make me think he might be more than a dumb shopkeeper's son.

During the weeks I spent with Aunt Agna, I wandered no farther than the shops nearest her house. On the day I finally accompanied Hannolt and Marcus toward what I hoped would be my new home, I had only the vaguest notion of what the castle looked like, based solely on the glimpse I'd seen during the ride into town.

I expected it to be large and well fortified. But when we finally emerged from St. Elsip's warren of crooked streets, I was overwhelmed by the sheer mass of the fortress that sprawled defiantly atop the hill before me. Thick walls of rugged stone seemed to have burst forth from the earth to encircle the jumble of towers within. Behind the battlements, turrets stabbed the sky, with a few narrow windows giving the only indication that people lived within. For a moment the weight of it chilled my spirits, and I was seized by a sudden reluctance to enter. Raised in the open air, with land extending in all directions, I had never considered what it would mean to live enclosed within walls.

Hannolt and Marcus had continued ahead, joining a crowd of carriages, carts, and fellow travelers along a steep upward path. I forced myself to shake off the foolish presentiment of danger and hurried to catch up with my companions. The castle's grim exterior must hide wondrous luxuries, I told myself, else why would the king live there? Though I was seduced by the beauty within soon enough, I was never able to forget that first visceral reaction. Most saw those walls as protection from danger, but I had recognized, somewhere deep in my soul, that not all threats came from without.

The press of people moved toward an arched gatehouse, with guards posted at either side.

"This way," Hannolt said, pushing me in front of him and jerking Marcus to his side. Marcus stared straight ahead, as he had done since we left my aunt's house, seemingly aloof. He had the slight build of a boy some years from manhood, but his straight nose and clear skin presaged future good looks. His thick, dark hair was raggedly cut and fell unevenly over his forehead, and his eyes intrigued me with their seriousness. The few boys I had known in my village had been either braggarts or awkwardly shy when conversing with girls their own age. None had ever appeared so at ease in my presence as Marcus did. Even his silence, so disconcerting at first, had become oddly comforting. His father babbled enough for the two of them.

Hannolt nodded to one of the guards and pulled the sack he was carrying off his shoulder. Opening it, he began lovingly describing the shoes inside. The guard glanced into the bag with scant interest and waved us through the gate.

We stepped into a large courtyard, so filled with activity and shouting that I did not know where to set my eyes first. Carriages swept by so close that I could feel the whip of wind as they passed, while my way forward was blocked by a circle of men boastfully comparing swords. Servants dressed in royal livery were shouting out orders to a group of workers—masons, by the look of their tools. I peered up, above the mass of people before me, and saw the castle rising toward the sky. A soaring vision of gray stone bordered by four great towers, each standing guard over the tiny figures swarming below. How well I remember the moment I paused there, face-to-face at last with the object of my dreams! I can still summon the tingle that ran from my scalp to my toes, that exhilarating mix of fear and anticipation, as I stood on the threshold of a new life. My earlier doubts cast aside, I longed to join in the drama surrounding me, to play a role—no matter how small—in upholding such magnificence.

Ahead, a paved drive led up a short rise to the entry doors, emblazoned with gold crests.

"That's how the quality enter," Hannolt said. "The rest of us fight our way to the back."

He took my hand and tugged me alongside him as a cart came crashing toward us. I saw that most movement in the courtyard was swelling and ebbing around an arch to the left side of the castle. Cramming ourselves into the passageway with the others, we emerged into another courtyard, of similar proportions but even more crowded. Opposite us, groomsmen were leading horses in and out of paddocks. Immediately to my right, a series of doors opened into the lower level of the castle; judging by the huge hearths I saw inside, I guessed they led to the kitchens. To our left, workers were loading supplies off carts into storerooms. As we passed, I glimpsed a basket the size of a horse's trough, filled with nothing but onions. Next to it were sacks of flour and meal that stood almost as tall as I was.

"Careful!" Hannolt shouted.

Distracted by the sights, I had come close to stepping into a mix of mud and rotting food. I pulled my skirt above my ankles and wrapped it tight around my legs.

A voice from behind me barked, "Look sharp!" Before I had time to turn around, Marcus had wrapped his arm about my shoulders and pulled me back from an almost certain collision with a barrel that had been tossed from the storerooms. It was the closest I'd ever been to a young man of my own age, and I was surprised by the sturdiness of his grasp, the firmness of his chest when I fell against it.

"Oy!" shouted Hannolt to the men inside. "Watch it!"

"Watch your lassie, more like it!" someone shouted back. "This is no place to prance about!"

I began to thank Marcus for his vigilance, but he drew back and turned his face before I could finish. Had the seemingly imperturbable Marcus been shaken by our near miss? Or, like me, had he been momentarily unsettled by the sudden press of our bodies together?

"Best get on," Hannolt urged. "I don't know where to find the housekeeper exactly, but we'll ask in the kitchens."

We walked gingerly through the muck, following Hannolt until we entered a room with three blazing fireplaces, each filled with a hanging cauldron. The heat was stifling.

A sweaty woman in a stained apron and matted hair stepped before us. "What d'you want?" she asked suspiciously.

"I have a delivery for Lady deWey," Hannolt said, as grandly as a knight readying for a royal audience. "I am expected in the Great Hall. This young lady is to see Mrs. Tewkes."

She looked me up and down. Evidently unimpressed, she sighed in annoyance. "You'll find her in the Lower Hall." She pointed across the room. "Through that door, down the passage, and up the stairs."

"This is where we part, then," said Hannolt. "I will tell your aunt we saw you here safely."

I looked at Marcus. We had barely spoken, but he had a steadiness of demeanor that made me regret the briefness of our acquaintance. He appeared to be on the verge of telling me something, but his father interrupted with a flurry of good wishes before turning to go. Marcus dropped his head in a brief nod and then followed his father out of sight.

Lonely and afraid, I felt my spirits falter, but I would not risk the cook's wrath by dawdling in that chaotic kitchen. I followed her directions, walking with one shoulder pressed against the walls to avoid being knocked down by men and women carting bags and buckets around me. The dogged procession brought to mind the ants that used to march across our dirt floor in search of crumbs dropped by my brothers. Flushed from the kitchen's heat, then jostled in the narrow passage, I felt light-headed as I climbed up a set of wide wooden stairs and emerged into a long room that extended as far as I could see.

I later learned that this Lower Hall—so named because it was beneath the castle's Great Hall—was the central gathering place for all who worked in the castle. It was here the servants ate their twice-daily meals, received their orders from the housekeeper, toasted the New Year, and mourned the death of one of their own. I took in the long expanse of space, calmed by its impression of symmetry and order. Simple wooden tables and benches were lined up along either side. Above my head, gray stone walls soared upward toward the massive beams supporting the ceiling.

Slowly, I walked forward, glancing into the workrooms that opened off the hall. One held looms and baskets of yarn, another engraved serving plates and candlesticks. The next was filled with bolts of cloth and spools of thread. The sewing room. I froze, trying to conjure up an image of my mother as a young seamstress, bent over a swath of silk. But, to my despair, I could only envision the mother I had known, ruined by years of hard living, and the memory brought on a throbbing ache of pain.

"May I help you?"

I turned abruptly, disoriented. A tall, willowy young woman with pale skin and equally pale hair, wearing a pristine white apron, was watching me with an expression somewhere between suspicion and curiosity.

"I'm looking for Mrs. Tewkes."

Pondering me for a moment, she appeared to decide that I posed no danger.

"This way."

She guided me to the opposite end of the hall, toward a door carved with a pattern of vines and flowers. I marveled that a mere housekeeper should live in a place more elegantly embellished than the finest home in my village.

The door stood ajar, but the girl paused before it and knocked.

"Come in," a voice commanded.

Compared to the shadowy Lower Hall, the room was bright and welcoming. Opposite the door a large window overlooked the courtyard. A table covered with papers and a few books sat against one wall, beneath a tapestry depicting a lion and a unicorn. Along the opposite wall lay a bed and a trunk inlaid with a pattern of multicolored wood. If this was the housekeeper's room, I could not imagine how fine the queen's must be.

Mrs. Tewkes sat at the table, saying nothing as I entered the room. I learned later that she ruled through silence rather than shrillness. In a castle where activity never ceased, her serene presence set her apart; she could draw the attention of an entire room with a few well-chosen words. I could not be certain of her age; her round face bore the creases of middle age, and her hair was more gray than brown, yet her eyes carried none of the weariness so common in the women of my village. She wore a simple black dress, its loose shape enveloping a figure that had widened and softened with time.

I bent my head, as Aunt Agna had taught me to do in respect of my elders.

"My name is Elise Dalriss," I said. "I believe you knew my mother, Mayren."

"Mayren." Mrs. Tewkes slowly whispered the name, as if her voice were unaccustomed to forming the sound. She rose from the table and walked over to examine me more closely. Then she placed a hand on my shoulder and smiled.

"Yes, I see it now," she said. "You have the same carriage. Mayren always held herself well."

"Yes, ma'am," I said, remembering my mother hunched beneath the weight of a baby on one side and a pail of water on the other. Mrs. Tewkes might not have recognized the woman who raised me.

"Where is she living these days? Is she doing well?"

The words did not come easy. "She died, not a month ago." I felt the tears ready to well up in my eyes.

"Oh, what a shame." The polite words were tinged with genuine sadness.

"She told me to come to you," I said, holding my voice steady through force of will. "I hoped there might be a place for me here."

"How old are you?" she asked.

"Fourteen."

"If you grew up on a farm, you're accustomed to hard work."

I nodded.

"Usually I caution girls that chambermaids here do not have an easy time of it," she said. "But it's likely an easier living than you've seen. At least you won't reek of cow muck at the end of the day!" Mrs. Tewkes laughed, and I found myself smiling along.

She reached out and used her fingers to stretch my lips apart, checking my teeth as one would when buying a horse. Her eyes ran up and down my body, pausing at my arms. She took one of my hands and turned it palm upward. My coarse fingertips testified to my life of labor, though I was proud I had avoided the cracked and reddened skin so common in farmers' families. Mrs. Tewkes nodded approvingly.

"Your mother, what skills did she teach you? Needlework, I presume?"

"I learned to embroider not long after I learned to speak. She also taught me to read and write passably well."

"Ah." Mrs. Tewkes looked pleased and motioned toward the table behind her. "The housekeepers before me barely knew their letters, and none could tend to the kitchen accounts as I do. The queen is a great proponent of education for ladies. She has even been gracious enough to give me a few books. If you can read, it may serve you well here, once you've proved yourself."

"Thank you," I said. "Whatever learning I have is thanks to my mother."

"I am glad she did right by you."

There was a pause in the conversation, long enough to make me fear that Mrs. Tewkes was searching for a polite way to reject me. I have wondered since if she considered telling me all she knew of my mother's disgrace. Was she weighing, even then, the danger that might fall on me as a consequence? She could have warned me off, sent me away. But she did not. She kept my mother's secrets—and her own.

"You're very presentable for a country girl," Mrs. Tewkes said at last. "Still growing into yourself, of course, but you have great potential. Never discount the importance of looks, especially here. You also have a modesty I find very pleasing. Yes, yes, I think you will be quite to the queen's liking."

The queen? Before I had time to ask Mrs. Tewkes what she meant, she was saying, "I will put you in Petra's charge. You'd do well to learn from her example. Petra!"

The maid who had escorted me to Mrs. Tewkes's room rushed into the doorway, so quickly I wondered how closely she had been listening outside.

"Show Elise to the chambermaids' room. There's a spare bed, is there not?"

"More than one."

"Good. Have her follow you the next few days. If all goes well, she can take over your duties, and I'll move you to the hall."

"Thank you, ma'am," Petra said with a delighted smile.

Mrs. Tewkes turned her attention back to me. "Come here the first day of each month for your pay. Two gold pieces to start, and we'll raise it to three if you perform well."

It was more than I had ever dreamed of. "Thank you."

"Off with you, then," Mrs. Tewkes said with a good-natured laugh. "Petra, see me Saturday and we'll talk about your prospects, shall we?"

After Mrs. Tewkes and I finished saying our good-byes, Petra grabbed me by the elbow and pulled me back into the Lower Hall.

"You're a sly one, aren't you?" she said, looking me over appreciatively.

"I don't know what you mean."

"Mrs. Tewkes doesn't take on every groveling girl who appears at her door! Are you a relation of hers?"

I shook my head.

"Yet she places you in the royal apartments rather than setting you to haul kitchen slops. Quite a mark of favor."

All I had done was invoke my mother's name, yet something told me to keep that revelation to myself. There would be others here who remembered Mother's disgrace, and she would not have wanted me tainted by her shame.

Petra, unperturbed by my silence, linked her arm in mine and led me forward. "Well, thanks to you my days of carting wood and chamber pots will soon be over. We're friends now." She spoke in a quick, lively manner that immediately put me at ease.

We walked to a small alcove off the hall, where a narrow circular staircase wound up above our heads into darkness. The smell of the dank, musty air provoked a sudden moment of panic. My entire body protested against entering such a place, cut off from all light, encased in a ring of stone.

"Come on!" Petra called out from the stairs above me. I hurried to follow, terrified of being left behind. She must have seen the fear on my face, for she paused a moment to reassure me. "It's rather a maze, I know, but you'll find your way around soon enough."

The staircase traversed the center of the original fortress, built in the time of the king's forefathers, when the building had been little more than a soldiers' fortification. Over time, towers and wings had been added, each constructed to house the growing number of nobles who made the court their home. As we walked upward, I tried to follow Petra's rapid descriptions of each floor we passed. One hallway led to the state apartments, where official business was conducted; the royal family's sleeping quarters filled the floor above. Up and up we continued, until the stairs ended at a narrow passage.

"Here we are," Petra said. She motioned me to follow her, and we walked by a series of rooms, most with doors closed. "The highest-ranking staff and those who are married have private rooms," she explained. "The rest of us are not so fortunate." She led me to the end of the hall, where we entered a large room with a sloping ceiling, under the very roof of the castle. Rows of simple beds extended from the doorway, each with a wood trunk placed at the foot.

"The maids' quarters," Petra announced. "Come, I'll make sure you sleep next to me." I examined the room as I followed her; there must have been twenty beds lined against the walls.

Petra pointed out her bed at the end of a row. "Sissy's next to me now, but I'll move her down one. Put the blame on Mrs. Tewkes." She opened a trunk and pulled out an armful of clothes, piling them haphazardly into another farther down. "It's much better on this side. You won't be bothered by the door opening and closing."

"All the girls in service sleep here?" I asked.

"Not hardly!" Petra laughed. "There's another room this size across the way, and the boys have rooms at the other end of the hall. Far enough to resist temptation, for the most part. Mrs. Tewkes doesn't tolerate any sneaking about, and any girl caught on the boys' side is sent off without her wages. She runs a strict household. But you don't seem the sort to fall afoul of her rules."

Petra took my small sack and placed it in the trunk. My few possessions appeared even more meager inside that vast emptiness.

"Once you start collecting wages, you'll fill this up," Petra said. "We'll see the seamstresses about getting you a new dress as well."

"What are my duties?"

"Chambermaid, same as all the other girls when they start. Lighting the fires each morning. Emptying and cleaning out the chamber pots. Doing whatever needs to be done. I'm in charge of the queen's rooms, but she's away at the moment, so I have time to get you trained. Then Mrs. Tewkes will decide which of the ladies you shall attend to."

"These ladies, are they very demanding?" I asked, worried that my inexperience would displease them.

"Some are," Petra said with a wry smile. "For the most part, you'll find they take no notice of you at all. Mrs. Tewkes instructs us to work as invisible spirits, never conversing with or looking at our betters unless addressed directly. I've seen maids dismissed on the spot for acting overly familiar. However, if one of the ladies does engage you in conversation, do your best to charm her. The right ally can make all the difference in your progress here."

The right ally. Though it seemed unlikely a girl such as me would attract the notice of any wellborn lady, I remembered something my aunt had told me not long before: *Power is the true currency at court. Those who have it brandish it without mercy, be they servants or knights.* I had entered this world without ties to any family or faction. If I intended to retain my position and earn enough to secure my future, I must have a champion. One powerful enough to protect me from threats I did not fully comprehend.

"Don't worry," said Petra, "I'll show you everything. But let's get your dress sorted out first. Mrs. Tewkes will give me a scolding if you're not properly attired."

She flitted off toward the door, and I rushed to keep up with her. I expected to return to the stairs we had climbed, but Petra guided me toward a different set. On either side of the staircase, a labyrinth of dark, narrow corridors pierced the thick walls, allowing the servants to pass through the castle unseen. The thought of making my way alone through those dank passages made my heart sink with dread, and I kept close to Petra, terrified I'd be lost forever if she vanished out of my sight.

As we approached the bottom of the stairs, I heard the sound of trumpets faintly in the distance.

"It's King Ranolf, back from hunting." She looked at me with a teasing smile. "He'll be passing through the Great Hall. Would you like to see him?"

I nodded eagerly.

She led me from the stairs toward an arcade of columns that lined a wide corridor. We stood behind one of the columns halfway along, peeking out from either side.

I heard the commotion a few seconds before I saw anyone: a rattle of chains and armor and swords, along with the thunderous sound of heavy boots. A few young pages passed before me, followed by a group of men crowded together, carrying longbows and quivers full of arrows. I feared I would not know the king in the crush of people.

Then he strode past, close enough to touch. It is an image I carry with me still, for that is how I would most like to remember him: at the height of his power, supremely confident that his destiny could be molded as he pleased. The king was not the tallest man among those who surrounded him, and he wore hunting clothes rather than a robe and crown, but he carried himself with such authority that my attention was riveted. I saw a long, prominent nose and a jutting chin, a profile distinctive enough to be recognized on a coin. His disheveled hair and beard were dark auburn with tinges of gold, and muscled arms swung from his broad shoulders. My skin prickled with excitement, and I understood how men could follow such a leader into battle without a thought for their own safety.

Within seconds the band of men had passed and the hall returned to silence. Slowly, other servants dashed out from the colonnade where they, too, had scurried out of the king's path.

"Is he as you imagined?" Petra said.

"Even finer-looking," I gushed, then turned away, embarrassed by my fervor.

Petra laughed. "Ah, you should have seen him a few years ago. He's aged since then."

"And the queen?" I asked. "Is she handsome as well?"

Petra shrugged. "Most say so, though her looks are quite different from his. You can judge for yourself when she returns to court. Now let's see about your dress. They'll be serving supper in the Lower Hall before long, and you don't want to miss that. There's no servants' slop here. We dine almost as well as the king."

I can still recall how it felt that first night, lying beneath those freshly laundered sheets, my legs exploring the novelty of an unshared bed. Despite the muffled sounds of the other housemaids, I felt utterly alone. Untethered from my past, yet a stranger in this new world. I wanted so desperately to belong in that magical place, where women boasted of their learning and men marched accompanied by the clang of swords. My mind summoned the memory of King Ranolf striding proudly down the hall. If the queen was half as striking, they would make for an imposing pair. How could I possibly be worthy of them? And if I were found wanting and sent away, how would my already shattered heart survive the blow?

Three

LADY OF SORROWS

I did not meet the woman who was to transform my life until my second week at the castle. It was an encounter that remains vivid in my memory to this day, for it was the first time I glimpsed the darkness that lurked beneath the pageantry of court. The first tiny step in my loss of innocence.

I had spent the previous days trailing after Petra, tending to the rooms of the queen's ladies-in-waiting. There were a dozen or so of these women, distant relations and daughters of noble families who lived at the castle under the king's protection. They were expected to serve as companions, but in the queen's absence they devoted themselves mostly to flirting and gossip. Cautiously, I had begun taking on tasks alone: rising before dawn to sweep away the previous night's ashes and light new fires, emptying chamber pots, filling basins with fresh water, retrieving breakfast trays from the kitchen and delivering them by the time each lady awakened. With the queen and her closest companions gone, the work was lighter than usual, yet I crumpled with exhaustion each night, worn out as much by the strain of fitting in as by the actual work. Lying in bed in the dark, I longed to turn to my mother for advice. The fact that I could not often left me racked with sobs; I muffled the sound with my pillow to avoid disturbing Petra and the other sleeping maids.

Despite my inner turmoil, I was able to fulfill my duties competently enough that Mrs. Tewkes agreed to move Petra to the Great Hall, where she would serve at meals. Petra could barely control her glee at leaving the chamber pots behind.

"You are not released yet," Mrs. Tewkes admonished. "I expect you to assist Elise for a time, to assure that her work is acceptable."

But when the royal traveling party arrived a day earlier than expected, we were caught unprepared.

"One of the queen's escorts has just arrived!" a footman cried out in the Lower Hall, where I was finishing my midday meal. "Her carriage is only a few minutes from the gates!"

I ran up the stairs to the queen's sitting room to see if I could be of assistance. Two other maids were sweeping the floor and polishing the chairs. The chamber was impressively large, in accordance with its occupant's rank, and adorned with decorative touches that feminized the space. The walls were hung with tapestries depicting maidens in gardens of roses, and images of flowers were carved onto the backs of the tall wooden chairs. A harp stood in one corner; in another a table was stacked with neat piles of fabric and colored thread. Through a door in the back of the room, I could see the queen's canopy-covered bed standing in solitary splendor, surrounded by drapes of purple velvet.

Mrs. Tewkes appeared behind me and nodded approvingly. "Good, good," she muttered. "Off to the kitchens now. The queen may request a bath after her journey, and we'll need plenty of hot water." I was starting to follow the other girls out the door when Mrs. Tewkes put her hand on my shoulder.

"Elise, light a fire. There's still a chill in the air."

Years at my family's hearth had taught me how best to coax a flame from twigs and tinder, and my skill had already attracted both praise and envy from the other maids. Only the day before, Mrs. Tewkes had decreed that I was to light the morning fires in all the noble ladies' rooms, including that of the queen when she returned. To my horror, I found that the logs piled in the basket next to the queen's hearth had been touched by damp, and it took longer than usual for the fire to catch. Only a single meager flame had taken hold when I heard a high-pitched chatter approaching from the hall. Standing, I pressed myself against the wall as a group of ladies entered. I kept my face turned toward the floor but raised my eyes enough to see a flurry of skirts. A floral scent wafted toward me as they passed.

"My lady, this fire has only just been lit," someone said close to me. "Perhaps we should retire somewhere warmer."

"It will do," a distant, weary voice replied.

I looked up toward the sound, but my gaze was blocked by an older woman who fixed me with accusing eyes, her lips thin with disapproval. Her sharp nose looked capable of stabbing me if I did not move quickly enough.

"Go on, then!" she snapped, waving her hand at the fireplace.

"Madam, I cannot hurry a flame," I tried to explain, but my retort must have been taken as impertinence, for the woman knocked my ear with the back of her hand.

"I'll tolerate no clever talk from you," she snarled. "Tend to your duties."

I sank to my knees and added another log, turning my back so she could not see the tears filling my eyes. I had spoken without thinking, ruining whatever chance I had to make a good impression on the queen. Would I be sent packing for a few thoughtless words?

"Leave the girl be, Selena," said the same hushed voice I had heard earlier.

The woman before me must be Lady Selena Wintermale, who Petra had told me served as the queen's first lady-in-waiting and closest companion. I did not doubt the woman's ability to keep order in these chambers; a few minutes at her side and I was already afraid of her. I stuck a poker in the growing blaze, angling my body slightly to catch a glimpse of the room behind me. Lady Wintermale strode back and forth, dictating to a young man wearing the purple-and-green tunic of a page. He nodded continuously, but from the look on his face I wondered how many of her commands he would remember.

"Bring my lady's doves from the tower, and make sure they have water in their bowls. The gold ones, not the silver."

"Yes, ma'am," said the page.

"Next, tell Cook my lady's stomach is troubled by her days of travel. A simple broth for dinner will do. . . ."

I looked past Lady Wintermale, toward the ring of chairs arranged in front of the fireplace. At the center stood one chair larger and wider than the others, its seat covered with a pillow of gold velvet. Four ladies in shimmering dresses stood around it, talking in quick, chirpy voices. Partially hidden behind their figures sat a woman dressed in a simple black gown. At first glance I might have taken her for a nun. Only the jewels braided into her hair marked her as royalty.

This, then, was Queen Lenore. She sat so quietly in that busy room, distancing herself from the commotion around her. Even her black hair and dusky skin set her apart from the light coloring of her ladies. She had the carriage and elegance of an aristocrat—I could not imagine those graceful hands washing linens or kneading dough—yet her dark eyes had the faraway look I had seen on many an overworked farm wife. I had never expected to see such sadness in a person so blessed.

I looked toward Lady Wintermale, wondering if she would indicate when the fire was acceptable. Catching my stare, she twisted her face in annoyance.

"You are dismissed," she ordered. "Make sure the fire is going before daylight tomorrow. My lady rises with the sun."

"Yes, ma'am." I curtsied quickly and left, reassured that I was to retain my position after all.

Later that night I told Petra I had been surprised by the queen's downhearted manner. "Is she always so?"

"Shush!" Sissy, the maid who slept on the other side of Petra, woke easily and often complained of the noise in the maids' room after dark.

"Shush yourself!" Petra hissed. There was nothing Petra enjoyed more than court gossip, and it would take more than Sissy's complaints to silence her. She turned back to me and whispered, "You should have seen the queen when she was first married. She's much changed since then."

"You were here?"

"I was just a girl, but my older sister was in service," Petra said. "For years, from what she said, the castle was quite a dull place. The old king, Ranolf's father, kept to himself after his wife died, and

King Ranolf and his brother, Prince Bowen, were rarely at home. They preferred to seek out novelty elsewhere. No doubt the king had his share of conquests during those travels, but there came the time when he was expected to do his duty and marry. The story is that the old king presented his son with a list of eligible young women in the kingdom. He had only to point to a name and she would be his. Yet Ranolf told his father he had his heart set on a young princess from a country so far distant that his father could not place it on a map. From the moment Ranolf met her, he would have no other. Can you imagine?"

Love at first sight. I smiled to know that such things were possible.

"No heir to the throne had ever married a foreigner. They say the queen's family was equally hesitant to send their child so far from home. But she was the youngest daughter and much indulged. Her father acquiesced to her wishes."

"Did you see any of the festivities?"

"Princess Lenore slept at the Convent of St. Anne's the night before," Petra said. "Her procession passed through the valley that morning, and people cheered and threw flowers toward her carriage. I stood along the road with my parents, and I had never heard such a commotion. The princess kept her face hidden, as is the custom, but she reached her hand out the window to wave, and I just about fainted with the thrill of it.

"When her carriage arrived at the main gate of the castle, the old king himself walked out to greet her and escort her inside. The wedding ceremony was held in the chapel, with only the highest-ranking families in attendance. But afterward, before the wedding feast, King Ranolf took his bride by the hand and led her upstairs to the Gold Chamber. I heard from one of the ladies' maids that they giggled like children. Ranolf threw open the doors that look out over the castle courtyard and the town, then brought her out onto the balcony.

"'I present your future queen!' he announced. My sister was in the courtyard, readying tables of food and wine for the servants' feast, and she said they were the most beautiful couple she had ever seen. We'd heard talk of this foreign woman who would bring wicked customs to our land, but she charmed the whole court from that moment. Her husband, too. From what I heard, their wedding night lasted well into the next day."

"What?" I asked, shocked. "Surely her servants would not speak of such private matters?"

Petra laughed. "Not just the servants!" she said. "Both families expected a report on the consummation. The news that King Ranolf could barely drag himself from his bride's arms was seen as a good omen."

Petra lay quietly for a few moments. I wondered if she had drifted off to sleep. She yawned, then adjusted her pillow and continued.

"The old king died not long after the wedding, and once the period of mourning was over, there were grand entertainments every week: jousting, riding excursions, balls. Anyone would have described the king and queen as the happiest couple alive. When I first came here, a few years ago, I happened upon them once in her chamber, holding hands like young sweethearts. At dinner she would feed him bites from her plate or wipe a trace of food from his mouth. That's long over, though. Ever since she proved herself barren."

"Oh, no," I murmured.

"Eight years the king has waited for an heir, in vain," Petra said. "The queen spends more time consulting doctors than verses of poetry these days. And now that the king lies with her but once a month, she is even less likely to find herself with child."

"Once a month? How do you know?" I asked.

"The laundress who changes the bedsheets reports to Lady Wintermale whenever there are relations. I suppose it's no surprise the queen has turned desperate."

"What do you mean?"

"Her pilgrimage." Petra drew out the word disdainfully.

"I thought she was visiting a hot springs, for her health," I said.

"That's the story put about, but I heard from Lady Wintermale's maid that the ladies traveled to a shrine in the mountains. The queen must be close to losing hope if she begs intercession from a saint that only country folk care about. Especially if it meant spending a week in the company of Madam Millicent." She drew out the final word, her voice sharp with contempt.

Did a shiver of warning speed through my body the first time I heard that fateful name? It would make for a more dramatic tale if I could claim such a premonition. In truth I was more curious than concerned.

"Who?" I asked.

"Ah, I forgot, you haven't seen her yet. Lady Millicent, the king's maiden aunt."

Many spinsters lived off the king's generosity, most of them irritable old women who complained that the fire was too cold or the food too hot when they were lucky to have a roof over their heads at all. But the hardening of Petra's expression implied that this woman was a more formidable presence than the rest.

"She was the one who convinced the queen that a week of prayer in a freezing chapel would cure her womb," Petra continued. "The king was against it. Said God would hear her prayers just as well from the royal chapel. But Millicent got her way, the old witch."

I could not believe that a servant would speak so disrespectfully of a member of the royal family.

"Forgive me, I should not have said such a thing," Petra said, seeing my shock. "I do not mean that she conjures up spells over a black kettle, though some believe her capable of such nonsense. Best to avoid her, that's all. She takes offense easily, and those who cross her pay the price. Drove her own sister round the bend, they say."

"What happened?" I asked.

Petra shook her head, brushing off my question and the subject of Millicent. "I've already said more than I should."

She turned from me and lay down, the hair splayed across her pillow shimmering in the darkness. The heavy breathing and shifting bodies of the other maids reminded me that we were not alone, that I must be mindful of what I said.

"Petra?" I whispered.

"Hmm?"

"There may be hope yet for the queen. I will pray for her."

I did not expect a response, but after a few moments Petra's hushed voice broke the silence.

"My father says it's a family curse. Time and again the fate of the kingdom has hung on the life of a single boy. The king's father was his parents' sole surviving son, as was his father before him. The king and Prince Bowen were the first brothers in generations to live to adulthood. Everyone thought they would usher in a new era of prosperity. Yet both remain childless."

Raised in a large family, I was accustomed to shouts and chatter and babies' cries. Was it the lack of such sounds that made the castle's vast, silent hallways so eerie?

"Will Prince Bowen inherit the throne if the king has no children?" I asked.

"I suppose so."

"Poor Queen Lenore. No wonder she looks sad."

What I did not know then was that the queen's suffering went deeper than I could ever imagine. At my young age, I could not understand how the glowing young bride of Petra's story had become the withdrawn woman I saw seated before the fireplace, for I knew nothing of the lengths to which a desperate woman will go in order to bear a child.

The next morning I crept into the queen's bedchamber as the first shafts of sunlight brightened the windows. The queen herself was visible only as a slight rise in the middle of the bed, almost entirely hidden under an embroidered coverlet. I tiptoed around her personal attendant, Isla, snoring on a straw mattress on the floor, and swept the previous night's ashes from the fireplace. Gingerly, I placed fresh logs inside, trying not to make a sound, and started a fire. When the flame was well established, I returned to the hall and carried in a bucket of water, pouring it into the elegant china basin that stood on a long table underneath the window. As the water fell, my eyes wandered to a piece of parchment lying on the table before me. Idly, I read the words written on it in an elegant, meticulous hand:

Where love has bloomed,
It surely must fade,
A memory of its perfume
All that remains . . .

"Girl."

I swung around, terrified of being called to task for idling. Queen Lenore was sitting up in the bed, looking directly at me. Her dark eyes were bloodshot and her cheeks damp with tears.

"Pass me a cloth." Her accent gave the simple words a melodious rhythm.

I took a square of folded linen from a pile next to the basin and handed it to her. She ran the fabric over her eyes and beneath her nose before passing it back to me. As she reached out, the sleeve of her nightdress fell back to reveal an angry red gash on her inner arm, a wound that had only recently begun to heal. How could a woman of such privilege have come by such a cruel injury?

I should have taken the cloth from the queen without speaking and disappeared as I was expected to. But her drawn expression made me want to linger, to divert her from that grief.

"Madam, the poem," I said, glancing back at the paper on the table behind me. "Did you write it?"

Her eyes widened with surprise as she nodded.

"It's beautiful," I said.

"You can read?" Her tone carried no hint of mockery. "What is your name?"

"Elise."

"That will be all, Elise."

I curtsied and turned away, belatedly shocked by my own forwardness. I had taken a great risk, yet the encounter had gone in my favor. Despite Lady Wintermale's glares, my position might be secure after all.

And so it appeared in the following weeks. Every morning I lit a fire as the queen awoke and brought her a cloth to wipe her face, as if it were perfectly normal to greet each day with tears. Day after day we followed the same routine. The queen never said more than a few words to me, yet I felt a bond of affection for her out of all proportion to the time I spent in her presence. She had an innate warmth of manner that made me sympathize with her plight, despite the vast difference in our ages and ranks. Like me, she was an outsider, cut off from her family, an object of disparaging gossip with no natural allies at court. Yet, like my mother, she carried herself with dignity and resolve. Is it any wonder I should feel drawn to her?

As Petra had predicted, my appointment to the royal ladies' chambers had set off a storm of complaints to Mrs. Tewkes, and jealousy cut me off from those who might otherwise have been my friends. The other maids' distaste for me was only reinforced by my ignorance of the Lower Hall's pecking order, where the hierarchies were murkier than in the royal apartments. One night at supper, finding the bench where Petra was seated already full, I slid onto an empty seat at a nearby table. The women seated there—clearly fellow maids, for we all wore the same gray wool dresses—glanced at me in silence, then at one another.

I introduced myself, and still not a sound was uttered. Confused and ashamed, I stared down at my bowl and ate as quickly as possible, my face flushed with humiliation. As I rushed out from the hall, tears trickling down my cheeks, I heard Petra calling after me.

"Never mind them," she said airily as I wiped my face with my apron. "It was an easy enough mistake."

"Why wouldn't they speak to me?"

"They're seamstresses." Seeing my continued confusion, she sighed and explained. "They think they're better than us, just because they've never had to pour out a pitcher of piss. Fancy themselves quite the fine ladies."

A smile began to creep up one side of my mouth, and Petra went on, gratified by my reaction.

"You'd think no one else here could even thread a needle, the way they carry on. As if I'd want to be trapped in the sewing room all day, bent over a pair of Lady Wintermale's underclothes. You watch, they'll all end up hunchbacks and we'll have the last laugh."

I did giggle then, and Petra convinced me to return with her to the hall. In hushed tones, she explained the seating patterns that so mystified me. The pages sat with the valets, never the footmen. The footmen occasionally ate with the carpenters and other skilled laborers, but anyone from the stables who dared to join them would be shunned—unless of course it was the head groom, in which case his company would be an honor. As a chambermaid I was expected to sit with the greenest, youngest maids; in a pinch I was permitted to join the upper housemaids at their table, but to do so often would be considered presumptuous. The ladies' maids, who attended to the needs of the noble ladies-in-waiting, sat at their own table at one side of the room, speaking only to one another and pointedly ignoring the rest of us. They were the Lower Hall's royalty.

Petra, bless her, found me an intriguing novelty rather than a nuisance. It seemed half the castle staff was related to her in some way, and she enjoyed conversing with someone whose life was not already known to her. She would ask me about the farm with the wistful expression of one who has never had to milk cows at dawn. When I told her about my mother and my brothers—slowly and briefly, for the wound still ached—she wept along with me. And when she found out I could read and write, she asked for my help in learning her letters. *This is what it must be like to have a sister,* I thought as we sat companionably together, poring over scraps of parchment begged from Mrs. Tewkes. Without Petra my life would have been dismal indeed, and anything I made of myself at the castle was due in part to her generous spirit.

During those brief moments when my duties were complete and Petra was not available to act as my defender, I lingered outside the queen's rooms, hoping to take on any humble errand that might bring me into her presence. It was there that I came face-to-face with the woman who had intrigued me ever since her name passed Petra's lips.

I have vowed to recount my tale without benefit of hindsight, depicting events as they happened. So while it is difficult for me to separate my early memories of Millicent from the knowledge of what she would one day become, I speak the truth when I say our first encounter left me shaken. I had seen the king's aunt occasionally from a distance, among the other elderly ladies of the court. Up close, however, I was taken aback to realize she had once been beautiful. Though age had whitened her hair and loosened her skin, it had not altered her most striking features: a straight, narrow nose; large green-gray eyes; full lips; and a broad, curved forehead. She wore her hair pulled back tight in the old-fashioned way, without tendrils to soften the lines of her cheekbones, drawing all the more attention to her regal face. She walked with a determined stride, each step punctuated by the tap of a cane I suspected she carried not from necessity but to warn others of her approach.

Her eyes bored into mine with such intensity that I felt frozen to the spot, unable even to curtsy as etiquette demanded.

"Have you nothing better to do than idle about?" she demanded. Her voice was husky and rich, each word issued with commanding authority.

The lie slipped effortlessly from my lips. "I have been given leave to assist the queen's ladies."

"Hmph." I could not tell if the sound indicated satisfaction or doubt. "In that case make yourself useful. I left a cape on my bed. Go fetch it."

"Yes, madam," I said, dropping my head respectfully. "Begging your pardon, but where will I find your room?"

Millicent exhaled sharply, put out by my ignorance. "The North Tower. First door at the top of the marble staircase. Go."

Her words were a jumble to me, but I would not risk her displeasure with further questions. As Millicent marched off toward the queen's rooms, I made my way toward the central servants' staircase. At the time I knew nothing of the North Tower's sad history, and I could not have imagined the terrible role it would play one day in my own life. Yet a sense of foreboding sank over me as I followed the narrow passage pointed out to me by one of the footmen, a lonely, deserted extension of the castle's otherwise bustling service corridors.

I put my nervousness down to fear of disappointing Millicent, a fear that only heightened after I emerged from the passage into a grand hall. I was immediately struck by the sensation of openness and light the room imparted. Unlike the rest of the castle, which retained the feel of a fortress, this section had large windows and whitewashed walls. Statues of knights in heroic poses were arranged in alcoves, interspersed with tapestries of nature scenes. The room had a sense of proportion and grace that even Lenore's apartments lacked. Why, then, were these quarters deserted, save for Millicent?

Millicent. I knew I mustn't provoke her wrath by dawdling, yet I could not see the marble staircase of which she had spoken. I turned one way, then another, eventually losing my bearings completely. The angles of the stone walls caused my footsteps to echo back from unexpected directions, so that I felt myself pursued by a foe who was first one step ahead, then one behind. Willing myself to remain calm, I used the windows to orient myself and discern where the tower joined up with the central fortress. A few more turns and I came upon the object of my quest: a staircase lined in pink marble. At the top stood two doors, both closed.

I walked upward, looking for signs of habitation, but could find no discernible difference between them. Then I heard a faint, quavering sound, coming from behind the door on the right. I took a step closer. The sound moved higher in pitch, then lower. It was a woman's voice, singing. The words were indistinct, but the notes had a melancholy beauty that carried the weight of loss.

I knocked gently, calling, "Hello?"

The sound abruptly ceased. I reached out and took hold of the handle, but the wood did not shift when I pushed against it. My skin prickled with the awareness of another's presence, willing me gone, and I felt a sudden urge to run from the tower and whatever strange doings it concealed. I stepped quickly to the neighboring door, which yielded with a creak to my touch. As soon as I entered, I knew I had found Millicent's room.

Most of the women passing their final years in the castle had few possessions, their lack of wealth being the primary reason they lived off the king's charity. A few had brooches painted with likenesses of their late husbands; others gave small ivory or silver crosses pride of place. As the king's aunt, Millicent would be granted larger quarters than most, yet I was still shocked by the grandeur of her room, with its soaring ceiling and dazzling glints of gemstones and gold. A massive bed filled the center of the room, with elaborately carved posts that extended well over my head; a crest of four trees surrounding a boar and other wild game was etched into the headboard. On either side of the bed sat heavy chairs and storage trunks, all of a size and luxury unheard of for a spinster's room.

As I stepped farther inside, I noticed objects scattered across every flat surface, from the heavy stone mantelpiece to the tops of the trunks to the edges of the table where Millicent kept her washing basin and hair combs. Delicate silver spoons, rings inlaid with stones in colors I had never seen, a bowl of aromatic flower petals—each new discovery filled me with wonder. But what intrigued me most were the miniature figures arrayed over the fireplace. A few had the look of saints, but others depicted women whose manner of dress was foreign to me. One tiny, rough wood carving had no clothes at all, drawing all the more attention to her swollen breasts and pregnant stomach. Another, no bigger than my thumb and crafted from a strange green stone, was polished to such a gloss that my hands were involuntarily drawn toward it. This woman was naked as well, and though the immodesty disturbed me, I found myself oddly soothed as I ran my fingertips along the smooth curves, wondering who could have made such a thing.

"What are you doing?"

Mortified, I turned to see Millicent standing in the doorway. I dropped into a hasty curtsy, my legs wobbly with fear.

"Thought you'd help yourself to whatever caught your fancy, eh?" she snapped.

"No," I protested. "I lost my way, I've only just arrived—"

Millicent cut me off, her voice icy as she pointed to my hand. "And what do you have there?"

She reached out toward my clutched fingers and pried them open. She seemed taken aback when she saw what I held; the green statuette remained cradled in my palm for a moment as she looked at me suspiciously, then back at the strange little woman. I felt sick with fear. If Millicent chose to believe I was stealing, she could have me turned out in disgrace. My word would count as nothing against hers.

Desperate to avoid such a fate, I fell to my knees.

"Please, madam, I was only admiring it. I have never seen such a thing before."

"I am sure of that," Millicent said tartly.

I held out the figurine and pressed it into her hands. My subservient posture and obvious distress appeared to mollify Millicent, for she snorted and motioned me to stand.

"My cape," she said briskly.

A swath of deep green velvet was draped along the bottom of the bed. As I picked it up, the fabric rippled over my arms and I saw that the edges were embroidered with a pattern of alternating diamonds and stars. Instantly, I knew. Mother had painstakingly stitched the same pattern on the bodice of my Sunday dress; I could see the tiny diagonal thread lines that were typical of her work. I had searched in vain for a trace of my mother since arriving at the castle; now, here in my hands, I had found it. My fingers lingered on the stitches, following the lines laid out years before. Millicent stared impatiently, and I held up the cape behind her, gulping down a sob as I was overcome by a wave of grief. She twisted around and stared in confusion as my face crumpled in anguish.

"I am so sorry," I mumbled. "The cape looks very much like the work of my mother. My late mother."

"You must be mistaken. It was made by one of the castle seamstresses."

"Mayren?" I asked softly.

The name caught her by surprise. Then confusion gave way to understanding, and she reached out, cupping my chin with one hand. As she gazed into my face, it was as if she saw past the chambermaid's uniform to the young woman within, all the way down to the relentless ambition I kept hidden beneath a humble façade. My hopes for advancement, my fear of humiliation, the shame of my bastard birth—she did not condemn me for any of it. The power she commanded flowed from her skin into mine, and my body tingled with expectation.

"Yes," she murmured. "I see it now."

She dropped her hand and pulled the sides of the cape around her body and walked to the fireplace, reaching toward the mantelpiece to replace the green figurine. Then she paused, her hand in midair, reconsidering. With a swirl of fabric, she turned and passed the piece to me.

"If this of all things caught your eye, then you shall have it."

I sank into a deep curtsy and thanked her. The tiny woman both fascinated and repulsed me, yet I could not stop my fingers from sliding repeatedly across the lustrous stone.

"Who is she?" I asked. "A saint?"

Millicent snorted in amusement. "Hardly. These sorts of carvings are called wishing stones. Rub the belly and your deepest desires will come to pass. So they say." She uttered the words with a smile, but her eyes gleamed mischievously. Was she making light of the servants' suspicions that she could harness the powers of witchcraft? Or was she acknowledging that the whispers were true?

I scurried to keep up with Millicent during our return to the royal apartments; despite her age she walked at a brisk pace on legs that were longer than mine. At the doorway to the queen's rooms, she stopped abruptly and asked my name.

"Elise, madam."

"You are a most curious girl, Elise. I do wonder what you will make of yourself here."

It was impossible to tell from her enigmatic look whether she foresaw success or failure. Curiously, the uncertainty did not trouble me. I was now known by name to the king's aunt, proof I was setting myself apart from the other maids, although I could not yet guess what advantages her favor would bring.

That night I retrieved the wishing stone from my trunk and tucked it under my pillow. Each night from then on, my fingers rubbed against it rhythmically, calming me for sleep. Did that heathen trinket possess magical powers? I will not risk damnation by saying so. But it is also the God's honest truth that the queen unexpectedly appointed me head housemaid of her apartments mere days after the stone came into my possession. On the first day I undertook my new duties, Millicent swept by me in the hallway, pausing briefly to nod in my direction. It was a passing gaze, no more, yet I understood her meaning instantly. She was watching me, taking note of my progress, assessing my talent. To what end?

⟡

Though Millicent was an elderly woman, dependent on her nephew's generosity, she did not carry herself as a supplicant. Quite the opposite. Born and raised at the castle, she marched through its halls flush with self-importance, quick to reprimand servants and courtiers alike. According to Mrs. Tewkes, she had once played a prominent role at court, even sitting on the Royal Council after the death of the king's father, but King Ranolf had tired of her hectoring and relegated her to a minor position, overseeing the needs of her fellow spinsters. Yet she had never stopped trying to insinuate herself into affairs of state, and her attentiveness to Queen Lenore made her a regular presence in the royal apartments.

As the days drifted toward midsummer, it seemed Millicent was always there, at the edge of my gaze, hovering over the queen, delighting in Lady Wintermale's jealous glares. How can I explain, in mere words, the effect she had on me? It was as if the very air sparked in her presence. Enthralled by her air of mystery, I found myself standing straighter and going about my tasks with fresh vigor, swelling with pride whenever she looked my way.

The other ladies grumbled about Millicent's growing sway over the queen, and I wondered what the two women discussed during their hushed, private conversations. There remained something unsettled about my mistress, as if her thoughts were far removed from the everyday routines of court life. Whenever she was granted some measure of solitude—in the late afternoon when her ladies dispersed to dress for supper or early on Sunday morning before services in the chapel—I would find her staring out the window, her expression troubled. Although I did see her smile, even laugh, she had the lethargy that comes from troubled sleep, and she moved through the castle halls with the hesitant pace of one pushing through waist-high water. On the few occasions the king arranged for evening entertainment, she usually excused herself and retired early.

The place Queen Lenore seemed most at ease was her workroom, a chamber adjoining her sitting room where she had set up a loom, a spinning wheel, and tables piled with the most luxurious fabrics I had ever seen. Though a woman of her rank was expected to have a certain expertise in fine needlework, she preferred the humbler pursuits of weaving and knitting, going so far as to spin her own yarns and threads. Though such diversions may have caused eye rolling among certain noble ladies, I admired her skill in those womanly arts. Seen at her spinning wheel, lost in the task at hand, she might have been any other wife, taking pride in her accomplishments.

Though I was spending more time in her presence, Queen Lenore and I had never exchanged more than a few pleasantries on the day that her personal maidservant, Isla, summoned me into the royal bedchamber for a private audience. The queen stood beside her bed, her dark hair and eyes in striking contrast to her deep crimson gown. Had she a more imperious manner, I would have been cowed by her regal bearing. Instead she smiled warmly and beckoned me over.

"Elise, I have been much pleased by your service," she began.

I suppressed a foolish grin of delight into a modest smile.

"My husband informs me that we will be graced with a visit from his brother, Prince Bowen, before the month is out," she said. I had yet to meet King Ranolf's younger brother, who was said to prefer a life of travel and adventure to the routines of court. My heart began thudding with anticipation. Was I to take part in the preparations for his arrival?

"Prince Bowen's valet, Hessler, has been courting my Isla for more than a year," Queen Lenore continued. "They have been separated much of that time, but now he has written to ask her hand, and I have given my consent. They shall be married when Prince Bowen returns."

I knew that Isla had accompanied the queen from her homeland on her marriage and that the women shared a close bond. Indeed, the queen's eyes held a hint of sorrow as she added, "Much as I wish Isla at my side, I will not keep two lovers apart. Upon her marriage Isla's place will be in Prince Bowen's household, not mine."

I nodded in what I hoped was a gracious manner, impatient to hear what plans Queen Lenore had for me. Would I be given the honor of waiting on Prince Bowen during his visit?

"As a result I will soon be in need of a new personal attendant," the queen continued. "I have informed Mrs. Tewkes that I would like you to take on those duties."

In my most fantastical daydreams, I had never imagined such an offer. A rush of delight washed over me, until I realized, aghast, the consequences of taking Isla's place. I could light a fire well enough, but a lady's maid was expected to be as refined as her mistress. I could not allow myself to be an embarrassment to a woman I so revered.

"My . . . my lady," I stammered, "you do me the greatest honor, but there are countless others more suited to such a role."

"You are very young," she said, looking at me kindly, "yet all you need to know can be learned in time. I made this choice because you have qualities that cannot be taught."

She approached closer and leaned in, her smile fading and her voice dropping to a low whisper. "Every morning you see me weep. You have told no one of my tears?"

I shook my head.

The queen glanced around to assure that none could overhear us. "I am accustomed to scrutiny," she continued. "Lady Wintermale keeps me informed of the court gossip; it is perhaps her most important duty. If you had been confiding my secrets to your fellow servants, she would have had word of it soon enough. Yet she has made no mention of my weakness. You have proved your loyalty."

I wanted to serve the queen more than I had ever wanted anything in my life, but I feared I was not ready for such a leap. I could only disappoint her and shame myself. Yet as I gazed into Queen Lenore's dark, penetrating eyes, I felt enveloped by her grace. This woman, so kind and yet so mournful, trusted me. And I would do anything to make her happy.

"I am yours," I said.

Had I known the sacrifices my service to Queen Lenore would ultimately entail, would my answer have been the same?

I arrived in the Lower Hall for supper that evening, anxious to tell Petra my news, but I saw no sign of her at the table where we usually took our meals. One of the other chambermaids quickly shook her head as I approached.

"That's your place now," the girl said curtly, pointing to the table where the ladies' maids gathered.

Surprised and embarrassed, I hesitated.

"Yes, we've all heard of your good fortune," she said. "News spreads faster than a fire in the servants' quarters. Congratulations." There was no warmth in her words, nor on the faces of the young women seated around her.

I turned and walked away, dropping my eyes downward to avoid the curious stares of the other servants. When I arrived at the table where Isla was seated, she slid from the edge of the bench to make space for me to sit. None of the other attendants did more than nod in my direction. To shun me completely would be an insult to the queen, but their near silence made clear I would not be welcomed into the inner ranks of their fellowship.

Worse was to come. When I retired to the maids' quarters that night, I found Petra in bed, eyes closed, but I could tell by her breathing that she was not asleep.

I whispered her name, then poked at the bedsheets.

"What?" she mumbled.

"Please, Petra. I want to talk."

"I did not think you could spare the time, with your new duties." I had never heard this bitter tone from her before.

"I wanted to tell you earlier," I tried to explain. "But the queen had so many instructions I couldn't get away before supper."

Petra's voice was muffled against her blanket. "I am sure you were quite overwhelmed. Forgive me, I have limited experience with the many duties of a lady's maid."

"I have rather limited experience myself," I said with a weak smile.

Petra, always so quick to laugh, didn't acknowledge the joke. I watched her icicle-blond hair slide across her pillow as she turned to face me, propping her head in one hand.

"Why you?" she asked with a mix of puzzlement and wounded pride. "I served her for more than a year, and she had no complaints with my work. Yet I remain a serving maid while you become the queen's personal attendant. Why?"

I thought of the lucky stone hidden under my pillow, of the nights I had caressed it, hoping for fortune to smile upon me. Now it had, beyond my wildest imaginings.

"I swear, I knew nothing of this offer before today," I assured Petra. "It took me as much by surprise as it did you."

Petra's head collapsed back onto her pillow. "I'm sorry. I cannot help but speak my mind when I feel I have been wronged."

"All that matters to me is that we remain friends," I said.

"I have no doubt we shall."

Her voice proved the words a lie, for they had the formal tone she used when serving at table. From the day of my arrival at the castle, Petra had been the person I looked to for guidance, yet as of this day I outranked her. And with our change in status, the easy bond between us unraveled. Petra was too kindhearted to cut me off completely; once the hurt faded, she greeted me with the same pleasantries as she did the rest of the household staff. But I feared that our days of sharing confidences were over. It was a loss that stung more than I could have imagined.

Though I continued to sleep in the maids' quarters, my waking hours were spent almost exclusively in Queen Lenore's company. My new duties were even more daunting than I had expected. I watched as Isla consulted the queen on her clothing for the day, assisted her with dressing, arranged her hair, and shadowed her throughout the day, stepping forward to smooth her gown or fetch her needlework. On my first attempt at twisting the queen's hair into the intricate style she favored, my fingers caught in a tangle and I felt her flinch. Though she assured me it was no matter, I carried the guilt of having caused her pain and hoped desperately she was not regretting her choice.

One evening, after snarling the laces of Queen Lenore's gown so thoroughly that she was late for supper, I slumped against the wall in defeat.

"Come, now," Isla said, her voice rising and falling in the same melodic rhythm as the queen's. "Are you crying?"

I turned away so she would not see my tears. Outside the window, shadows stretched across the garden, a tranquil retreat fenced off from the hubbub of the stables and storerooms at the south end of the castle. It had been cunningly designed with a series of curved pathways that revealed distinct vistas: a fragrant herb garden, a small field of wildflowers, a stone fountain carved with mermaids, and a mass of rosebushes transported from Queen Lenore's native land. I eagerly took any chance offered to fetch fresh blooms from the gardeners, for that haven was the one place where the vista was one of trees and leaves rather than gloomy gray stone. For a few minutes, I could imagine myself in the open lands of my childhood.

As I looked downward, watching shadows create filigreed patterns along the paths, my eye was caught by a sudden flash of white in a far corner, opposite the entrance. I followed the movement for only a moment before it disappeared behind the bushes.

I must have tensed in surprise, for Isla asked, "What is it?"

"The garden," I said hesitantly. "I thought I saw . . ." A ghost? It was the first thought that came to mind, though I dared not say it aloud.

"Saw what?"

"Nothing," I said. "A trick of the light."

Meek and quiet by nature, Isla rarely spoke of personal matters. So I was surprised when she pressed one hand against my arm and said, "Do not trouble yourself with worry. The queen is pleased by your progress."

"I have been a great disappointment," I said, my voice shaky. "You cannot deny it."

"You have been discreet, and that is more important than anything else. She needs such loyalty, now more than ever."

I wondered at Isla's meaning, but she had already begun clearing off the dressing table. Had I been more practiced at reading the signs before me, I might have guessed the matter that lay so heavily on the queen's mind. But I passed those days fretting about hairstyles and anticipating Prince Bowen's return, little aware of the monumental changes looming before us.

Four

HEIR APPARENT

With Prince Bowen's arrival imminent, I became most curious about this royal brother, who was rumored to rival King Ranolf in looks and far surpass him in female conquests. Queen Lenore, however, was put out that Bowen's messenger had only a vague notion of when his master might arrive.

"How are we to arrange a suitable homecoming if we are not apprised of his plans?" she fretted, after passing yet another fruitless day waiting for her brother-in-law.

"Bowen has a long history of disregarding others," King Ranolf said with a scowl, pacing back and forth in front of the fireplace. "He's likely to halt his journey altogether if struck by the urge to hunt along the way."

"From what I've been told, foxes and pheasants are not the only creatures that fear his weapon," one of the younger ladies said suggestively. "Is he not likely to brandish his sword before any comely lass who crosses his path?"

The assembled women dissolved into laughter, and even King

Ranolf smiled. Queen Lenore shook her head in disapproval, but I could tell by the way her lips curved up on one side that she was stifling her own amusement.

"Hang Bowen and his whims," the king declared after the giggling had died down. "This talk of hunting has me missing the saddle. Tomorrow I'll ride out with my men."

So it was that the queen was left to welcome her brother-in-law alone when he appeared without warning the following day. As soon as a page announced Prince Bowen's arrival, she allowed herself a quick glance in the mirror, then took her place in the chair before the fireplace, pointing to where her ladies should array themselves around her. I arranged the skirt of her gown so it cascaded in rippling waves to the floor.

I had just finished when Prince Bowen strode into the doorway and paused, admiring the scene before him and allowing himself to be admired in turn. He was, by any measure, an exceedingly handsome man, with the same broad frame and dark auburn hair as King Ranolf, and he bristled with the tightly suppressed energy of one who prefers action to conversation. As he approached us, however, his appearance called to mind a poorly executed painting: possessing a certain grandeur from a distance yet revealing a shabby technique upon close inspection. His eyes, which twinkled flirtatiously at Queen Lenore's attendants, were watery and tinged with pink. His skin was weathered from hours spent in the saddle, and though he was only in his late twenties, a good decade younger than the king, he already appeared to have lived a harder life.

"Beloved sister," Prince Bowen announced, reaching for Queen Lenore's hand and bowing low over it. His lips brushed lightly across her skin.

"Brother." Her mouth curved into a smile that was not reflected in her eyes. "How was your journey?"

"I rejoiced at each mile that brought me closer to you."

"I see you have perfected the art of flattery." Queen Lenore nodded toward the chair beside her. "Come, tell me of your travels."

She caught my eye and motioned toward the door, where a footman had entered with a pitcher of wine and two crystal goblets upon a brass tray.

"Mrs. Tewkes sends word that she is preparing Prince Bowen's usual rooms," the man said.

"I will tell the queen," I said, taking the tray and clutching at the edges to stop my hands from shaking. I had developed one important attribute of a handmaiden, the ability to read my mistress's mind, and I could see that Queen Lenore was uneasy entertaining her brother-in-law alone. Why?

Prince Bowen was finishing up a tale.

"And *that* is why the women of Romany have such a reputation," he concluded with a rascally grin.

Queen Lenore laughed politely, while the silliest of her ladies gasped with mock horror or threw their hands over their mouths in exaggerated modesty.

"Mind, you're not to tell my brother I've been filling your head with such scandal," Prince Bowen admonished Queen Lenore. "He would not approve."

"You expect me to keep secrets from my husband?"

"How could you, my lady? Lips as sweet as yours were made to tell only truth."

Queen Lenore caught my eye and smiled gratefully. "Ah, here's the wine." She nodded at me to pour it. I crossed the room and set the tray on top of a large wooden trunk that sat directly under the window. I was aware of Prince Bowen's eyes on me as I walked, and I fumbled with the pitcher's handle. It slipped in my hand, and wine splashed onto the tray.

"Have a care, girl!" he cried out. "Leave some for us to drink!"

My face flushed with embarrassment, I left the wet tray on the trunk and carried the glasses over, serving Prince Bowen first. His hand reached around mine as he took the goblet, imprisoning it for a moment.

"Straight off the farm, are you?" he asked.

The insult stung, but I stared straight down, silent. Better he think me slow than insolent.

"I can feel it in your hands. Rather rough for a lady's maid."

Queen Lenore reached for her glass, and I pulled away from Prince Bowen's grasp.

"One can have both a modest upbringing and gracious manners," Queen Lenore noted.

"Wise words, and a wise choice. Simple girls are less likely to turn your husband's head."

"Is this how you would speak of your brother before his wife?" Queen Lenore asked stiffly.

Prince Bowen laughed. "I beg your forgiveness. Too much time at decadent foreign courts has given me a taste for lewd humor."

He drained his glass and motioned me to refill his goblet. "Do you know why Ranolf summoned me here with such urgency?"

Queen Lenore's face tightened. Prince Bowen's visit had been discussed among the ladies as a social call; this was the first I had heard of the king's sending for his brother. Apparently the news was a surprise to the queen as well.

"Wives are not privy to all their husband's decisions," she said.

"God help us if they were!" Prince Bowen laughed.

We heard footsteps approaching, and a slim young man in a long cloak and muddy riding boots stepped inside.

"Beg your pardon, my lady," he said with a bow. "My lord, I was sent to inform you that your rooms are ready, if you wish to change."

"Thank you, Hessler."

This, then, was Prince Bowen's valet, Isla's future husband. I could see how she would have been dazzled by him, with his clear blue eyes and tall, elegant bearing. Were it not for his servant's livery, I would have mistaken him for a gentleman. His eyes searched the room quickly, then lighted upon Isla, who smiled shyly but with evident pleasure.

Prince Bowen stood from his chair and wagged a finger in my direction. "Enough gawking, miss, my man is already spoken for." I blushed, mortified at being singled out, and Prince Bowen's eyes flashed with amusement.

Ducking his head toward Queen Lenore, he said, "I must make myself presentable before Ranolf returns."

"Until supper, then," she said, rising to see him off. "Isla, you may take your leave as well. I am sure you and your intended have much to discuss."

After Prince Bowen strode off, followed by Hessler and Isla, the queen collapsed into her chair, spent of her charm.

"Ladies, you may see to yourselves," she said. "We must welcome our guest and his men with suitable ceremony tonight."

The ladies-in-waiting chattered brightly as they left the room, relishing the opportunity to preen before a new group of potential admirers. The queen and I remained alone. She had not moved.

"My lady?" I asked cautiously.

"It has always been this way between us." She sighed. "Bowen flirts and flatters, yet does everything in his power to lessen my influence with the king."

"Shall I leave you to rest?"

"Yes. Please tell Lady Wintermale that I am not to be disturbed for the next hour. After that you may help me prepare for this evening."

"Yes, madam." I placed the glasses on the tray and picked it up. As I walked toward the door, she called out my name, and I paused.

"How did the prince strike you? Speak plainly."

Taken aback by her familiarity, I tried to order my thoughts. My immediate reaction was to tell her that Prince Bowen made my skin crawl. But he was the king's brother. I had to consider my words carefully.

"He appears very confident. A man accustomed to having all eyes upon him."

"So he is," said the queen. "Yet he remains a younger brother without a title, and these are treacherous times."

I was not sure how to respond. Isla and the queen had an easy rapport, but they had grown up together. How could I presume to offer advice to a noblewoman? I simply nodded, my face impassive.

"With no heir, the king and I find ourselves in a precarious position," she continued. "Bowen is next in the line of succession, and he is young and vigorous. He may covet the title before we are ready to release it."

My heart sank at the thought of arrogant Prince Bowen ruling over us. But he was the rightful heir.

"Elise, will you inform Mrs. Tewkes that my digestion is unsettled? I would like to be served plain chicken and bread this evening." She looked so distressed that I wished I could embrace her, the way my mother had comforted me when I was a child. Of course, such an intimate gesture was unimaginable. Queen Lenore was a porcelain figure, to be set on display and admired from afar. She would shatter if I touched her.

She looked up at me with worried, exhausted eyes. "Do not be fooled by the fine manners. At court, enemies hide in plain sight."

Mrs. Tewkes and the kitchen staff prepared a splendid banquet to celebrate Prince Bowen's return. I peeked into the Great Hall as the festivities began and was awed by the opulence before me: silver platters piled high with roast quail, cured ham, and other delicacies; cut-glass goblets catching and reflecting the candlelight; the sparkle of gemstones adorning the ladies' wrists and headdresses. Prince Bowen was huddled with a group of knights, their raucous laughter provoking a frown of disapproval from his aunt Millicent. Wrapped in a voluminous black cape, she was the only woman who had not clad herself in bright colors, and she drew my eye as a raven would amid a gathering of songbirds. Perhaps that was her intention. Millicent was never one to blend meekly into a crowd.

I made my way to the Lower Hall for the servants' dinner and took a seat beside Isla and Hessler, curious to know more about the man who might one day rule the kingdom.

"Congratulations on your upcoming marriage," I told him after we had been introduced. "Have you made plans for your wedding?"

Though I genuinely wished Isla happiness, I had begun to dread her departure. Without her help, I worried that my clumsiness and ignorance would be on full display.

"We will be saying our vows in a few days," Isla said. "The queen has made all the arrangements." The placement of her arm suggested she was touching Hessler's leg under the table.

"Where will Prince Bowen be traveling next?" I asked.

"He has been courting a daughter of the king of Grenthia, so I imagine he has plans to return there." Isla turned to Hessler. "Has there been a formal announcement of their betrothal?"

He shook his head quickly. "The girl's father has objected to the match. We will not be going back."

I was impressed by his discretion. Gossip is rampant among servants, especially those who bask in the glory of their patron. But I had heard nothing of Prince's Bowen's courtship—or his rejection.

Hessler refilled Isla's wineglass and addressed himself to her. "Have no fear. We'll be well taken care of. My lord is resourceful."

It was not long before they were exchanging the affectionate glances and whispers of a couple who wish to converse in private. I finished up my food quickly and returned to the queen's chamber. As I expected, she had left the Great Hall early, avoiding the post-supper entertainments.

"Madam," Lady Wintermale was protesting as I entered. "Prince Bowen was preparing to sing a song in your honor. To leave before he has done so . . ."

"I have no interest in Bowen's false adulation," Queen Lenore snapped. I had never heard her speak with such bitterness.

Lady Wintermale's face froze in an expression of scandalized dismay.

Queen Lenore sighed, then waved her hand, pushing her hard words away. "Forgive my outburst. I spoke without thinking."

"You must not forget they are brothers," Lady Wintermale said urgently. "Bowen has always been a rogue—I know that as well as anyone, after all my years here. Yet he remains heir to the throne. A situation for which *you* are directly responsible."

"As I am forever reminded."

"Hate him if you must, but conceal it with honey. You may depend on his mercy one day."

Mercy was not a quality I sensed that Prince Bowen possessed. Was that the reason I found myself so uneasy in his presence?

"Please, rejoin the festivities," Queen Lenore urged. "Make my apologies."

Lady Wintermale nodded, her silent stare bristling with words unspoken. After she had swept out, I moved away from the wall and asked the queen if she wished to prepare for bed.

"I have asked the king to join me this evening," she said. The king's and queen's bedchambers adjoined each other, connected by a door concealed behind a hanging tapestry. In the weeks I had been an attendant, the king had availed himself of it on only a handful of occasions.

"Shall I fetch a nightdress?" I asked.

Queen Lenore smiled, her expression tinged with sadness. "Alas, it is not that sort of visit. I will receive him as an adviser, not a wife." She fidgeted with the rings on her fingers, twisting them in circles, and I realized she was nervous. How had it come to this, that the queen was afraid of speaking to her own husband?

She sat in the chair before her dressing table, and I took my place behind her. Carefully, I unclasped her necklace, a three-tiered marvel formed of delicate gold flowers so lifelike they might have been blooms dipped in liquid metal. She smiled when she saw how my gaze lingered upon it.

"It was a wedding gift from my mother," she said. "I planned to pass it on to my own daughter one day."

Many maids would have offered false comfort, reassuring their mistress that her prayers for a child would be answered in time. But Queen Lenore valued my honesty. I had no words to lift her melancholy, so I simply took the necklace and placed it gently on her dressing table. Then I released her thick, rich hair from its pins and ribbons. The fashion at court in those years was for hair to be braided and tied in elaborate arrays, but Queen Lenore looked most beautiful when her dark locks hung simply around her face and over her shoulders. Seen like this, without jewelry, she could have been a maid of eighteen rather than a woman who had already passed her thirtieth birthday.

I brushed her hair until it shone, sending both her and me into a trance with the rhythm of the strokes. The knowledge that I was able to release the queen from her cares for these few moments brought a rush of satisfaction, and I smiled at her reflection in the mirror even as her image smiled back at me. The sound of a door opening jolted us both from our reverie, and we turned to see the king walking in, alone. He held up his hand as his wife rose to greet him.

"Sit, sit," he urged.

She walked to the bed, where the king took a place next to her. His hand lingered a moment on her hair. He must love her still, I thought, if he could touch her so. But his face betrayed no tenderness; he watched Queen Lenore as if she were any other subject come to make a plea before him. I wondered if I should leave the room but did not want to draw attention to myself by asking. In truth, I did not want to go; I was desperately curious to know what Prince Bowen's return portended for all of us. If power was the true currency at court, as my aunt had warned, then I must know whose hands would command our fates. I slid into the corner behind the dressing table, where my figure would be partly obscured by shadows.

"Forgive me for retiring early," Queen Lenore said. "I am too tired to join in the revelry."

"It's all as it was years ago," the king said. "Bowen preening before the blushing young ladies as Aunt Millicent scowls with disapproval. You've seen it a thousand times before."

They smiled at each other, understanding flashing between them. I was accustomed to seeing them in public, presenting the united front of rulers joined by marriage. But this was the first time I had heard them speaking a private language of shared memories. It did not seem right that I overhear such a conversation, but they appeared unmindful of my presence. Raised in privilege, both had been surrounded by servants and attendants since birth, never knowing what it was to be truly alone.

"Bowen told me you summoned him," Queen Lenore said. "I had not known that his visit was your doing."

The king shrugged. "I've told you often enough our situation is precarious. And now Marl deRauley has been heard questioning the line of succession."

I had not heard the name before, but from the king's tone this mysterious figure carried some weight in the kingdom.

"Such talk must be stopped, and soon," the king continued.

"How?"

"Bowen must be acknowledged as my heir."

Queen Lenore's fingers picked at the embroidery in her skirt, even as the rest of her body remained still.

"I know he is a man of many vices," the king said wearily, the weight of the decision evident in his grave expression. "I wish better for my subjects. Still, he is my brother. We have no choice."

Queen Lenore nodded slowly but her expression did not change. This could not have come as a surprise. I felt a pang of compassion for her plight, knowing that her own failure to conceive a child had brought Prince Bowen to the throne.

"Millicent says he will be the ruin of this kingdom," she said quietly.

"Nonsense!" the king exclaimed. "They've never gotten on, ever since he was a boy. He's the only person in the family who has ever stood up to her."

"She told me of a portent. . . ."

"Aunt Millicent's ramblings are of no importance!" the king exclaimed. "I have already summoned all the nobles in the kingdom to an assembly, where I will publicly welcome Bowen as my heir."

"No!" The vehemence in the queen's voice was so uncharacteristic that I almost rushed to her side to offer comfort. "Why did you not tell me? Surely there is no need for such haste."

"The messengers already have been sent," the king said firmly. "It is done, and we must congratulate Bowen as if we could think of no greater successor. He may surprise us all, you know. Once his claim to the throne is acknowledged, his marriage prospects will improve. With the right woman, he may well settle down and reform his ways."

"It's the rare husband who grants his wife the power to transform him," the queen said.

"Rare, yet not unheard of."

King Ranolf reached for his wife's restless fingers and stilled them. Gently, he pressed the back of her hands to his lips, then brushed them against his cheek. The gesture was so unexpected, so tender, that I caught my breath. Instantly, a much-loosened bond tightened between them, and I watched, moved almost to tears, as the queen's body softened at her husband's touch. He gazed at her, his eyes offering silent comfort, and she smiled in reply, the expression transforming her face into one of radiant beauty. I had not seen many affectionate marriages in my life, but Petra had told me the king and queen had once loved each other deeply. I hoped it was not too late for them to recapture their past happiness.

Just as a good servant can anticipate her mistress's demands for food or drink, she also knows when to disappear. I edged toward the door leading to the sitting room and pulled it closed after me. I thought of going down to the Great Hall to peek at the dancers but was afraid I might be called to prepare the queen for bed. I sat on the floor near the door, which was thick enough that I could hear only muffled voices inside.

I must have drifted off, for I jumped to attention when a log crackled in the sitting-room fireplace. I had fallen asleep with my arms wrapped around my knees, my head leaning forward, and my neck ached from the unnatural position. The candles in the sitting room had burned out, and the fire was close to dying. Pressing my ear against the door, I heard nothing from the bedchamber.

I opened the door a crack. A candle by the bedside still burned, and in the dim light I could see Queen Lenore's face peeking out from under the covers. Next to her, with one arm wrapped around her body, lay the king. I could tell from the pattern of their breathing that they were asleep. I pulled the door shut and curled under a blanket in the doorway, protecting their sleeping figures from any disturbance. When Isla returned and roused me, close to dawn, the king was gone.

In the week leading up to the assembly, Queen Lenore's silent reveries became more frequent, forcing me to repeat myself two and three times before she paid mind. When she was not wrapped up in her thoughts, I often found her conferring with the king or Isla, her face taut with concern. Did I sense the danger of the scheme being put into place? Or is it hindsight that makes me pause and reexamine those mysterious whispers, the looks I could not decipher? I do know that the king and queen's hushed complicity made me nervous, and I felt the disorientation of one who spins her head back and forth in a search, only to become dizzier than ever in the attempt.

At the time I put the queen's distraction down to her dread of the assembly, which would confirm to the world that she was a barren failure. Who would welcome such public humiliation? Her fears could hardly have been eased by Prince Bowen's boorish behavior; he comported himself as if the castle staff were already his to command and openly mocked his aunt Millicent when she chided him on his unbecoming conduct.

"He said a man of his appetites wouldn't take orders from a dried-up old maid," Petra told me, eyes wide at the memory. "You should have seen her! She berated the king for not keeping Prince Bowen in check, yet he did nothing. Sat there with his face frozen as stone."

I thought such incidents proved that King Ranolf had accepted his fate. More concerned with the occasional leering glances Prince Bowen directed my way, I remained ignorant of the true cause of the queen's agitation, just as I underestimated the king's pride.

Driven, perhaps, to escape her brother-in-law's increasing influence inside the castle, Queen Lenore began passing hours outside, in the garden. It was during one of these excursions that I once again glimpsed a flash of movement among the shrubbery, a glimpse of white that was gone almost as soon as my eyes lit upon it.

I flinched, and Queen Lenore stopped beside me.

"What it is, Elise?"

"Did you see that?" I whispered.

"See what?"

The garden lay silent around us. Queen Lenore would think I had taken leave of my senses if I began babbling of ghosts, but I was too terrified to take a step farther.

"I thought I saw someone. Up ahead."

To my surprise, the queen smiled. "Ah, it must be Flora."

Unsure if the name referred to a castle legend or a real, living person, I waited for her to explain.

"The king's aunt. Millicent's sister."

I remembered Petra's offhand mention of a sister when she first told me about Millicent, but I had never heard her spoken of since. Was she the mysterious occupant of the locked room in the North Tower, the one whose mournful song lingered in my memory?

"She has become quite a recluse, I fear," Queen Lenore explained. "She tends to a small herb garden here, but otherwise she keeps to her chambers. According to Ranolf, she had a nervous collapse years ago. He thinks her quite mad."

"Is she?"

"I find that any woman who acts contrary to expectations risks such accusations," she said. "What the truth is, I cannot say. I have hardly spoken to her for years."

My curiosity piqued, I raised Flora's name with Petra later that evening. She shared what she knew of the castle gossip; the sad decline of the king's aunt was blamed on a sudden illness, a doomed love affair, even witchcraft. The only person who knew the truth was Millicent, and I would never dare address such questions to her.

The day of the assembly began inauspiciously, with drenching rain and a damp chill that seeped through the castle walls. I felt a pang of sympathy for the downstairs maids, who would spend the day on their knees, wiping the floors clean of muddy footprints. To my great surprise, the queen announced I would be dressing her for the day, as Isla was otherwise occupied. It seemed odd that the queen's attendant would have a more pressing engagement on such a momentous day, but Isla had appeared tired and wan recently. I supposed Queen Lenore was allowing her some rest before her wedding.

My first duty was to fetch the queen's ceremonial robe from the laundresses' room off the Lower Hall, where it had been given a thorough cleaning. Hastening up the wide central staircase with the garment laid across my arms, I hurtled into a figure who suddenly veered from his path into mine.

It was Prince Bowen.

He had arrayed himself in a costume suitable to the occasion: a tunic of deep blue velvet, leather boots polished to a gleam, jewels adorning his fingers and the handle of the sword that hung at his hip. Flanked by companions who mirrored his haughty manner, Prince Bowen regarded me, amused.

"I know you," he said. "One of Lenore's girls."

I nodded, bowing my head submissively.

"A meek one, eh?" Prince Bowen said, addressing his friends rather than me. "Perhaps there's more here than meets the eye."

He reached forward and pressed his palms along either side of my head, assessing me as if I were a dish he was about to devour. Then he took hold of my shoulder, forcing me to follow as he maneuvered my body into an alcove off the landing, one of the countless openings that provided access to the cramped, dimly lit servants' passages. The muscles in my shoulders tightened as Prince Bowen pushed me against the clammy wall. Footsteps away, courtiers and guards passed to and fro, but I was hidden from view.

"Yes, there's something here I quite fancy," he murmured, moving his fingers along my cheeks, then my chest. I shivered as he thrust against the curve of my breasts. Mistaking my reaction for pleasure, he flashed a self-satisfied grin.

"Just as I thought. You're young but hardly innocent."

His hand shoved aside the robe I was holding and forced my skirt between my thighs.

"My lord," I begged, terrified. "I am an honest girl."

"Ah." His hand did not cease its examination of my trembling body. "All innocents are ruined in the end, my dear. Why not have the deed accomplished by one skilled in such matters?"

I did not know if his words were meant as reassurance or threat. I did not care. Horror gave me the strength to heave my shoulder into Prince Bowen's chest, and the sudden jerk was enough to break his hold. I tore up the stairs, terrified he would order his men to drag me back. I could hear raucous male laughter from below, mocking my every panicked step. Suddenly a hand reached out to clutch my forearm, and my feet slid to a halt. Before me stood Millicent, her face twisted in an expression of disgust.

It took a moment for me to realize that her anger was not directed my way. I turned to follow her gaze and saw Prince Bowen bow with exaggerated reverence. Summoning his men with an impatient wave, he disappeared down the staircase, out of sight.

"What has he done?" she demanded sharply, eyeing me up and down.

"Nothing, madam," I murmured. I would gain little by disparaging Prince Bowen to his aunt.

"He's a brute." She practically spat out the words. "He could have made something of himself once, yet he refused to heed my counsel. More fool he."

The intensity of Millicent's distaste encouraged me to speak frankly. "How am I to avoid another such encounter? He can summon me to his presence whenever he pleases."

Millicent let out a sharp laugh. "You will be safe from his groping soon enough. Fear not!"

I did not see how she could make such a promise, but her confidence helped shore up my own strength. Once again, it seemed, Millicent had chosen to be my champion. Why? What interest could one of the highest-ranking women at court have in a maidservant's struggles? I was ignorant then of the ways courtiers stage their conversations for public effect. Millicent had intended her harsh judgment of Prince Bowen to be heard by the dozens of servants and nobles walking past. By slinking away from a confrontation, he had allowed his aunt to claim victory in this skirmish.

The weight of Queen Lenore's robe had begun to make my arms

ache. "I hope you will agree that my mistress should not be bothered with this matter," I said. "Her thoughts are burdened enough."

Millicent smirked, as if she were privy to a secret that she took great pleasure in hinting at but not sharing. "As you wish."

She gave a quick nod of dismissal, then swept away, the rap of her cane echoing down the hall. I managed to compose myself before approaching Queen Lenore in her bedchamber, but it took some effort to fully calm my shaken body. I dressed her in a deep green velvet gown and looped her hair into an intricate pattern woven through with strings of pearls and rubies. Isla could have done the same in half the time, yet I was proud of the result. Shameful as this gathering might be for the queen, she would not appear a woman defeated.

I brought forward her looking glass, and she peered at her misty reflection.

"You've done well."

For a moment our faces were caught in the glass together: a regal, beautiful woman beside a girl determined to show a poise beyond her years. Already I looked different to myself, displaying an outward confidence I did not yet feel inside.

Queen Lenore's hands passed across her skirts once, then again. Her face was impassive, but I knew the meaning of her fluttering fingers. She was afraid.

"Well then, Elise," she said, collecting herself. "Are you ready?"

"Am I to come?" I asked, taken aback.

"Yes. I may need your assistance."

My fear of Prince Bowen nearly overcame the pull of duty. How could I stand at the queen's side, a few paces from the man who had attacked me? I came close to blurting out what had happened on the stairway, until I remembered my place. My duty was to support the queen, pushing my own feelings aside.

The king soon arrived, ready to escort his wife downstairs. On his head sat the royal crown, worn only for the most important ceremonies, and his shoulders were swathed in a red velvet cape edged with fur. Together the king and queen presented an image of such nobility that it seemed impossible they were about to acknowledge the end of their rule. King Ranolf might remain on the throne for another twenty years, but this announcement would forever diminish his authority. Anyone hoping to curry favor would go to his brother, not to him—a bitter path for an elder brother to follow.

The Great Hall was more crowded than I had ever seen it. Usually the room appeared vast, for even when all the tables were pulled forward for a feast, great open spaces remained. Today, however, there was barely room for the king and queen to move through the crush of people toward their seats on the dais. The heads of all the landed families in the kingdom had been summoned, and it appeared none had declined the invitation. Members of the Royal Council sat at a long table directly in front of the dais. Other titled families received chairs directly behind them. Standing, and filling the rest of the room, were the landowners, some finely dressed and most likely residents of town, others in country clothes years out of fashion.

Heralds sounded their trumpets when the king entered the room. Pages cleared a path for the king and queen through the throng, and I followed close behind. A murmur of greetings rustled around us as we passed. As we neared the front of the room, I saw

Millicent sitting with the other elderly ladies of the court. She stared intently at the queen, who passed by without turning her head.

Only one person stood on the dais as we approached: Prince Bowen, watching with an expression of grim pleasure. I wondered at the recklessness that had led him to claim his place before the king entered the room. Already, it seemed, the protocols of the palace were shifting in his favor. Would that further embolden him to do as he wished with me? Looking at his haughty, arrogant face, I felt sick with apprehension. I could still feel the violation of his hands pressing between my legs.

"Stay by my side," Queen Lenore whispered as we walked up the steps. I took a place behind her chair and watched the mass of people filling the hall, waiting with an unnatural stillness.

"My lords," the king began. "Ladies." He nodded to his wife and the women of the court. "I have requested your presence here today on a matter of the utmost importance. A matter, one might say, of survival. The survival of this kingdom."

The silence was so complete it was as if all had forgotten to breathe.

"For some time I have been aware of rumblings of discontent. An heir, my people demanded! My prayers and those of my queen joined your own, yet God did not grant us our most fervent wish. The question of succession has grown more insistent in recent years. My distant cousin, Marl deRauley, has been especially vocal in his concerns."

I remembered the king saying the name in the queen's bedchamber. Was it possible someone else had a claim to the throne?

"Nothing would pain me more than to see these lands descend

into war upon my death," the king continued. "My father, and his father before him, labored hard to bring harmony to our realm. I wish it to remain so. We must secure a future as peaceful as our present."

Prince Bowen stirred in his seat, anticipating the moment when he would rise to be acclaimed by the crowd. To those watching he might appear suitably regal, but to me he would always be the man who leered with pleasure at my helplessness. My stomach lurched in disgust, and I shifted my body farther behind Queen Lenore's chair, anxious to avoid his attention.

"My younger brother, Prince Bowen, is next in line for the succession. That is common knowledge, yet he has not been formally recognized as my heir. My doing so would settle the whispers that have plagued these lands."

Prince Bowen was smiling. His moment had arrived.

"When I sent word of this gathering to all of you, I was prepared to proclaim my brother as my successor."

Was prepared? Had he chosen another course?

"My intention was to urge you to accept him as your next king. Yet I find my circumstances much changed. Today I stand before you to announce something far more momentous. My wife is with child."

I heard a gasp to my right, from the women. I looked at Queen Lenore, whose face was turned modestly downward. With child? I had been by her side for months and knew nothing of it. My mind reeled, caught between joy at the news and hurt that she had not trusted me enough to tell me.

Gradually a sound began to sweep across the room. First a few claps, then muttering rising louder and louder until it was a unified cry of delight. The wave of sound rose to a peak, filling the hall. The king rose from his seat, basking in the rejoicing, then raised his hands for silence.

"I welcome your good wishes, as does my wife. In celebration of this blessed news, I invite the members of the court to join me for prayers in the chapel. This day cannot pass without thanks to He who brought this miracle. After the service all are invited to the hall for a feast. I promise, our cooks have outdone themselves today!"

There was another smattering of applause, and then the crowd parted to allow the king and queen to leave the room. I found myself staring at Prince Bowen, who sat utterly still, his mouth pressed in a rigid line. Though relieved beyond measure that he would soon be gone from the castle, I was chilled by the ferocity of his gaze. Shaken, I turned away and caught sight of Millicent, her face set in a self-satisfied smile. *She knew,* I realized with a flash of understanding. She knew that the queen was with child, and she knew how this announcement would unfold.

Blind to the ways that a lust for power can entrap a man of strong will, I could not understand why King Ranolf would choose to publicly humiliate his own brother. The king had established his dominance, but he had created a dangerous enemy. One who would never forget what had been done to him.

I joined the rest of the court for the chapel service, mouthing words of thanksgiving even as my mind reeled. Sitting directly behind Queen Lenore, her head bowed in prayer, I could not ward off my feelings of betrayal. How had I missed the signs of my mistress's condition? Why had she not told me?

When the queen requested leave to retire afterward, the king dismissed her with a kiss on the forehead. Upstairs, the queen and I found ourselves alone in her rooms. I stood behind her to unclasp the brooch that fastened her cape. Knowing it my duty to conceal my own hurt in favor of my mistress's happiness, I offered my congratulations on the blessed news.

Queen Lenore reached up and wrapped her hands around mine. "Thank you, Elise." Her voice was so warm, her gratitude so genuine, that my childish anger withered.

"You cannot imagine how difficult it was to remain silent. But I had been disappointed so many times before, I did not want to raise false hopes until I was sure. Isla and I even kept the news from the king, until Bowen's return forced my hand."

Isla. She would have known if her mistress had no cause to use women's cloths for some months. Their shared secret was yet further evidence of their bond, one I could never hope to replace once Isla was married.

Married. To Prince Bowen's manservant.

"Isla!" I exclaimed. "What will she do?"

Queen Lenore looked at me sadly. "She has followed her future husband, as I insisted she must. She packed her things earlier, in readiness for a hasty departure."

So there was to be no castle wedding for Isla, no leisurely leave-taking from the woman who was both her mistress and her friend. My sometime rival was gone, leaving me responsible for all the queen's needs. I can still remember the terror that washed over me at the magnitude of the task ahead. Though accustomed to carrying myself as one older than my years, I found that the thoughts racing through my mind were those of a frightened child: *I am not ready! I need more time!*

"This should be a day of great happiness," Queen Lenore said quietly. "Yet I fear that my husband has made a terrible mistake."

I remembered Prince Bowen's face, the hatred that blazed from his eyes. Was it my place to warn my mistress about what I had seen? It is hard to believe I was once so fearful of speaking my mind. But I was young, and inexperienced, and I believed that proper etiquette dictated respectful silence over honest conversation. So I said nothing.

"I did protest." The queen almost whispered the words, as if assuring herself she had been in the right. "I told my husband we must inform Bowen of the news in private, to prepare him beforehand. But there is no convincing Ranolf once he has made up his mind."

She sighed, worn out by the day's events. "Would you like to bring down your things? Best you got settled in now, before the feast."

A lady's maid slept in her mistress's chambers, ready to be of assistance at all hours. For the last time, I made my way to the servants' quarters under the eaves. As I pulled together my few possessions, I set aside a slim volume Mrs. Tewkes had given me, a collection of prayers I had long since memorized and the only book I had ever owned. I placed it on Petra's bed, remembering the nights we'd huddled together with a precious candle stub, sounding out the letters as I praised her progress. Her desire to learn was only one of the qualities I cherished in her, and I determined that despite our different stations and paths I would not allow our friendship to fray.

It was only later that night, as I lay in an alcove off Queen Lenore's bedchamber, that I began to revel in all I had achieved. Leaving the company of jealous chambermaids was no great sacrifice; I now slept within footsteps of the queen herself. Soon there would be a baby in these rooms, and perhaps another after that. I had soared to a position of great prestige in only a few months and found favor with the kindest of mistresses. I smiled to myself in the dark, thinking how my mother would have marveled at my change in circumstances.

In one hand I clutched Millicent's wishing stone. I prayed—to God? to Millicent?—for the health of Queen Lenore's baby, for an heir who would brighten the future of the kingdom. Most of all I prayed that Prince Bowen would never return. How ignorant I was, to think that distance would weaken his ability to do us harm. The prince would have his revenge. And I would learn that every wish granted comes at a price, one we cannot foresee until it is too late.

Five

A CHILD IS BORN

If fate had made Queen Lenore suffer in her wait for a child, it was done with her once her womb proved fertile. She bloomed along with her stomach. Her cheeks flushed with color, and her skirts rustled as she walked with a bounce to her steps. She dreamed up patterns for blankets and swaddling clothes and urged me to sit by her side at her loom as she brought those designs to life. I marveled at her swift fingers just as I marveled at my own ability to converse easily with a woman who treated me more as a younger sister than as a servant. On the day I turned fifteen, she presented me with a hand-crafted shawl, the loveliest piece of clothing I had ever worn, made all the more valuable by the knowledge that my mistress had woven the garment with me in mind. Those were the days that I first heard the queen laugh—not her usual polite acknowledgment of a jest but outbursts of unabashed delight. How it breaks my heart that I can no longer recall that sound, for it would bring me great comfort to remember her when she was capable of such joy.

The change in Queen Lenore's demeanor rippled through the court to those around her. King Ranolf abandoned his daily hunting trips and doted on his wife like a love-struck suitor. Millicent was just as solicitous, though her visits were far less convivial than the king's. She ordered Queen Lenore about in an imperious manner I thought unseemly for one who had never borne a child herself. She brought flasks of foul-smelling concoctions for the queen to drink, telling her they would make the baby strong, and nagged at her to lie abed into midmorning. Queen Lenore smiled politely and thanked Millicent for her concern, but she began spitting the drinks into her washing bowl when Millicent's back was turned.

"Something that tastes so horrible cannot possibly do the child any good," she told me.

Indeed, she put more stock in my own advice; since I had seen my mother through half a dozen pregnancies, there was little I did not know of the changes a woman's body undergoes during those nine months. It was a heady feeling, realizing that my words were having some small influence upon the future heir to the throne. At times it almost felt as if I were mothering her, sharing the reassurance and nurturance she would have received from her own family, had she not been living so far from her homeland.

By all indications Queen Lenore's pregnancy progressed with none of the troubles that can so bedevil a woman at such times. But as the queen's stomach grew more prominent, filling even her roomiest gowns, Millicent began to insist she recuse herself from public life.

"A royal wife should keep to her quarters once her condition becomes manifest," she said authoritatively.

"In my country it is very important that a queen be seen with a full belly," Queen Lenore argued. "If not, it could be whispered that an heir had not been borne of her body."

Millicent rolled her eyes dismissively. "Such reassurances may be necessary in your part of the world, but no one here would dare insinuate such a thing. You simply cannot be seen prancing about in your delicate state." The king, mindful of family tradition, took his aunt's side.

The queen felt the loss of her freedom deeply, and I was no less affected. As autumn announced itself with cool breezes and shorter days, the castle took on a grimmer, more shadowy cast. I began to dread the upcoming winter and the months of confinement it would bring, for I had few opportunities to escape those gloomy halls. I received the occasional invitation to dine at my aunt Agna's, but the bond between us had not deepened with time. Her home was a self-contained world with little place for outsiders, and my cousins treated me with barely disguised snobbery. I might answer to the queen herself, but in their eyes I was still a servant, while they were the favored children of one of the town's leading citizens.

So it came as a great relief one afternoon when the queen threw aside her embroidery with an irritated sigh and sent for the king, declaring that she could not tolerate another minute of imprisonment. He came quickly, his face tight with concern.

"Do not fear, all is well with the child," she said. "But I am so very melancholy, shut away in here. Could I perhaps join you in the Great Hall for supper?"

The king narrowed his eyes but did not say no.

"Is this not a happy time, love?" she asked.

"Indeed it is."

"Then why must I pass these months as if I were in mourning? Should we not celebrate our good fortune?"

It would have been impossible to resist her then, with her eyes sparkling and her voice calming him like a caress. The king's sense of propriety was no match for her charms. He moved his hand from her cheek to her hair, smoothing it under his fingers.

"I see no reason I should deny myself the pleasure of your company this evening," he said.

"Might we have music?"

"Music, eh?" I could see from the twitch at the edge of his lips that the king was teasing her. "Who could say no to such a pretty plea?"

"Oh, thank you!" she cried, embracing him with a delight that caught him off guard. He rocked back for a moment, then righted himself and laughed.

Thrilled by this turn of events, I could have embraced the king myself. Catching sight of my relieved smile, Queen Lenore waved me forward.

"Did you hear, Elise?" she exclaimed. "Music! Perhaps even dancing!"

"Now, now . . ." the king admonished.

"I would not dream of dancing myself. I meant only that it would give me great pleasure to watch." She tilted her head back and planted a peck on his cheek, then turned to me. "Come, we have work to do. Do you think my violet gown could be let out enough that I might wear it?"

That night was the first of many banquets Queen Lenore attended even as her stomach grew more pronounced. After eating my own meal with the servants, I would creep upstairs and watch them through the doorway of the Great Hall, the graceful ladies and courtly gentlemen embodying all that was noble. On those nights the menacing shadows that so unnerved me were banished to the farthest corners of the room, and scores of candelabra bathed everyone in a youthful, golden glow. I can still remember Queen Lenore's dark eyes reflecting the sparkle of the silver candlesticks, King Ranolf watching the proceedings with benevolent delight. I had never seen them as beautiful as they were on those nights, nor would I ever again.

"To my son!" the king would announce, raising his glass for a toast. Courtiers would cry out, "To the future king!" and the hall would echo with the sound of brass and silver goblets clinking together, a metallic clash that I imagined sounded like swords on a battlefield. None of us doubted that the child would be a boy, a solace for all the years of waiting. We did not allow ourselves to picture any other outcome.

Yet it would be a lie to say the days passed in a haze of happiness. Deftly pushing aside Lady Wintermale and the other ladies-in-waiting, Millicent clearly relished her role as the protectress of the future heir, and she turned to me as an ally, demanding I reveal the most private details of Queen Lenore's health: what she ate, how often she used the chamber pot, whether the king spent the night in her bed. I attempted to feign ignorance or said I could not recall, but Millicent was relentless in her questioning. Time after time I gave way and told her what she wanted to know. When she smiled and said I had done well, I felt a rush of pleasure that blotted out the shame of my disloyalty. For despite the warmth I felt for Queen Lenore, a love that rivaled the love I felt for my own mother, Millicent's approval was harder earned and therefore the more valuable. I believed it possible to serve two mistresses, thinking it within my power to keep peace between them.

If only Millicent had been content with our private bargain, savoring her knowledge of the queen's life in secret! But that was not her way. She boasted openly of her influence and laughed dismissively when King Ranolf grumbled that her constant hovering was overtiring his wife. And I allowed it to happen. I told Queen Lenore nothing of Millicent's intrusive questions or her snipes at the king. I did not understand—how could I?—that Millicent and her nephew were drawing ever closer to war, with Queen Lenore as their prize. I was the one person who could have warned against Millicent's deviousness. Yet I stood dumbly aside. For that I shall never forgive myself.

The cataclysm, when it came, was swift and devastating. Queen Lenore's pains began in the middle of the night; with typical selflessness she suffered them in silence for some time before her restless turning awoke me. I pulled myself up to my knees and saw her lying on her side, arms clutching her belly.

"It has begun," she whispered. In the darkness the only things I could see were her eyes, looking at me fearfully.

I leapt up and lit a candle. Then I poured water over a cloth and put it to her forehead.

"I will inform the king," I said.

I rushed into the hallway, stumbling in my hurry with only the candlelight to guide me. I rapped on the door to the king's chambers, and one of his guards emerged, wiping his bleary eyes.

"Send for the midwife," I said. "The queen's time is come."

Immediately the guard straightened and nodded. I waited while he pulled on an overshirt and a coat. Then he lit a candle from mine and hurried away. The midwife, Ursula, had already been paid a healthy sum to check the queen's stomach throughout the pregnancy, and she had pronounced the baby hearty. She had a jolly, confident manner that I thought would serve Queen Lenore well during her ordeal.

After whispering the news to the king's valet, I rapped on the doors of Lady Wintermale and the other ladies-in-waiting, then returned to Queen Lenore's side. She remained as I had left her, with the cloth lying across her forehead.

"Elise," she said, stopping to wince for a moment. She panted for a few breaths, then continued. "It's early. Ursula said the baby would not come for a month or more."

I, too, had worried at the timing as I dashed back and forth in the halls. But it would not help the queen to linger on such things. She would need all her strength for what was to come.

"A child arrives when it's ready," I said, in what I hoped was an assured manner. "My mother was never correct in her calculations. One of my brothers appeared a full two months before she expected, and he was as healthy a child as she had."

"Really?" She seemed to believe me.

I was spared any further lies by the arrival of Lady Wintermale. If I had seen her under different circumstances, I would have been amused by the sight of her bedraggled hair and ill-wrapped robe. But tonight I felt simply gratitude that she had come so quickly. The woman usually took such pride in her appearance; it was a testament to her love for the queen that she had dashed from her rooms attired thus.

"How does she?" Lady Wintermale demanded, looking at me.

"I am well," Queen Lenore said with a brave smile. "Well enough to speak, at least."

"Good, good. Elise, light the candles. We must make it as bright as possible. You've sent for the midwife?" I nodded. "We must ready the supplies."

Roused from the servants' quarters, a huddle of maids arrived to take Lady Wintermale's orders. Sweaty-palmed with nerves, I stepped aside, only to hear Queen Lenore call out my name.

"Yes, my lady?"

"You must fetch Millicent. She promised me—" She winced as her stomach contracted. "She promised me something to ease the pain."

Lady Wintermale rolled her eyes but said nothing. I hurried to the North Tower, concern for the queen overpowering my fear of those dark, echoing hallways. Millicent did not answer the door until my third, pounding knock. With her hair covered by a nightcap and her eyes sagging with weariness, she looked, for the first time, like an old woman. Defying that first impression, however, she quickly readied herself once I announced my mission. She swept out of the room and paused at the door next to hers, giving it a sharp rap. The door creaked open almost instantly, as if Flora had been perched in readiness, waiting to be called into action.

For months I had wondered about Flora, pitied her, even feared her. My imagination had conjured such visions of madness that I'd forgotten she was a real woman, aunt to the king, flesh and blood of a royal family known for its striking good looks. And Flora, in her prime, would have been the most striking of all. She had the same strong nose and chin as Millicent, but her large, smoky green eyes gazed at me softly, almost wistfully. Her mouth curved naturally in the hint of a smile, and her cheeks were tinged a delicate pink. Framing her angelic face was a mass of fine white curls, so fragile they could have been made from a spider's silk; the rest of her hair was tied back with a girlish ribbon. She must have been past sixty, but in her virginal white nightdress, lit by the flame of a single candle, she appeared ageless.

"The queen has gone to her childbed," Millicent said briskly. "Do you have the herbs?"

Flora disappeared into the darkness of her room. From the little I could see, it had the same imposing proportions as Millicent's and similarly lavish furnishings. I was puzzled by several dim shapes that hung from strings tied to the bed frame, until I recognized the jagged edges of leaves and branches. It seemed odd that a noble lady would dry herbs like a common apothecary, and I wondered if this was a proof of her disturbed mental state.

Flora returned and handed her sister a small glass vial filled with a dark green substance.

"It should be placed under her tongue," Flora said in a quiet, breathy voice. "No more than could cover her smallest fingernail."

"Yes, good," Millicent said.

Flora looked at me curiously, and Millicent hastily explained that I was the queen's attendant. At this, Flora asked, "How does your mistress fare?"

Disarmed by Flora's evident concern, I answered honestly. "The queen fears the ordeal before her."

"So she does, poor thing. So she does."

She spoke as if she were privy to the queen's most secret thoughts, and I felt a ripple of unease.

"Come," Millicent announced, motioning me toward the stairs. I dropped a quick curtsy to Flora, and she smiled wistfully, her expression such a mix of sweetness and sorrow that I was momentarily baffled. Only the rapping of Millicent's cane brought me out of my trance and reminded me that my duties lay elsewhere.

As we entered the hallway leading to the queen's rooms, Millicent suddenly stopped, her path blocked by the king and two of his knights.

"The queen is being attended to by the midwife," he said sharply. "She needs no other distractions." Jaw clenched and arms crossed before him, the queen's loving husband was transformed into a self-righteous ruler who would tolerate no threat to his authority. The same man who had publicly shamed his own brother, regardless of the consequences.

"There is something I must give her," Millicent insisted.

She stepped to the side and made as if to walk around the king. The insult of the gesture fueled the fire already simmering within him.

"You shall not enter!"

The knights each took a step forward, and Millicent retreated. Smiling as if amused by the whole scene, she waved the glass vial in front of her.

"My dear Ranolf, you misunderstand my intentions. I have been summoned here on your wife's orders. Ask Elise."

I hugged the wall, reluctant to be drawn into their skirmish. "The queen sent for a tonic to lessen the pains of childbirth."

"The last thing the queen needs is one of your potions," the king said to Millicent with obvious contempt. "This is another feeble attempt to insinuate yourself with Lenore, hoping she will take your side against me. I will not allow it! You will not drive a wedge between me and my wife!"

Despite Millicent's propensity for troublemaking, I was alarmed that the king chose this moment to make such a stand. Would he deny Queen Lenore relief from her agony simply to spite his aunt? Millicent held herself perfectly still throughout the king's tirade, her face never shifting from its impassive expression. Only I, standing so close, could see the way her fingers clutched her cane until the veins popped from the skin. Then she smiled, as if she had remembered the final weapon in her arsenal.

"You still fail to grant me my due, dear Ranolf. I spent hours with Lenore at the shrine of St. Agrelle, praying even as our bodies shuddered with cold. Now, thanks to me, she presents you with an heir. Yet have you shown me gratitude?"

King Ranolf's eyes narrowed as she continued.

"I was with your wife when she cried at the barrenness of her womb. I caught her tears with my hands. I will not be denied my rightful place beside her as she welcomes our heir into the world."

"Our heir?" The words came out in a whisper, as if King Ranolf could scarce believe he was saying them. Then his face flushed and he waved a hand contemptuously in her direction, the same gesture he used to dismiss servants who displeased him. "You have no place here, not today. Begone!"

Stunned, Millicent stumbled backward, and I leapt forward to steady her. Her breathing was heavy and deliberate, her chest a bellows pumping up her rage. Terrified of where her anger might lead, I bowed obsequiously to the king and tugged at Millicent's sleeve, urging her to return to the North Tower. King Ranolf turned away with a stomp of his boots, followed by his men. Lady Wintermale's face peeked around the edge of the doorway, and she nodded when she saw I had Millicent in hand. I only hoped the voices had not carried as far as Queen Lenore's bed. She must not be upset, today of all days.

I can still see Millicent as she was in that moment, a vision that haunts me even now. Tall and regal, her striking face set in an expression of arrogant determination, she had a terrible splendor that weakened my already shaky resolve. Could I have stood against such a force? If I had bent Millicent to my will and pulled her away, would I have prevented the scene that followed? These are questions that still trouble my sleep, when exhaustion allows such thoughts to creep in. I tell myself a servant girl of fifteen could not have altered the course of events. My affection for Queen Lenore was no match for Millicent's dark powers.

"Elise," she said, reaching out to clutch my forearms, and I was lost once again, lulled into obedience by her commanding voice. "You must go to the queen."

"I will, as soon as I've seen you back to your room."

"No, no, it cannot wait. Tell her that Ranolf has forbid me entrance but she must insist upon my presence. I am the only one who can assure she receives the proper dose."

She pressed the vial into my hands, urging me on my way. I heard a sharp cry reverberate through the thick stone walls. It was Queen Lenore, screaming. I nearly cried out myself; the thought of my mistress in such pain made my stomach twist in sympathetic anguish. The concoction I held in my hand would relieve her suffering, but my offering it to the queen would only bring on another, far worse, confrontation with the king. Palms sweating, I hesitated by the door, miserable with indecision. Millicent stared at me, and the full force of her attention washed over me like a searing-hot wind, flushing my face despite the castle's midwinter chill.

"Go," Millicent said coldly.

Had she shown but a glimmer of kindness, of gratitude, I would have done her bidding. But she shot me a look of disdain, as if I were still spattered with country mud. In a flash of devastating insight, I saw her attentions toward me for what they were. She had not singled me out for special notice because I was smarter or more able than the other maids. No, she had flattered me into thinking I was exceptional so I would obey her under any circumstances.

Humiliated and betrayed, I buckled at the knees and pressed my face into my hands, pushing back the tears that threatened to overcome me. My collapse enraged Millicent, and her carefully maintained self-assurance cracked. She straightened her shoulders to stand at her full height, enjoying her advantage over me, then pulled her cane back and struck me on the shoulders with crippling force. I cried out and dropped to the floor, curling my arms around my rib cage.

"You wretched fool!" she shrieked. "How dare you defy me!" Again and again she struck me, her vile words as painful as the blows. "You would be *nothing* without me! A dung-stained chambermaid unfit to lie at the queen's feet!"

Dimly, through half-closed eyes, I was aware of thudding footsteps surrounding me. The beating stopped, and a footman wrested Millicent's cane from her hand. As I slowly rose, my back throbbing, King Ranolf appeared before us.

"What is this madness?" he demanded, eyes blazing.

Millicent spat out her words. "This insolent wench must be dismissed at once."

"Sir, I beg you," I said in a rush. "She told me to bring this to the queen, against your orders."

I showed him the vial, and he snatched it from my hands. Holding it up to one of the torches mounted on the wall, he swirled the contents with a flick of his wrist, then hurled it against the floor. Millicent gasped as a slimy green puddle oozed from the fragments of shattered glass.

King Ranolf stepped forward to stand directly in front of Millicent, his proud bearing the mirror image of hers.

"My tolerance is at an end," he said, his voice rumbling with barely controlled fury. He motioned to the knight at his side. "Thendor, escort my aunt Millicent to her room and keep her there, under guard."

"Perhaps you should consult your wife before making such rash pronouncements," Millicent murmured.

"The queen obeys *me*!" the king thundered. "In this and all other matters!" He turned to the men hovering behind him. "Take her away! I can no longer stand the sight of her!"

Suddenly Millicent was grabbed on either side by two burly guards and pulled nearly off her feet. The woman whose majestic bearing had so awed me was reduced to a pathetic, shrieking crone, struggling futilely against her captors. Her white hair slipped from its fastenings and cascaded over her face as she hurled insults at the king, horrible words that lingered in the air like smoke long after she was out of sight. King Ranolf stood for a few moments in the hallway, silent and clearly shaken. Then he marched off past me, into his room, crashing the door shut after him.

Slowly rising from the floor, I saw that a crowd had gathered behind me. The queen's ladies-in-waiting huddled together, uncharacteristically silent. A group of footmen muttered darkly, while a lone chambermaid stared at me in loose-jawed shock. All had witnessed my humiliation, as well as the king's rage. The story of this confrontation would be spread throughout the castle within minutes.

Indeed Lady Wintermale took me aside not much later as I stood in the queen's sitting room, gazing out as daylight crept over the garden, involuntarily shivering whenever I heard a cry from the bedroom.

"Is it true?" she asked, wide-eyed. "Millicent has been sent away?"

"The king has confined her to her room."

"Thank heaven for that."

"How is the queen faring?" I asked. Ursula, with the king's approval, insisted that only she and Lady Wintermale be permitted at the childbed, and thus far the two women had shared little of the labor's progress.

"Her spirits are good," Lady Wintermale said. "Though she continues to ask for the potion."

"Tell her it could not be procured," I said. "She does not need to know why."

"Poor dear. I fear it will be some time yet till the baby is born."

She was correct in her prediction, for Queen Lenore fought through a day and a night of pain. Concern for my mistress denied me sleep, and I spent the evening drifting between the royal apartments and the Lower Hall, where a group of maids and footmen kept vigil along with Mrs. Tewkes. As I stood at the sitting-room window again the following morning, witnessing yet another dawn, I feared I could not bear a single hour more. Ominously, I had heard no cries or groans from the bedchamber for some time.

Ursula emerged from the room, summoning a weak smile. I could see from the way she held herself that her arms and legs ached. I had brought her a bowl of soup, but she pushed it aside.

"The time is near," she said. "Come, I may need you."

Inside, Lady Wintermale sat on a chair, limbs crumpled with exhaustion. Ursula leaned down at the head of the bed. Queen Lenore was a pitiful sight, with her usually lustrous black hair matted against her drawn, sallow face. Her eyes stared dully, showing no flutter of recognition when I entered.

"The time has come, my lady," Ursula said. "You must push."

Queen Lenore moaned, a sad, faint sound that made my heart ache. If I could have put myself in the bed and pushed for her, I would have.

Ursula's voice took on a hectoring tone I had not heard before. "You must! Your baby is ready!"

Clenching her teeth and fists, Queen Lenore began to push. And God took mercy on her then, for the remainder was arduous but quick. Within no more than ten painful breaths, she had sent her child into the world.

For a moment that felt like hours, there was no sound. Then I saw Ursula rise, beaming, with the baby cradled in her arms. A firm slap on the child's back was quickly followed by an insistent wailing. Relief flooded through my spent body, and I almost burst into sobs myself. Lady Wintermale took the baby from Ursula and wiped it deftly and expertly with a damp cloth, then wrapped the tiny creature in a wool blanket the queen had embroidered for the occasion. She opened the door to the antechamber, clasping her precious bundle.

"Summon the king," she announced.

The king must have been pacing the hall outside, for he appeared almost immediately. The ladies parted to make way for him as he passed.

"A daughter," Lady Wintermale said, extending the arm where she held the baby. "Healthy as can be."

The excited whispers died away, and the room descended into silence. A daughter. I stared down at the floor, afraid to see the devastation on the king's face. How quickly a moment of joy could be transformed into a scene of mourning.

I caught sight of Queen Lenore on the bed across from me and realized she was crying. Not the euphoric tears of a new mother but sobs of anguish and regret. I grabbed a fresh cloth and dried her face, then dabbed lavender fragrance on her neck.

"Hush, madam," I whispered. "Your husband is come."

"A daughter," she moaned. "All this for a daughter."

I brushed her hair smooth as quickly as I could. Ursula was removing the bloody sheets from the bottom of the bed in preparation for the king's entrance. I wrapped Queen Lenore's shoulders in one of her best shawls, doing my best to make her presentable for the king. But no matter how well she looked or how sweet she smelled, the king would not be able to see past the despair on her face. After all she had suffered, she still had not produced an heir. In a sickening flash, I thought of Prince Bowen. How he would rejoice at this news!

Behind me I heard Ursula say, "She is ready, sir." I turned from the bed and saw the king hand her a bag of coins. Judging by Ursula's delighted expression, it was larger than she expected.

"You have delivered a healthy child," he said. "I will be forever in your debt."

He walked over to the bed, standing on the opposite side from me. Queen Lenore did not meet his eyes.

"My dear." He reached out and brushed his fingers along her cheek.

"I am so sorry for this disappointment," she whispered.

"Disappointment?" He turned back to where Lady Wintermale stood at the door. "Bring the child to me."

Lady Wintermale gingerly placed the baby in the king's arms. He carried her to the bed, gently tucking her under one of the queen's arms, and knelt beside them. "Have you not admired her?" he asked.

Queen Lenore glanced down without moving her head. The baby lay silently, her dark eyes and deep red lips peeking out from the swaddling.

"I prayed every day for a son," Queen Lenore said.

"If my daughter proves as beautiful as her mother," said the king, "will that not provide me with more joy than a loutish boy?"

Queen Lenore's lips twitched in the beginning of a smile.

"I prayed you would be delivered of a healthy child, and those prayers have been answered," the king said. "A woman may never have inherited the throne before today, but that does not mean our daughter cannot be the first."

The queen began to cry again, but these were tears of relief, for I could see her smiling and looking at the king tenderly. I heard a sniff and saw that Lady Wintermale was struggling to hold back tears herself. The king rose and addressed himself to the crowd waiting in the antechamber.

"Send word throughout the land that my heir has arrived!"

The ladies clapped, and I could hear the exultation echoing through the hallway outside, where dozens of other courtiers awaited.

"I'll have no one claim I didn't welcome this child," the king said, turning back to his wife. "We will have the grandest baptism this kingdom has ever seen. What do you think?"

Queen Lenore smiled and nodded, her eyes bright despite the dark circles of exhaustion that shadowed them. "Yes, we must give thanks."

Elation melted the usual social barriers, and I found myself embracing ladies-in-waiting and servants alike, until my mouth ached with smiling. Queen Lenore waved me over to admire the baby, and I cooed with delight, falling in love with her instantly.

If the king had been moved by the spirit of that moment to surrender his pride, all might have been well. Thankful for the birth of a hearty child, he might have forgiven his aunt's insults. But it was not in his nature. King Ranolf, benevolent and generous with those he loved, was an obstinate man, as obstinate as Millicent. Arrogance may confer certain advantages to a ruler, but it can also blind him to the benefits of diplomacy. It was the reason I was never able to shake a certain fear of the king, for who knows what a man convinced of his own infallibility might be capable of?

Two mighty forces had been set against each other. And such struggles can only end in disaster.

Six

A CURSE UPON US

They named the child Rose, a tribute to Lenore's love of flowers as well as the baby's deep red lips. From the beginning she was welcomed with as much pomp as any son: Trumpets announced her arrival from the ramparts, and the queen held her, swaddled, in the chapel on the Sunday following her birth, so that members of the court could admire the new arrival. Her baptism, the king declared, would be held in the cathedral of St. Elsip, so his subjects could rejoice alongside him. Following the public celebration, noble families from throughout the kingdom would gather at a grand banquet in the Great Hall.

Only one person of rank was denied an invitation, for the king had banished Millicent from the kingdom on the day after Rose's arrival. Queen Lenore's pleas on behalf of his aunt only hardened his resolve.

"Look at yourself!" he barked. "Groveling for a woman who treats me with contempt. I never paid heed to gossip, but perhaps it's true. Perhaps she *has* put a spell on you!"

"Stop!" the queen cried. "Don't say such things!"

An unwilling witness to their confrontation, I moved discreetly from the bedside, inwardly scolding the king for berating his wife when she was still weak from childbirth.

"She has a hold over you, I've seen that well enough," the king said. "I'll not have her do the same to our daughter."

"And the baptism?" Queen Lenore asked, wiping her eyes with the sleeve of her gown. Months before, through her usual cunning maneuvering, Millicent had convinced the queen to appoint her the baby's godmother.

"She is not welcome," King Ranolf said firmly.

"She is your father's sister!"

"I will never allow that woman guardianship over my child."

"Please." Queen Lenore's voice was desperate. "She need not stand as godmother. Invite her as a guest, as a gift to me. It is all I ask."

"Enough!" the king shouted. "Aunt Millicent may have kept my father under her thumb, but she will not do the same to me—or to you! I have sent guards to escort her from the castle, and I will not hear her name spoken within these walls from this day forward. As far as I am concerned, she is dead."

He stalked off in a fury, and Queen Lenore broke into sobs.

"He does not understand," she moaned.

"Hush, my lady." Without thinking I ran my hand along her head, imitating the manner in which my mother used to comfort me. To my surprise she reached for my hand and kissed it, then pressed it against her cheek.

"Thank you, Elise," she said. "You bring me strength."

Her tender words touched me deeply, but I could not rid my mind of Millicent's cruel pronouncement: *You would be* nothing *without me!* Was it true? Had Millicent urged the queen to choose me as her attendant because she knew I would do her bidding? Was all I had achieved not the fruit of my own labor but rather the result of sorcery, a charm cast by the green wishing stone I had pressed between my fingers? Such thoughts so disturbed me that I sneaked to my sleeping alcove while the queen was distracted with the baby and pulled the stone from under my pillow, slipping it between the folds of my skirt. Excusing myself, I ran to the servants' latrines and hurled the stone into one of the foul pits.

Yet Millicent's influence was not so easily cast off. Rather than return to my mistress, I found myself following the route to the North Tower, to assure myself that the woman who had been both my protector and my tormentor was truly gone.

She was not—not yet. As I approached the marble staircase leading up to her room, the commanding voice I knew so well echoed downward, and I froze in place. Then she appeared, flanked by two guards whose grim expressions signaled their distaste for the task at hand. Millicent, who had been haranguing them for keeping an overly tight grip upon her arms, laughed when she saw me. It was such an unexpected sound that I could not fashion a response. I simply stared, appalled by her expression of near-madness, yet enthralled all the same. Even as she was dragged from the castle in disgrace, she carried herself with an air of righteousness I could not help admiring.

"Elise!" she announced. "How fitting that you should bear witness to my downfall." The last word was uttered mockingly, almost as a boast. "Have you come to gloat?"

I shook my head.

"Then why are you here? Why would you possibly seek me out?"

The guards had loosened their hold, and Millicent strode directly in front of me, weakening my defenses with her piercing stare. "Ah, yes. I see. You wished an assurance that your rival for the queen's love is well and truly gone. So I am. You shall have dear Lenore entirely to yourself, for all the good that will do you."

Embarrassed that my emotions could be so easily read, I protested, "My only concern is for the queen's health and that of her child."

"Yes, the child. The focus of Ranolf's every hope. A girl!" She cackled bitterly. "And so the throne will be Bowen's after all. What a fitting end to Ranolf's disastrous reign."

"The king has declared his daughter as his heir."

"Nonsense! Women have never been allowed in the line of succession."

"They are now."

I did not expect those few words to strike such a blow. Millicent looked as if I had hurled an unforgivable insult; her mouth hardened into a grimace, and her eyes blazed with fury. When she finally spoke, expelling her words with brutal force, spittle dotted her lips.

"So it has come to this. Ranolf breaks with centuries of tradition, yet he banishes the one person who could be a model for his precious daughter. Does Lenore know anything of what it means for a woman to wield power? No! She is content to spin and weave, no better than a peasant's wife. And Ranolf—he is blind to the forces gathering against him. I am the only one who can save this realm from conquest and destruction. The only one! Yet I am cast aside!"

Her escalating shrieks shook the guards from their lethargy. One took firm hold of her upper arm and tugged, pulling her away from me.

"You know I speak the truth! You know it!"

I did not want to believe her. It was easier to discount her warnings as the ravings of a madwoman than to believe our kingdom truly in danger. As the grumbling guards wrestled Millicent to the bottom of the stairs, I heard a rustling sound from above. I looked up and saw Flora standing at the top of the stairs.

I remained motionless, but she seemed unaware of my presence. She was watching her sister, tears streaming down her cheeks. I had given no thought to Flora in all the ferment over Millicent, but now I realized what a terrible blow this must be. She was losing her closest companion, the one person who retained her trust even after she had withdrawn from everyone else at court. Yet it was not heartbreak I saw in Flora's face. Sadness yes, and perhaps regret. But also a certain resolve. As if she must cry for the past before facing a new future.

I intended to slip away, but as I turned around, Flora called out my name.

"Yes, madam?" I asked.

"The child, is she well?"

"Yes, strong and healthy."

"What do they call her?"

"They have named her Rose."

"Rose." She pondered the sound of it for a moment, then curved her lips in a shy smile. "Queen Rose."

I waited for more, but silence hung between us as Flora drifted into whatever thoughts haunted her troubled mind. Wishing to make a gracious departure, I said the first words that sprang to mind: "I am sorry about your sister."

"Do you know, had my father been as bold as Ranolf, Millicent might be our queen? She was the eldest, and more cunning than my brother and I put together. But of course women could not inherit the title."

Until now. When it was too late for Millicent.

"She left Ranolf no choice," Flora said softly. "Yet I fear where her anger might lead. I fear it very much."

She turned quickly, her crumpled skirts forming a tangle around her, but not before I recognized the other emotion that had swept across her face as her sister disappeared from sight. It was relief.

In the following weeks, I tended to Queen Lenore as she gradually regained strength. She insisted Rose's cradle be placed in her own sitting room, rather than in the nursery on the castle's third floor. A wet nurse tended to the child's feedings, but in all other matters Queen Lenore took charge of the baby herself. The ladies-in-waiting felt sure that King Ranolf would object, particularly if he heard the crying infant from his own bedchamber. But the king made no complaint. Indeed he was often seen holding the child himself, beaming down at her peaceful, sleeping face.

"My Beauty," he would murmur. "My Beauty."

On the morning of the baptism, the king, the queen, and their tiny daughter proceeded through St. Elsip in a golden carriage. Undeterred by the frigid winter wind, townspeople lined up three and four deep along the streets to see them pass. A procession of courtiers followed the carriage, with Rose's newly chosen godmother, Lady Wintermale, leading the ladies and Sir Walthur Tilleth, the king's solemn chief counselor, at the head of the knights and noblemen. A boisterous gaggle of jesters and musicians followed behind.

I formed part of the tail of this parade, jostling among the other servants. Queen Lenore had given me one of her old gowns for the occasion, made of a sumptuous velvet that caressed my skin. The hem was frayed and the style of the sleeves years out of fashion, but it was the loveliest dress I had ever worn, and a fur-lined cloak protected me from the chill. Clad in such luxury, I moved differently, as if the fabrics conveyed the noble bearing of their original owner. At fifteen I was years younger than any other lady's maid, and self-doubt still plagued me despite the queen's kindness and patience. But on that day, in that dress, I took my place in the procession as if born to it, smiling graciously to the well-wishers. Even after I entered the peace of the cathedral, my ears were still ringing from the cheers of the crowd outside.

The baptism service was long and tiring, as such ceremonies often are, but Rose acquitted herself well, crying only at the end as the water was poured on her head. Crammed in among merchants and minor landowners at the very back of the church, I hardly saw the baby at all, only fleeting glimpses of Queen Lenore at the altar, holding a bundle of white lace. When the service ended, the king and queen walked down the aisle beaming, then emerged onto the cathedral steps to present Rose to her new subjects. I heard a wild cry of voices outside, after which cheers erupted inside the cathedral as well, ringing back upon us from the stone walls.

I waited until the crush at the church doors had cleared before attempting to leave. Outside, hundreds milled around in the open square, hoping to prolong the celebratory mood of the day. I looked around to see if others from the castle still lingered but saw no familiar faces. I was preparing to walk back alone when a voice called out, "Miss Elise!"

It had been some time since I'd been addressed so formally. I looked around and saw a rotund figure panting up the church steps toward me. As he approached, I recognized Hannolt, the shoemaker. Though I had passed the entrance to his shop on occasional visits to my aunt's house, I had not seen him since the day he escorted me to the castle.

"What a pleasant surprise!" he exclaimed.

He reached out to take my hand and kissed it with an extravagant flourish. As ever, the words tumbled from his mouth with barely a pause for breath.

"Your aunt tells me you serve the queen herself—how you have come up in the world since we last met! Well done, my girl, well done. Are you in town for the baptism? It's been very good for business, I can tell you. Ladies and gentlemen both have been ordering new shoes for the festivities. I've been working through the night for the past week, and that's with my wife and Marcus helping."

I looked over Hannolt's shoulder to see if his son lurked silently behind. "Is he with you?"

"Marcus?" Hannolt looked so puzzled that I immediately regretted my question. How brazen I must have appeared to him, asking after a young man I barely knew. I compounded my foolishness by stammering a too-hasty excuse: "It's only . . . I thought perhaps your whole family might have come to see the princess."

"Good luck catching a glimpse of her in this crowd!" Hannolt scoffed. "No, this may be a feast day at the castle, but my work continues all the same. Marcus is off making deliveries on the east side of town. I was just coming from Mrs. Hilsker's house, right around that corner, when I saw the procession, and I couldn't help but stop and take a look."

"It is a pleasure to see you," I said, attempting to extricate myself gracefully from further conversation before he delayed my return any longer. "However, the queen expects me back at the castle."

"I say, now that you keep such royal company, perhaps you might speak well of my work, if the opportunity should present itself. I do so enjoy working for the fine ladies of the court."

"I would recommend you without hesitation."

"Spoken like a true gentlewoman. Yes, your voice has become quite refined. And such lovely manners, too. You've made your aunt proud. She has much to celebrate—from what I hear, there will be another baptism celebrated before the year is out?"

"Yes, my cousin Damilla is expecting."

"Joyful news all around. I will send Mistress Agna your regards, and Marcus as well."

I told him it was not necessary, feeling the redness rise in my cheeks, but Hannolt was bowing and did not appear to hear. I could picture the scene later that day: Hannolt blathering on about my interest as Marcus struggled in vain to remember me. Since we met, I had crossed paths with dozens of young men with finer prospects than a shoemaker's son. Why, then, did Marcus's face remain so clear to me, and why had my heart sunk with disappointment at his absence?

⊶═⊷

Upon my return to the castle, I passed through the kitchens, where the cooks were flushed with the effort of their labor. Pigs roasted on spits in every fireplace, and the tables were covered with dough and pies. At any other time, I would have stopped and stolen a few bites—my stomach was rumbling at the smell—but that day I knew it meant risking a shout and a slap from the head cook. I walked on without stopping.

In the Lower Hall, pitchers of ale and platters piled with meat and cheese had been set out on the wooden tables. Stableboys and chambermaids were toasting one another and picking at the platters, though I guessed Mrs. Tewkes had not yet given leave for the party to begin. A cluster of grooms stumbled across my path, preparing to greet the visitors' carriages. One of them, a particularly sour driver named Horick, cursed me as I stepped on his foot after another jostled me to the side. A word from me to the queen could cost him his job, and I thought to tell him so but walked away instead. There would be no more certain way to turn the other servants against me, and I felt the loneliness of my station keenly enough as it was.

A few maids dashed past toward the Great Hall, their hands clutching precious goblets and bowls. Petra had described the feast preparations to me the day before: All the finest gold and silver serving pieces had been polished, the best crystal laid out, tapestries brought down from throughout the castle so every wall would be covered with color. The king and queen would sit at their table on the dais, with Rose in the royal cradle at their side. After dinner and the usual songs and poems in honor of the child, the highest-ranking guests would present their gifts. This procession was expected to take hours, by which time the crowd would be hungry again and supper would be served.

A hand tugged at my shoulder, and I turned to see Petra, eyeing me approvingly.

"What a lovely dress," she said.

"The queen gave it to me, for the baptism."

"You were at the cathedral?"

"In the back, crammed in a corner," I said. "Hardly a place of honor."

Petra glanced at the servants bustling past us. "I can't talk now. I'm risking an earful for being late as it is. Shall I look for you here later?"

"I'm not sure. The queen may need me." It was a convenient excuse, one I had used often to avoid servants' gatherings.

"Surely she'll allow you an hour or two of fun?" Petra asked. "All the girls will be dying to hear about the ceremony. And I hear that a certain huntsman will be singing."

We exchanged smiles, mine tentative and hers mischievous. The young man who tended to the king's hunting dogs was the subject of much conversation among the castle's female servants. Grateful for the friendly overture, I told her I would try to come.

Petra grinned and turned to go. "I'll be expecting you," she said over her shoulder as she ran off.

When I arrived in the queen's chambers upstairs, one of the maids told me she had already made her way to the Great Hall. I hurried back downstairs, weaving my way between extravagantly dressed ladies and gentlemen who sashayed along the hallways, preening for one another's benefit. When I entered the hall, I saw the king and queen across the room, greeting guests I did not recognize but whose elaborate cloaks signaled their noble rank. Counts, lords, and princes from throughout the land would be in attendance, and the king was determined to dazzle them all.

I elbowed through the press of people in the hall until I caught Queen Lenore's eye. I began to offer apologies for my late arrival, but she simply tilted her head to the side, indicating that I was to take my place. I pushed through the crowd until I reached the wall behind the dais, where I could watch the proceedings yet be within easy reach.

Suddenly the blast of trumpets rang out. Guests rushed to take their seats in a buzz of conversation and a rustle of skirts. The king rose from his chair. He was resplendent in his purple-and-gold robe, radiating happiness.

"Fair ladies and good gentlemen," he began, "it is my honor to welcome you to this glorious celebration. On this day I present my daughter, Rose, to you as my heir, with all the rights such a title entails."

I saw guests glance at one another, acknowledging the momentousness of the king's break with tradition, and I remembered Millicent's warning about forces arrayed against him. If any disloyal subjects lurked in this crowd, I saw no sign of them.

"The future of the kingdom has been a matter of great concern, to you as well as to my family," the king continued. "Whatever fears may have been raised in the past, I trust that Rose's arrival has eased them. Let her birth herald a new era of glory for us all."

He raised his golden goblet, inlaid with a rainbow's worth of jewels, and the guests stood and raised their glasses as well, a mass toast that exploded through the room. I tried to capture the sight in my mind, imagining I might one day tell Rose of this moment. Was it possible that a tiny child, and a girl at that, could preside over an era of peace? I wished it with all my heart.

After the toast, trays of food were brought in by an army of servants; I noticed that even the chambermaids and pages had been pressed into service. It was surely a mark of my favor with the queen that I had not been ordered to wait on the guests as well. She signaled to me a few times during the meal—once to fetch her a cool cloth, for the room was warm from the press of bodies, and the other to wipe a small puddle of wine that had spilled at her feet—but for the most part I stood aside and watched. By the time the jugglers and dancers arrived and attempted their entertainment in the narrow aisle that crossed the room, my face was flushed and my feet ached.

But there was still more to be endured: the endless parade of gifts. In order of rank, guests were escorted to the dais, where they presented gifts chosen for their power to impress the king and queen. The pile of jewels, furs, and gold grew, was carried away, and then grew again. I could see the hours wearing on the queen; she leaned sideways in her chair, her smile gracious as ever but her body slumped with fatigue.

The last of the gift givers, an elderly noblewoman whose back was bent in a permanent bow, shuffled toward the dais. The room's previously lively spirit had dissipated through the course of the afternoon. Now guests yawned and whispered to one another, long since bored by the proceedings. The gown I had worn with such pride that morning was wrinkled and damp with sweat, and my precisely arranged curls had wilted. I yearned for nothing more than to collapse upon my pallet and sleep.

In my distracted haze, it took me some moments to realize that the mood of the room had shifted. It was the rustle of mumbling voices I noticed first, near the doorway. I rose to my tiptoes, peering about to discover the cause, but the crowd was too thick. I listened to the commotion gather and swell, as a ripple passes across a pond. And then a figure emerged from the press of courtiers, and I gasped.

Millicent did not appear a woman disgraced. She held herself as regally as any queen, her black cape swirling around her tall frame. She wore a gown of green and purple—the royal family's colors—and her golden earrings flashed in the candlelight. I will never forget the sight of her as she marched, radiating strength. In that moment she was both beautiful and terrifying, and I felt myself succumb once again to her mysterious allure. Had she commanded me to bow before her, I would have, without question.

She stopped at the edge of the dais, directly in front of the king, and all sound ceased. She motioned toward the pile of riches at his feet.

"I fear I have arrived unpardonably late." Her resonant voice rang throughout the silent room. "Have all the gifts been presented?"

Queen Lenore sat perfectly still; to the guests she might have appeared indifferent to Millicent's arrival. Only I recognized the stiffening of her jaw and the way her hands clenched in her lap. The king's cheeks flushed, and I saw the effort he made to control himself before speaking.

"Madam, the celebration is at an end."

"I wish only to pay my respects," Millicent said, lowering her head in supplication.

Queen Lenore reached out and laid her hand on her husband's

arm. He glanced at her, then nodded at Millicent, his eyes narrow with suspicion.

"Thank you," Millicent said with an elaborate bow. "I do have a gift for both of you, but it is one you have already received." She stretched her long, bony fingers toward the crib. "Your beautiful daughter."

The king began to protest, and Millicent spoke quickly to silence his objections. "Ask dear Lenore. She will tell you how my efforts brought this miracle to pass."

The king turned to his wife, but she stared straight ahead, watching, waiting, her body so still that it was as if she had forgotten to breathe.

"Yet did I receive your gratitude? No. Instead you chose to shame me, casting me off like a common beggar. You have taken everything: my home, my good name, my happiness. And so, good King Ranolf, I will take your happiness from you."

Queen Lenore, as if sensing what was to come, reached toward the cradle and clutched Rose's tiny fist.

"Your child, your wife, your beloved kingdom—you shall lose it all," Millicent went on, her voice rising in triumph. "Not today and not tomorrow. No, I want you to clutch at your throne as you watch your power dissolve. I want you to live each day in fear, not knowing when the final blow will fall. I want you to see your child grow, loving her more with each passing year, until she is snatched away forever."

Despite my revulsion I remained enthralled by her voice, her spellbinding presence. The entire court must have been so affected, for not one us of moved to stop her.

Millicent dropped her voice to a murmur and leaned in toward the king. "There are so many ways to take a life. An elixir poured in a goblet. A potion spread on a pillow. Perhaps a trace of poison on the tip of a spinning wheel. Lenore, you are fond of such womanly arts, are you not? Imagine your girl at the height of her youth and beauty, pricking her finger and falling dead before you. What would you do then?"

I can still hear her cackle. That chilling sound is lodged in my memory for eternity, Millicent's revenge on me from beyond the grave. Queen Lenore cried out, and the sound roused the king from his horrified stupor. He leapt from his seat and made as if to attack Millicent himself in a battlefield rage. But she was prepared for such an onslaught. She sprang back, laughing, as the king tripped off the dais and tumbled to the floor.

"You will spend the rest of your life in fear," she said with a terrible smile. "That, my dear Ranolf, is my gift to you."

Then she disappeared. Later, through the years, people would say it happened by magic, that she vanished in a puff of smoke. Though I can swear there was no such scene, what I witnessed was barely more believable. One moment Millicent was standing at the center of the room; the next she had wrapped herself in her cape, turned, and lost herself in the crowd. The king shouted for his guards to go after her, and there was a roar of outrage and confusion as the knights pushed their way through the press of people, but to no avail. Millicent slipped out of the Great Hall without being seen.

She left behind a wake of shock and horror. Some guests huddled together and argued about what was to be done; others were struck dumb by what they had seen. Queen Lenore was shaking with sobs as she pulled Rose from the cradle and curled her body around the baby, as if to shelter her from Millicent's hatred. Rose began to scream, finding no comfort in her mother's embrace.

The sound roused me from my horrified stupor. I knelt before the queen, anxious to protect her from the frenzied scene.

"Come, madam," I urged.

Gently, I pried Rose away from the queen's arms and told the nurse to take her upstairs. The baby's shrieks and the surrounding mayhem made me dizzy with confusion. Looking to the king for direction, I ushered Queen Lenore through a small doorway behind us that led to the Receiving Room, the chamber where she had cheerfully greeted visitors throughout her pregnancy, with a preening, proud Millicent by her side. As soon as we entered, King Ranolf waved to his guards and they pulled the door shut behind him, silencing the bedlam outside. The king reached for his wife's hands, but she erupted with fury, pummeling her fists against her husband's chest.

"What have you done?" she shrieked.

I had never seen her so unhinged, and the sight horrified me almost as much as had Millicent's threats. King Ranolf gripped her elbows, and she sagged against him as her fury melted into despair. It was all I could do not to break down in tears myself.

"I begged you to invite Millicent," Queen Lenore sobbed, pausing between words to catch her breath. "You refused, and this is the price we pay."

"She is a madwoman! How dare she say Rose is her gift to us?"

"Because she is," Queen Lenore said, her sobs subsiding into a moan. She did not meet her husband's eyes.

"How can that be?" King Ranolf asked.

Behind us I heard a gentle rap at the door. Not wishing the king and queen to be bothered at such a time, I ran over and opened it a crack. To my surprise I saw Flora standing before me, a frail vision wrapped in an ivory cloak.

"Lenore. Ranolf. I must speak to them."

I pulled the door just wide enough to admit her. She moved shyly, hesitantly, like a sheltered maiden of sixteen rather than a woman well past middle age. She held her hands before her with fingers intertwined, in an attitude of prayer, and seemed to float rather than walk in her trailing skirt. The edges were tattered and grimy, evidence of years of wear, and her wavy white hair had been shoddily pinned in a ramshackle mass that threatened to collapse with each movement of her head.

Queen Lenore cried out and pulled away from her husband's arms.

"Help us!" she begged, falling at Flora's feet. "We are doomed!"

Flora's fingertips smoothed the queen's hair. "I feared that Millicent would come," she said slowly, her voice rusty from disuse. "You must believe I did my best to stop her. But it was not within my power."

"What can we do?" Queen Lenore moaned.

"Take hold of yourself!" the king ordered. "I will not have you undone by my aunt's wicked lies!"

"Ah, but what she said is true," Queen Lenore repeated wearily, rising from her knees. "Without Millicent I never would have given you a child."

"What do you mean?"

"The pilgrimage." Queen Lenore's voice was soft and hesitant, her eyes despondent. "It was Millicent's idea that we seek the intercession of St. Agrelle at the convent named in her honor. It was only after we arrived that she told me the full story. The reason St. Agrelle herself made the journey there so many years ago."

As the king waited for his wife to continue, Flora's face fell. "No," she whispered.

My stomach tightened with dread. What had Millicent done?

Flora turned to the king. "There have been stories, passed down from woman to woman. Claims that barren women bore children after visiting that hilltop. Some whispered that terrible sacrifices were made to a goddess there in ancient times, but I cannot believe that Millicent—"

"Black magic?" scoffed the king. "Nonsense!"

I remembered the figurines in Millicent's room, the carved pieces depicting naked, round-bellied women. Months later I could still feel the strange pull they had exerted, as if begging to be taken into my hand. I had known, in my heart, that those creatures were tinged with danger, yet I had taken one. Lain with it underneath my pillow. Had I put my very soul in peril?

Queen Lenore looked at each of us in turn, taking in the king's suspicious scowl, Flora's anxious eyes, and my fearful concern. Her delicate shoulders straightened, and she faced us directly, captivating us with her husky, musical voice.

"We were there three days," she began. "We prayed, we ate with the nuns who watch over the sanctuary, we walked the grounds. It was all as I had expected, until our final night. Millicent waited until Isla and the other ladies were asleep, and then she crept into my room and awakened me. She told me to come as I was, in my night-dress. It must have been past midnight. The moon was hidden behind clouds, and I could barely see my way down the path that led from the convent.

"She took me into the church and lit a candle. I thought she meant us to pray one last time, but she led me to a small anteroom. Underneath the woven mat that covered the floor was a wooden door. She pulled it up, and I saw narrow dirt steps leading into the ground. A wave of air wafted into my face. It was so cold and damp I felt I was staring into a grave. I stopped, shook my head, and said I wouldn't go.

"I cannot explain what happened next. The thought of entering that pit terrified me. And yet, when Millicent stepped down inside, I followed. I knew from that moment I would do whatever she demanded."

Flora nodded slowly, acknowledging the force of her sister's will. Had she spent her whole life subject to Millicent's commands? I felt a deep stab of sympathy for her, as I did for poor Queen Lenore. Had I been in her place, I would have followed Millicent down those stairs just as readily.

"The way gradually opened before us," the queen went on, "revealing a large chamber hollowed into the earth. Flat stones engraved with strange letters and crude carvings of women were arranged in a circle on the floor. In the very center was a patch of black soil, the size of a well. Millicent gripped my hands and began babbling, words I could scarce follow in my bewildered state. She spoke of a Great Mother and the power granted to those who served her. I knew it for blasphemy, but I did not have the strength to resist."

"It is as I said before," the king declared. "The woman has lost her senses!"

"I do not expect you to understand," Queen Lenore said, her tone wistful rather than dismissive. "I only ask for mercy when I tell you what happened next. One moment I was listening to her ramblings, and the next I saw a flash of silver as she raised a knife into the air above us. I wondered if she meant to kill me, and yet I was so in thrall to her that I did not fear such a death. Millicent grabbed my arm and held the knife over my wrist. I had only to make a blood oath accepting Millicent's dominion over me and my deepest wish would be granted. It was then that I realized the nature of the dark stains scattered across the stones and the dirt floor."

The king scowled in disgust, and my stomach churned with revulsion. Queen Lenore turned her despondent face to her husband, as if only he could offer absolution.

"I may be forever damned, but it was my last hope. I watched a red stream burst from my skin as Millicent cut into my wrist, and I swore to do whatever she demanded. Millicent told me the goddess's wishes would be done, that if I lay with my husband on my return home, I would find myself with child. I returned to my room as if in a dream. For hours I drifted in and out of sleep, and by morning I was wretched with guilt. The entire journey home, I agonized over what I had done. I hesitated before inviting you to my chamber, I was so fearful of what the outcome might be.

"And then, when I found out I was having Rose . . ." Queen Lenore's eyes had misted over with tears. "I was so happy and yet so afraid. I could not deny Millicent anything."

"Enough of these lies!" the king commanded, breaking the spell cast on all of us by the queen's tale. "It was a dream, brought on by my aunt's devious whispers."

"You do not believe me?" Queen Lenore pleaded, her face incredulous. "Look! Look upon the proof carved into my flesh!"

She thrust her arm at the king, palm upward, and the shimmering fabric of her sleeve slid backward. A puckered scar was all that remained of the raw gash I had noted on the morning I first spoke to her. Now, as I saw the evidence of her blasphemous bargain, my heart sank. The woman I looked to as a model of grace and kindness had shown herself capable of evil, and I feared that my love for her would be forever tainted by the memory of that slashed skin. It was only many years later, when I carried the grief of childlessness myself, that I was able to look upon the queen's decision with understanding, not judgment. None of us can know what we are capable of until we are tested.

The king pulled roughly at Queen Lenore's sleeve to conceal the wound.

"I will hear no more of this," he said sharply, his tone that of a father reprimanding a wayward daughter.

Flora, who had stood wide-eyed but silent throughout the queen's story, took a small step forward. "Ranolf," she said. "Do not doubt my sister's resolve. If she has sworn revenge, she will find a way to take it."

Queen Lenore choked back a sob, and Flora took her hand. "All is not lost," she said soothingly. "I cannot undo Millicent's curse. But I can keep Rose and the family safe."

The king looked at her doubtfully, but the queen was eager to take hope from Flora's words.

"The herbs in my garden can be used to heal. Millicent may have the power to sicken Rose, but she will not die, I promise."

"I'll not have you practice dark arts on my daughter," the king muttered.

"Dark arts!" Flora shook her head quickly as a blush flooded her cheeks. "My cures ease pain and lighten fevers. There is nothing dark about them."

I was doubtful that the king's eccentric aunt had the skill to cheat death, but I could see from the way the queen's eyes brightened that she took heart from Flora's assurances. Could the kingdom's salvation lie in the hands of this timid, disheveled woman?

King Ranolf stood silent for a moment, and I was not the only one who feared what words he might utter next. His eyes seemed to stare miles into the distance, and his chest quivered with the effort of maintaining steady breaths. Just as his wealth outdid that of any man in the kingdom, so did his passions. Would this terrible story forever destroy the tender feelings that had so bound him to his pregnant wife? Or would that love be strong enough to temper his rage?

"I will do whatever I must," he said at last, reaching for Queen Lenore's hands. "If it sets your mind at rest, we shall install tasters in the kitchen for our food. It is the custom at other courts. No one will think it amiss."

"The spinning wheels," Queen Lenore said. "I can't stop thinking of what she said, about Rose pricking her finger. . . ."

"If you wish it, I will burn every spinning wheel in the castle."

"People will think me mad," she whispered.

King Ranolf had always inspired more fear in me than love, but my heart swelled with affection in that moment, for he did not mock his wife or disparage her fears. He simply drew her closer and spoke as if they were the only two people in the room. "Your will is the will of the people. Whatever you wish shall be done."

Queen Lenore nodded.

"Banish Aunt Millicent's poisonous words from your thoughts," the king urged. "Her actions were those of a traitor, and she will reap a traitor's punishment."

Flora's eyes flickered nervously from the king to Queen Lenore to me. With that glance she and I became allies, silently promising to do what we must to spare the queen further agonies of guilt. Despite the king's assurances, I felt no safer now than I had in the moments immediately following Millicent's tirade. I knew too well her cunning, her ability to mold others' actions to her purposes. I might hate her for what she had done to my mistress, but even I could not swear before God that I was resistant to her influence. She knew my weaknesses, as no one else did, and she would not hesitate to use them against me.

"That witch will not destroy us," the king vowed.

And yet, by sowing the seeds of mistrust and fear, Millicent already had begun to do just that.

Seven

NEW BEGINNINGS

The bonfire blazed through the night, blistering the skies with its defiant light. All the spinning wheels in the castle had been smashed and burned in the front courtyard, and by the following day, in a gesture of loyalty, women from St. Elsip were dragging their own wheels to the foot of the hill outside the gates. The stack soon towered above the heads of the tallest men, and ladders were propped along the sides to carry the latest arrivals to the top. I joined a group of the queen's ladies at the windows of Lady Wintermale's room, overlooking the town, and watched a guard mount the ladder at sundown and set the pile alight. It was a stirring sight, and I found myself captivated by the crackling, sparking mass. Queen Lenore's empty, silent workroom made me mourn for all that had been lost, but I hoped the fiery display outside the walls would show Millicent—wherever she might be—that the king's subjects stood united against her.

But the following day I heard a group of footmen muttering that the king's precautions had gone too far.

"He's ordered the church of St. Agrelle destroyed," said one whom I had often seen standing outside the Council Chamber. "The convent as well, down to the foundations. The king says it's a favorite retreat of Lady Millicent's, and he'll not have her hiding there."

"I wish her dead as much as anyone, but that's hardly a reason to tear down a house of God, is it?" asked one of the other men.

"It'll be more than torn down," said the first man. "It's to be set aflame and left to rot. 'Leave the earth scorched and barren,' he said. The northerners will use it as another mark against him, you can be sure of that."

He ceased talking abruptly when he noticed I had stopped to listen. Turning swiftly away, I hid my face from them, as I would not have word spread through the castle that I had smiled in relief at the destruction of a church. Such an action would no doubt be proclaimed sacrilege by the deRauleys, the king's disloyal relations who held sway in the north of the kingdom, but it would also risk offending even the king's staunchest subjects.

If the obliteration of that blood-spattered pit beneath the earth was meant to reassure my mistress, it did not have the desired effect. She insisted Rose sleep in her bed, against the wishes of her ladies and the king.

"I'll not have her raised like a peasant," he said. "It's time she was moved to the nursery."

"Not yet," Queen Lenore begged. "Not when she's so small."

I saw the pain flash across the king's eyes and knew he would relent. "I will do everything in my power to protect her. I promise you."

He was true to his word. The number of guards at the castle gates was tripled, and each visitor and parcel was searched thoroughly before being permitted entrance. This caused much grumbling among the tradesmen forced to wait in line for hours along the road, and noble families protested formally when they learned they, too, would have their cloaks and bags inspected. To those of us behind the gates, the castle might as well have been under siege. I barely left the royal apartments, as Queen Lenore insisted on my presence at all hours. Over the following months, I ventured beyond the grounds only once, to observe the baptism of Aunt Agna's new granddaughter. I held baby Prielle and smoothed my lips across her downy head, breathing in her sleepy scent, wishing Princess Rose could have been welcomed into the world with such serenity. Prielle at least would live a simple, normal life, unencumbered by the terrible burdens of royalty.

Of Millicent we heard nothing. The king sent his best men after her, but perhaps she had magical powers after all, for they returned empty-handed. She had vanished, like a phantom. The thought that she might yet be plotting against the family weighed heavily on Queen Lenore, and I saw the toll it took on her in sleepless nights. She fretted if Rose was not within her sight and did not allow any of the other ladies to hold her. The baby was quieter than any I had known, but rather than give thanks for Rose's peaceful disposition, the queen worried that the tranquillity presaged illness.

The only assurances of Rose's good health that held any weight with the queen were those given by Flora. The king's aunt did not fully relinquish her eccentric habits in the weeks following the baptism, but little by little she emerged from her prior isolation. She tended to her herbs in full sunlight, rather than at dawn or dusk, and became a regular visitor to the royal apartments. Casual conversation did not come easily to her after so many years of self-contained silence, and she skittered away like a frightened hare when groups of ladies swarmed through the garden in a chattering mass. Yet it was Flora, our unlikely savior, who delivered the queen from the fear that threatened to imprison us all.

It was a bright spring afternoon, the sort that once would have sent Queen Lenore to the garden to consult on new plantings or choose cuttings for her rooms. Yet she had not set foot outside in the three months since Rose's birth. I lingered at the window in the sitting room, gazing at the trees and newly flowering bushes. Below, a familiar figure emerged from the herb garden and strolled leisurely along the winding path, a route I longed to follow myself.

Flora looked up, and I raised a hand in greeting. In return she held up a bright yellow bloom, the first flower of the season.

Delighted, I beckoned her to join us. Before long she had arrived in the queen's sitting room, clutching her floral offering.

"My lady, come see," I enthused. "The daffodils are blooming!"

Queen Lenore glanced up briefly, taking in Flora and the blossoms without emotion. Everything that had once given her pleasure—flowers, music, poetry—had been forgotten, replaced by fear for Rose. Flora gave a heavy sigh, and the weary sound encompassed all our despair.

"My dear, this can't go on," she said gently.

Queen Lenore's finger traced the pout of Rose's lips. The baby's mouth twitched in response and curved upward into a cheerful, gummy smile, her first. Queen Lenore caught her breath and looked up at me.

"Elise, did you see that? Did you see our Beauty's smile?"

"Indeed, my lady," I said, nodding happily.

The smiling must have been contagious, for Queen Lenore was

soon laughing and clucking at Rose in delight. It moved me to see her as any other mother, delighting in her child rather than fearing for its every breath. She rose and proudly showed off the baby's new trick to her ladies, then peered through the pane of rippled glass toward the garden below.

"How time passes," she murmured. "Perhaps a walk outside would do us all good."

I rushed to fetch her shawl before she changed her mind. The other ladies must have felt the same urgency, for they leapt from their seats and hovered near the door. By the time we emerged from the castle doors, you would have taken us for a merry band of adventurers, a dozen or so ladies and attendants who anticipated a walk in the garden as much as they once would have looked forward to a royal ball.

Flora drifted off from the group, and I followed, curious about the tucked-away beds she tended so carefully. My mother had grown some of the same plants in her vegetable garden throughout my childhood, and Flora smiled with satisfaction when I identified a few of the tiny shoots. Within her private domain, the shyness that shrouded her like a cloak gradually slipped away.

"Do all of these have medicinal uses?" I asked.

"Yes," she said, her mass of hair bobbing as she nodded. Her voice, once unleashed, flowed quickly, even eagerly. "Most in combination with other tonics. Some ingredients are not so easy to come by."

"It is a wonderful gift," I said. "The power to heal."

"Ah. You think it a gift?" For a sudden, disorienting moment, I was reminded of her sister, Millicent: the way she arched her eyebrows, regarding me with a look that seemed to bore into my most private thoughts. It is a troubling sensation, to feel yourself utterly without defense against another. But while Millicent's attentions had always held an undercurrent of danger, I did not feel the same fear with Flora. *She is considering me,* I thought. *For what?*

"There is no magic to my cures," she said at last. "My mother taught me all I know, passing down what she had been taught by her own mother and grandmother. As I must teach it one day to another. It would be a great loss if this knowledge were to die with me."

She focused her gray-green eyes upon mine. I understood the meaning behind her words but could not believe she would entrust me with such secrets.

"You are so very young, yet your devotion to the queen and the child is clear. We shall see. We shall see."

Before I could respond, we were interrupted by the head gardener, who was showing Queen Lenore where he planned to plant new hedges. She was lost in the conversation, forgoing her usual fretting over Rose as her ladies-in-waiting rejoiced at the sunlight and the gentle breeze. By the time I turned back around, Flora had drifted off, as was her way. I was left both intrigued and apprehensive at the thought of serving as her apprentice. The ability to cure illness would be a wondrous power, yet the responsibility would weigh heavy as well. Perhaps it would be a fitting repentance for the many times I had done Millicent's bidding.

The queen's hold on Rose may have loosened, but the threat overhanging the child was never forgotten. Rose slept at her mother's side until after her second birthday, when she was moved into what had previously been the queen's workroom. I held her and played with her as often as her own two nursemaids did. As I watched her sound out her first words or cackle in triumph as she plodded her way on shaking legs, I was haunted by memories of my lost brothers. Time and again I had watched my younger siblings pass through these same stages, though in my family's cottage the children were mostly ignored until they were able to work. I had tried so hard to avoid thoughts of my life before the castle, for dwelling on the losses I had suffered might have undone me completely. Yet I saw echoes of their faces in Rose, and at times, in the dark, I wept with regret for all the moments I had pushed them away or grumbled at having to share my food. Rose received more affection in one day than my brothers had in their entire lives.

I had tried to do right by my one surviving brother, Nairn, who remained on the farm with my father. Whenever I heard of a carriage traveling in the direction of my village, I would prepare a small package of food, with a coin or two wrapped inside, and ask that it be delivered to the farm. I would instruct that it be given to Nairn alone, not my father, but I did not know if these offerings were ever received. Nairn never sent word to me, though I told myself this was because he could not read or write. I allowed myself to imagine he was hiding the money away, saving up for the day when he could escape as I had done.

Millicent's curse had left a permanent scar on Queen Lenore, who never again laughed with abandon or sat flushed with pleasure at a loom, as she had in the days before she bore Rose. The nights in particular were a torment to her, dark hours when she hovered over her sleeping daughter, listening for each intake of breath. I do not think the poor child ever enjoyed a full night's rest, for her mother would shake her into wakefulness whenever her breathing grew too shallow, fearing that Millicent's dark arts had triumphed over her husband's precautions. But throughout those two years, as Rose thrived, Queen Lenore's gentle smiles gradually returned and the sadness in her eyes lessened, though it never completely vanished. Spinning wheels were restored to the seamstresses' rooms—though they were never again seen in the royal apartments—and noble visitors who passed through the kingdom were entertained at feasts in the Great Hall. Still, lavish entertainments remained rare, so it was cause for considerable rejoicing when the king and queen announced they would be reviving a tradition that went back to the time of the king's grandparents: a midsummer tournament.

Preparations began weeks beforehand, with all the noblewomen in the castle fretting to replace their outdated clothes with more fashionable finery. Even the servants were caught up in the ferment, for the celebration was to extend into the Lower Hall on the final night, and Petra had made me promise I would come. Though always conscious of the strain caused by our differing stations, we had both done our part to rebuild our friendship, a process eased by our growing maturity. Petra's abilities and charm had assured her rise among the serving staff, and she was now widely discussed as an eventual replacement for Mrs. Tewkes.

"The king is never stingy with the ale," she assured me, her eyes sparkling. "If you've got your eye on someone, that will be the night to claim a kiss."

I blushed, as she knew I would, for I could claim no special someone; I hadn't as much as held hands with a man. Confusing, lustful feelings had coursed through my now seventeen-year-old body in the silence of night, as I lay on my pallet and remembered Petra's tales of the servants' quarters after dark. With so many young, unmarried people living together, there was a shifting pattern of couplings and uncouplings. But just as I slept apart from the other servants, I kept my distance from such goings-on. The only love affairs I indulged in were creations of my imagination. I had learned the lesson of my mother's life all too well.

"And you?" I teased, anxious to take the attention off myself. "Who will you be batting your eyelashes at?"

"A certain young page may have caught my attention," she said with a sly smile, daring me to guess.

The castle pages were a varied and often changing group, mostly young men of noble family sent to court to learn both battleworthy swordsmanship and elegant manners. Some came for a few months and left without distinguishing themselves; others remained for years, the best earning their way toward knighthoods and positions in the king's service. I knew only a few by name.

"Go on," I urged. "Tell me."

"Dorian."

I knew instantly of whom she spoke, for he was the son of the king's chief counselor, Sir Walthur. His father's rank gave him certain privileges; unlike other, less fortunate pages, he was not expected to act as a messenger or an errand boy but attended to the king's most favored companions and was often brought on their hunting parties. To my surprise I felt a sudden stab of jealousy. Dorian was strikingly handsome and the subject of much interest among the queen's younger ladies. Though his air of self-regard held little appeal for me, I could not help following him with my eyes when our paths crossed. Surely, I had assumed, such a man would never stoop to converse with a maid. Yet here was Petra, giggling in anticipation, unafraid to flirt with the best-looking youth in the castle. If only I were not so shy! While I might admire a young man from a distance, I did not know how to speak to one in any way that did not pertain to my duties.

"The pages will hardly forgo the Great Hall celebration for our humble servants' fest," Petra said, "but it does no harm to daydream, does it?"

"Of course not," I said, smiling in relief. Dorian was a passing fancy, nothing more. I would not have to stand by, silent and uncomfortable, while my friend danced and whispered conspiratorially with a new beau. But I knew that day would come, by and by. Petra was too pretty and well liked to remain unmarried much longer. And when she met her mate, would jealousy embitter me to their happiness?

Perhaps it was because such thoughts lay heavy in my mind that a chance meeting the following day struck me with such force. I was returning to the queen's rooms from the garden, where I had made my weekly excursion for flower cuttings, when I almost walked headlong into a short, rotund man who had stopped directly in my path outside the Great Hall.

"Miss Elise! What a pleasure, after all this time!"

It was Hannolt, the shoemaker, accompanied by a young man I might not have recognized had he passed me in town. Marcus had grown a good head taller since I saw him last, so that he now towered over his stout father, and I had to tilt my head upward to look at his face. His shoulders and arms had broadened somewhat, though his shirt still hung loose from his lean frame. Through the dark hair that partly obscured his face, I saw eyes framed by thick lashes and ruddy, healthy cheeks. Dressed in something other than a shopkeeper's tunic, he could have passed for a man of quality.

Hannolt and I exchanged greetings, and Marcus bobbed his head.

"Say something for yourself, boy," Hannolt urged. "You remember Elise, do you not?"

Marcus stumbled over his first words, a blunder that further endeared him to me.

"Um . . . it is . . . um, a pleasure to see you, Elise—that is, Miss . . ."

"Elise will do," I said quickly. "It is my pleasure to see you as well."

I might have been one of Queen Lenore's ladies, conversing politely at a reception, yet my belly tightened with giddy anticipation. Marcus smiled, and it was enough to make my heart race, for his face reflected my own delight at our sudden reacquaintance. Warmth tingled through my body, unbidden and unexpected. I had never felt such a strong physical response to a young man's attention, and I had to glance downward to hide the blush that burst across my cheeks.

Hannolt, as ever, was quick to launch into conversation.

"It seems every fine lady demands new shoes for the tournament," he said, "and the castle shoemaker has been kind enough to spread word of my talents. I've been given a commission by Lady Wintermale herself!"

"You will find her a demanding patron," I said.

"Nothing I have not been subjected to before. I imagine you must encounter Lady Wintermale a great deal in your service to the queen." He lowered his voice as if he were discussing great matters of state. "Do you still attend on her?"

"Yes, I was just bringing these flowers to her chambers," I said, indicating the bouquet in my hands.

"Oh, my dear, I hope I have not caused you to neglect your duties. If your mistress expects you, please do not linger on our account."

Anxious that the encounter not be cut short, I allayed Hannolt's concerns by fobbing off the flowers on a passing chambermaid. I was almost certain I saw Marcus's shoulders soften with what could only be relief. Glancing about in search of a diversion, I offered to show them the Great Hall, where the servants, including Petra, were finishing up their preparations for the evening meal. I escorted my awestruck visitors around the edge of the room, explaining the intricate seating arrangements and describing some of the lavish dishes that had been served at the king's feasts. Hannolt gaped as he took in the intricate tapestries and silver serving pieces. Marcus's response was more measured. Was I flattering myself to think that his glance fell more often upon me than on the wondrous extravagances of the hall?

Nervously, I babbled on. The few questions Marcus asked were thoughtful and well considered, but for the most part he was content to listen, as if my words were important and worthy of consideration. In a court where everyone, even the servants, strove to be noticed and admired, I found his reserve strangely compelling. He did not preen or invite my attention; indeed he seemed somewhat cowed by the magnificence surrounding him. Yet when our eyes met, those shared, secret glances revealed an intensity of feeling out of all proportion to our brief acquaintance. He was curious about me, just as I was drawn to him for reasons I could not fully understand. As we passed through the doorway to the entrance hall, side by side, Marcus's presence a mere handsbreadth away exerted a physical pull, tempting me to brush my fingertips against his. I could almost feel the spark of pleasure race up my arm.

I was quickly distracted from such thoughts by a commotion on the main stairs. In a flurry of footsteps and chattering voices, the king, the queen, and other members of court descended for their meal. I swiftly escorted Hannolt and Marcus aside, but not before catching Queen Lenore's attention, and she stepped over to speak with us. I made hurried introductions, mortified to have been discovered dawdling rather than tending to her dress and hair. She did not appear displeased, however, and she smiled when Hannolt bowed so low that his forehead nearly scraped the floor.

"My lady, it is truly an honor," he said in his most obsequious manner. "For a humble man such as myself to be in the presence of such glory is an experience I shall treasure all my life, you may be sure. . . ."

Well versed in the signs of long-windedness, Queen Lenore was quick to cut him off. "Elise, would you speak well of Master Yelling's craftsmanship?"

"Yes, madam. I still wear the shoes he made for me when I first came to the castle."

"Hmm." Queen Lenore allowed Hannolt to quiver with anticipation for a moment, then delighted him by saying, "Perhaps I will have a commission for you myself one day."

Hannolt's grin was so wide it looked as if his cheeks might crack under the strain. It was all I could do not to giggle, and Marcus glanced at me with a conspiratorial smirk, acknowledging my amusement. Outside, a rumble of thunder announced the arrival of the storm that had been threatening all afternoon.

"Time we were off," Hannolt said with another bow. "I do apologize for keeping you."

Queen Lenore glanced at his cane. The sudden, wrenching sound of lightning made us all jerk in surprise.

"I can't have you walking back to town in this weather," she said. "Please accept the use of one of our carriages."

"I couldn't possibly," Hannolt said.

"I insist." She turned to me. "Did you say Master Yelling lives in the same building as your aunt?"

I nodded.

"You have my leave to visit her, if you wish. Tell the driver to wait and bring you back."

My aunt was the kind of woman easily put out by unexpected guests at suppertime. But I could bear her muttered grumbling if it meant more time with Marcus.

"Good," Queen Lenore said, taking my silence for assent. "Stay as late as you wish."

After bidding the queen farewell, I led Hannolt and Marcus down the hallway toward the stairs. Now that I had been granted my wish, I could not think of a thing to say, and Marcus appeared to be suffering from a similar lack of inspiration. Luckily, Hannolt had words enough for all of us.

"What an honor!" he gushed. "To be in the presence of the queen herself! What a fine lady she is. I had heard tales of her beauty, yet she was even more gracious than I imagined. You're a lucky one, Elise. Taking after your mistress in looks as well, wouldn't you say, Marcus?"

Seemingly mortified by the question, Marcus merely mumbled a barely intelligible "Hmm" and looked downward. It was true, I had learned to arrange my hair in the queen's manner, taming my wild curls into elegant twists that framed the edges of my cap. I mimicked her walk as well, trying to keep my footsteps silent so it would appear my skirt was gliding across the floor. I had been struck by Marcus's taller, more manly stature, and he must have noted the changes in my appearance since our last meeting. But perhaps, to a townsman, my manner of speech and dress were off-putting. Worse, given my humble background, he might think me one who enjoys putting on airs above my station.

I led Hannolt and Marcus through the courtyard to the stables in back. Horses and carriages were apportioned according to rank, as with any other castle honor. When not traveling with their masters, servants were given simple wooden carts for journeys into town, and this is what I expected to be offered when I brought the queen's orders to Mr. Gungen, the stablemaster.

"It's a quiet night," he told me. "Take the green one if you like." He pointed to a covered carriage with cushioned seats, the sort reserved for noblewomen.

I looked at him doubtfully, and he shrugged.

"You may as well. We can't have the queen's maid soaked and covered in mud on a night like this. Horick!"

My smile faded. So this would be the price paid to travel in comfort. Horick was the sour groomsman often charged with shuttling servants and goods, duties he clearly thought beneath him. His bitterness at being denied royal passengers only assured that he would never be given that honor, for he was known to shout oaths and wave his whip at passersby who did not clear his path quickly enough. He had driven me occasionally on errands for the queen, and I found him poor company.

Mr. Gungen went to rouse Horick, who emerged brandishing a chicken leg, his face crumpled in its usual expression of misery.

"Just as I was starting my supper," he complained.

"Get on!" Mr. Gungen barked. "These orders are direct from the queen."

The greatest benefit of the enclosed carriage was that it blocked the sound of Horick's grumbling as we rode. Hannolt had insisted I enter the carriage first. He followed and climbed into the seat facing me, spreading his arms wide and patting the plush seats with a delighted grin. Marcus took the place next to me. Though I was intensely aware of his presence, I kept my eyes straight ahead, and I could tell from the corner of my eye that he was doing the same. As we approached my aunt's house, my heartbeat counted down the seconds before we must make our farewells. When would I see Marcus again? I remembered Petra talking about the tournament and the handsome page she meant to charm. The carriage rounded the final corner, turning onto my aunt's street. There was no time left.

"There will be a celebration, the final night of the tournament," I blurted out, facing Marcus.

"Oh," he said, taken aback by my sudden outburst. But not displeased. No, for he leaned closer to hear what I might say next, giving me the courage to continue.

"You are welcome to come if you wish."

"You are sure?" he asked quickly, anxiously. "It is not intended only for those who live at the castle?"

"No, no, guests are welcome," I assured him. "Some of the other maids have invited their sweethearts from town."

No sooner had I said the words than I began to blush furiously, mortified that Marcus might think I included him in that category. Or perhaps he was already spoken for? What a fool I would look!

"A fine offer," Hannolt spoke up, ever ready to insert himself into a conversation. "Marcus would be delighted, wouldn't you, my boy? Ah, here we are!"

When the carriage stopped, Marcus was quick to push open the door and clamber down, standing below to offer me his hand and holding up his cloak to shield me from the rain. I tried to descend as gracefully as possible, allowing my skirts to swirl around as Queen

Lenore would have done. If I held Marcus's hand a minute longer than necessary, he showed no eagerness to release his steady grip.

"I'm to wait?" Horick scowled from his driver's perch.

"Would you have the queen's maid walk to the castle alone after dark?" Hannolt said indignantly. He urged me toward the doorstep of my aunt's house, where an overhang sheltered us from the storm. When my aunt Agna opened the door, she stared at our damp, windblown figures in surprise.

"Greetings from the castle," Hannolt announced, eager to boast of his brush with royalty. "The queen herself ordered us escorted back to town in one of her own carriages and urged your niece to pay you a visit. Is that not kindness itself?"

"Begging permission to wait in your stables, ma'am?" Horick shouted from the carriage. The surliness of his tone tarnished the civility of the words.

"To the left, round the back," my aunt ordered. Suddenly she stopped and peered out from the doorway to regard the driver more closely.

"It's Horick, is it?" she asked.

They looked at each other, and recognition fluttered across his face. His harsh voice softened into little more than a whisper. "I remember you. Mayren's sister."

I perked up at the sound of my mother's name, but Aunt Agna put a quick end to the exchange. Stepping back into her doorway and turning her face away, she said briskly, "Speak to my groomsman. He'll see you're fed."

Horick shook the horses' reins and drove off.

"Miss Elise," Hannolt said with an elaborate bow, "it was a pleasure to serve as your escort, and I hope to see you at the castle during my next visit."

"Thank you for your kind invitation," said Marcus stiffly. Under the watchful eyes of his father and Agna, he was obviously flustered, and I felt a rush of sympathy. What might we have said to each other if we'd been granted a few moments unobserved? All I could do was smile pleasantly and tell him I would meet him at the castle gates at eight o'clock on the following Sunday night. The delight on his face was enough to fuel a fortnight's worth of daydreams.

"Come along, Elise," Agna ordered. "Join us for supper. You'll want to see Prielle, I'm sure, before she's sent off to bed. She has become a regular chatterbox since you saw her last."

I took hold of her arm before she could call out to the others to join us. "The driver, Horick," I said. "He knew my mother?"

Agna pursed her lips, considering what to say. I stared at her, my eyes pleading. She sighed and drew me into the front room.

"I take no pleasure in revisiting the past or speaking ill of the dead," she said. "What's done is done, and we all suffer the consequences of our actions as God wills. However, if you're set on hearing what happened to your mother, I'll not spare you. Take what I tell you as a cautionary tale."

I nodded. Agna did not know I had been told of my birth out of wedlock, and I had no wish to revisit my mother's shame by speaking of it. But I had never stopped wondering how her life had taken such a tragic turn.

"I knew Horick many years ago," my aunt continued. "He is much changed, and for the worse. When I first met him, he was a stableboy, not yet twenty. He cut a fine enough figure, though he was far from handsome and smelled of horses, as groomsmen do.

But he had all his teeth and a full head of hair, an easy laugh. Mayren could have done worse."

"Horick was Mother's beau?" Impossible. My graceful, beautiful mother drawn to that bitter man? But, as Agna said, it was many years ago, when Horick was quick to laugh. I could not imagine it.

"They had an understanding, though I do not know the exact words exchanged," my aunt said. "I suppose Mayren thought herself betrothed, though Horick soon proved otherwise." She stood, lost in thought, as I tried to follow her meaning.

"Why did they not marry?" I asked.

"He played her for a fool," Agna said, though her tone made it clear she blamed her sister more than Horick. "Led her to believe they were betrothed, then refused to marry her."

My mother. Horick.

"Mayren made many mistakes," Agna continued. "You'd do well to learn from her example. A young woman in service at the castle must be mindful of her reputation at all times. One roll in the hay can be enough to ruin you."

The truth of my birth hovered between us, an invisible thread intertwined in her words. Despite her sharp tone, I knew that Agna thought herself kind for not saying aloud that I was a bastard. I did not want to tell her I already knew.

"Mayren paid a heavy price for her foolishness. Mind you, it doesn't look as if he's done well for himself either. I'd be surprised if he had half his teeth left."

For so many years, I'd wondered about the man who had fathered me, weaving tales of star-crossed lovers and forbidden passion. Now I had reached the end of my quest, but there was no satisfaction in it. My very soul wilted with disappointment.

"You've done well at the castle," Agna said, "far better than I expected. Don't let pretty words and good looks distract you from all you have accomplished."

It was as if she'd divined my lustful thoughts of Marcus. Frightened by my aunt's prescience, I nodded and assured her my behavior was above reproach.

Throughout the meal I imagined confronting Horick on the drive back to the castle. What would he say when I threw out my mother's name? Beg forgiveness? Offer up a feeble defense of his betrayal? As he pulled open the carriage door for me to enter, I searched his scowling face for a familiar feature but could see no reflection of my own appearance in his craggy cheeks and jowly chin. Inwardly cursing my own cowardice, I remained silent as I entered the carriage and rode back to the castle through the darkened streets. Had Horick uttered the slightest pleasantry as I alighted in the courtyard, I might have gathered my nerve to speak. But his curt disrespect made me fear what he would say if confronted. To hear my mother insulted would be more than I could bear. Worse, any acknowledgment of my parentage might give Horick some claim over me, and I would not be beholden to such a man.

That night, though I felt capable of soaking my pillow with tears, I set my mind resolutely to thoughts of Marcus. My mother's sorry fate, and Horick's part in it, was a piece of my past that must be walled off and forgotten. I was on the cusp of a new beginning, with Marcus beckoning me forward. At last I would know what it was to have a suitor, a person who longed for my touch as much as I longed for his.

Yet a troubling thought repeatedly pierced my girlish imaginings. Was this how my mother had felt, the night she gave herself to Horick?

Eight

LOVE'S FIRST BLUSH

"So who's your young man?" Petra demanded with a teasing smile.

It was the third and final day of the tournament, and we sat in the stands overlooking the jousting. Carpenters had worked day and night in an open field just outside the castle walls, erecting a series of raised wooden benches surrounding a central track. The king and queen sat under a canopy of purple velvet; along with certain favored attendants, I had been granted a place on a bench directly above them, and I had invited Petra to join me. With preparations for the tournament keeping us both busy over the past week, we had exchanged only brief, hurried greetings, and I was looking forward to her always amusing company.

"My young man?" I asked. A knight wearing the colors of a neighboring kingdom was riding in to face Lord Steffon, a cousin of the king and a favorite of Queen Lenore. It was the most anticipated match of the afternoon, and for a moment Petra's voice was drowned out by cheers.

"The good-looking lad I saw you with in the Great Hall. Dark hair, soulful eyes? Or do you have many such admirers?"

"Marcus." The way I said his name clearly revealed my feelings, for she clapped her hands with delight.

"Marcus! How well the name goes with yours. Marcus and Elise. Rather like poetry, don't you think?"

"Hush!" I urged, laughing. "He's an acquaintance, nothing more. He and his father are shoemakers."

"Then he must have skilled hands indeed!" Petra exclaimed. "Or have you learned that for yourself already?"

I slapped her arm in mock horror, hoping to distract her from the warm blush rising over my cheeks. A cry erupted from the crowd around us as the king's cousin caught his lance against his opponent's armor and fell from his horse. The sound continued to build as he lay still for a moment, followed by cheers when he raised himself to his knees. His attendants rushed forward and helped him stand.

"Look!" Petra exclaimed, pointing to the huddle of people around Lord Steffon. "There he is."

Slightly above average height, Dorian carried himself with a swagger that made him appear even taller, and his strong chin and chiseled features embodied the image of a fairy-tale hero. With his thick blond hair, green eyes, and ready wit, he might have been crafted for the express purpose of making women swoon, and, like Petra's, my attention was fixed upon him as he followed Lord Steffon from the field.

"Have you seen him dance?" Petra asked. "Such fine legs! I may trip over myself in admiring them."

"From a distance, I presume."

"Oh, I'll find a way to turn his head. A man such as that likes a girl with spirit."

I was surprised to hear Petra speak so boldly. Many maids thought themselves lucky to catch a kiss and a fondle from a young nobleman before they settled down with a suitable but less heart-stirring husband, yet Petra had never been one to indulge in that sort of escapade. Though his family was not a noble one, Petra knew that the son of the king's chief adviser would never consider a serving girl a serious prospect.

"Have you spoken to him?" I asked, trying to judge the depth of her interest.

"Of course," she said. "I will admit that our conversations haven't strayed much further than 'I'll have more bread' and 'Yes, sir,' but in my head he has already declared his undying love."

I smiled, remembering similar conversations I had imagined with Marcus.

"Some men have no need of words," I said. "They show whom they favor in other ways." My tone was lighthearted, but I remembered a story one of Queen Lenore's ladies had recounted some months before, an incident involving Dorian and a certain woman of ill repute who had greeted him by name when the king's hunting party was passing through town. It made me wary of Dorian's reputation, for it seemed he had been flattered rather than shamed by the harlot's attention.

The sun was beating down upon us, and Petra ran a few fingers under the edge of the scratchy linen cap that was part of each maid's uniform. "Have no fear," she said. "My honor has not been sullied. Dorian hasn't given me so much as a pat on the backside, which is more than I can say for other so-called gentlemen of the court."

She laughed, and my stomach tightened in disgust as I remembered my narrow escape from Prince Bowen. I had told no one of our encounter, not even Petra, for to speak of it would be to relive the horror anew. But the memory of that shameful episode lingered, and to me the liberties that courtiers took with serving girls would never be a joking matter.

Petra pushed the cap off her head, releasing a cascade of icy-blond hair. I wished I had such self-assurance, for it would have been a welcome relief from the heat. But I was far too modest. Petra combed her fingers through the shimmering strands, and I noticed heads turning around us at the sight. She had a natural grace that set her apart from the rest of the maids, and for a moment I was convinced her beauty might be enough to spark Dorian's affection after all.

Petra twisted her hair into a tight knot and returned the cap to her head, transforming herself back into a simple, anonymous servant. "Dorian is no more than a pleasant distraction," she said. "Plotting to catch his eye helps pass the time during a long night at the tables."

Lord Steffon and his men had moved into the stands just below the king and queen. I watched Dorian laughing and jostling his fellow pages, as young men do when they want to make a show of their manliness. It was clear from the way the others deferred to him that they looked to Dorian as a leader.

And what was I thinking, on that summer day so long ago? Though I have never been drawn to those who push themselves to the center of attention, I remember watching him, intrigued. Even then he seemed a man destined for great things, though I never could have imagined the role he would one day play in my own life.

"Enough of Dorian," Petra said. "Let's return to your beau."

"I told you, Marcus is not my beau."

"But you wish he were, don't you?" Petra laughed in delight as I blushed, then admitted I had invited him to the party that night.

"But it has been nearly two weeks since I saw him last," I said. "I have no idea if he'll come."

"If he's seen you this giddy, he'd be a fool to stay away."

The servants' fest was uncomfortable in the way such events often are: too many people drinking too much ale, forced into conversation with acquaintances they usually avoid. I had no desire to linger, and were I not awaiting Marcus, I would have eaten quickly and left. As it was, I spent an excruciating half hour looking for him in the crowd around the gates, occasionally greeting a fellow servant before returning to my search. My heart pounded with both anticipation and nerves.

"Fancy a spin?"

I turned, surprised, only to be assaulted by an odor of spirits and sweat. It was Elgar, one of the stableboys. His body swayed slowly from side to side as he fixed me with a crooked smile.

I shook my head. "No, thank you."

"Aren't we fine?" he asked, attempting a mocking imitation of my accent. "Should have known you'd be snooty about it. You're no better than the rest of us, darling."

Infuriated, I strode away before I made the mistake of speaking my mind. For I did consider myself better than Elgar and his drunken friends. My time in Queen Lenore's service had changed me. I had grown to appreciate the same things as my mistress: beauty, poetry, gracious manners, and clever conversation. Strangely, I felt more at ease with her than with those of my own station, most of whom could not even write their names.

"Elise!"

I turned and saw Marcus across the press of people, his height giving him an advantage in seeking me out. In an instant the noise and throngs surrounding me ceased to exist. So great was my relief that I waved and hastened toward him, not caring if my behavior was too forward for our limited acquaintance. He was wearing what must have been his Sunday best, a white linen shirt and brown woolen trousers that were immaculately clean but showed signs of mending. Most of the servants around us were clad in clothes of higher-quality fabric, for the king set great store in appearances and provided new uniforms every two years. My own gown, another hand-me-down from the queen, was trimmed in lace and velvet ribbon. Marcus struck me as a more than usually observant young man; the humbleness of his clothing in comparison to mine would not escape his notice.

He dropped into a quick, awkward bow, then smiled wryly and shook his head. "I am sorry. I do not know the proper form for such events."

"This is a servants' fest, not a royal audience," I said with an encouraging smile. Then, hoping spirits might ease my nerves, I offered him a cup of ale, and together we braved the knots of boisterous revelers who surrounded the barrels.

Our first attempts at conversation were forced and tentative, as I clumsily tried to ascertain whether he was spoken for and he just as clumsily confirmed he was not. By the time we had drained our first mugs, we were speaking easily enough of court gossip and the news from St. Elsip, even as our bodies hinted at other, more tantalizing subjects. Jostled by the crowd, Marcus would press his arm against mine, or my hand would brush against his shoulder when I leaned in to whisper a scandalous rumor. When a soused craftsman staggered toward me, looking perilously close to retching, I veered from his path directly into Marcus, almost knocking us both down. Wobbling, trying to regain my balance and my dignity, I heard Marcus laugh as he took hold of my waist to steady me. Not the mocking laughter another man would have thrown out on witnessing my befuddlement. It was a gentle, happy sound.

All around me, men and women were coupling off, their inhibitions loosened by drink and the excitement of the tournament. It was a night when servants were released from their duties and allowed a few precious hours to follow their own desires. For once I wanted to join them. I wanted to please only myself, with no thought for what others might think.

As Marcus freed me from his grip, I reached out and grabbed his hands. "It's too crowded here," I said. "Follow me."

I led Marcus through the courtyard and into the castle, hoping my face gave no hint of the fluttering that rippled through my chest. In silence we walked along the corridors that snaked through the walls of the main floor, past the Great Hall where the nobles were enjoying their own revelries. Emerging into the queen's empty Receiving Room, we continued toward the door that led outside, into the walled garden. The midsummer sun had nearly completed its descent to the horizon, burnishing the scene with a golden haze. The flower beds were at the height of their glory, and fragrant aromas drifted on the air as we passed. A short distance away, hundreds of people were gathered, yet here, within this hidden sanctuary, Marcus and I stood alone.

Alone and unobserved. My heart thudded with expectation.

"Shall we sit?" I asked, pointing toward the semicircular wooden bench in the middle of the rose garden. Marcus left a handsbreadth between us as he took his place.

"Do you ever . . ." He paused and fixed me with a look of such intensity that it shattered the polite formality between us. "Do you ever marvel at your change in circumstance? To find yourself here, in such company?"

Such a direct question deserved a direct answer. "I do marvel, every day."

"It suits you, this life," he said with a touch of wistfulness.

"The queen suits me. But the castle is a very different world than the one I came from."

"And where was that?"

I had not spoken of my past at any length to anyone but Petra. My story could be told in a few short sentences, yet Marcus listened—truly listened—and I found myself revealing more than I intended. I told him of Father's hardness, of Mother's last moments, of my desperate hope that the castle would offer some kind of salvation. Even as I praised the queen's kindness, I spoke of the loneliness that plagued me when I was not in her company, the fear that I would always be regarded an outsider within these walls.

"Perhaps that is why you treat me differently than the others," Marcus said quietly. "All the servants look down on tradesmen from town. You are the only one who does not."

"When we first met, I was fresh off the farm, most likely with straw still caught in my hair. Yet you treated me kindly."

"You remember that day in my father's shop?"

"Of course I do," I said with a shy smile. "And you?"

"I've never forgotten it," he said, his voice husky. "I have not forgotten any of our encounters."

We looked into each other's eyes, seeing our hopes reflected in the other's face. I reached out my hand and found his, and then our fingers were intertwined, caressing with the lightest of touches. He leaned downward and grazed his lips along my knuckles, and I giggled in delight, provoking his own laughter.

"Does this please you, my lady?" he asked with exaggerated courtesy. "You must have dozens of admirers who beg the privilege of a kiss. Perhaps one who sings of love while strumming a lute?"

Behind his joking tone, I heard fear. I would always think myself a poor country girl, ill suited to her position. But to a cobbler's son, I might appear out of reach.

"I am the same girl you met in your father's shop," I said. "I have no interest in courtiers who fancy themselves poets."

We sat companionably together, hands joined, my heart racing. Eager to further the bond of honesty between us, I told stories of how poorly I had carried out my duties during my earliest days as Queen Lenore's attendant, delighting in his laughter.

"Look at you now, as much a lady as those you serve," Marcus said. "I knew from our first meeting that you were fit for more than a chambermaid's duties."

"Anything I have made of myself is a credit to my mother," I said. "We had no money and no prospects, yet she made me believe I could be more than a peasant's wife."

"And a shoemaker's wife?" His voice was lighthearted, yet I felt the import of the words.

"I care only that my future husband be kind."

"I would ask the same of my future wife."

I so longed for him to kiss me that when his lips suddenly met mine, I thought the force of my desire had pulled him forward. Or perhaps I hurried the result by bending my body toward his. If so, he was not offended by my forwardness, for he responded instantly, caressing my mouth with his, raising one hand to rest softly on my cheek. A rush of heat coursed through my body, and I leaned closer, pressing my lips harder against his, demanding more. It was Marcus who drew away, Marcus who warned that someone was approaching.

We sprang up from the bench and moved a decent distance apart as the sound of laughter and thudding footsteps grew closer. I peered out through the bushes and saw Lord Steffon and one of Lenore's ladies-in-waiting tumble to the ground in an embrace, their exploration of each other's body advanced well beyond kissing.

Putting my fingers to my lips to urge silence, I guided Marcus away from the intruders, toward Flora's herb garden and the hidden door that led back into the castle. Once inside, we laughed conspiratorially at our near discovery, but the presence of other people dampened the ease we had felt when we were alone. I did not offer him my hand, and he did not reach for it.

Marcus followed me back through the servants' corridors, past the kitchens and into the rear courtyard. The flagstones in front of the stables had been given over to dancing, and the sound of stamping feet and raucous singing almost drowned out the fiddles and drums.

"It's very late," Marcus said. "My father will fret if I'm gone much longer."

I could not hide my disappointment. I had hoped he would ask me to dance, that I might revel in the feel of his hands on my shoulders and waist.

"It's only . . . he's not been well lately," Marcus explained. "He's had some rheumatism in his legs, and now it has moved to his arms. He'll be counting on me to be up early tomorrow to help him."

"I understand, of course. Let me show you out."

Together we wove through the crowd, each step taking us closer to the castle gate and the moment we would say farewell. Groups of guards lingered against the walls, guffawing and calling out to pretty girls. My hands clutched my skirt, desperate with frustration. How could we part in such a manner, talking politely of his father's health as if nothing had changed? During my time at court, I had listened to Queen Lenore recite countless poems celebrating romance. In the stories one kiss was enough to seal eternal love, yet Marcus had not swooned and declared his devotion. I was no fairy-tale heroine, speaking in elegant rhyme, and he was far from a prince. How did two such people read each other's hearts?

We arrived at the gate. "I am glad you came," I said, willing my voice to remain steady.

"Me, too."

I thought that would be all. But then Marcus leaned down toward my neck, so close that his breath tickled my skin. "I must see you again. When?"

I felt the ache in my stomach that had lurched to life when his mouth met mine. He brushed a fingertip along my palm, a gesture small and swift enough to be unnoticed by the guards, and I slid my arm against his, feeling the fabric of his shirt ruffle my sleeve.

"I am relieved of my duties most Sunday afternoons," I murmured. "But there are few places here for me to receive guests."

"We could meet in St. Elsip. I will take you anywhere you like."

"Anywhere?" I asked with a mischievous smile. Our thoughts circled each other, unspoken yet understood. *I will go anywhere, as long as I can embrace you once again, feel your mouth upon mine and match my breath with yours, look into your eyes and know that here, at last, is the one I have waited for. . . .*

I knew that Marcus would not kiss me in view of the rowdy guards. But I allowed myself to imagine it. His fingers reached out and gripped mine, and it was all I could do not to wrap my arms around him. But I held myself composed. I was skilled at presenting a blank front to the world, tamping down whatever feelings raged within.

"Sunday, then," I said. "I will send word to your father's shop once I have received the queen's permission."

It was only after I watched his figure receding slowly down the hill that I allowed my delight free rein. I raced toward Queen Lenore's chambers, feet skipping up the stairs, a puppet's legs pulled by invisible strings. I tiptoed into the bedroom, expecting the queen to be asleep, but found the room empty. I walked back to the sitting room in time to see her emerge from Rose's room next door.

"My lady," I said, surprised. "I am so sorry. Were you waiting for me to prepare you for bed?"

"No, no," she said softly. "I was sitting with Rose." She did not meet my eyes, and I wondered if she was reverting to her vigilant habits, watching each rise and fall of her daughter's chest, prodding the poor girl until a whimper assured that she still lived.

"Did you have a good time?" she asked, forcing a smile.

A minute earlier I could not have kept myself from burbling with happiness about Marcus. But something in the queen's face stopped me. Tonight was not the time for girlish confidences.

"I did not think so many people could pack into the courtyard and still breathe," I said. "Toasts are being made in your family's honor throughout the castle."

"We shall tell my grandchildren of it one day, shall we?"

I saw it in her eyes, the desperate desire to believe that Rose would grow up and marry and have children, continuing the king's bloodline into future generations.

"Indeed we will," I said confidently. "Along with a lifetime of other happy memories."

Such foolish promises came easily to a girl still giddy from her first kiss. For me, Millicent's curse had faded to a whisper, its harshness worn smooth with time. I did not know then how her hateful words still lingered in Queen Lenore's mind, poisoning any joy she took in her daughter. For she could not look upon Rose without remembering the terrible bargain she had made, promising subservience to Millicent in exchange for a child. When Millicent's name echoed through the castle once again, the queen was the only one who was not surprised, for she was the only one who had never lost sight of the shadow that hung over us all.

It was a sweltering evening, not long after the tournament, and my thoughts were still caught up with Marcus, whom I was due to see again in a few days. Although I had told the queen I would be spending Sunday afternoon in St. Elsip, I had allowed her to assume I was seeing my aunt. My cautious nature warned that the events of a single evening were too unstable a foundation on which to pin all my hopes, and I dreaded facing her questions if the encounter did not go well. What if Marcus and I did not perceive each other the same way in daylight, without ale to loosen our tongues?

I was brushing out Queen Lenore's hair in preparation for bed when the king suddenly strode through the door that linked his bedchamber with that of his wife.

"She is found!"

Confused, I paused, holding the brush in midair. But the queen's shoulders stiffened, and her face took on a harsh cast. She knew immediately of whom the king spoke. Through the open doorway behind him, I could see figures huddled in conversation. The queen reached for her husband's arm, and her skin whitened with the force of her grip.

"Where?" she whispered.

"Far from here, love, have no fear."

King Ranolf began to pace back and forth across the room, his words tumbling out in rhythm with his steps.

"Aunt Millicent is cunning, I'll give her that. To remain hidden all this time, despite the gold I offered as a reward for news. Now, at last, we know where she has sought refuge. Brithnia."

What little I knew of Brithnia was from stories my mother told at bedtime, when she calmed my brothers and me for sleep. She had spoken of a harsh, rugged land, a country where rocky fortresses guarded stark mountaintops and the people dug ore from eerie caverns deep in the earth. To me the place was no more real than a fairy tale.

"A godforsaken country if ever there was one," said King Ranolf.

"I traveled there in my youth, and a week was enough to last me a lifetime. Be that as it may, the king did share my love of horsemanship, and he is one of the many I sent word to when Millicent disappeared, though I doubted she would flee in that direction. Crossing the mountains to reach Brithnia is an undertaking that defeats even the young and healthy. But it seems she has managed it."

Queen Lenore's eyes widened. "Why would she go there?"

King Ranolf shook his head. "Whatever her reasons, it has delivered a way out of her predicament. When Millicent arrived at the court, she begged refuge from the queen and was granted protection. The Brithnians treat their elders with the greatest respect, and it would be seen as an abomination if the king betrayed that promise of shelter."

"She lives there as an honored guest?" the queen demanded, her voice rising to a near-hysterical pitch. "Gathering strength for another attack?"

My own pulse quickened in sympathy. Were Millicent to return, what revenge might she take on me for defying her orders on the night of Rose's birth? Or would she work more deviously, using her wiles to ensure I was her puppet once again? Deep down I feared I would never be sure of my own loyalties.

King Ranolf took hold of his wife's shoulders. Bending, he looked directly into her eyes, calming her with the force of his attention.

"In his letter the king states that he can take no action against her. But he will not stop me from doing as I see fit."

He sank onto his wife's bed, his body sagging with the weight of his decision. It was the only time I had seen his mantle of certainty slip. Whatever softness the king had once possessed had been chipped away by his aunt's treachery, and he had become a brusquer, more demanding ruler, one who could be goaded into a smile only by the daughter he called Beauty. Yet his precautions had kept us safe.

"If I order my own kinswoman killed, it will play into the hands of my enemies. They will paint me as a monster."

To me the decision was so clear that I was astonished by his hesitation. *She wished death upon you and your child!* I wanted to cry out. *She is the monster, not you!*

"What shall you do?" Queen Lenore asked.

"I will ask the Brithnians to keep us apprised of her whereabouts, but that is all for now. She is an old woman. Nature will take its course soon enough, and her death will not be on our heads."

Lenore's voice was cold, her face set in an expression of grim resolution. "If you think it best."

Why, oh, why did she not demand Millicent's head? The king would have done anything for her had she set herself to pleading. But she chose to be a good wife, acquiescing to her husband's wishes, and Millicent slipped from our grasp. How could any of us have known that this moment was a turning point, the last chance to thwart her monstrous plans? In granting Millicent a reprieve, the king had signed his own death warrant.

Lady Wintermale's strident voice rang out from the sitting room. "Is it true?"

She burst through the doorway in her usual imperious manner but stopped as soon as she saw the king. "Beg your pardon, I did not mean to interrupt."

"If you are referring to the rumors about Millicent, they are true," King Ranolf said calmly. "The queen will inform you of the details. I must be off."

His words were curt, but his manner was tender as he paused to kiss his wife's cheek. Her body softened at his touch.

Once the king had gone, Lady Wintermale demanded a full accounting, huffing in disgust when she heard of the king's decision to leave Millicent be. Had she been a man, I have no doubt she would have set off for Brithnia to strike down Millicent herself.

"The Brithnians are no better than savages," she fumed. "Imagine, giving refuge to one who has cursed a child, heir to the throne!"

"There's nothing to be done," Queen Lenore said. "My husband has made his decision. We must find consolation in knowing that Millicent is so far away."

"A certain person could have spared you the worry," Lady Wintermale muttered.

Queen Lenore's mouth tightened in disapproval. "Flora has assured me repeatedly that she knows nothing of Millicent's whereabouts." She turned to me. "Elise, you must inform Flora of this news at once. See if she has any advice on how we should proceed."

"Advice!" Lady Wintermale sputtered. After I had taken my leave, she followed me out the door and into the corridor, then grabbed at my sleeve to stop me.

"The queen may believe what Flora tells her, but I do not. She is Millicent's sister, remember that."

"Flora promised the queen she would protect Rose," I said.

"Words, words," Lady Wintermale said dismissively. "Easy to say and easily forgotten. Flora has spent her entire life under Millicent's thumb. The bond between them . . ." She hesitated, her wary eyes silently acknowledging that she was treading dangerous ground. "It's not natural. I was raised here, in this very castle, and I saw how their father spoiled them rotten. He built the North Tower for Flora and Millicent, did you know that? Created the most sumptuous living quarters ever seen in the kingdom, all so his daughters would stay and raise their families here, by his side. Yet, rich and beautiful as they were, neither married. Is that not strange?"

"They must have had suitors?"

Lady Wintermale shrugged, her face hinting that she knew more than she was telling. "Millicent frightened most men off. She never tried to hide her cleverness, and no husband wants to be bested by his wife. Flora did have one serious prospect, for a time, but Millicent's jealousy drove him away. He died young, and poor dear Flora went mad with grief, or so the story goes. I am sure you have heard some version of that sorry tale, but I hope you will not be gullible enough to indulge her whims because of it. It may not even be the truth. Some say the sisters never married because they preferred to share a bed with each other and the guilt of such wickedness is what addled Flora's brain. Though I would never spread such vicious rumors myself."

In telling me she had done just that, but I would not argue the point.

"I am only telling you this because I've seen you and Flora chattering away in the garden. I know she has taken to you. She may appear harmless, but she can call upon the same dangerous powers as Millicent. Never forget what she is capable of."

Lady Wintermale's warning stayed with me as I proceeded on to Flora's room in the North Tower. As I passed by the silent statues, over floor panels inlaid with exotic marble, I envisioned the empty spaces as they were meant to be: a home for two royal sisters, their husbands and families, echoing with children's laughter and scurrying servants' footsteps. All that remained of the old king's hopes were the rooms themselves, beautiful but mournful, heavy with the weight of unrealized expectations. How could Flora bear living here, alone?

I had been sent to Flora's room on occasion to deliver messages but had never been admitted into her shadowy chamber. On that night, however, as soon as I told her the news of Millicent, she pulled her door open a touch wider than usual.

"Come in. We must talk."

The bedroom was larger than it appeared from the entrance, for it extended a good twenty paces inward, with alcoves on either side that held additional chairs and storage trunks. The furnishings glinted with luxury, from the marble tabletops to the golden candlesticks positioned over the massive fireplace. But what struck me most was the smell: a pungent mix of spices and more earthy scents completely at odds with the opulent surroundings. As I moved farther inside, I saw that one wall was covered with wooden shelves, where dozens of glass bottles and vials were arranged in neat rows by size. Directly in front was a worktable covered with the tools of an apothecary's trade: mortars and pestles, mixing bowls, and racks where leaves and flowers had been laid out to dry. More than two years had passed since she spoke of training me as her successor, yet I had heard nothing on the matter since. Had I been assessed and found wanting? The thought had caused me some distress, but with Lady Wintermale's suspicions fresh in my mind I was no longer sure if I should crave such a heavy responsibility. Flora might teach me skills I would be better off not knowing.

"How did Lenore take the news?"

"She is upset. She believes that Millicent is still plotting against us." I gazed directly at Flora, my eyes begging for reassurance. *And you?* I silently asked. *What do you know of your sister's plans?*

"And Ranolf?" Flora asked.

"He will not move against her. He believes that her age makes her less of a threat."

Flora shook her head slowly. "Millicent may be weakened, but she is nowhere near death."

So Lady Wintermale was right: Flora had known where her sister was all along. I was shocked that she was capable of such deception.

Seeing my stricken face, Flora rushed to explain herself. "She has not contacted me, I swear to it. But I do not need a letter to know her state of mind. Millicent and I, we have always shared more than the usual family bond, almost as if we could read each other's thoughts. If she were hurt or her health were failing, I would feel it."

She spoke with such conviction that I believed her immediately. Lady Wintermale might sneer at the sisters' unnatural closeness, but I knew how easily Millicent's thoughts had been able to insinuate themselves among my own. If she were able to provoke such intense feelings in me, a comparative stranger, how much stronger her influence must have been on her own sister!

"So what can be done?" I asked.

"I do not know," Flora said, and there was no mistaking the anguish in her voice.

Why? I nearly cried out in frustration. Flora was surrounded by concoctions that could conquer illness and pain; she was gifted with the power to fight off death itself. Yet she professed herself helpless against her own sister. What a girl of my age could not know was that salvation does not always come through grand public gestures. Flora was standing watch over us all, eternally vigilant to any sign of her sister's return. But I did not see a heroine before me, only a timid old woman.

"I must return to the queen," I said abruptly. "She will be retiring shortly."

Flora gave me a mournful look but said nothing. By the time I returned to the royal apartments, my anger had weakened into pity. For decades Flora had mourned her lost love in that deserted tower; now she mourned the sister who had been her closest companion. I wondered again, as I would so many times, at the nature of the bond between them. Could Flora feel both love and hate for Millicent?

Queen Lenore was singing softly to herself when I entered her bedchamber. Glad to see my mistress's mood improved, I laid out her best nightdress, hoping King Ranolf would return after dark to whisper reassurances beneath the covers.

I still remember how it felt to hold that nightdress, made of a lace so delicate it might have been crafted from butterfly wings. I used to imagine myself enveloped in that fabric, seeing Marcus's eyes light up at the sight of me in such a garment. The man in my daydreams moved with self-assured ease as he nudged the gown off my shoulders, confessing his passion with flowery words of devotion. Such grand gestures went against everything I knew of plainspoken Marcus, who would most likely stammer in mortification if asked to recite a love poem. But that did nothing to impede the wild imaginings that left my body flushed with longing.

At seventeen I would have been betrothed or even married had I remained on the farm. The women at court said their vows later than country folk, but any not spoken for by twenty-one were called old maids. Petra, who would be reaching that milestone within a year, had already received two offers of marriage, but she was the only daughter in a large family, with a father who was not particularly anxious to marry her off, so she was granted the luxury of choosiness. A maid not blessed with her looks would have been long since wed to the first man who asked for her hand.

In many ways the castle was an ideal hunting ground for marriage-minded young women. Had I the inclination, I could have set my cap for any of the highest-ranking servants: one of the king's valets, perhaps, or the castle's master carpenter, an amiable fellow who winked when he saw me in the courtyard. But Marcus was the object of my daytime thoughts and nighttime desires, for I recognized a quality in him that I shared. Even at our first meeting in his father's shop, when we were little more than children, I had understood that we both preferred to observe the world from a certain distance, keeping our emotions in check. Yet he had granted me brief, tantalizing glimpses of the self he kept hidden from others, a gift all the more precious for being so rarely bestowed. Surrounded by courtiers who struggled to be noticed and admired, I could not help being drawn to someone who presented himself without artifice.

It was a quality evident during our first outing together. Where another man might have labored to impress me, Marcus simply greeted me with a broad smile and said he was mine to command for the afternoon. I suggested a walk through the north end of town, where I had never been. Polite questions gave way to easy conversation as Marcus guided me through the winding streets, pointing out the best-known shops and the fine homes of the town's leading citizens. We bought meat pies from a woman who called Marcus a handsome boy while he cringed with embarrassment, then walked with our food to the curved stone bridge topped with statues of the king's forefathers.

Marcus's learning was beyond that of most cobblers—like me, he could read and write with ease—and he showed endless curiosity about the world. I shared stories the queen had told me of her country, and he listened with interest, asking questions until I laughed and said there was no more to tell. Had he been born into a different family, he might have escaped to sea, for he watched the ships in the harbor with an expression of wistful longing. I could picture him on the deck of a great sailing vessel, his steady confidence giving men heart in times of danger.

Walking together in public, we found it impossible to recapture the intimacy of our encounter in the garden. Yet every smile and nod of understanding further solidified the connection between us, reminding me that one day we would do more than converse. When we bade each other farewell at the castle gates, he kissed my hand with unexpected tenderness, then murmured, in a voice meant only for me, "To future kisses."

How I wish I could recapture every detail of that afternoon, for to relive those exchanges with Marcus would bring solace during the nights I am pierced with loneliness. But memories can resist all attempts to tame them, flitting away at the moment we think them ours to control. At times I can still feel the press of his lips against my skin; at others I can only gaze at the image of us from a distance, my sight shadowed by what was to come.

As I arranged Queen Lenore's hair for dinner shortly afterward, she held up her hand mirror and frowned.

"Did we not say the red?" she asked.

I looked at the green ribbon entwined in her hair, then at the red ribbon that lay on the dressing table.

"Beg your pardon, my lady," I said, threading my fingers through her hair to pull the locks apart. "It will take but a minute to set right."

"You are not yourself today, Elise. Pray tell, what occupies your mind so thoroughly? Or should I say *who*?"

My hands froze, and I could see the reflection of Lenore's smile in the mirror.

"Elise, do you think me blind? You go off on a mysterious outing and return dreamy and fumbling. There can be only one reason."

Her tone was light and teasing, and I tried to smile as if I shared in the joke. The force of my effort must have shown, for she put down her mirror and turned around to face me.

"It's true, then? You went to see a young man?"

I nodded, and the queen's face brightened with delight. This reaction was the very reason I had been so evasive about my plans earlier. Queen Lenore, a woman who had given up all she knew for love, savored tales of romance, and I feared her questions when I was not yet sure how matters stood between me and Marcus.

"From your manner I take it the meeting proved satisfactory?" she asked.

My flushed cheeks gave her my answer.

"Oh, you must tell me," she urged. "Who is it?"

"Marcus Yelling, the son of the shoemaker who visited the castle a few weeks ago."

"Oh."

Queen Lenore was considerate enough of my feelings to try hiding her surprise, but I knew she was mystified that such a seemingly unremarkable young man should have caught my eye.

"You're a sensible girl, Elise," she said firmly. "If you think him worthy of your attention, then I am sure he is. You are hardly the kind to lose your head over someone like Dorian!"

Dorian? Ever since Petra had spoken of her admiration for the handsome page, I could not help letting my gaze linger upon him whenever we passed in the halls. I was far from the only woman at court to do so, but I was mortified that the queen had noticed. She might think me as infatuated as some of her ladies, but in truth I thought of Dorian as a mystery to be solved rather than a prize to be won. Would he become an acclaimed leader of men? Or would vanity—and those admiring female gazes—be his downfall?

Queen Lenore turned her head back and held up the red ribbon for me to re-dress her hair. I slid it through my hands, feeling the velvet caress my skin. To be in the presence of such lovely things calmed my mind, reminding me of my great fortune. In the distance the trumpets sounded for the start of supper. I gently pulled her hair into a twist and wrapped the ribbon around it, securing the roll with diamond-encrusted pins. The queen stood up and smoothed her skirts, then turned to me, reaching out her hands and placing them gently against my cheeks.

"Do not forget that I was young once and very much in love with a young man from a kingdom far away," she said. "Courtship rarely runs smooth, and you may always turn to me if you have need."

Her manner was so tender, so kind, that I felt an almost painful pang of adoration. She should have been blessed with more than one child, I thought, for she had a gift for divining the exact words and gestures that would best soothe a troubled mind. Would my own mother have looked at me with the same compassion, urging me to confide in her? Would she have been happy for me?

After the queen left for the Great Hall, I could not stop smiling. Never before had my future held such promise. My confession had bonded me closer than ever to my mistress, and Marcus's affection seemed assured. But happiness, fleeting by nature, is often savored only after it has flown. For me, thinking on that day will always be tempered by memories of the sadness that followed. Much as I try to relive the hours spent at Marcus's side, I cannot fully summon the pleasure that coursed through my body when he looked at me and smiled. I want to weep for that innocent girl, who believed so fervently that love conquered all. For the queen was right. Love's progress is rarely smooth, and my way was to become rocky indeed.

Nine

THE PATH OF COURTSHIP

I recall that autumn and winter not as an orderly procession of days but in a jumble of memories. When life follows the course of our desires, it is easy to be swept along without thought. It is only now that certain incidents take on an importance they did not possess at the time. Much as one discounts a gentle breeze until it is recognized as the harbinger of a brutal storm, I overlooked any signs of trouble brewing. Lost in a love-struck haze, I forgot that we were all in danger, every one of us, from distant forces intent on revenge. Our enemies were content to lie low as they plotted our downfall, fading into the background of our thoughts. And so, through simple carelessness and ignorance, our fates were sealed.

But who among us can foresee the end result of our day-to-day decisions? I myself willfully ignored the consequences of falling in love with Marcus. Early on, in an endearingly mortified manner, he had explained that apprentices could not wed; any talk of marriage would have to wait until he had been accepted into the Merchants' Guild in a year's time. I was in no rush to leave the life I had made for myself at the castle, nor was the queen eager to release me from my duties at her side. Though she took a kindly interest in my romance, she remarked more than once that I should not rush into marriage, and I was quick to agree. And so, for a time, my daily routines continued much the same as before, even as I myself was transformed by love.

Under Marcus's intent, admiring gaze, I became the woman I had always longed to be. I walked with a confident stride and spoke more freely, open to him with my thoughts as I was with no one else. Yet beneath my self-assured manner was a giddy girl who fidgeted with anticipation before each encounter, so eager was I to feel the warmth of his hand clasped around mine. Marcus, a gentleman in every way, never hastened me down the path of temptation, and I took inordinate pride in our chaste courtship. But the promise of more was always there, simmering beneath our lively conversations. I could feel him quiver on the rare occasions we stole a kiss in the shadow of a doorway. I had been intrigued by Marcus's calm restraint from our very first meeting, yet it was the glimpse of those feelings—the very mirror of my own—that sent me hurtling into infatuation.

During our visits to town, Marcus never took me to his home, though he assured me repeatedly that Hannolt sent greetings and best wishes. He made passing references to his father's ill health, and from this I understood that his parents did not welcome visitors. Seeing such a man laid low by sickness must have been painful for his son, and I avoided speaking of Hannolt unless Marcus did so first. In truth I was relieved to be spared awkward chitchat with his parents, as I treasured every moment we had to ourselves. At times I could not resist testing the limits of our flirtation, pressing my body against his when we kissed, feeling his arms tighten about my shoulders, watching his regret as he pulled away, cheeks flushed. It was exhilarating to see the effect my body had upon him, just as his every touch provoked the same breathlessness in me.

In my memory those golden months are intertwined with images of Rose as she grew from a toddling baby to an enchanting little girl. She was beautiful even then, trilling songs through the hallways of the castle, skipping through the garden and pulling off flowers to place haphazardly behind her ear. Queen Lenore tried in vain to keep her daughter's reddish-gold hair smooth and her dresses clean, for Rose was always off on another adventure, anxious to see what lay around the next corner.

It was during one of these outdoor excursions that Flora took me aside, her thin fingers gently tugging at my sleeve. Eyes flickering over toward Rose, giggling among the wildflowers, she whispered, "It is time."

I stared into her face, set in an expression of firm resolve, free of its usual air of melancholy. For a sudden, chilling instant, it was as if I were gazing at Millicent, hearing her thoughts overpower my own. *I will teach you all my secrets. Under my guidance you will learn to conquer death itself.* It had been so long since Flora had hinted at making me her apprentice that I had all but forgotten about her offer. Now I was overwhelmed by an intense hunger for the knowledge she promised. The force of that sudden, inexplicable desire scared me. Was this evidence of Flora's own dark powers? Could she be trusted?

"My first loyalty is to the queen," I said warily.

"Lenore will give you leave to visit me. She understands the importance of our work."

Our work. So it had already been discussed and decided between them.

"If you are sure," I said.

"I am." She took my hands in hers, and a warm tingle of contentment flowed through me at her touch. The hint of danger that had so frightened me dissipated. For the first time, I believed myself capable of healing. Capable of rising to whatever challenges lay ahead.

Which is not to say that I performed my first tasks with any great skill. As the days grew shorter, I helped Flora cut the last of her herbs and hang them before the fireplace to dry, then began the slow, laborious work of crushing them into powders. Since I had little experience with mortar and pestle, my mixtures were lumpy and uneven, and my earliest attempts at blending an ointment had to be discarded completely. But I was captivated by the possibilities at my fingertips. I happily pored over Flora's ledgers, filled with mysterious ingredients I had never heard of, and tried to match the names to the labels on her bottles. As is often the case when we set ourselves a challenge, I was inordinately proud of any small accomplishment, and my meetings with Flora became a welcome distraction from the gloom of winter.

With St. Elsip battered by icy winds, Marcus and I were forced to retreat to the Lower Hall for our Sunday meetings, where I would beg hot cider and warm bread from the cooks. Petra had admitted, reluctant to hurt my feelings, that some of the ladies' maids mocked me for being courted by a shoemaker, and I was ever conscious that we were objects of gossip. For the first time, I saw Marcus through the eyes of my fellow servants: his drab, coarse clothes; his ignorance of court manners; his wide-eyed awe of luxuries we took for granted. The flickering light of the castle's wall torches cast his many virtues into shadow, illuminating only the flaws of the man I thought my perfect match. Never granted a private moment or a private touch, we saw our interactions become more those of brother and sister than would-be lovers.

The dreariness of that winter took its toll on three-year-old Rose as well. Her sleep, never easy thanks to her mother's fretting, became even more unsettled, and she began waking in the night, screaming from a horror she could not put into words. The first night the commotion was loud enough to wake both me and Queen Lenore in the next room, and despite the nurse's assurances the queen insisted on tending to her daughter. Rose refused to close her eyes, terrified of what she would see in that darkness, and her mother held her tight for hours, soothing Rose until their eyelids drooped closed near dawn.

The following evening the screams returned, and again the night after. The queen's face began to sag with exhaustion, and Rose dragged through her days red-eyed and irritable. On the fourth night, Queen Lenore jumped from her bed at the first sound of shrieking from Rose's room. Drifting up from sleep, I watched her scurry past my pallet. I leapt from the floor and caught up to her.

"My lady," I insisted. "I will go."

"I must. I am the only one who can comfort her."

"May I try? You have barely rested for days."

Weariness slowed Queen Lenore's response. "She may still call for me."

"If she does, I will fetch you," I promised. Rose's sobbing was taking on a wild, wobbling tone, and I could faintly hear the nurse's attempts to soothe her. "Please."

Queen Lenore nodded and leaned her body against the doorframe. "I will wait here, in case I am needed."

When I entered Rose's room, her howls took on a higher, more desperate pitch. In the darkness I could faintly see the nurse's arms wrapped around Rose's shoulders as she struggled to break free. Only scattered embers remained in the fireplace, and the air was dank and cold.

"Mama! I want my mama!" Rose demanded.

"Hush, hush," I said. "She is asleep. We must be quiet, so we don't wake her." I nodded to the nurse, who released Rose and went to light a candle. I ran one hand over Rose's flushed face as I knelt by the side of the bed. Her eyes sought mine, wild with terror.

"I will stay with you tonight," I said soothingly. "Only you must tell me what you are so frightened of."

Rose clenched her eyes shut and shook her head defiantly back and forth.

What child refuses the chance to unburden herself? I thought frantically. Then the answer came to me: a child who fears she will be punished for speaking the truth. "Has someone told you to say nothing to your mama?"

Rose nodded, lips trembling.

"But you may tell me. It will be our secret."

Rose considered my offer, her face twisted with indecision.

"Who came in your sleep, my darling? Who has scared you so?"

"The witch!"

I froze in shock. My first thought, horrible in its clarity, was of Millicent, calling out her curse at Rose's baptism. Had she found a way to haunt Rose's dreams?

"A witch?" I asked carefully. "What does she look like?"

"Horrible!" Rose whispered. "She has pointy teeth. And a black hat. And red eyes!"

I almost laughed with relief. Not Millicent. I must have been caught in a nightmare myself to imagine that the woman could disturb Rose's slumber.

"Will she eat me?" Rose's lips quivered as if she were about to burst into tears again.

"Of course not," I scoffed. "Witches would get sick if they ate sweet girls like you. Don't you know? They usually have rat tails or frog legs for supper, the rottener the better."

"Eww!"

"Oh, yes." I saw the hint of a smile emerge and did my best to tease it out. "The next time the witch tries to scare you, tell her to stop that nonsense. Or better yet, tell her your father is on his way. He's a brave knight, is he not?"

"The bestest."

"That will do, then. Just think of your father in his armor. He'll have that witch flying off on her broomstick in no time." I ran my hand over the top of her head and down her hair. "Do you feel better?"

Rose nodded.

"Do you think you could sleep?"

She reached out for my hand. "Will you stay?"

"Of course."

I whispered to the nurse that I would lie down with Rose, and then I tucked us both under her blankets. Within minutes Rose was breathing in a steady drone, and it seemed the next moment that I was shaking off sleep as the sky lightened outside the window.

The following night Rose slept without waking, though her peaceful rest did not prevent the queen from standing over her bed for some time, taking note of each slow breath. The witch returned to Rose's dreams off and on throughout her childhood, though she did not speak of the creature during waking hours. I came to suspect that Rose's nightmares were an unintended consequence of her parents' vigilance. Wondering why her safety caused such concern, she imagined her worst fear come to life. It was only much later, after I had seen the unspeakable consequences of Millicent's anger, that I wondered if my first instinct had been correct after all. Did Millicent, from her far-off sanctuary, have the power to corrupt an innocent child's dreams?

Perhaps as a result of my success in comforting her at night, Rose began demanding my companionship more frequently, always in search of a new diversion during those months when the weather confined her indoors. One Sunday she refused to leave my side when Queen Lenore dismissed me for the afternoon. I took her by the hand and led her to the castle's front entrance, where Marcus stood before the guards, who were waiting for my approval before allowing him to pass.

After I waved him through, he stepped into the entryway, stamping snow from his boots on the stone floor. Rose stared at him curiously.

"Who is that?" she demanded.

I watched his face quickly rearrange from surprise to interest as he looked to me for guidance.

"This is my friend Marcus," I said. "Marcus, may I present Princess Rose?"

Marcus bowed, keeping his head lowered so he could address her face-to-face.

"It is an honor to meet you," he said.

"Marcus is paying me a visit, and you must be off to your room," I told Rose. "Come, I'll take you."

"What's that?" she asked, pointing to the white flakes that dusted Marcus's coat.

"Snow," Marcus said.

Rose pulled away from me and approached him, staring in wonder. She had watched snow fall outside the castle windows but never felt it. She held out her hand, and Marcus placed a fingerful of icy crystals on her palm.

"Ooh!" Rose exclaimed. She turned to me, eyes sparkling. "I want to see it!"

This was one of her favorite phrases, usually followed by "You mustn't" or "Not now" from her mother. Rose chafed against her imprisonment, and I felt a swell of sympathy for the girl. Surely a few minutes outside would do her no harm?

"Sir, may I have your cloak?" I asked one of the men standing at the door. The guard pulled the heavy woolen garment from his shoulders, looking at me with a doubtful expression. I folded it over to prevent the bottom from trailing on the ground and wrapped it around Rose.

"Would you mind?" I asked Marcus.

"Of course not." He smiled at Rose, and she clapped her hands in gleeful anticipation.

It took two men to tug open the massive wood doors. We stepped out into a frozen world. The usual bustle of the courtyard was gone, replaced by a hushed stillness as snowflakes floated downward and dusted every flat surface. Rose gasped as the freezing air hit her face.

"Is it too cold? Shall we go back?" I asked, knowing what her answer would be.

"No, no!" she squealed. She reached out her hands to grab the flakes and looked mystified as they melted against her skin.

"Where did they go?" she demanded, holding out her palms to me and then Marcus.

"Let us see if we can catch one," Marcus offered, glancing toward me questioningly. I smiled and nodded, relieved to see that he did not begrudge Rose's company. If anything, her presence had brought out a playful side I had not seen before.

Marcus leaned down and took Rose's dainty hand in one of his own. Pulling her slowly alongside him, he waved their arms gently through the snowfall, their fingers brushing against the tiny white specks that surrounded them. Rose was silent, her face intent.

"Ah!" Marcus exclaimed. "I think we've got one. Elise, what do you think?"

I walked over to join them, stepping gingerly through the drifts of snow. I peered down at Rose's finger, coming so close that my nose almost touched her skin. Seen thus, the snowflake was unexpectedly beautiful, an intricate pattern of sparkling white threads.

"It's perfect," I said.

This outing, though it was mere steps from the castle, would have caused the queen to fret with worry and brought on a tongue-lashing from Lady Wintermale, but I did not care, for I had forgotten everything but the look on Marcus's face. He was happy, unabashedly so, and I could suddenly glimpse him as a father. He would be a good one, a man who cherished his children, and my stomach fluttered at the future I imagined for us. I had known that Marcus could provoke my interest as well as my lust. But I had not truly known until that moment that I loved him.

"Ooh, look!"

Rose had knelt down in the snow, and when she stood, the front of the cloak that enveloped her was covered with a swath of white.

She brushed her palms against it and laughed as it scattered outward. I leaned down and gathered a handful, releasing it over Marcus's head, so that his hair was sprinkled with white. Soon we were tossing fluffy white handfuls in all directions, creating a shower of icy crystals as Rose whooped with joy. Marcus, cheeks flushed red from the cold, laughed with an abandon I'd never heard, and the sound was so infectious that I joined in, not caring how we might look to the guards and any other observers at the windows above.

Is this how I should remember them, those two people I cherished so dearly? It is tempting to bask in the memory of that magical day. Yet I cannot help but ponder how that simple outing planted a dangerous seed in my dealings with Rose. Though I knew she was forbidden from leaving the castle, I allowed myself to be swayed by her pleading. I watched her prance through the snow, never thinking that she might have caught a chill and fallen ill. I did not correct her when she addressed Marcus as an equal, though he was of lower rank than her own attendants. Like an indulgent older sister, I let her run free—indeed I delighted to see her so.

Even at that young age, Rose possessed a charm that could overpower my better judgment. She fought against her restrictions, more so with each passing year, and I sympathized with her plight, discreetly taking her side against that of her parents. I could not know that when Rose defied their final orders, so many years later, the outcome would be disastrous.

Much to my relief, another liaison soon replaced mine as the prime topic of castle gossip. Faced with the open admiration of a maid as pretty as Petra, most men of Dorian's position would have brashly grabbed their chance. She would have enjoyed the chase and perhaps allowed a grope or two before cutting off his advances. Though well versed in the ways to catch a man's eye, Petra retained a virtue that castle intrigues had not tarnished. She believed in love.

And Dorian was smitten enough—or cunning enough—to promise it. What began with lighthearted words exchanged while Petra served supper turned to whispered conversations in the Great Hall before meals, then bold, open gazes across the room. For weeks Petra laughed off my questions, assuring me it was no more than a flirtatious game. I was not so sure, and my suspicions increased when I came upon her in an alcove off the back stairways and saw her hastily slide a piece of paper into her apron.

"What were you reading?"

It was not my way to be so forthright, but something in her furtive manner concerned me. To Petra's credit she did not drag out the moment with false reticence. She withdrew the note and handed it to me.

Writing was scrawled across the page in a firm, confident hand. The letters had been formed in a way unfamiliar to me, with dramatic rises and falls in the *f*'s and *h*'s, and it took me some moments to decipher. It was a love poem, describing the passion of a knight for a lady who could never be his. I had read far worse compositions, and when I saw the enormous *D* at the end, produced with maximum flourish, I was surprised that Dorian should be the author of such skilled prose. He had always struck me as more suited to youthful boasting than to contemplative thoughts. Perhaps he had copied it from another source, though I did not voice that suspicion to Petra.

"It's from Dorian?" I asked.

"Yes." Her lips curved in a tentative smile. "He gave it to me before supper."

"So he fancies himself the knight?" I asked.

Petra looked at me blankly. Suddenly I understood. Petra could read, but she had learned from a book in which the letters were printed with careful precision. The words of Dorian's poem might as well be a different language.

"The writing is of a very unusual style," I said, trying to spare Petra embarrassment. "Shall I tell you what I think it says?"

Pointing with one finger so Petra could follow my progress, I sounded out each word with no emotion, careful to avoid emphasis on any particular passage. Petra would be imagining these words in Dorian's voice, not mine. When I had finished, I felt a perverse stab of jealousy that Petra had inspired such a work. Marcus, for all his kindness, was not one to declare himself in flowery words of passion, and I doubted I would ever receive a love note or a poem written in his hand.

Petra took the paper back and folded it into a neat square.

"I know you disapprove." The defiance in her voice took me aback.

I was quick to assure Petra that I had never questioned her judgment. It was a lie, but she appeared eager to believe me.

"It's been so difficult, Elise. Keeping the true nature of our bond a secret. He values my opinions and speaks to me as he would a woman of his own rank, with the greatest respect. He takes notice of things I say in passing, as if my every utterance were precious." Her voice dropped to a whisper. "He says he adores me."

I was shocked. A lighthearted flirtation was one thing, but ensnaring the affections of a high-ranking gentleman could be dangerous. If Dorian was truly infatuated with Petra, for her to reject his attentions could mean the end of her service at the castle. And if she gave in to his pleas, she would lose her hard-earned reputation for chastity, a reputation she counted on to make a good marriage.

"What will you do?" I asked.

Petra shook her head slowly. "I do not know. I envy you, Elise. There are no obstacles to your marrying Marcus. Yet I can see no happy resolution for Dorian and me."

Neither could I. "No matter what happens, you must stay true to yourself," I urged. When she nodded, I believed she understood the importance of safeguarding her virtue.

It was not until some days later that I learned she had taken a very different meaning from my words.

I was on my way to visit Flora in the North Tower. With the worst of winter past, she had begun sorting her seeds for the spring planting, tedious work that I felt better suited to a gardener than a healer. For all my initial trepidation, the remedies Flora had shown me thus far would have been common knowledge to any village midwife. Accustomed to being the only one traversing that wing of the castle, I was surprised to hear the sound of voices floating down from the upper level of the staircase that cut through the center of the tower. Had Flora wandered upstairs? Who could she be talking to?

I walked cautiously upward, an instinct for potential danger silencing my tongue. By the time I reached the top of the stairs, the voices had stopped. Ahead of me was a large arched entryway, leading into a wood-paneled room. A rustling sound caught my ear. Curiosity won out over apprehension, and I tiptoed forward. Pressing one hand against the doorjamb to balance myself, I peered inside.

Though Petra's face was buried in Dorian's shoulder, I knew her instantly from the gleam of white-blond hair that dangled from her cap. Her back was pressed against a column in the center of the room, her arms taut with the effort of clutching his waist. One of Dorian's hands cupped the nape of her neck, while the other had reached up her skirt, exposing one leg to midthigh. The stocking had already been loosened and lay crumpled around her ankle. Petra let out a faint moan but remained as still as the statues that adorned the North Tower's halls.

Aghast as I was, I could not look away. This was not the sort of grunt-and-thrust encounter that pages and kitchen maids were known to indulge in behind the stables or in the storerooms. Dorian's fingers were caressing Petra's inner thigh, teasing her with their proximity to her most intimate parts. Her body pressed against his, giving willing assent, yet his hand moved unhurriedly. He dipped his head to nibble at her ear, and with that slight shift of position his face turned directly toward the doorway.

My stomach dropped. For an instant Dorian froze. Then, just as my body tensed in preparation to run, his mouth twisted into an amused smile. Slowly, deliberately, his lips kissed Petra's cheek and neck as she murmured with pleasure. Still watching me, he pushed his hand further up her skirt. Petra made no protest; indeed she seemed to thrust herself even closer against him. I could not turn away. Overcome by lustful cravings, I imagined myself touched in that way, lost to everything but my lover's caress. Dorian saw it all: my envy, my shame, my desire. For that I could never forgive him—or myself.

Snatched out of my confusion by the sound of Petra's voice, I ducked out of the room right as she whispered to Dorian that she loved him. He repeated the words back to her in a firm, confident voice, loud enough to ensure I heard him.

It was a few days later, during a particularly bleak afternoon, that a visitor was announced for Queen Lenore. The man in question did not live up to her ladies' hopes for an entertaining diversion, for he turned out to be a traveling metalsmith, who wandered from village to village repairing pots and pans. He bowed low and said he had been paid to deliver a letter into the queen's hands alone. Examining the blank paper that enclosed the message, she asked, "Who sent you?"

The man shook his head. "'Twas given me by a woman in Greysgate, the day before last. She said it came to her from another such as me." Tradesmen often carried letters for a small payment; few had the means to hire their own messengers.

Frowning, Queen Lenore pulled open the outer layer, but her suspicion turned to delight when she saw the writing inside. "It's from Isla." She told Lady Wintermale to give the metalsmith two gold coins for his trouble and turned to her letter with a smile.

I busied myself with pulling faded flowers from one of the vases in order to hide my annoyance. I could never replace Isla in the queen's affections; the two grew from girls to women together, sharing secrets that would never be passed to me. But accepting the childishness of one's feelings does not always quash them. Did Isla regret choosing the love of a man over the love of her mistress? I wondered. It was no great honor to serve in Prince Bowen's entourage since his fall from grace, and he and his men were said to be traveling foreign lands as soldiers for hire.

"Elise!" Queen Lenore exclaimed.

I attempted to produce an expression of interest. The ladies-in-waiting had drifted to the other side of the room, where Lady Wintermale was admonishing one unfortunate woman for an unsuitably low-cut gown.

"Prince Bowen has married," she said, her eyes surveying the page. I drew closer and glanced at the paper, enough to see it was written in the queen's native language and therefore meaningless to me.

"And guess who he has taken as his wife? Jana deRauley."

So Bowen had allied himself with the notorious family that had been stirring up trouble since before Rose's birth. As far as I knew, their clamoring about a claim to the throne had been quashed once Rose had been proclaimed King Ranolf's heir. Why, then, did news of this marriage make me so uneasy?

"A strange choice of wife for a man of his stature," Queen Lenore noted. "The deRauleys may be lords of their lands, but their territory is small and their fortune smaller."

"Prince Bowen is hardly one to marry for love," I said, then immediately regretted my biting tone. I had never told the queen of his attack on me. But she did not seem surprised by my evident dislike.

"More likely," she said dryly, "the woman is with child and he was forced to marry at the point of her father's sword."

I remembered Prince Bowen pawing at my skirts, telling me I was his to command. The hatred in his face on the day of the Royal Assembly. I could not escape the suspicion that this alliance was part of a larger scheme. And from the troubled look on Queen Lenore's face, she thought the same.

"Isla gives no explanation?" I asked.

Queen Lenore shook her head. "The rest is remembrances from when we were young."

Isla had given up everything to follow her husband, and I wondered if writing that letter was a form of escape from her present diminished circumstances into the days of her youth. I knew that her departure had left an ache in Queen Lenore's heart that I could never fully heal, and I wondered if the fear of losing me as well was the reason she was so hesitant to encourage my courtship by a townsman. Were I to marry a man who lived at the castle, I could remain at her side, and it was not long after she received Isla's letter that she asked the king to grant me a small dowry.

"I want you to have every advantage when it comes to your future," the queen told me with a reassuring smile. "You've grown quite pretty, you know, and there are many fine men at court who will consider you a serious prospect once there's money involved."

Though she had never disparaged Marcus in my presence, the jab at him was clear. I could not help contrasting Marcus's careful avoidance of any talk about our future with the overpowering, reckless desire that Petra and Dorian had for each other. Her submission to him, I soon learned, was not a momentary lapse of judgment. She had opened her body to Dorian's caresses because he had given her something in return: a promise of marriage.

We were sitting before the fireplace in the Lower Hall, enjoying the relative quiet of a Sunday evening, when she told me they were planning to wed. I hugged her and offered my congratulations, feigning a joy I did not feel.

"Dorian asked me not to say anything, but I knew I could trust you," Petra said, giddy with delight. "Marrying me means defying his father, so it must be done quietly."

Dorian's father, Sir Walthur, was a sober, hard-nosed man, one unlikely to be swayed by young lovers' pleas. Having risen from a relatively humble background to a position of great importance, he would be furious at the thought of his son marrying so far beneath him. But it was pointless to warn Petra of the obstacles in her path; she knew them better than I did.

"If Dorian's father cuts him off, he must find a place in another lord's service," Petra went on. "He does not want to announce our intentions until such arrangements have been made. But it has been difficult, carrying such news in secret."

"You needn't have secrets from me," I said.

Petra shook her head. "I won't. Not anymore."

And yet I kept secrets from her. I did not tell her of the look Dorian and I had exchanged in the North Tower. I did not tell her my doubts about his fidelity or describe the scene I had observed in the kitchen the day before, when Dorian ran his finger audaciously through a bowl of batter and held it upward, asking which of the giggling kitchen maids would sample a taste. She had seen his flirtatious ways for herself. If she forgave such behavior, I must do the same or risk losing her friendship. Still, I wondered, as I had so many times before, what manner of man Dorian was underneath the golden exterior. Lust alone could not have induced him to make an offer of marriage. Taking Petra as his wife would ruin his prospects at court and embarrass his family. He could be making such a sacrifice only for love.

Would Marcus have taken such a risk for me? The sorry truth was that I did not know. For my eighteenth birthday, he presented me with a braided leather bracelet in which he had carved our initials. I told him I would cherish the bracelet, and I did, pressing it against my lips as I lay in bed at night, imagining his strong fingers working the leather until it yielded to his commands. With the changeable nature of youth, I had begun succumbing to the lustful cravings I had once derided as a weakness in others. In my fantasies Marcus's lips moved from my mouth to my cheek, then to my neck, then on to the swell of my breasts in a tumbling progression of breathless discovery. Such liberties could be taken only once we were married, or formally engaged at the very least. But Marcus did not raise the subject. And I felt a shameful relief that he had not.

Deep down I could not help comparing Marcus's tender affection to the ardor I had seen on Dorian's face when he touched Petra. Once, to my belated horror, I dreamed of Dorian lying beside me, his hands entwined in my hair, murmuring wicked promises of what he would do next. Was Marcus capable of such passion? Or had I fallen in love with a man who was largely a creation of my own longings?

Queen Lenore and Flora believed I could be more than a shoemaker's wife. Though I hated myself for harboring thoughts so disloyal to Marcus, I began to wonder if they were right.

Ten

A PROMISE MADE

It was Flora who unwittingly nurtured my worries about marriage to Marcus, and it was she who just as unwittingly inspired me to bring matters to a head. Over the course of our meetings, she had begun to show me some of her more exotic concoctions, and each new discovery only increased my appetite for more. None of what she revealed could be called magic, but there was wonder in it all the same: how a simple mixture of crushed herbs and seeds could calm a rash or a syrup of honey and rose water ease an aching throat. I was soothed by the satiny feel of a fine powder against my fingertips, entranced by the colored liquids arrayed on the shelves. Flora herself seemed rejuvenated by her role as teacher, and she guided me with a new, zealous vigor, as though her talents were enhanced by my admiring presence. For the first time, I could see her as Millicent's equal, a woman capable of miracles. Though her eyesight was poor and her hands occasionally trembled, at her core she maintained a quiet strength. She may have suffered; she may even have toyed with madness. But she had not succumbed. She had taken the defense of the kingdom on her frail shoulders, and she would not release that burden until her secrets were securely in my care.

It was a heady thought. And it was an honor, I came to realize, that might never be mine if I married Marcus. Would a humble craftsman's wife be entrusted with the safety of the heir to the throne?

On the day after Petra told me she was to marry Dorian, I spent the afternoon with Flora, helping her sort through dusty boxes she had pulled out from a storage trunk. Distracted by jealous thoughts, I paid Flora little attention until a few muttered words caught my ear: "'Forever the color blue / Shall signal a love that's true.'"

I turned abruptly. Flora was holding a small vial that held a vibrant blue powder, a shade that called to mind the sapphires that studded one of the queen's favorite necklaces.

"What did you say?" I asked.

"Ah, it was a song, long before your time. This made me think of it. It is a mixture of crushed flowers that some call Lover's Delight."

"A love potion?" I asked, surprised.

Flora tipped her head sideways and widened her eyes in exaggerated innocence, a faint echo of the coquettish looks she must have perfected years ago. "You know there is no such thing! My cures affect the workings of the body, not the mind.

"However," she added slowly, drawing out the moment for maximum suspense, "if one inspires love, one may receive it. Imagine a woman who is painfully shy. She is tongue-tied in the presence of the man she favors, afraid to draw his attention. Imagine she drinks a tonic that brightens her cheeks and raises her spirits. She becomes self-assured and therefore desirable to the man who once overlooked her. Is that magic?"

Something in the way Flora recounted her story made me suspect she was speaking of herself. I had been curious about Flora's long-ago romance ever since hearing of it from Lady Wintermale, though I was never bold enough to raise the subject myself. In conversation Flora could be as skittish as a colt, pulling away unexpectedly from even the most innocuous subjects. I would have to tread carefully.

"What does it feel like?" I asked. "Once you've taken it?"

Flora gazed at me, carefully considering her next words. "It feels," she said at last, "as if you've swallowed joy."

She rolled the vial in her hands, gently detaching the powder that had stuck to the sides. "I tried it only once. I have lived with the consequences ever since."

I waited in silence, afraid that intrusive questions would scare her off.

"His name was Lorenz." She spoke calmly, as if recounting a tale told to her long before. "He didn't come to court me, of course—he was intended for Millicent. Everyone knew that the elder sister must marry first. I suppose I brought it all upon myself, with my foolishness. He was so dazzling, you see, so charming. He sang more beautifully than my father's minstrels. I craved his attention for myself, if only for a few hours. So I crushed the flowers and sprinkled them into my drink one evening at supper. And my shyness fell away, and I looked at him openly across the table, and he looked at me, and Millicent was forgotten. Would you believe me if I said we fell in love that instant?"

I nodded. "I believe such things can happen."

"Lorenz went to my father and begged for my hand. He had money, a title—my parents could make no objection. Had Millicent agreed, we would have married. How innocent I was, to think she would give us her blessing! She fumed and raged and accused me of stealing him solely to humiliate her. My mother took my side, but Father wavered. And then Millicent was attacked."

"Attacked?"

"She claimed that Lorenz, in a rage, had forced himself upon her. Not one person who knew him thought him capable of such an act. But my father had no choice. His duty was to protect his daughter's honor. Lorenz was sent off in disgrace. My parents forbade all contact between us, and I was confined to my room until he was gone. A few weeks later, he died."

"I am so sorry," I said gently. I had never heard her speak for this long, and the effort was clearly taxing. She sighed deeply before continuing.

"His family made it out as an accident, but he had taken his own life. Hanged himself from an oak tree on his estate. My family thought it proof of his guilt. 'An innocent man fights to clear his name,' Millicent told me. 'Only the guilty resort to suicide.' As if she were satisfied that all had worked out for the best. For months I tortured myself, trying to work out what had happened. The man I had known was kind and gentle. Had there been another side he kept hidden? I did not think it possible. But if my judgment of his character was correct, it could only mean that Millicent had ruined a man simply for the satisfaction of besting me. How could I think such a thing of my own sister?"

I pictured Flora as a young woman, still beautiful, pacing her lonely room, tormented by thoughts of Millicent and the man she loved, agonizing over who was to blame. The betrayal had marked her for life.

"In the end, I found, the truth did not matter, for the result was the same. Lorenz was dead. And I could not imagine a life without him."

The agony of that loss still lingered in her girlish voice, her sorrowful eyes. I reached out for her hand and squeezed it lightly. The touch brought her back to the present day, and she looked down at the glass vial, sitting on the table between us.

"Is there a reason this interests you?"

I saw the same cunning alertness I had once seen in Millicent; like her sister, Flora had the ability to instantly gauge a person's deepest, most hidden desires.

"I have wondered, every day since then, what would have happened if I had not swallowed that powder," Flora said, staring at me intently. "When it comes to matters of the heart, the answer is best found within yourself, not in a bottle."

Within myself. Was the ache I felt for Marcus's touch the longing of true love or no more than shameful lust? Could I marry him and still fulfill my duties to the queen and to Flora? No potion could ease my way to the truth. I must force a resolution by my own actions.

Flora turned back to her bottles and began humming a lilting melody that seemed vaguely familiar. Then I remembered: It was the same tune I had heard on my first visit to the North Tower, coming from behind the closed door of this very room. Flora had told me the man she loved had a beautiful voice. Was this a song he had sung to her, embedded in her memory as an eternal reminder of all she had lost?

The arrival of spring had allowed Marcus and me to resume our meetings in town, and on the following Sunday he suggested an excursion to the hill overlooking St. Elsip's harbor. However, an unseasonably oppressive heat descended upon us as we made our way upward, and the warmth brought out the putrid smell of the rotting food and waste floating atop the water. It was hardly the setting for romantic confidences.

"It's so hot," I grumbled. "There must be somewhere else we can go to escape this sun."

Marcus looked thoughtful. "I know of a place, off the Allsbury Road."

The town he spoke of lay in the opposite direction of the village where I had grown up, nestled in the foothills of the mountains I could see from the castle windows. During the hottest summer months, many noble families retired to homes there, where the mountain air was said to be cooler.

Offering his hand, Marcus pulled me to my feet, and we set off. The heat had sent St. Elsip into a torpor, and the few fellow travelers we passed moved with the dazed shuffle of sleepwalkers. No more than five minutes after we had crossed over the Bridge of Statues, Marcus left the main road and took me down a cart path that led into a ring of trees. I heard birdcalls above me, but otherwise we were completely alone.

"This leads to the tannery where we buy our leather. Father's known the family forever." Marcus spoke quickly, not meeting my eyes, jittery in a way I had never seen before. If it had been any other young man leading me through a deserted forest, I might have turned and run.

"Here it is."

Marcus waved me toward an opening in the trees, so narrow that my skirts brushed against the trunks as I passed. Before me was a clearing, a tranquil expanse of green dotted with wildflowers. A creek trickled through the middle, ending in a pond as still as a mirror. Sunlight streamed down through the leaves in golden streaks. Marcus smiled to see my delight.

"It's lovely," I said, my heart swelling with emotion, but Marcus had turned away and occupied himself with unpacking our lunch from the leather bag tied to his belt. We spoke few words as we ate, lethargic in the peacefulness of the setting. Yet my heart beat faster every time his gaze turned toward me, and my entire being prickled with anticipation.

"You have been here before?" I asked.

"Not for some time."

"It seems the sort of place a man brings a woman to woo her," I said lightly. "I find myself quite at your mercy."

"I . . . I assure you . . ." Marcus stammered. When he was nervous or offended, words often failed him, and he looked at me helplessly.

I breathed a sigh of annoyance and stood. If Marcus could not declare himself here, perhaps he never would. I took a few steps toward the pond, drawn to the shimmering water. I had put on my winter-weight dress that morning, never imagining it would be so warm this early in the season. My skin was coated with a sticky layer of sweat, and I was tempted to walk in fully clothed. Had I been back at my family's farm, I would have.

I sat at the pond's edge and reached under my skirts to pull off my stockings. Boldly hitching my dress to my knees, I stepped into the blessed coolness. The water was even more soothing than I had imagined, and I reveled in the feel of it against my skin. Marcus remained on the grass, utterly still, staring with rapt attention. Daring me to shock him further.

I walked out slowly, keeping my skirts lifted, leaving a trail of drops behind me. I stood before Marcus in the middle of the clearing, and he stared at my bare calves, then up toward my face. I stared back, offering a silent challenge. Slowly, he stood and reached for my cap, tugging it free. Emboldened by my acquiescence, he moved his hands along my hair, releasing the thick brown locks from their pins. The touch sent a ripple of pleasure from my scalp down my neck to my stomach. I closed my eyes to experience the sensation more fully. Gently, he shook out the waves of curls. No one other than my mother had ever touched my hair. Never had I imagined that it could provoke such a mix of serenity and longing.

"You are so beautiful," he whispered.

At any other time, I would have protested modestly. But in the quiet of that clearing, blood racing, I basked in his admiration.

He smoothed wisps of hair off my face, his fingers brushing along my cheeks and forehead. When I opened my eyes at last, I saw him bend toward me for a kiss. A kiss unlike any other we had shared, for it provoked a desperate hunger that overpowered my senses. Urgently, my hands clutched at his arms, his back, the hair pressed against the nape of his neck, and we collapsed into each other, falling downward in a frenzy. I understood then how Petra could have given herself to Dorian, how she had chased these sensations to their conclusion.

"Elise," Marcus murmured in my ear. "How you tempt me."

His fingers traced a line down my cheek and neck, but his body pulled away from mine. The abrupt shift jolted me from my rapturous haze, and I stared at him, confused, as he sat up.

"You know I have no way with words," Marcus said, twisting with discomfort. "But I will not have you think me a dishonorable man. If we are to—that is, if you are to allow me . . . this . . . my intentions must be clear. Elise, I have always intended to make you my wife, and now we can be married whenever you say the word. Tomorrow, if you wish."

Taken aback, I said the first thing that sprang to mind. "I thought you would not be admitted to the guild until the winter?"

"The guild has voted to amend the rules in my case, because I have been taking on so much of my father's work. Just this week they agreed to accept me as a full member. Is that not wondrous news?"

Marcus looked at me with such hopefulness, such devotion, that my heart sank. All I could think of was my work with Flora, of all I had yet to learn. And Rose, still so young, so desperate for my reassurances when the nightmares came. *Not yet,* I thought. *Not so soon.*

"So . . . you will marry me?" he asked, his face radiant.

"Yes," I said. Then again, more forcefully, "Yes."

Further conversation could only risk revealing the truth of my conflicted feelings. I stood up, reaching out my hands to Marcus.

The two of us hand in hand, I led him toward the pond. He yanked off his shirt and scooped water onto his face and chest; soon we were splashing each other like children. Gradually our laughter faded, and my heart raced as Marcus placed his cool, wet palms against my cheeks. He looked blissfully, foolishly happy. I ran my hands over his forearms, his shoulders, reveling in his solidity.

"I do not give my love lightly," he told me with a sigh, tracing the edge of my neckline with his finger. "You have it, Elise. Forever."

I felt his hands move to the back of my dress. With a whisper of assent, he would loosen the laces and push the bodice from my shoulders. My bare skin could press against his, and the thought of that sensation made me ache with longing. How easy it would be to succumb to my desires, now that we were betrothed! But opening myself fully to Marcus would seal our marriage in a way my words had not. A wary inner voice told me to hold back. Gently, I drew Marcus downward, until we were kneeling in the water, my legs propped against his. We kissed again and again, lost in the taste and feel of each other. When we paused to catch a breath, he ran his lips along the curve of my shoulders, whispering the words of devotion he had kept in check for so long. I felt his hand tentatively move under my water-soaked skirt and upward along my thigh. The touch provoked a shudder of delight, but it also served as a warning. Were I to grant Marcus access to such pleasures, there would be no turning back.

I glanced sideways; the sun was well advanced on its downward journey.

"The queen expects me back," I said hastily, rising and wringing out my dripping dress. "I lost track of the time."

"And no wonder." Marcus watched me with amused affection.

My passionate response to his proposal had loosened something within him, and he grinned with an easy confidence I had not seen before. *He loves me,* I thought with sudden clarity. *He truly loves me.* And the thought of such devotion was both thrilling and terrifying.

On the journey back through St. Elsip, walking the streets we had traversed so many times before, the desperate need Marcus had provoked in me took on the quality of a dream. We were now promised to each other, but we walked together seemingly unchanged. Should I not feel transformed?

"I planned to ask your family's blessing, but with your parents dead I was not sure whom to speak with," Marcus said. "Your aunt and uncle? Or is it the queen who must grant permission?"

As I had no intention of seeing my father again, I had led Marcus to believe he had died of the pox. For an instant the extent of my deception struck me: How could I enter the sacrament of marriage when I had kept so much from my future husband?

"The queen is aware of our courtship," I said. "She can have no objection."

Or would she? I was a free woman and could not be denied my husband of choice. But the suspicion that she did not approve of Marcus troubled me as much as if she had been my own mother. When I returned to the queen's chambers, she immediately noticed my soaked skirt and began asking teasing questions. Hurriedly, I changed into a fresh, dry gown, trying to conjure the right words to share my news. In the end I simply said that Marcus had asked for my hand and I had accepted.

"Oh, Elise," she said, summoning a smile. She embraced me, and I came close to tears, knowing she was making a show of happiness for my sake.

"Now you must tell me everything," she said with forced brightness. "Have you a date in mind?"

"Not before the end of the year, when he completes his apprenticeship," I said. How easily the lie came! All I needed, I told myself, was more time. Time to sort out how I might marry Marcus without losing everything I had achieved.

"I will admit, the thought of your leaving tears at my heart," she said. "And poor Rose, she will be devastated."

Slowly, gently, she explained the consequences of choosing Marcus as my husband. As a shoemaker's wife, I would no longer be a suitable companion for Rose. A townswoman of my rank could not be admitted to the royal apartments, or speak freely to anyone of noble rank, or wander the gardens with Flora. In all my mooning over Marcus's soulful eyes, I had never appreciated how much he was a social inferior to the queen and the rest of the court. Was marrying the man I loved ample compensation for all I would lose?

It was the thought of bidding farewell to Rose that brought tears streaming forth down my cheeks.

"I never . . ." I stumbled, "I never meant to cause her grief. Or you."

Queen Lenore's own eyes welled up in sympathy. "Now, now. There is always a need for men of talent at court. What if I found a place for your Marcus here?"

The queen proposed a plan so well thought out that it was clear she had contrived it sometime before. Mr. Rees, the castle shoemaker, was always in need of assistance, and he would welcome Marcus onto his team of craftsmen. We could live at the castle as husband and wife, and I could retain my position as Queen Lenore's attendant.

"Oh, my lady, he will be greatly honored by your offer. Thank you!"

"No, I must thank you, for considering my selfish feelings in this matter. I will do whatever I can to keep you by my side."

"I will not leave you," I said with the fervor of a blood oath. The air of melancholy that hung about Queen Lenore like a spring mist briefly dissipated, and I caught a glimpse of the woman I had once known, whose inner beauty and outer serenity were in perfect alignment. She had known such sadness, carried such a heavy burden of guilt. I could not bear to cause her further unhappiness.

There was one person I felt sure would welcome the news of my betrothal with delight, and I sought her out later that evening. I did not see Petra cleaning the Great Hall after supper, and none I asked in the Lower Hall could tell me her whereabouts. It was long after dark by the time I ventured upstairs to her private bedroom in the servants' quarters, an honor she had been granted recently in honor of her appointment as head housemaid.

I knocked lightly. There was no response. I pushed the door inward and saw Petra lying on her bed, facing me. Her eyes gleamed in the dark.

"May I come in?" I asked.

She did not forbid me, so I walked through the doorway, sheltering my candlestick with one hand.

We had not spoken in private for more than a week, and I was shocked by the change in her. She lay utterly still, misery etched across her face. In a voice cold as the castle's flagstone floors, she told me Dorian had broken off their engagement, on his father's orders. Her eyes were blank and clear of tears; she had cried them all out, she said.

"Oh, Petra," I said, devastated by my friend's misfortune. "I am so sorry."

I placed the candle on the floor and knelt down to embrace her. She twisted her shoulders to escape my touch and shook her head.

"You must think me such a fool."

"No, of course not." Despite my mistrust of Dorian, I had hoped to see them wed, for Petra's sake.

"I could manage if I did not see him," she said quietly. "It would take all my strength, but I could put him from my mind. Yet how can I forget when we walk the same halls? When I see him laughing with the kitchen girls every night?"

"It will be summer soon," I said. "He'll be off hunting or traveling to tournaments. The pain will ease."

"Will it?"

I had no reply. She rolled onto her side, turning her gaze from me to the wall.

"Please, leave me be," she pleaded.

Once again I was not wise enough to understand that women can loudly demand the very opposite of what they crave. Curing Petra's heartbreak was beyond my power, but I could have lessened the burden of her loneliness. Instead I backed away.

"There is one thing," I said, pausing on the doorstep. "I wanted you to know first, before word spread. Marcus has asked me to marry him."

She did not flinch. "I wish you the very best."

Her voice was muffled but steady. She might have been one of Queen Lenore's ladies, offering polite good wishes to a slight acquaintance.

There was no more to say. I left Petra alone with her misery and tried to push away the disloyal thought that I had been proved right. To my everlasting shame, I avoided her in the days that followed. I told myself it was to spare her feelings; she would hardly welcome the company of a newly betrothed companion when her own heart had been so recently broken. But my motives were not selfless. I stayed away from Petra because I could not bear to witness her pain. A pain I might one day inflict on a man I claimed to love.

Eleven

THE TRUTH WILL OUT

I wrote to Marcus, inviting him to the castle to meet Mr. Rees and hear of his future prospects. To my dismay he greeted me at the gates not with an embrace but with a terse nod.

"I have no intention of groveling before the castle shoemaker," he said sharply, and I was alarmed by his unexpected coldness. I had left him foolish with love after our last meeting. What had changed?

I insisted he accompany me inside, to an alcove just beyond the Great Hall, where we would be somewhat hidden from the comings and goings of the castle's inhabitants and visitors. It was the sort of place where Marcus once might have taken advantage of the semi-darkness to slip his hand into mine and sneak a furtive kiss. Instead he glared at me with an expression halfway between anger and bewilderment.

"How could you accept such a bargain on my behalf?" he demanded.

"It is a great honor! The queen has made the offer out of affection for me. You should be grateful."

"Grateful to start over as someone else's apprentice? When I have just been admitted to the Merchants' Guild?"

"I am sure you would not start as an apprentice," I said, but he cut me off with an adamant shake of his head.

"You cannot understand, can you? How much it means to me and my father that we have our own shop, that we have made something of ourselves. My father worked all his life to ensure that I would never have to answer to a master."

Dazzled by the majesty of court life, I could not imagine anyone choosing to forsake it. How blind I was, not to see that Marcus's self-sufficiency, the quality that first drew me toward him, also guaranteed that he would never follow me into royal service. I did not understand that a modest man can also be a proud one, unwilling to do what others might perceive to be in his best interests if it conflicts with his own deeply held beliefs. Marcus had always been so kind, so accommodating, that I underestimated his will when it counted most.

Thinking him still capable of being swayed, I tried again. "It would be an easy life for you here. You've told me you never know from month to month how much money you will make. There will be none of that uncertainty here, and I am sure the queen will see that the pay is generous."

"Oh, yes, it will be a comfortable living," he said. "But for how long?"

"The queen is not fickle in her affections. Once you prove yourself—"

"That is not what I meant," Marcus interrupted, looking quickly to either side to make sure we were not overheard. "The queen may protect those she favors, but who is to say how long her word will be obeyed?"

I was shocked. I had heard of men being imprisoned for publicly disparaging the king.

"You cannot say such things," I hissed.

"I am hardly the only one," Marcus said. "The king's position will never be secure as long as his brother has a claim to the title."

Prince Bowen. I could imagine farmers such as my father proudly exchanging tales of Bowen's exploits while sourly rejecting the prospect of a woman taking the crown.

"The complaints most likely will come to nothing," Marcus assured me. "The queen may even bear a son, now that she's proved herself fertile. But you must see, a life at court is no guarantee of prosperity or safety. I'd rather take charge of my own fate."

It was a motto that might have been my own. How could I fault Marcus for having the same yearning?

"We are agreed, then," Marcus said, taking my silence for assent. He smiled, relief flooding across his face, and my heart ached. His trust in me was complete. And undeserved.

"You must come to supper soon, so we may tell my parents together," he went on, his voice eager. "When might you be granted permission for an evening off?"

"You have not told them of our betrothal?" I asked, surprised.

"Not . . . not yet." His stammer betrayed him; there was something else he was afraid to say. I fixed him with my best no-nonsense stare, and he rubbed his hands across his cheeks and back around his neck, a gesture he often resorted to when gathering his thoughts.

"You remember that day, in the woods?"

I blushed at the thought; how could I not? But Marcus did not join me in conspiratorial remembrances. Hurriedly, he spoke on. "I told you that path leads to a tannery. The tanner has a daughter, his only surviving child. Some years ago he and my father agreed on an alliance. . . ."

Even then I did not understand. "A business arrangement?" I asked.

"Of a sort," he said, looking downward. "Sealed by their children's marriage."

"You are promised to another?" I asked, stunned.

"There is no contract," Marcus objected. "This is why I never spoke of it, for fear you would misunderstand. Hester and her father have no formal claim on me."

"Hester? So you know her?"

"I have met her a few times. But I feel no affection for her, I swear."

He reached one hand around my waist to pull me toward him. A group of chambermaids appeared around the corner in a clatter of pots and brooms, and we froze as we were, Marcus's eyes staring searchingly into mine. Curiously detached, I avoided his gaze as the women passed, and then I leaned forward, cradling my face in the curve of his shoulders. How easy it was to melt into his sturdy body, allowing the touch of his fingers along my neck to chase away thought in favor of sensation.

Marcus spoke quietly, his breath rippling the edge of my cap. "Once my father sees us together, how happy we are, he will understand."

This could be mine forever, I told myself. *The feel of this embrace, the kindness of this man who cannot bear to see me hurt.*

"I love you, Elise," he said, caressing my lips with his. "Never doubt my love for you."

I did not. The doubts were mine to bear, unspoken.

With the feel of Marcus's kisses still fresh, I sought refuge in the castle's chapel. It was surprisingly simple, given the rest of the building's majestic sprawl, but to my eyes the room's modesty heightened its holiness. A statue of the Virgin Mary stood to one side of the altar, and a gold cross hung on the wall behind, but otherwise there were none of the jeweled adornments common to royal churches. When sunlight streamed through the tall, narrow windows, burnishing the cross and bringing it to blazing life, it was as if God himself had reached down to bless us. I knelt before the altar, praying for guidance. I could continue to serve Queen Lenore or I could become Marcus's wife, but not both. Whichever path I chose would cause pain to someone I loved. Deep in my heart, I knew that the answer must come from within; I had little faith in signs. But I was wrong.

The following day the castle was shaken by devastating news, setting in motion a course of events that made clear where my loyalties lay. The king's face was heavy with grief when he informed us his cousin, Lord Steffon, was dead. A hunting accident, the messenger had said, in a forest beyond the mountains, where the lord had been visiting his sister and her family. A stray arrow had felled him instantly. Lord Steffon and the king had come of age together and enjoyed a camaraderie close to brotherhood. The loss of such a favored companion would have caused heartache enough, but King Ranolf raged that the death was no accident, that it was part of a treasonous strike against him and his reign. Lord Steffon, he vowed, would be not only mourned but avenged.

Buried beneath the castle foundations was a dungeon, reached from a heavy iron door near the stables. I had heard the place described as a desolate, airless pit, and the castle guards who rotated through prison duty grumbled when their turn arrived—no one went willingly into such a place. Once I had happened to walk by when the door was opened, and all I could see were a few rough stone steps, leading down into utter darkness. It was down those steps that Lord Steffon's three men-at-arms were dragged, arms bound tightly behind their backs, feet stumbling, their faces drawn with fear.

A crowd of us watched in silence as Sir Walthur announced that the men who accompanied Lord Steffon on his ill-fated hunting expedition had been charged with murder and treason. After he strode off into a huddle with the other advisers, I watched two of the castle carpenters wrestle with a bundle of long wooden rods and planks that they were attempting to fit through the prison doorway.

"What are they doing?" I asked one of the guards standing nearby.

"They're building a rack, on the king's orders," he said.

Innocent that I was, I did not know what a rack was and how it might be employed. The guard was happy to dispel my ignorance, and I wish he had not. In the following days, I could have sworn I heard the screams of those terrified men cutting through the layers of stone to beg salvation from the torments they suffered. All three protested their innocence to the last, even after they were sentenced to hang in St. Elsip's cathedral square.

Most servants happily accepted the king's permission to witness the execution. I chose to stay behind, sickened by the day's air of celebration. King Ranolf's public humiliation of his own brother—announcing the queen's pregnancy on the very day Prince Bowen expected to be hailed as heir—had shown he could be ruthless with those who insulted his honor. But I had never thought him cruel until that day, when he condemned three innocent men to death. The soldiers who were to hang had served Lord Steffon for years; many of those who would watch them die had ridden beside them, eaten with them, laughed at tales of their adventures. How could anyone believe they had intended to harm their master? What purpose would their deaths serve?

In search of solace, I wandered the empty garden. Seedlings had begun sprouting from the herb beds, and I wondered if I would be here to see the plants spring fully into bloom. The thought of life continuing here, without me, was inconceivable.

"Elise."

It was Flora, who had appeared in her usual silent manner. Had I not known the true benign nature of her powers, I might have believed her capable of appearing and disappearing at will.

"Is it done?" she asked.

I could sense that she was as troubled by the soldiers' fate as I was. I glanced up at the sky, where the sun sat almost directly overhead.

"By now I suppose it is," I said. Then, emboldened by Flora's gentle, sympathetic stare, I said bitterly, "Three men dead, and for what? A bow pointed the wrong way in a dark forest. A mistake anyone might have made!"

"No, not a mistake," Flora said quietly. Her face was weighted with sorrow in the same way the king's had been when he announced his friend's death; never had I been reminded so vividly that they were blood relations. "The arrow pierced Lord Steffon's heart. It was intended to kill."

"I cannot believe it of any of them!" I argued.

"Nor can I."

Flora began to pace, the hem of her skirt tracing a path in the dirt. "The arrow that killed Lord Steffon was tipped with a dark green feather. None of the king's men carry such arrows. It was intended as a message to the king. And to me."

I remembered the bold green dress that Millicent had worn when she cursed Rose. The strange green figurine she had pressed into my hands. The green velvet cape she had so often tossed over her shoulders with a dramatic flourish.

"Millicent?" I asked in horror.

Flora nodded, her expression mournful.

"But how?"

"She has ways of making others do her bidding. You know that as well as anyone."

Stung as if rebuked, I stiffened. But she did not mean it cruelly, simply as a statement of fact.

"Did you tell the king of your suspicions?" I asked.

"Ranolf has never put great stock in my counsel. He agreed that Millicent might have instigated the plan, but he was sure that one of Lord Steffon's men shot the fatal arrow. He was willing to hang them all rather than risk one guilty man going free. But I believe that the culprit was someone else, someone who took care not to be seen. The king ordered men to Brithnia a few days ago, in secret, to hunt down my sister, but she will be gone by the time they arrive. I do not know where she will seek shelter next or what form her revenge might take, only that she will never give up. That is why I need you, Elise. To continue my work after I am gone."

"Do not speak of such things—" I urged, but she cut me off.

"I must. I do not know how much time I have left. Were I to die tomorrow, Millicent would know. And she would come for Rose."

She halted her pacing before me, and I saw for the first time that she was truly afraid. When she had promised the queen she would keep the royal family safe, we had believed her. Now I saw the cracks in her certainty, the doubts that had begun to torment her. And I was terrified.

"I cannot," I whispered, my face crumpling with shame. How could I possibly be trusted to hold off a woman such as Millicent? A woman intent on evil, who could twist my mind to her own desires?

"I would not wish this burden upon anyone," Flora said wearily. "But you are the only one I am sure of. I am so very tired, Elise. I do not know how much longer I can stand against her."

Should I shy away from this duty, I would hold myself forever responsible if Rose or Queen Lenore came to harm. I thought of the queen's face, aged in so short a time, and my promise never to leave her side. I imagined Rose sickening, wasting away before my eyes. *No,* I vowed. *I will not allow it.*

"Tell me what I must do," I said.

Flora smiled, her face shining with relief, and I saw how beautiful she must have been once, when she was young and free of cares. She took my hand and patted it, her dry, papery fingers as fragile as onionskin.

"The only sure weapon against hatred is love," Flora said. "You love deeply, Elise, and that is a more powerful protection than you know."

Flora held off any further questions, saying we would speak of such matters in due course. After she had excused herself to rest, I paced the pathway for some time, until the confusion that had clouded my vision of the future cleared. When I emerged into the castle courtyard, bracing myself for what must come next, I found the area already swarming with people returned from the hanging, chattering and smiling as if they had just witnessed a tournament rather than an execution. They thought justice had been done, knowing nothing of the danger that still threatened us all, and I wanted to shout them out of their self-satisfied contentment.

At the front gate, I had to stand aside as a procession of carriages entered. Thinking the way clear as last, I stepped forward, only to cower in terror as a horse suddenly startled in front of me, its hooves pounding into the earth mere inches from my feet. The animal was skittish amid the crowd; it needed a strong, steady hand to keep it in line, and I shouted angrily at the driver.

It was Horick, slumped on his seat, the reins slack in his hands. "Watch yourself, missy," he drawled.

"Watch your horse," I snapped.

The carriage stopped, blocked by others ahead. I looked up at Horick's sour face, and he mumbled something, rolling his eyes. Had it been anyone else, I would have turned my back and ignored him, but Horick's disrespect enraged me.

"What did you say?" I demanded.

"I merely observed that I need no advice from the likes of you on how to handle a horse."

As if to infuriate me further, he cracked his whip against the poor creature's back, though it could only proceed a few paces.

"You watch your tongue!" I shouted. "The queen shall hear of your insolence!"

Heads turned as Horick regarded me with exaggerated dismay. My loss of control had given him the upper hand, and I walked away before the situation could degenerate further. My somber mood only worsened as I marched along the streets of St. Elsip. The town that had so impressed me a few short years before now appeared drab and provincial to my jaded eyes, a place where people were content to live in ignorance, celebrating the death of innocent men.

I pushed open the door to Hannolt's shop and saw Marcus sitting at a simple wooden desk in the corner, a ledger before him. For a moment I could vividly picture him in middle age, sitting contentedly in this same room, jotting numbers at the same desk. He looked up in surprise, then his face brightened with pleasure.

"Elise! What brings you to town? The hanging?"

"No," I said abruptly. "I came to talk to you."

My tone appeared to take him aback, and he regarded me questioningly as he rose and tipped his head toward the door. I could hear the muffled voices of his parents from behind the curtain that closed off the shop's living quarters. I followed Marcus outside. Throughout our courtship we had hardly ever been alone together, unobserved. Perhaps it was fitting that this life-altering conversation be held within hearing of dozens of townspeople making their way home.

He reached for my hands, but I resisted his touch, knowing that such affection would weaken my resolve. "Marcus, I cannot leave the queen."

"I thought I made myself clear," he said, more mystified than angry. "I am not meant for a life among the nobility."

"How can you know if you have not tried?"

Marcus's expression hardened. "Do you think I did not notice when your fellow attendants sneered at my clothes? When they addressed me as 'the shoemaker' rather than by name? I chose to ignore such insults because their approval did not matter. But it would if I were to live at the castle. I would be forced to seek favor from simpering courtiers who care for nothing but gossip and who sits at which table."

"They are not all like that. . . ." I tried to explain, but Marcus ignored me.

"I see only too well where it would end, Elise. I have no talent for flattery and obsequiousness. I would never fit in, and you know it."

I remembered the winter afternoons we had spent in the Lower Hall. Those gloomy hours when I first saw Marcus through my fellow servants' eyes, when the perception of others had caused me to doubt my own feelings. Could I swear that I would not fall prey to such disloyalty again?

"You told me once you did not care what trade your future husband practiced, only that he be kind. Do you remember?" he asked.

I nodded. I remembered everything about that night in the garden, when one kiss from Marcus could provoke shivers of delight.

"Was it a lie? Would you be content as a shoemaker's wife?"

After all Marcus had given me, I owed him the truth. "Not if it means renouncing my duty to the king's family."

Marcus looked down, away from me, but not before I saw he was close to tears. His shoulders caved forward, and he clenched his arms across his stomach, as if protecting himself from further blows.

"Please reconsider the queen's offer," I begged. "You could accustom yourself to court life, given time."

"Ah, but I couldn't, Elise," he said bitterly. "Not as you have."

"I would never ask it of you if I had any other choice," I said. "Rose, the queen, Lady Flora—they depend upon me." In all the time I had known Marcus, I'd been reluctant to speak of Millicent and the danger that kept me tied to the castle; intensely practical, he had no patience for superstition or tales of enchantment. Even then I might have told him everything, but when he snorted in disgust, I knew he would not believe me.

"Yes, it is quite clear that the fine ladies of the court have a hold on you," he said. "So I must ask you, one last time: Will you marry me, Elise? As I am?"

"I love you," I said softly. It seemed very important he know that at least.

"But not enough." His breath came out in an anguished sigh. "I would make any sacrifice for you, do you know that? I would give up everything my father has worked for. But I will not marry a woman who thinks me beneath her."

"I never said any such thing—" I began, hoping to delay the final reckoning, but he stopped me with a mournful shake of his head.

"Do not lie to me. Not now."

Strengthened by his quiet dignity, I looked at Marcus head-on. Here were the dark eyes that had regarded me with such tenderness, the mouth that had met mine with passionate hunger, the tousled hair I had clutched when he ran his hands over the curves of my body. That man I knew so well was slipping away, hiding himself behind a stern, protective shell. I had not understood until that moment how very precious a gift he had offered me. A man such as

Marcus feels deeply and truly, and such a love, once offered, does not waver. My chest ached from the burden of carrying his heartbreak as well as my own.

"Perhaps there is still a way," I begged. "If you could wait a year or two, until the princess is a little older—"

"No, Elise. I will not be your second choice."

There was no last touch, no final embrace. Marcus turned from me and walked back into the shop, shutting the door behind him. Bereft, I stumbled away from the man I loved. How I made it back to the castle remains a mystery, for I was blinded by tears the whole way.

When I returned to the royal apartments, Lady Wintermale told me Queen Lenore was in the chapel, praying for the souls of the executed soldiers, but Mrs. Tewkes had asked to see me. I had hoped to nurse my sorrow in private, but perhaps it was best to be pulled back into the routines of castle life. I had been raised to believe that hard work was a virtue. Only the lazy and foolish had time to fret over a love affair gone wrong.

When I knocked on Mrs. Tewkes's door, she bade me come in with a more subdued expression than usual. For a moment I was convinced she knew what had befallen me. It was impossible, of course, but Mrs. Tewkes had an uncanny ability to follow all the twists and turns of the servants' personal lives. It would not have surprised me if she confessed the power to read minds.

"We have not spoken for some time, have we?" she asked with a concerned smile. "You are well?"

Such a simple question, and yet so difficult to answer. I nodded.

"An incident has been brought to my attention. A minor matter, concerning you, and I wish to set my mind at ease by determining the true state of affairs. Mr. Gungen spoke to me a few hours ago, on behalf of one of the grooms."

"Horick," I guessed.

"Yes. So you know of what I speak? Mr. Gungen told me Horick is in a rage, going on about your manner toward him earlier today."

"The disrespect was on his part, I assure you."

"I am sure it was," Mrs. Tewkes agreed. "He's a most unpleasant man, and slow in his work to boot. I made it clear to Mr. Gungen that your wishes are to be respected as those of the queen, and that's the end of it. Though I would suggest you avoid Horick for a few days at least."

"Consider it done." I rose from my chair, but Mrs. Tewkes waved me back down.

"Elise, I must confess, I was quite surprised to hear of such behavior from you. Horick is an oaf, but I did not think him capable of enraging you so. Has he provoked you in other ways? If he has made your life difficult, you must tell me so I can put a stop to it."

I shook my head and began to say there was no bad blood between Horick and me. Yet under Mrs. Tewkes's watchful gaze, I found the truth slipping out.

"I cannot abide him," I said.

"I agree he is surly and disagreeable, but hardly enough to warrant such hatred. There must be more. Come, my dear, what has he done?"

His was the ultimate betrayal, I thought. He denied me an honorable birth and my mother an honorable life. I had told no one of my past and did not think I ever would. I glanced at Mrs. Tewkes, then away. She sat unmoving, waiting. Like me, she understood that silence often provokes others to speak freely.

"I suppose you know why my mother left the castle," I began. Mrs. Tewkes nodded. "Though she never told me who seduced and abandoned her, I came to find out it was Horick. I will always hate him for what he did to her."

Mrs. Tewkes raised her eyebrows. "Horick? He told you this?"

"No. My aunt said my mother was pledged to him, and I guessed the truth."

"Then you have misunderstood your aunt, for poor Horick is quite blameless," said Mrs. Tewkes.

"Horick is not my father?"

"Oh, no." Mrs. Tewkes frowned dismissively. "You could not be more wrong."

Stunned, I stared at her dumbly. All along she'd known who had fathered me. Why had I not thought to ask her before? Mrs. Tewkes and my mother had been friends, close enough for her name to be on my mother's lips at her death. In whom else would my mother have confided?

"But my aunt—she said Horick was Mother's sweetheart."

"So they were. Mayren was fond of him, though he was far more besotted with her. That's what turned him, you see. Knowing that the woman he loved had been with another man."

"Who?" I asked, but Mrs. Tewkes continued as if she had not heard me.

"There was no formal engagement, you see. Horick was still a stableboy, with hardly a penny to his name. Once he became a groomsman, there was an understanding that he would ask for

Mayren's hand. She said she would wait. But then a certain nobleman took notice of her. She had Horick to thank for that, strange as it sounds. His love gave her a self-assurance she had lacked before. She went from avoiding attention to courting it. When this man began to pursue her, Mayren simply lost her senses. As soon as she found herself with child, he abandoned her, just as I suspected he would.

"He could have paid her off and set her up in town under a new name, posing as a widow. Many a noble mistress has lived quite well in that sort of arrangement. But his family kept him on a tight leash when it came to money, so he cast her aside and ensured she would be banished from court forever. And of course Horick wanted nothing to do with her after that. Her betrayal was his undoing, and he only grew more bitter as the years passed. Poor girl, how she cried! I did my best to help her, but I could not risk my own future by taking her part in public. I had no choice."

"We do what we must," I said, knowing all too well the sacrifices that a life at court demanded.

Mrs. Tewkes took her time, mulling over what she should say next, as my stomach churned. "If I tell you the name of your true father, you must promise you will do nothing with the knowledge," she said at last. "This man spared no pity for your mother—he will hardly welcome a reunion with his bastard."

The word stung, and it was meant to. Mrs. Tewkes had often cautioned the staff to remember their station, at all times and in all matters. Whatever my father's rank, the circumstances of my birth meant I would never be more than a servant.

"It was Prince Bowen."

Speechless with shock, I stared at Mrs. Tewkes, half expecting her to shake her head and laugh in jest. I could not imagine my sensible, clear-eyed mother falling victim to Prince Bowen's wiles. With a wave of disgust, I remembered his hands—my father's hands—groping at my body, enjoying my powerlessness. And yet the dissolute man I knew had once been devastatingly handsome. My mother would have been flattered by his attention, even welcomed it. I thought of Petra smiling at Dorian across the Great Hall and remembered how quickly my friend had succumbed to his advances. I, too, had weakened under Marcus's touch. With my own heartbreak so fresh, I felt the pain of my mother's all the more deeply.

"No one must know," Mrs. Tewkes admonished. "Not even the queen." Quickly, she explained the danger I faced. It would not matter that I had served the king and queen faithfully for years or that Prince Bowen had no knowledge of my parentage. As his daughter I would be an object of suspicion, my motives questioned. I would have all the burdens of royalty with none of the advantages.

Royalty. Had my true father passed on the deep, unshakable ambition that had brought me from a country farm to the queen's favor? I might hate Prince Bowen for his betrayal of my mother, but his noble blood flowed within my body. Had he acknowledged my mother as his mistress, I might have been raised as a cousin to Rose. The thought brought a quiver of pleasure.

"Best you put all this from your mind," Mrs. Tewkes concluded. "I've no doubt you can. You have a cool head. It's what makes you such a fine attendant."

She stood and peered down at my face.

"Most would not see it, but you have a trace of him, about the eyes," she said, regarding me as she would a painting. "A fine, proud posture as well, very like the king's mother."

I sat stiffly under her gaze. Stepping back, Mrs. Tewkes asked brightly, "I hear you're to be married?"

Though she had shared the truth with me, I was not ready to do the same. Saying my engagement had been called off would make it true, and I could not yet bear to accept a future that did not include Marcus. I simply smiled and nodded before making a hasty exit.

God showed his mercy that afternoon, for he granted me a few quiet hours alone to collect my thoughts and mourn what I had lost. When I shared the news of my broken engagement with Queen Lenore, I wove a tale that mixed truth and fantasy, putting the whole episode down to youthful infatuation. Now that I had reached the womanly age of eighteen, I told her, I realized the importance of choosing a husband suitable to my position. When I cried into my pillow that night, my body shuddered with withheld sobs, and I vowed that my mistress would never know the sacrifice I had made on her behalf.

The progression of weeks, then months, softened my stabbing pangs of regret into a dull ache. Every time I watched Rose scamper across the garden or received a grateful smile from the queen, I told myself I had made the right choice. I was well fed and well clothed, living a life that most in the kingdom would envy. If at times my mind wandered to thoughts of what might have been, to visions of myself in Marcus's arms, sharing a bed as man and wife, I pushed them forcefully aside. I fixed my eyes firmly on the road ahead, on my work with Flora and my duty to the royal family, hoping time would act as a salve and fade Marcus from my memory.

For poor Petra the castle offered no such refuge from heartbreak. So she escaped in the only way she could. Within a few months of Dorian's rejection, she married a blacksmith in town, brother to one of the castle grooms, who had already buried one wife and sought a new mother for his two small children. I met him for the first time at their wedding dinner, a quiet affair held at her new husband's modest house. He was a brawny man, as blacksmiths often are, yet quiet almost to the point of sullenness. I could not imagine a greater contrast to elegant, witty Dorian.

Petra looked lovely in her bridal gown, made of a delicate silk I had bought her as a wedding gift. Her hair, liberated from its servant's cap and arranged in a pattern of braids and rolls, glistened in the sunlight that streamed through the windows. The children appeared much taken with her, and the smaller girl clutched Petra's skirt for most of the afternoon.

When we finally stole a moment together, I clinked my glass of wine against hers in a toast. "I wish you much happiness."

"Wish me peace."

Petra's face was weighted down with weariness. Gone was the girl I had once known, who chattered with delight in the bed beside mine and laughed as she pulled me behind her through the Lower Hall.

"Do not pity me," she said with a brief, wry smile. "I am told he is a good man. His brother assured me he never beat his first wife."

"Is that all you require in a husband?" I had intended to be humorous, but Petra's smile wilted.

"I saw no other way."

Her grief-stricken expression told me all she dared not say aloud. Anything, even keeping house for a tight-lipped blacksmith and his demanding children, was preferable to living alongside Dorian. He continued to flirt and preen in front of the castle ladies, and I was convinced his promise of marriage had been no more than a ploy to lure Petra to his bed. She—like my mother before her—had been used and cast aside.

I grasped her hands. "I understand."

Had it been mere months since Petra and I giggled over tales of our sweethearts, basking in the pleasure of being loved? It seemed so very long ago. Time enough to transform us from hopeful girls to heart-hardened women.

Though we parted with tears and vows of friendship, Petra and her husband soon moved to a village across the kingdom that had lost its blacksmith and would pay well for a new one. She promised to write but did not. At first I thought her disappearance a betrayal of our friendship, but with time I came to understand and honor her decision. Whatever her affection for me, I was part of a life she had left behind, and any news I sent from the castle would only prolong her pain. The Petra who had been my friend no longer existed.

I, too, had changed. Rather than gazing hopefully toward the future's horizon, I learned to be content living out each day as it came. Each morning I awoke with the sunlight, rising from my pallet in the alcove off Queen Lenore's room. I dipped a cloth in cool water to wash the sleep from my eyes, then helped my mistress do the same. I fetched the breakfast trays from the chambermaid, laid out the queen's clothes for the day, accompanied her to services in the chapel, and sat at her side before the fireplace, embroidering pillows or reading poetry. I played with Rose, delighting in her clever way with words and her infectious laughter. I accompanied Flora on her rambles through the herb garden and, in time, took over the planting and harvesting as her fingers stiffened with age. In the evenings I arranged Queen Lenore's hair for supper, then brushed it out hours later as the candle on her dressing table dripped away. Seasons passed as I watched flowers erupt on the rosebushes, then fade and fall. The tumult of youthful emotions became a distant memory.

I thought those unremarkable years the end of my story. I did not know I was destined to be part of history once again, at the center of events terrible beyond imagining. This time I would play a leading role.

Part II

The Shadow of Death

Twelve

SECOND CHANCES

Is it possible that ten years could pass as one? A single afternoon with Marcus could demand an hour's telling: the feel of the sun on my face, the looks that passed between us, the things he said to make me blush. Yet I can recount the decade after our parting in a few words: My life carried on, unchanged. Within the castle, day followed day, month after month, the rituals of court unaltered by the passing of time. Yet beyond our walls the shadows gathered. The evil we had sought to hold off for so long swirled inexorably closer, spreading suspicion and panic in its wake.

The kingdom had become a land ruled by fear rather than strength. Lord Steffon's was the first in what would be a series of mysterious deaths, the victims all nobles traveling in far-off regions. A year would pass without incident, even two, but by and by word would come of a terrible fall or an unexplained collapse suffered by a relation of the royal family or a courtier's nephew. Was it Millicent's doing? We could never be sure, and the uncertainty pushed

King Ranolf to govern with an ever-harsher hand. Soldiers were sent northward, where they confiscated the homes of the deRauleys and their supporters, then fortified the dwellings into citadels from which they could patrol the region. Networks of paid informers sifted through even the most innocuous gossip, and the castle dungeon filled with those who had foolishly uttered disloyal thoughts aloud. Queen Lenore turned inward, spending hours at prayer in the royal chapel. Desperate for God's forgiveness and protection, she traded in most of her finery for humble black gowns and became easy prey for traveling nuns and so-called seers who sold her religious talismans meant to ward off evil.

And yet, despite the anxious rumors that were our constant companions, we thought ourselves safe inside that towering ring of rough-cut stones. Until the very end, we believed that the castle would protect us.

I was no longer the shy country girl who had quaked at the sight of the castle's imposing gates. Unmarried at the age of twenty-eight, I might have been an object of pity to some, but never to myself. I was a fixture of the court, confident in my role and my position. The touchstones of my former life were gone: My sole surviving brother, Nairn, sent word that our father had died, unmourned, and that he was off to seek his fortune at sea. Marcus and his parents had long since moved from their shop in town, and Flora, my teacher and ally, had become a sickly, bedridden recluse. I spent an occasional Sunday with Aunt Agna, whose household had grown less lively as her children married off and moved away. Only my cousin Damilla and her husband, who had taken over the family's cloth business, remained, along with their daughter, Prielle. She had grown into a quiet but curious girl who reminded me of myself at her age. I did my best to draw her out with my tales of court life, which she listened to with rapt attention.

Prielle's reticence could not have been a greater contrast to thirteen-year-old Rose, who delighted in lively conversation and did not hesitate to make her opinions known. She was a beacon of light in those somber times, her sturdy health a daily defiance of Millicent's hatred. She had her father's rich auburn hair and the large, expressive eyes of her mother's people; her full red lips brought to mind the bud of her namesake flower. Such looks would have inspired marriage proposals even without her title and vast wealth, but the king did not wait to secure her future, betrothing her at the age of ten to Sir Hugill Welstig, a distant relation whose family owned a vast estate in the western part of the kingdom. A girl of royal blood often said her vows at fourteen or fifteen, but Rose begged not to be married until her eighteenth birthday, and King Ranolf, as always, acceded to his daughter's pleas. He could never deny her anything.

Feeling no great pull toward marriage myself, I sympathized with Rose's reluctance. I could have married a fellow servant, kept my place, and done no more than move my bedroll to a different room. More than one man had signaled with admiring stares or flirtatious jokes that he'd have me. But my sights had been set perilously high. I never came close to feeling what I had for Marcus. I'd had love once, and modest affection was not enough to tempt me.

I was not such a fool as to think love necessary for a successful marriage. Women marry to be assured a roof over their head and food on the table. They marry because they need a protector or because they wish for children. All perfectly sensible reasons, and none to do with love. But my needs were met: I had a fine home and fine food and fine clothes. As the queen's attendant, I was respected and respectable even without a husband. Having seen what I had of childbirth, I was relieved to have been spared that suffering, but I did feel a pang whenever I held a swaddled baby. I wondered how it must feel to be bound by flesh and blood to such a tiny creature. The love I might have showered on my own children went to Rose and Prielle instead.

Only once in all those years did I question my decision not to wed. Walking the streets of St. Elsip after a visit to my aunt, I was jolted out of my daydreaming by a familiar face. Marcus had lost all trace of boyishness in the five years since we'd parted, and he carried himself like a man of substance, walking through the cathedral square with a short, stout woman and a young girl. He pressed his hand against the woman's back, guiding her through the crowd, and I remembered, immediately and viscerally, how it felt to be the object of his gentle concern. Here, before me, was the life that might have been mine. A wave of longing churned in the pit of my stomach, and I turned to go before he could see me.

But it was too late. Marcus had stopped cold, his eyes fixed upon me. Waiting for me to determine what would happen next.

My first impulse was to flee. But the queen had trained me well. I set my mouth in a polite smile and walked forward. Marcus greeted me as he would any old acquaintance, with formal good manners, and introduced me to his daughter, Evaline, and his wife, Hester. Looking at her up close, I saw her roundness for what it was: proof of another child on the way. I took petty satisfaction in noting her dowdy dress and freckled, plump face; my hair was braided in the latest style, with curly tendrils framing my face, and my skin, protected from the sun by the castle walls, was smooth and unblemished. Yet she had claimed the prize I once thought mine.

"You are well?" Marcus asked.

Unlike so many who ask the question, he appeared genuinely interested in my reply. I answered as best I could, but there was little to tell. His life had been transformed since we last saw each other; mine had not much changed.

"So you have not married?"

I shook my head. If Marcus was surprised by the news, or pleased, he did not show it. "I have found life at court rich enough without a husband," I could not resist adding.

Hester scowled in disapproval, and Marcus made a halfhearted attempt to rein in a smile. Whether it was my words or his wife's reaction that amused him, I could not tell.

"I am glad your loyalty to the queen and Princess Rose has been well rewarded," he said.

Our eyes met, and the stiffness between us softened. For a moment it was as it had been, when Marcus was my friend. Time had eased the pain of our parting, and I remembered the easy rapport we had once shared, when we could make ourselves understood with no more than a glance.

"It is good to see you," I said, glad I had resisted my first impulse to avoid him. "Good to see you happy."

He smiled warmly, and I could sense, without a word said aloud, the message he wished me to hear: *My love is not easily given, nor is it easily revoked. No matter what happened between us, I will always care for you.*

As I care for you, I replied silently.

Hester tugged at the girl's hand to pull her along. "Come," she ordered Marcus. "The service will be starting."

"The cathedral," Marcus explained. "It is Evaline's birthday, and we thought it right to give special thanks on this day."

"Yes, of course. The queen will be expecting me back as well."

And so we parted, with kindness and forgiveness. We were both healthy and content, which was more than most could say. It was enough.

The passing years were a kindness, for they had dulled the memory of Marcus's hungry kisses and the feel of his fingers upon my skin. The longer I went without a man's touch, the less I felt the need of it. Not until I had fully resigned myself to a life alone did a suitor come along who could not be easily refused. A suitor who showed me how little I understood my own desires.

It was Queen Lenore who told me. I had just returned from a visit to Flora's room, my spirits dampened by the signs I had noted of her further decline. Her cures were helpless against the relentless ravages of old age: weakened legs that could no longer walk to the garden, faltering eyesight, a mind that lit more easily on stories of the past than on events of the day before. I came to her now as companion rather than student, my presence an assurance she had not been forgotten.

"Elise! What news!" the queen trilled with uncharacteristic enthusiasm when I entered her chamber. She patted the bedcover next to her, urging me to sit. Proper etiquette between a maid and her mistress did not concern her when we found ourselves alone. "You will scarcely believe it. You have received an offer of marriage."

The thought so stunned me that I took a moment to reply. Over the years Queen Lenore had asked me occasionally if I had a special man, and I always replied no. In time she no longer asked.

"It cannot be," I protested, thinking the offer could result only from a misunderstanding. "I have no suitors."

"Surely you are aware of a certain person's interest in you?" she asked, her eyes wide with delight.

"In truth I am not."

My bewilderment was plain, for Queen Lenore's smile faded, and she regarded me curiously.

"Dorian has said nothing?"

Dorian? The name was so unexpected, so mystifying, that it must be proof that I had been confused with some other woman. Dorian's talent for riding and hunting had brought him into the king's inner circle, and he had recently returned from two years commanding a troop of soldiers in the north, a commission that was considered a sign of special favor. From what I had seen, his knightly exploits had only enhanced his appeal among the castle's young noblewomen, any of whom would have wed him in an instant. That he might ask for *my* hand was absurd.

"We have scarcely exchanged two words in all the time I have lived here," I said. "There must be a misunderstanding."

The queen looked puzzled. "I will send for Sir Walthur," she said. "It was he who told me of his son's intentions."

A visit by Sir Walthur to Lenore's chambers would set off a storm of gossip, with myself at the center.

"Please, my lady," I offered, rising to stand beside her. "It's best I clear up this confusion myself."

The king's advisers and their families were housed along a corridor just above the Council Chamber. As the king's chief counselor, Sir Walthur was granted the largest suite, blessed with more light and space than the inner apartments. When I entered his front room, I saw him seated at a large desk. Though not fat, he gave an impression of solidity, from his broad shoulders to his jowly cheeks and wide nose. His thick white hair sat like a cap over his forehead and ears, and it stood out even more against the somber black clothing he favored. Were it not for the heavy gold chain with the royal seal that hung around his neck, he might have been mistaken for a particularly well-fed monk. But he had none of a clergyman's humility, be it real or feigned. Sir Walthur wore his position proudly and cultivated his reputation as one who dared speak the truth to the king. His seriousness of manner was a striking contrast to his son's jocularity; I did not think I had ever heard Sir Walthur laugh.

He looked up as I entered, and I saw an echo of Dorian in the way his eyes moved over my face and down along my body. It was the habit of a man accustomed to surveying and assessing a woman's charms, or lack of them.

"Sir Walthur," I said, bobbing in a curtsy. "May I speak with you?"

He nodded brusquely, extending his hand toward the chairs that sat opposite him. For a moment I paused, torn. Customarily a servant would not be permitted to sit in the presence of such a high-ranking official. Slowly, I took a seat facing Sir Walthur, half expecting to be admonished for impertinence.

"The queen has told you of our offer?" he asked.

It crossed my mind to ask if both he and his son were intending to take me as wife. Instead I nodded and waited for him to continue.

"I hope you appreciate the honor done you." His voice rumbled as he talked, giving even the simplest words a ring of authority. "I mean no insult when I say Dorian has had other, better prospects. Yet, given the circumstances, we must make the best of things. I hope you will rise to the occasion."

"Excuse me," I spoke up. Sir Walthur was not used to having his monologues interrupted, for he scowled with irritation.

"Yes?"

"Begging your pardon," I said in my most obsequious manner. "Your son has said nothing to me of marriage. Indeed he has not spoken to me on any matter that I can recall. Is this an offer that comes from him or from you?"

Sir Walthur stared at me impassively, betraying no emotion. "Do you know anything of my family?" he asked.

I shook my head.

"I have two sons. Dorian is the younger, Alston the elder. Alston is a man of steady nerves and very little thought. He will never do great things, but he takes care of my estate in the country and performs his duties well. He married a respectable girl from a neighboring village some years ago, and they've produced three children, with more to come, God willing. With the family bloodline secure, there was no rush for Dorian to marry. Why should he? He had the run of the castle, and young men of his disposition need time to sow their oats before they settle down."

I wanted to cut off his smugly confident flow of words, to tell him that rich young men such as Dorian left a trail of brokenhearted women behind them. But I kept my mouth closed and my expression respectful.

"These are uncertain times," Sir Walthur went on. "We have kept the peace, thanks to the efforts of my son and his fellow soldiers. But the deRauleys are wily devils, and they continue to foment discontent. It is only a matter of time before we face an open rebellion."

I was shocked. Isolated as I was from the rest of the kingdom, I had no idea that the king's rule rested on such a shaky foundation.

"Dorian is young enough to welcome the thought of bloodshed. I trust his skills on the battlefield as much as any man's, but I cannot push aside the thought that he may never return. It would set my mind much at ease if he left an heir. If the unthinkable should happen and he were to be killed, he must leave a legacy behind. Do you understand?"

I nodded, thinking it the right thing to do, though I still did not see how this story might wind its way around to me.

"I did my duty as a father and found a girl for Dorian to wed, a distant relation of my late wife. He was betrothed a few years ago, with the wedding to take place this summer, once the girl was of age. Alas, we received word that she has been taken by a fever. The other women I had considered as possible brides have all been married off or promised to others. I was preparing to look farther afield for a match until Dorian came to me with a suggestion. You."

The thought had come from Dorian himself. I still had no idea why.

"A servant, and one of your age, was hardly the partner I imagined for my son," Sir Walthur continued. "However, it has come to my attention that your bloodline is less humble than I thought."

Sir Walthur watched me with his large, bulging eyes, fixing me with the glare that caused weaker men to crumble before his demands. He knew. He knew that Prince Bowen had fathered me, and that was the only reason he favored this union.

"I have never spoken of my parentage, with good reason," I said hastily. "Please, I beg you to say nothing of it, not even to the king and queen." If I were revealed as Bowen's child, I might lose everything: Queen Lenore's trust, my position at court, Rose's friendship.

"I agree, we should keep it quiet. Now, what do you say?"

My first inclination was to say I was unworthy of such an honor; I was well schooled in feigning humility. But as I stared at Sir Walthur's haughty face, my obsequiousness hardened into anger. Sir Walthur had concocted this plan as if my own preferences were an afterthought. He expected me to agree without question, to fall to my knees in gratitude. But I would not. A surge of recklessness burst through my body, pounding against the restraint I wore like armor. It was the same feeling I had when I walked off the farm, determined to forge a new life for myself. The same feeling I had when I lay in Marcus's arms in that meadow, ready to throw aside caution and virtue. It was a feeling that overcame all reason, demanding only to be satisfied.

I fixed Sir Walthur with my sweetest smile and said, "I could hardly accept a proposal of marriage without seeing what my future husband has to say for himself. I will speak to Dorian before giving you my answer."

Let him fume at my rudeness, I thought recklessly as I strode from Sir Walthur's room. Before I faced Dorian, I must seek out the only other person in the castle who knew the truth of my parentage. A person I thought would never betray me.

I stormed into Mrs. Tewkes's room without knocking. She was sitting at her table, writing in an account book, and started when I entered.

"How could you?" I demanded. Though my chest was tight with fury, my voice came out as a whimper.

"Elise, take hold of yourself," she said briskly. Years of experience with hysterical housemaids had taught her well. She put down her pen and took me by the shoulders, planting me firmly on a stool by the fireplace. She sat in a rocking chair opposite me and leaned forward, her hands on her knees.

"Now, what is this all about?" she asked gently.

"Sir Walthur," I said. "He knows, about me and Prince Bowen. You were the one who said that knowledge must be kept secret."

"When I thought it might be a danger to you, yes," Mrs. Tewkes said.

"The queen herself does not know!" I exclaimed. "What business is it of Sir Walthur's? And what does Dorian want with me?"

Mrs. Tewkes sat back and folded her hands across her chest. She regarded me with an expression I knew well, one that proclaimed her wisdom in the ways of the world. It was a look she used often to silence any young servant who dared question her edicts.

"I can see it's been a shock, and I'll make allowances for that, but you must see you've been offered a great privilege. I expected thanks rather than a scolding."

I stared at her, perplexed.

"Yes, I'm the one who put you forward as a possible wife for Dorian, and I'm glad I did. Do you think your mother would have wanted you to remain unmarried? I know you had your heart broken—most of us have. But we learn to pick ourselves up and move on.

"When you were twenty or twenty-one, you could have made a good match. Yet you cut off any man who showed an interest. What do you think happens to an unmarried woman as she ages? When you're no longer lively enough to tend to the queen? You have no family, no home of your own. Oh, you may have saved enough to live in a rooming house, with enough for a meal or two a day. But do you not wish for better?"

I might be considered an old maid, but I was hardly old; I'd never given a thought to what would happen to me in twenty or thirty years. Now, considering Mrs. Tewkes's words, I realized that there were no elderly female servants at the castle. Of course not. Room and board were granted only to those who could work. If you were heard gasping for breath as you climbed the stairs or your hands could not keep a firm grip on a tray, you would be dismissed. And what then?

"I will tell you what happened, and you may reserve judgment until I finish," Mrs. Tewkes said. "Yesterday Dorian strode up to me in the Great Hall, with that wide grin of his, and said, 'Mrs. T., I have a problem only you can solve.' He told me his father was pressing him to marry, and he wondered if I knew of any good prospects. 'You know everything that goes on at court, far better than my father,' he said, and that's true enough. I mentioned a few ladies of suitable age and family, and he hemmed and hawed, but I could see he had already considered and rejected them. I do not know what made me mention your name. It was a thrown-off suggestion, made in passing, but he perked up immediately."

My suspicious, stiff posture had gradually loosened, and I listened to her intently.

"I remember his words exactly: 'She intrigues me.' Fancy someone of Dorian's rank saying that about you! But it's often that way with men. A woman who succumbs quickly loses her charm, while one who holds herself apart retains her appeal. You may well be the most attractive woman at court he's never gotten his hands on."

"For good reason," I said indignantly.

"He's always been a rascal," Mrs. Tewkes agreed. "But he's older now, looking to the future. Imagine, being daughter-in-law to the king's counselor!"

"So you sweetened the pot by telling him of my parentage," I said.

Mrs. Tewkes shook her head. "No, Dorian was ready enough to take you. It was his father who needed convincing. He came barging in, much as you did a few minutes ago, demanding I give him an account of your background and temperament. I told him of your loyalty to the king and queen, along with assurances of your virtue. Still he wavered. So I offered a final point in your favor, and it was as I'd hoped. At the mention of your true father, he dropped his objections."

I sat hunched over on the stool, the strength of righteous anger drained from my body.

"Courage, girl," Mrs. Tewkes urged. "Your future is secured!"

The most handsome man at court wished to marry me, and his father, Mrs. Tewkes, and the queen favored the match. What did my own desires matter? As Mrs. Tewkes made so clear, such a chance would never come my way again.

I rose to leave and thanked Mrs. Tewkes for her efforts on my behalf. Just before leaving, I paused in the doorway.

"I have not forgotten the promises Dorian once made Petra, only to throw her aside," I said. "How many other maids has he seduced?"

Mrs. Tewkes shrugged. "He has had his way with those he wanted. Mind you, none of them were seduced unwillingly. I know of only one who bore him a child. Sir Walthur saw she was well taken care of."

I nodded, but Mrs. Tewkes noted my distaste. "Things are not always as clear as you imagine," she warned. "Karina was never one to deny a man her favors. The child may not even be his. She may have tricked Dorian into paying her to raise another man's bastard."

It was hardly comforting. All I had heard of my future husband only confirmed my worst suspicions.

When I returned to Queen Lenore's chambers, a few of her ladies were gathered in the sitting room, working quietly at their sewing.

"You've had a visitor," one of them said. Her eyes remained fixed on her stitches as she said Dorian's name, but I could hear the curiosity threatening to burst through her indifferent air. "He said he'll be in the armory should you wish to speak with him."

I wondered if rumors of his proposal had already wafted through court. As soon as I walked from the chamber, I could hear Lenore's ladies whispering. As one who had never been the subject of noblewomen's gossip, I found the sound troubling.

The armory was a brick building behind the stables, abutting the castle walls. It was defiantly male territory, filled with swords and spikes and noxious with the smoke that clouded from the blacksmiths' bellows. I stared into its murky depths from the arched entrance, then stepped cautiously inside, anxious not to be hit by an errant weapon. Directly before me stood two men drenched with sweat, trading insults in harsh, angry barks. Breaking off their argument when they noticed me, they assessed my nervous posture and delicate gown and scowled with suspicion. I feared I had made a mistake in coming.

"Ah! Miss Elise!"

Dorian approached from the middle of the dim room, holding a sword that flashed as it reflected nearby flames. With his broad shoulders and vigorous gait, he was the very picture of a soldier. His hair had lost the golden glow of youth, but his looks remained striking: clear blue eyes that appeared incapable of anger, a strong chin, muscular legs and arms. In the shadowy armory, he alone appeared lit by a magical glow. My eyes could not help being drawn toward him.

I held back, waiting. He nodded in my direction, then said a few words to the metalsmith at his side. He waved the sword quickly back and forth, perhaps for my benefit, for he did look striking doing so, and Dorian was well aware what effect his looks had on women. Satisfied, he handed off his weapon and walked toward me.

"It's time we talked," he said. "Come."

He was accustomed to being obeyed, and I was accustomed to being led. Without asking where we were going, I followed him past the stables and toward a staircase that scaled the castle wall.

"Have you ever been up there?" he asked, pointing to the walkway that led around the top.

I shook my head.

"The view is worth seeing. Besides, we are less likely to be overheard." He ascended the stone stairs two at a time; concerned for my skirts, I walked slowly, feeling my head reel as I approached the top. Standing on the narrow stone path at the top of the wall, Dorian held out a hand to steady me. He led me a few paces along the walkway, toward a small enclosed guard tower.

Dorian pointed out the window, and I saw lush farmlands spread below my feet, stretching far as I could see. To my right was St. Elsip; directly ahead the mountains of Allsbury loomed on the horizon. Surveying the land before me, I realized with a start that I was looking down on the woods where Marcus had taken me years before. Somewhere in those trees was the meadow where we kissed. And nearby the tannery, *his* tannery, the place he worked and lived with his wife and family. I pulled my eyes away and looked outward. Fields of late-summer crops covered the land in a pattern of golds and greens. Brown country lanes snaked across them like twisted vines.

"It's beautiful," I said.

"Soldiers grow accustomed to such sights," Dorian said. "You look upon it with fresh eyes."

The sound of his voice brought me back to the reason for our visit. "Dorian . . ." I began.

He pressed a finger to my lips. The familiarity of the gesture surprised me. I was not sure whether to be offended by his presumption or flattered.

"I must first offer my apologies," he said. "I had hoped to

approach you myself, to make my case as a gentleman. Instead I find that my father has spoiled my gallant plan with his meddling. I never intended to have my offer discussed by half the castle before we had a chance to speak."

His hand moved away from my face and came to rest on my arm. The skin beneath my sleeve warmed at his touch.

"We are little more than acquaintances, Elise, but you have all the qualities I seek in a wife. Loyalty, discretion, patience. And other charms not so easily apparent. Your modesty has kept your loveliness well hidden."

The warmth from my arm spread up toward my face. I remembered, with shame, the moment he had spotted me eavesdropping on his seduction of Petra. The pleasure he had taken in my attention. How I wished myself incapable of blushing, for it revealed emotions I preferred to mask.

"I am greatly honored," I murmured, pulling away from him. "Yet I believe you were pledged once to another more beautiful than I."

"Freydig?" he asked, puzzled, and I guessed she was the intended wife who had recently died. "She was hardly a beauty, God rest her soul."

How soon he forgot. I could see my friend's desolate countenance as clearly as if I had just come from her side, and my stomach lurched with anger at his treachery. Then his face fell, and suddenly I glimpsed another side to the man I had spent so long disparaging.

"Petra."

He said her name in a whisper, and it was enough. Enough for me to know that he had loved her.

"Is she well?" he asked, his voice returning to the smooth, polite tone of a courtier.

"She married and moved from town some years ago." I decided to say nothing of her husband. A man of Dorian's position would hardly consider a blacksmith a great match.

"And you have heard nothing from her since?"

I shook my head.

For a brief moment, Dorian's face was shadowed with disappointment. He turned and looked down into the courtyard, where a group of riders were preparing to depart with much jostling and shouting. If he had intended to be one of the party, he must have changed his mind, for he soon brought his attention back to me.

"She always spoke well of you," he said.

"She also had much to say about you."

He let out a whoop of laughter, and his unexpected joviality took me aback. Was he mocking me or admiring my spirit?

"I imagine she did. Petra never minced words. It was one of her most admirable qualities."

"Yet such qualities were not enough to make her your wife."

Dorian's eyes fixed on mine, the crinkles of amusement gone. Up close I could see the signs of hard living etched on his face, but they enhanced rather than marred his good looks. I'd felt little attraction to the pretty boy Petra had swooned over, but this Dorian had earned the right to carry himself with a knight's swagger.

"I never intended to wrong Petra," he said. "We were young and foolish, and we spoke of marriage as two besotted children would. With very little thought to the future."

For years I had thought Petra the victim of Dorian's cunning. But what if he was telling the truth? What if he believed his promises when he made them?

"Since I was knee-high, I've followed my father's commands," he continued. "He chose my companions and horse when I was a boy, and I knew he would choose my bride when the time came. Like any headstrong youth who fancies himself a man, I toyed with defying him. Yet I never had the courage to do so. Until now."

He reached out and pulled my hands into his. "Elise, I'll speak plainly. My father would like nothing better than to arrange another marriage with a suitably wealthy girl. But this time I will make the choice for myself."

"And you choose me? Why?"

"I believe we would make a good match. You understand the ways of court, and you can see to yourself if I am called to battle. I do not have the makings of a perfect husband, but I can promise you the full honor of my family's name."

His rough thumbs caressed the delicate skin of my wrists.

"Will you have me?"

It was by no means the declaration of love I had imagined from my future husband. But he made no false promises, and perhaps that was more valuable than poetry.

"I am hardly worthy," I said.

"Spoken like a true lady," he said with a delighted grin. "I have seen women far more wellborn become a discredit to their husbands. I do not fear that with you."

His hands moved to my waist, drawing me gradually closer.

"If you agree, we could be husband and wife by harvest time."

His hips pressed against mine, and his powerful hands pressed against my back, pulling me ever closer, until our bodies were melded together. I could have fainted yet remained upright, such was his hold upon me. Dorian leaned over to kiss my forehead, then my cheek, then my lips. I closed my eyes and surrendered to the warm sensation that rushed across my skin, numbing any resistance. Indifferent as I thought myself to Dorian's wiles, I could not deny the longing that his touch provoked, the sudden quickening of my pulse, the powerful urge that impelled me to return his kisses with ever greater force. Freeing my arms from his grasp, I ran my hands over his back, then downward; I could feel the hardness of his legs through my skirts, and the sensation weakened whatever resolve I had left.

Slowly, Dorian disengaged his lips from mine, smiling in amusement. "May I take this to mean you accept my offer?" he asked.

Blushing and avoiding his eyes, I nodded, belatedly mortified by my boldness. Dorian placed his hands on my cheeks and turned me back to face him. At first I thought his smile was at my expense, but I soon realized he was pleased by my fervor. Abandoning any attempt to compose myself, I acquiesced willingly when he ran his fingers under the edge of my cap and through my hair, drawing me toward him once again.

I had taken Mrs. Tewkes's admonitions to heart. I knew that the prestige and wealth of Dorian's family would assure a comfortable future, and as wife or widow I would be cared for in my old age. But that is not the reason I said yes to Dorian's proposal. I did not love him, and I did not entirely trust him. Yet the moment he kissed me, my body submitted to his. Once we were married, such passionate embraces would be no cause for shame. My thoughts raced to an image of our wedding night, and suddenly I could not wait to discover what pleasures I might find in my new husband's arms.

Thirteen

A WEDDED WOMAN

Dorian and I exchanged our vows in the Royal Chapel, with the king and queen as witnesses. Queen Lenore gave me a new dress for the occasion, made of a deep red velvet chosen to complement my brown hair and eyes, and insisted I borrow the gold floral necklace she had received as a wedding gift from her mother, the necklace that would one day be passed down to Rose. Dorian grinned with satisfaction when he saw me standing in the chapel entry. He looked utterly self-assured, as if this ceremony were a joust or a hunting excursion, a diverting escapade rather than a life-changing event. I followed him silently to the altar, still astounded that this striking, rugged knight had chosen me as his wife. The sunlight streaming through the stained-glass window lit him with a burnished aura as I followed the prompting of the priest, promising to obey my husband and put his cares above my own. It was not until I said the words aloud that I truly understood the consequences of my actions. As Dorian slid a gleaming gold band along my finger, the finality of the gesture made my hand tremble. Had I relinquished my freedom too easily?

After the ceremony we were given a feast in the Great Hall. King Ranolf presented Dorian with his wedding gift, a hunting dagger whose blade jutted from a handle inlaid with precious gems. Dorian's fellow knights exchanged envious glances at this extravagant proof of the king's favor, just as their wives shared looks of silent disapproval when I took a seat among them. Rose ran over and threw her arms around me, bubbling with congratulations, and I was further discomfited by this unexpected flouting of castle etiquette. To judge by the expressions of my table companions, my sudden rise in status was scarcely believable to them as well. Throughout the rest of the meal, I stared modestly at my plate to spare them the awkwardness of my attention.

Dorian alone appeared unaffected. He was his usual jovial self throughout the meal, trading jokes about his prowess as a lover with the knights who sat at our table. He ruffled my hair and kissed my hands, proud to publicly claim possession. As the hour for us to retire grew closer, I grew steadily more nervous. We had shared many passionate kisses since our engagement, but time and again I had stopped his wandering hands, determined that the consummation wait until our wedding night. But now that the moment was upon us, I feared disappointing him. I was ignorant in the ways a woman pleases a man, and Dorian had enjoyed a wide array of female companionship. Would I bore him?

After dinner and a series of rambling, drunken toasts, a group of Dorian's friends escorted us from the hall, taunting my new husband about the great test before him. Although I knew that such jests were a matter of course for a wedding night, they fueled my unease. I quickened my pace, hearing the voices fade in the distance behind me, and walked into Dorian's bedroom. I had seen it for the first time earlier that day, when I'd accompanied the porter who carried my meager possessions downstairs. Accustomed as I was to the expansiveness of the queen's rooms, the space looked woefully cramped and dark. A simple bed stood in the center, with posts at each corner but no canopy. Two chairs sat under a small window, which looked out over the stables. A plain wooden cross on one wall was the only attempt at adornment. Such a spare room bore little witness to the character of the man who slept there.

I paced between the bed and the chairs, the only part of the room with space to walk. I heard footsteps and looked up, preparing myself for further mockery. Dorian entered, alone, and closed the door behind him.

"Don't tell me those fools upset you?"

He carried himself as if this were any other night, walking past me as he pushed his coat off his shoulders and tossed it onto one of the chairs. His boots were cast aside in a similarly careless manner. Was I expected to disrobe with the same indifference? Dorian turned to stand before me, the form of his broad chest visible through his thin linen shirt. Gently, he removed my headdress and pulled my curls loose from their fastenings, sending tingles across my scalp. His hands moved down to my shoulders, along my arms, and to my back, where they expertly undid the laces that cinched my dress. The supple velvet slid to the floor, and I was left in my shift, shivering with nerves. Dorian leisurely took in the sight of me as I stared at the floor, unsure how to proceed. Then, suddenly, I was in his arms, lowered back onto the bed, trapped by the weight of his body.

"You have no idea how I've waited for this moment," he said, his voice a gruff whisper, as his hands pushed up my skirt and ran up and down my legs. My heart pounded so strongly it seemed the rhythm passed through us both.

"You'll do as I say, will you, wife?" he asked teasingly.

"I will obey you," I said, echoing the vows I had said a few hours before.

I thought his body an unknown land to be explored warily, but he treated mine as territory to be conquered. Guiding me through the motions that bind husband to wife, he issued commands like a soldier, but the words were uttered with the warmth of lovers' talk; the forcefulness of his callused hands might have been threatening had I not felt so protected in his powerful embrace. For he had a skill I imagine few men do: the ability to temper danger with tenderness.

In that shadowy bed, illuminated by the flame of a single candle, my nervousness fled under Dorian's assured fingers. When he unbuttoned my shift with a grin and pushed it down from my shoulders, I blushed as my nakedness was revealed. But the feel of his skin against mine as our limbs intertwined soon swept me into a realm of pure pleasure. With his delighted encouragement, my hands roamed from the tight muscles of his legs, hardened by years of riding, to the surprisingly soft skin at the base of his neck; when I reached up to kiss him there, he quivered with delight, and I reveled in my power to affect him so. Yearning for more, I followed as he urged me here, then there, tasting his musky skin with ever-increasing hunger. When his final assault made me gasp with a sudden, sharp pain, he pressed his face against mine and whispered reassurance, holding me tight as he shuddered to his conclusion.

Stroking my arm as he rolled to lie beside me, he said, "I was right to put trust in your virtue. A fine wedding gift to your husband."

He kissed me lightly on the forehead, then turned away; before long his breathing rumbled into snores. After so many years spent sleeping alone, I knew not how to position my body beside him. I lay rigid and alert, feeling the heat emanate from his skin, exhausted yet unable to sleep.

Marriage had transformed me from the queen's maid to a knight's wife. Queen Lenore took on a new personal attendant, an amiable young girl named Heva, and I became the newest of her ladies-in-waiting. Rather than stand to the side in the queen's sitting room waiting to be summoned, I was entitled to a seat among women of noble birth and permitted to speak as an equal. Though I continued to treat them with deference, the queen's ladies did not welcome me into their ranks. On more than one occasion, I walked toward a knot of them huddled in whispered conversation only to have all sound cease at my approach. One asked impertinently if I was with child, as if that were the only way the castle's most notorious bachelor could have been enticed into marriage. No doubt a few had fancied Dorian for themselves.

The occasional disapproving stare was a small price to pay for the advantages of my new position. I was no longer awake at dawn to serve another; I could now greet the morning at my leisure, hovering between sleep and wakefulness in my new husband's arms. The days were mine to spend as I pleased, for the queen's ladies could come and go at will. In truth, after so many years of service and with no friends of my own rank to help pass the time, I found it difficult to fill the empty hours that greeted me at the start of each day.

Out of habit and affection for the queen, I continued to spend much of my time in her apartments, which were a welcome escape from the cold, masculine rooms Sir Walthur and Dorian shared.

Rose, one of the few who reveled in my new position, became my closest companion. In her younger years, she had enjoyed a certain measure of freedom, escaping the castle's fortifications for rides with her father in the countryside or visits to nearby estates. Given the growing threats to her safety, such excursions now were denied her, as was the company of girls her own age, for most noble families raised their children away from court. Desperate for diversion, with no other friends to turn to, Rose came to me for conversation and guidance. Not long after I said my vows, she asked whether the wedding night had been as I expected.

"Do you mean after the feast?" I considered carefully how to phrase the words. "The consummation?"

"I heard the men making jests with Dorian, but I did not understand their meaning."

"Hasn't your mother spoken to you of such things?" I asked.

She shook her head. "She told me only that a wife must perform certain duties. The rest could wait until I was older."

Given my rustic upbringing, I could not imagine reaching the age of fourteen with no knowledge of how men and women lay together. From as early as I could remember, I had seen sheep rut in the field and heard my father grunt against my mother in the darkness of our hovel. I did not think it my place to educate Rose, yet I was touched she trusted me with such questions.

"I must respect your mother's wishes," I said. "I promise, I will tell you all you need to know when the arrangements for your marriage are made."

"You are happy with Dorian, are you not?"

Such a simple question, yet so difficult to answer truthfully.

"Of course," I said with great assurance.

"I hope to be happy with Sir Hugill." Rose had yet to meet her future husband, though she often pored over a small portrait he had sent. "I know nothing of his character or temperament, yet I am to be bound to him for life. Does that not strike you as cruel?"

"It is the way things are done," I said warily. No good could come of questioning her lot in life, and I would not be accused of encouraging such sentiments.

"I am more prisoner than princess. Never consulted for my thoughts or opinions, only informed of what I must do. Not once has my mother spoken of love when it comes to my marriage. How I envy you."

Rose, alas, was too young to remember when her parents had stared adoringly at each other before the whole court or read poetry aloud in Queen Lenore's sitting room. Now they were little more than figureheads, a king and queen who lived largely separate lives. Her father passed his days fixated on real or imagined threats, while her mother took solace in the teachings of her newest favored adviser, a traveling monk named Father Gabriel who could expound for hours on the sins of human vanity. Tall and ascetic, with a gangly, thin frame that called to mind a crane, he took pride in sleeping on the floor of the kitchens, rolled only in his cloak. With such a saintly presence hovering in the queen's rooms, I could hardly blame the king for seeking amusement elsewhere; according to Heva he no longer shared his wife's bed. It was little wonder that Rose considered my marriage a love match, compared to that of her parents.

Was my marriage happy? I could not say. Our vastly different natures often put us at odds; during rides in the country Dorian fretted at my slow pace, while his attempts to explain the intricacies of joust tactics left me yawning. Amused rather than impressed by Flora's tutelage, he referred to the collection of bottles and jars I stored in a corner of our room as witches' brews, though he was happy enough when I applied one of my salves on his sore muscles. Married or not, he would not relinquish the role of entertainer, and he sought the admiration of both women and men. In his eternal quest to amuse and be amused, Dorian enjoyed making me a topic of fun, lamenting his lost freedom or complaining of his wife's sharp tongue, when we both knew I had never spoken a word against him. When I told him that such complaints hurt my feelings, he rolled his eyes and said marriage had dulled my appetite for humor, thereby proving his point.

How, then, can I explain the way he enthralled me in private? On the nights I turned from him in irritation, frustrated by a thoughtless remark or gesture made earlier, he would run his fingers through my hair or kiss my chest along the neckline of my gown, until my body betrayed me by responding to his touch. Unlike so many men, who take what they need from a woman to suit their own tastes, Dorian took pleasure in giving pleasure. The fact that I was known throughout the castle for my discretion and modesty only heightened his wish to see me undone. I revealed a side of myself to Dorian that no one else had ever seen, and the knowledge of such secret selves can bind a couple in matrimony more sturdily than can their church vows.

I did not expect Dorian to be faithful to me, and he was not. I accepted it as the price paid to spend my days as I pleased, for he put few demands on me during daylight hours. Dorian could be coarse and arrogant but also generous and charming, unintentionally insulting but never purposefully cruel. My own parents had shown me that a wife's lot could be far worse. I hoped fatherhood might tame his wandering eyes and juvenile ways, yet a year, and then two, passed with no change to my cycle.

Fears for my own possible barrenness did not blind me to the looming dangers facing the kingdom. A seeming victory—the capture of the youngest deRauley brother—revealed itself in time as a further spur to the rebels. The young man's trial for treason was a sham, for he had little knowledge of his older brothers' scheming, and the cruelty of his execution, dragged out for maximum suffering, only hardened the hearts of those already disposed against the king. Sir Walthur spent his days closed off with the Royal Council, debating whether additional troops should be sent north, where talk of Prince Bowen's taking over the throne was now commonplace. Though Bowen himself eluded the king's spies, it was clear he was actively plotting in the area, stirring up discontent with his brother's rule.

Dorian spent his days on horseback, practicing battle formations with the other knights, overgrown boys playing at war until the real thing came along. In the privacy of our room, he taught me how to wield the jeweled dagger that had become his most prized possession, standing with his chest pressed against my back, clutching my hand as he demonstrated a thrust or a cut. It was the closest I had ever come to understanding the lure of soldiering, for my very bones seemed to take on the weight of that steel, filling me with unaccustomed strength. The undercurrent of danger proved exhilarating, and such encounters invariably ended with the dagger dropped to the floor as we reached for each other instead.

Though Dorian proclaimed himself eager to fight, the king and his advisers believed it was in their power to cow the rebels without resorting to a full invasion. It is only hindsight that makes a war inevitable. For months—years—we set our hopes on other resolutions. The eldest deRauley brothers might be captured, putting an end to their conspiracy, or Prince Bowen's arrogance might drive away his followers. The king invested great effort into building a network of allies that would make his hold on power unshakeable. The rulers of neighboring lands had every reason to support King Ranolf, for any upheaval in our country might spill over into theirs. The cornerstone of this strategy was Hirathion, the land that bordered us to the north and therefore was the most likely to be affected by possible bloodshed.

Were Hirathion's king to publicly stand with us, the rebels' stronghold would be encircled by territory loyal to King Ranolf, dealing a mortal blow to the northerners' conspiracy. So it seemed a most auspicious sign when the king of Hirathion sent word that a representative would be visiting the castle to discuss a formal alliance.

I did not see the delegation from Hirathion arrive; the men disappeared into the Council Chamber almost immediately to confer with the king. However, the news soon spread that the visiting party consisted of only a few officials, led by an ambassador whose name was unfamiliar to Sir Walthur. Dorian strode into our room, filthy and exhausted from a week of military exercises in the western region of the kingdom, and complained that the ambassador's youth proved Hirathion's indifference to our affairs.

Still, among the ladies of the castle any change to our usual routine was cause for excitement. A great feast had been prepared for his first night, and even Queen Lenore rose to the occasion, adorning herself in the precious jewels she usually forswore. I wore the red gown made for my wedding, which elicited a lecherous grin from Dorian when I emerged from our bedroom. All the members of court were present in the Great Hall when the men from Hirathion arrived, ushered by a hum of curious whispers. They were led by a dark-featured young man who moved with a dignity beyond his years. His eyes darted swiftly across the room, and I sensed immediately an intense curiosity, an eagerness to observe and remember all he saw. This, Dorian whispered to me, was Joffrey Oberliss, the ambassador on whom our fates might depend.

I noted his lack of title—further proof of his relative unimportance—yet he comported himself with the grace of one accustomed to aristocratic circles and was granted a seat of honor at the queen's side. Throughout the meal my eyes were drawn to him as he engaged Queen Lenore in conversation, listening to her answers with attentive concentration. Rose, separated from the guest of honor by both her parents, leaned forward repeatedly to catch his words, her expression openly enthralled. I shot her a disapproving glance, but I could not fault her for finding our visitor compelling. Joffrey exhibited a refinement and a thoughtfulness that were rare among the hardy, boisterous knights of King Ranolf's circle.

After the plates were cleared and a series of flowery toasts had been offered, the king signaled the musicians to begin. The younger courtiers rose from their seats and gathered in the middle of the room, arranging themselves in rows facing one another to dance. I had learned the steps only recently, after my marriage, and firmly declined Dorian's entreaties to join him; I would not risk tripping over my feet at such a formal affair.

As the musicians sounded out their first tune, Rose turned to her father and touched his arm. I could not hear her words, but the king stood and signaled for silence.

"One moment!" he announced. "My Beauty would like to join the company, but only if our guest serves as her partner."

He turned to Joffrey with a playful smile, delighting in the young man's surprise. A look of alarm passed across Queen Lenore's face, so quickly that few would have noticed, to be replaced with her customary polite smile. Rose's forwardness in requesting a dance with a man of drastically lower rank was a considerable breach of etiquette. But if King Ranolf had chosen to encourage his daughter's youthful high spirits, Queen Lenore could not be seen to disagree.

Rose had moved to the floor by the time Joffrey got up from his seat. Befitting her position, she stood at the head of the line of ladies, where she would be on full display to the surrounding guests. I wondered if Joffrey would be able to follow the steps; not all young men have a talent for movement, and his gait appeared hesitant as he took his place.

They stood opposite each other, his eyes staring directly into hers, for Rose at sixteen had spurted to above-average height. The music began, and Rose took two dainty steps forward, then slid smoothly past and around her partner, as if wrapping him in an invisible net. The warmth of her smile melted Joffrey's cautious reserve, and he succumbed further with each movement, his eyes following every dip and turn, lips parting with pleasure as he matched Rose's steps. When their hands met briefly at the end, his palm stayed too long against hers, and she pulled away with a delighted laugh.

We all saw it. The ambassador was so besotted by Rose that he did not care if the whole court noticed. They danced another round, then another. The king, who should have put a stop to such favoritism, was caught up in conversation with his courtiers; Queen Lenore, always deferential to her husband's wishes, made no move to admonish her daughter. A woman's honor is her most prized possession, and I feared that Rose was wearing hers too lightly.

During the next pause in the music, I stood and made my way toward the edge of the dancers. I saw Rose stare at Joffrey with raised eyebrows, daring him to flout etiquette and request her hand yet again. Moving into her line of sight, I shook my head slowly, hoping the darkness of my expression would compound the warning. Rose's smile dropped, along with her flirtatious manner, and she introduced me to her guest with formal politeness.

"May I request the honor?" he asked, extending his hand toward me. Flushed from the dancing, giving me the full force of his attention, he was even handsomer than he had appeared from a distance. It was no wonder that Rose had been dazzled.

I shook my head. "I must decline, with the greatest respect. Unfortunately, I am a poor dancer."

"As was I, until tonight."

His flash of wit disarmed me, and I found myself grinning along with Rose. Then, aware of all the eyes upon us, I discreetly nudged Rose back toward her table. "Time to take your place," I whispered.

"Yes, yes," Rose murmured, then raised her voice to include Joffrey in our conversation. "I would find some cold cider quite refreshing. There's nothing like dancing to awake a thirst."

"I'll have some sent," I said, searching the hall in vain for a serving maid. As usual, most had disappeared once the music had started, no doubt to indulge in their own revelry downstairs. I slipped through the doorway behind the dais that led to the Receiving Room, remembering how I had made this same escape years before, on the day of Rose's baptism. Here I had huddled with the king and Flora as Queen Lenore recounted the grisly tale of Millicent's dark powers. On this night the room was empty and still, and I moved through the dark space quickly, averting my eyes from the shadows that shifted as I passed. Alone, I climbed down the narrow staircase that led to the Lower Hall, shivering when the damp walls rubbed against my arm. The noise and gaiety of the feast had been left behind; the only sound was the tap of my shoes against the slabs underfoot. Despite the many years I had lived at the castle, I had never lost my discomfort walking these passages alone, secretly fearing that one wrong turn might lead me into a tunnel or dungeon from which I would never return.

Once downstairs, I accosted a half-drunk footman and charged him with bringing pitchers of fresh cider to the king's table. I darted back up the stairs, so distracted that I did not see the dark figure blocking my way out until I ran headlong into the solid mass of his body. His arms imprisoned me, pressing my face against his chest and muffling my scream with his shirt. His fingers spread across the nape of my neck and up through my hair before gently pulling my head back so that I could look at him. It was Dorian.

"I am sorry I frightened you," he said in hushed voice. "'Twas all in fun."

Fun? Furious, I twisted away from his grasp. He reached out for my hand and clasped it with unexpected tenderness, bringing my fingers up to his lips for a kiss. The sweetness of the gesture was enough to halt my steps, and Dorian drew closer, sliding his hands along my sleeves, up to my shoulders.

"How you torment me," he whispered, running his mouth along the arch of my neck. "It seems forever since I touched you. It was torture, watching you tonight, being denied this." His hand slid smoothly down my side to my thigh. I felt the skin of my calves prickle in the clammy air as he pulled up my skirt.

"What would you have me do, wife, with the blood risen up in me?" One hand pressed against the curve of my bottom to keep me in place; the other began a steady stroke along my inner thigh.

"I cannot stay," I said, my languid voice at odds with my words.

"Please."

The ache in his voice took me by surprise. Dorian's mouth moved from my lips to my cheeks, my forehead, my ears, desperate movements driven by a need he could not master. I grabbed his hips with my hands, pressing him against me until I could feel the hardness of his desire. His fingers moved between my legs, stoking my own hunger for what came next.

Suddenly I heard the distant crash of a falling pot, followed by faint laughter. Roused from a momentary madness, I remembered we were at the top of the servants' stairs, in full view of whoever might ascend. Terrified, I froze and stared at Dorian. He grinned devilishly and pulled my skirt almost to my waist. His boldness spurred on my own desire; I could not stop, not now. I reached under his tunic, fear of discovery hurrying my fingers. Dorian pushed me against the wall, taking me as we stood, grinding into me with a force that left me breathless. Even after he was spent, he held me there, lost in the moment, unwilling to see it past.

For those few, silent minutes, I held him. Though we had come together in a frenzy of lust, I felt an unexpected tenderness for my husband. Dorian had revealed a chink in his armor, a need of me I had never suspected. Perhaps, deep down, he even loved me.

Belatedly remembering my obligations, I pulled away and hastily smoothed out my dress. Dorian watched, amused, while I hid all trace of debauchery. As we walked out into the Receiving Room, I was surprised, then panicked, to see two figures hovering in the doorway opposite me. Who were they? What had they heard?

As I hesitantly walked closer, I saw that it was Rose and Joffrey, deep in conversation. Whatever sounds Dorian and I had made had not traveled this far, for they both startled at my approach and stepped backward to increase the distance between them. While Joffrey was abashed enough to avoid meeting my eyes, Rose addressed Dorian and me in her usual bright manner.

"I have been showing our visitor the tapestries."

"A challenge indeed, in this dim light," Dorian noted with mock concern.

I shot him a look and gave Rose's shoulder a firm push. "There will be time enough to see the sights tomorrow. Come, sir. It won't do to have our guest of honor go missing."

As we reentered the Great Hall, I was relieved to see that our appearance did not cause much stir. While Rose and Joffrey's absence could not have passed unnoticed, my presence as chaperone made their brief outing respectable. Only I knew that they had been together alone, unobserved, a blunder that could have stained Rose's reputation forever. Rose and Joffrey rejoined the king and queen, while Dorian and I made our way back to our table. He flung one arm possessively around my waist and leaned in close.

"If only they knew what you've been up to," he murmured, then laughed suggestively.

His breath tickled my neck, and my face flushed. I glanced around, hoping my husband's words had not been overheard. The buzz of conversation surrounding us continued, uninterrupted, but

I was suddenly aware of a gaze fixed upon me. I saw a tall figure looming in the doorway, standing utterly still with arms crossed, his very posture a stiff rebuke to the revelry before him. It was Father Gabriel.

I was surprised, then concerned. He often boasted of his indifference to worldly matters; why, then, should he make an appearance this evening? And why was his disdainful gaze directed at me? He could not possibly know of my encounter with Dorian in the stairway, yet I sensed that something in my posture, in my husband's easy, possessive touch, had given us away. Excusing myself hurriedly from Dorian, I walked over to the monk and greeted him with what I hoped was an innocent expression.

"I did not think I would see you here tonight, Father," I said. "Did you wish to speak to me?"

"According to the servants' gossip, Princess Rose made quite a spectacle of herself in the dancing." He sniffed. "Now I find you escorting her from a private meeting with the ambassador. I had not expected such permissiveness, from you or the queen."

"It is her father who indulges Rose," I said with a wry smile. "But I see no harm in her charming our guest. It may even bring the king of Hirathion to our side."

Father Gabriel's tight-lipped expression of disapproval did not change. "It's time that girl was married. She needs a firm hand."

His words in themselves were not shocking, but I was taken aback by the vehemence of his tone. His role at court was to tend to the queen's spiritual needs, not the princess's personal affairs. Was he using his influence with the queen to meddle in matters of state? *Of course not,* I quickly admonished myself, for I had seen no such signs. Chaste men of God, I have found, have little sympathy for young women of a flirtatious disposition, and I could not deny that Father Gabriel's censure was earned: Rose never should have been allowed to take such liberties.

When I asked Rose later what had transpired in the Receiving Room, she blushed and would not say. I could not tell whether her reticence was intended to cover behavior I would have disapproved of or to hide her disappointment that Joffrey had not attempted such behavior.

The following morning, irritable with frustration, Dorian told me Joffrey had made vague assurances of support but admitted that the king of Hirathion would send no soldiers to aid our cause. The king, furious, had hurled accusations of deception, and the delegation had quit the castle abruptly, without the customary formal farewells.

"We're on our own," Dorian muttered.

Sir Walthur had joined us in the family's sitting room. The hours of fruitless talks had brought dark shadows to his eyes, and his usual sternness was softened by exhaustion. "Hirathion remains an ally," he said solemnly.

"We are defending the rights of a noble family. A fellow king should find that a cause worth fighting for."

"You must consider his position. If he sends soldiers here, he'll be leaving his own lands sparsely defended."

"Hang all of them," Dorian said.

Sir Walthur sucked in his breath at his son's irreverence. I sat silent, as I usually did when father and son argued affairs of state. A woman's opinion was of no import to either man.

"King Ranolf commands the finest forces these lands have ever seen," Dorian continued. "It's time we proved ourselves."

Sir Walthur shook his head sadly. Then he turned to me.

"There is one matter I must address with you, Elise. When the men from Hirathion departed this morning, I accompanied them to the courtyard to see them off. As they were riding out, their ambassador, Joffrey, swerved aside to speak to someone who was standing by the gates. The person was wrapped in a dark cloak, and I would have paid the encounter little mind had the wind not shifted and blown at the hood. It was Rose. I knew her hair instantly."

I was surprised, but not shocked. I should have guessed that Rose would seek out a last dramatic farewell with the man who had so fascinated her. I only hoped none of Joffrey's men had witnessed her impetuous gesture.

"Did anyone else see?" I asked.

"I don't think so. Thank God. But I believe it my duty to notify the king."

"No, no, please don't," I begged. "I will speak to her."

Sir Walthur sat like an old man, his shoulders stooped and his arms flat and lifeless upon the table. "The young give no thought for consequences. Like those who yearn for battle." He looked at Dorian. "When word gets out that we have no reinforcements to call on, I don't see how war can be avoided."

"I welcome it," said Dorian, defiant, and I was momentarily chilled by his single-minded craving for bloodshed. As Sir Walthur had noted, his son was relentless in pursuit of his desires, no matter the cost. Just as Rose refused to admit fault when I chided her for running after Joffrey like a loose woman. When I appealed to her good sense, saying it was dangerous to hover so near the castle gates, she smirked.

"More dangerous than walking through St. Elsip?" she asked. "For I have done so and returned quite unharmed."

"You have gone out?" I asked, horrified. "Alone?"

"No one spares a second glance for a girl in a chambermaid's dress."

I understood that she struggled with the constraints of her position, but I had never imagined she would go to such lengths to escape them. I begged her not to slip out again and knew even as she said the words that she would not honor her promise. Yet I never told her parents or asked her maid to report to me on Rose's movements. I took no actions to stop her. Rose's outings beyond the walls fed a vital piece of her soul. If I did not tacitly support her furtive attempts at independence, I risked losing her trust—and her love—forever.

Sir Walthur's fears of war proved prophetic. It was not two weeks after Joffrey and his men had departed that we received devastating news. The fortress of Embriss, once the seat of the deRauley family but controlled for the past decade by soldiers loyal to the king, had been overtaken. I was in the front courtyard with Dorian when the rider arrived, breathless and terrified, his exhausted horse barely able to put one foot before the other. Dorian shouted to one of the stableboys to take the reins. The person who dismounted was little more than a youth, but his eyes were those of one who has seen misery far beyond his years.

Dorian half dragged the messenger to the Council Chamber, where the king was gathered with Sir Walthur and his other advisers. Though it was not my place, I followed at a discreet distance, accompanied by other members of court who sensed the importance of this sudden arrival.

The king bade the young man enter and say his piece. Lingering in the hall, I could only catch glimpses of the men inside, but I heard the boy's terrible tale clearly. Two days before, marauders had attacked Embriss without warning, storming through the gates like a pack of wolves, eager for blood. Their actions had been swift and ruthless. Bodies had been tossed from turrets and flames devoured the walls as the boy watched in horror from a nearby hill.

"Could you see the attackers?" the king demanded.

"The men leading the charge carried the standard of the deRauleys, three bear heads on a field of yellow," said the youngster. "One rode a black horse, the largest I've ever seen."

"Marl," the king said, his voice almost a whisper. Tales of the oldest deRauley brother had taken on the flavor of legend: He was reputed to stand a head taller than any other man and to ride a massive black beast that was more bull than horse. If Marl himself had made the attack, it was an act of war.

Yet how could such a mighty stronghold fall so quickly? Later, when the messenger was dismissed, I offered to take him to the Lower Hall to see he was fed.

"You saw the riders approach the castle?" I asked him.

The boy nodded.

"How did they enter? Surely the walls were well defended?"

"I could not see the gates from where I stood. But it seemed that no time passed before I heard screams from inside."

There had been no attack, no siege. A traitor had opened Embriss to its enemies, further proof that the king's hold on his people had grown slack with time. Dorian and his friends may have fancied themselves the bravest soldiers in the land, but swordsmanship is no defense against betrayal.

After years of whispered rumors and uncertain threats, making plans for war brought a cathartic relief to the king and his men. Commanders put soldiers through their paces on the vast tournament field to the south of the castle walls, and hoofbeats thundered through the air. The bellows in the castle armory stayed lit well into the night; I lay in bed listening to the clink of metal. Queen Lenore spent her days at prayer in the chapel, Father Gabriel at her side. She would rule in the king's name during his absence, and I feared that the weight of such duty would hang heavy upon her. Yet she faced the prospect of her husband's departure with serene acceptance, for which I grudgingly credited Father Gabriel's ministrations. I could forgive his aloof manner toward me and the rest of the court as long as his prayers gave strength to the queen.

Beyond the royal apartments, the days leading up to the army's departure saw an outbreak of lusty couplings, as many young women who had denied their suitors certain favors suddenly put aside their qualms. Any man in armor was much swooned over, his faults overlooked and his bravery praised. Even I found myself clinging to Dorian in a way much contrary to my usual reserve during the few hours he was not out training his men.

The night before the army was to march off, Dorian stomped into our room long past nightfall. Drained by the day's events, he collapsed onto the bed with a grunt of satisfaction. I fetched the water pitcher and washed off his grimy face as he lay back, eyes closed, worn out from his exertions. Gently, I pushed his disheveled hair back from his forehead, listening to his slow, even breathing.

Just when I thought he had fallen asleep, he reached up and drew me tight against his chest. I did not speak when he pulled off my dress, nor when I eased his tunic up over his shoulders. We came together silently, his rough soldier's hands stroking my delicate skin as if he could preserve memories by touch.

I expected Dorian to fall asleep afterward, as was his habit, but his impending departure sparked an uncharacteristic tenderness. He lay on his side, facing me, twisting his fingers through my curls.

"The thought of lingering with you is almost enough to make me regret the coming of war."

There was no teasing smile, no lighthearted laughter. For that brief moment, I saw us as we could have been, had we learned to speak honestly and openly to each other. Perhaps it was still possible for us to forge a true partnership when the war had passed.

"Linger a while longer, then," I murmured, rubbing my palms against his chest.

Flush with affection, I considered telling him the secret I had been holding for some weeks. Missing one monthly course was hardly sure proof that I was with child, and I was fearful of raising his hopes and mine until more time had passed. Would it be better to wait, I wondered, and present him with a full belly on his return? I envisioned a weary and mud-spattered Dorian riding home from battle, myself waiting at the castle gates to share the news.

"I shall miss these soft hands when I'm bedded down in a field with a horde of filthy soldiers," Dorian said.

"You won't have time for such remembrances," I said, teasing. "You will be too busy boasting."

"You know me too well," he said with a wry smile. "I cannot deny it, I am ready to fight. Ready to see this settled."

Already Dorian's thoughts were on those northern battlegrounds. Drawing his attention to other matters would be no kindness, and I decided to say nothing of my condition. If I was wrong and this monthly interruption was no more than woman's trouble, he need never know of it.

I fell asleep with Dorian's arms around me, cocooned in the sturdiness of his body. Awakened at dawn by a gentle kiss, I opened my eyes and saw Dorian standing beside the bed, already dressed.

"I'm off to muster the men."

"So soon?" I asked, groggy.

"There is much to be done." Then, softening, he said, "Will you be seeing me off?"

"Of course," I said.

Dorian hesitated, looking at my bare shoulders, the curve of my breasts beneath the cover tempting him to return for a final embrace. I ached with longing. He had not even left the castle, yet I already missed his warm, solid presence.

"I will look for you," he said at last, bowing his head in farewell. The husband who had whispered to me in the night was gone; Dorian was now a warrior, ready to face his destiny.

The soldiers departed with great ceremony from the front courtyard. A raised platform had been erected so the queen and her ladies could take leave of their men on horseback face-to-face. The walls were ringed with a crush of people; it seemed every inhabitant of the castle, noble or servant, had gathered to watch. Queen Lenore carried herself with dignity, as always, surveying the commotion impassively from her gilded chair. Only her dark eyes revealed the melancholy that had taken an ever-increasing hold over her. Rose sat beside me, but she could not keep her body still; her feet tapped under the front of her skirt, and her eyes moved restlessly across the scene.

The sharp call of bugles rang out from the back courtyard, where the army was gathering. Voices hummed with anticipation, and Rose's fidgeting stirred up my own nerves. The heralds were the first to march through the archway, their steps keeping time with the rhythm of their horns. They were followed by the flag bearers, walking six abreast, each proudly brandishing the king's coat of arms. Dorian had told me that these standards were of great importance during a battle, as they marked the position of each commander during the fighting. Dorian would be leading the king's cavalry, and I wondered which of these bearers would ride alongside him.

With clanging armor and stomping footsteps, row after row of soldiers in full battle dress emerged before us. The courtyard echoed with rapturous cheers. A few of the men waved and shouted out ribald suggestions to girls who caught their eye, but most marched solemnly and wordlessly past us and out the castle gates. I saw many faces I recognized, footmen and craftsmen who had asked to take up arms in the king's service. Some I had known since they were boys. And others, so many others, from loyal families who had traveled from throughout the kingdom to join our cause. Crowds lined the path that led into town, and their shouts soared up to join ours as the army paraded past them. Beside me, Rose's voice grew husky with cheering; only Queen Lenore remained silent.

Last to emerge were the king and his knights. They rode the finest horses from the royal stables, bred for speed and strength, draped this day in the royal colors. The animals jerked at their reins impatiently as the men steered them toward the viewing platform. These were the favored few who would be leading the charges, urging on others with their own bravery. Their servants followed behind, as ready to tend to their masters on a muddied field as in a bedchamber.

Only a few locks of Dorian's deep gold hair escaped from the front of his helmet, but I would have known his broad frame even if his back had been turned. Upon sighting me he flashed an elated smile. At last he found himself in the position he had trained for his whole life. My heart swelled with pride. Never had I been happier to call him my husband.

The king rode up to Queen Lenore and pulled his horse to a stop. She rose and presented him with a handkerchief embroidered with her family seal. He touched the cloth to his lips before tucking it under the front of his saddle. Then, breaking with the formality of the proceedings, he clutched his wife's hands and kissed them. A deafening roar broke out from the crowd; no doubt a similar sound had been heard when King Ranolf first embraced his beautiful new bride so long ago. Queen Lenore's eyes welled up with tears, obscuring what might be her last view of the man she had once loved so deeply. Years of threats had sapped them both, and that moment gave me hope that some remnant of their old affection still remained.

The king turned to Rose, who threw herself into his arms. He allowed his face to fall into his daughter's auburn hair, and his hands cradled her back. It recalled an image of heartbreaking clarity: those same hands cupping her tiny body on the day she was born, smiling with gratitude when other men would have been raging against fate. Gradually, gently, he pulled away from Rose's grasp and lowered the front of his helmet. This signal of resolve sent observers into another round of cheers, but I wondered if it was done to hide his expression after such a leave-taking.

The king's followers moved to take their places behind him at the gates. Dorian suddenly veered off and pulled his horse in my direction.

"Elise."

Surprised to be singled out, I walked to the very edge of the platform, so he would not have to shout his words.

Dorian's face softened into the same pensive expression I had glimpsed the night before. Stripped of his jaunty self-confidence, he appeared older, yet also more at peace.

"You've been a better wife to me than I deserve," he said. "I may have given you cause to regret your vows, but I have never regretted mine."

Flustered, I shook my head quickly, suddenly wishing I had thought to give him a token of my favor.

"When this is over, I'll do better," he said. "I don't expect you to believe a change will come easy, but I will make myself worthy of you."

I waited for the guffaw that would signal an elaborate joke at my expense. It did not come. Dorian took hold of my sleeve and drew me toward him, brashly kissing me on the lips before everyone. My face flushed with both shame and pleasure, and I buried my head in the curve of his neck, as I had so often in the privacy of our room.

How I wish I had told him! What joy it would have given Dorian to know he had fathered a child. Instead, noting the scandalized glances of the other ladies-in-waiting, I looked downward modestly and said nothing. Rose quickly turned her face forward in a vain attempt to deny her eavesdropping. The horns sounded as King Ranolf took his place before his men at the gates. Dorian dug his feet into his stirrups and urged his horse toward the men whose lives he commanded.

And so I watched my husband brace himself for bloodshed, praying with my whole heart for his safe return. For all his failings, he would be a proud, affectionate father, and I wanted my son or daughter to have what I never did.

Sheer numbers assured a certain victory for our troops, we told ourselves that summer. Sir Hugill, Rose's future husband, had raised an army of hundreds from his lands, and other nobles from throughout the kingdom joined up in support. On an open field of battle, the size of our forces would have had the clear advantage. But the reports we received told of skirmishes and teases, for the deRauleys and their followers were wise enough to avoid direct engagement. They tricked the king's lookouts into reporting false positions, then robbed the army's supply train while the troops were mustering elsewhere. They preferred to do their killing in stealth, without honor. Messages to and from the soldiers were delivered only occasionally, but the few lines I received from Dorian were sobering.

"Two of my men cut down by arrows today," he wrote in a rough, uneven scrawl. *"I have yet to see the enemy I came to fight."* The letter ended with promises of victory, not love, but I had not been so foolish as to expect such declarations. That he had taken the time to write at all was a mark of his affection.

It was easy for dark thoughts to take hold in those days. The grand rooms and wide passageways sat eerily empty without the shouts and heavy footfalls of the men who had gone off to fight, and I retired each night to a bedroom that felt hollow and lifeless without Dorian's boisterous presence. The uncertain times dampened

Rose's willfulness, and she no longer complained of boredom or begged for dancing after dinner. Dutifully, she consulted Sir Walthur for news of the war and requested a map be drawn up so she could follow the army's progress. But she had not entirely abandoned her secret wanderings. One day when I pointed out mud on the hem of her skirt, she admitted she had been to St. Elsip's harbor. I scolded her on the dangers of mingling among the unsavory characters who frequented the wharves, but she waved away my concerns.

"I felt drawn to the water, Elise," she said. "Perhaps it was the sight of all those boats, so full of possibility. Can you imagine sailing off for a land you have never seen? The thrill of not knowing where you will be next month—or next year?"

"I sleep better knowing exactly where I will be next month," I said tartly. "In my own comfortable bed."

She laughed, yet a certain melancholy hovered over Rose in the following days. As is so often the case, I did not recognize the depth of her discontent until I looked at her life through an outsider's eyes. Some months after the troops had marched northward, my niece, Prielle, came to the castle bearing the news of my aunt Agna's death. It was not unexpected—she had been in poor health for some time—yet I took the news hard. Another tie between me and my mother had been severed, and though Aunt Agna was not of an effusive nature, she had welcomed me in at a time when I had nothing, and for that I would always be grateful.

I ushered Prielle into the Receiving Room, though it was usually reserved for visitors of higher rank. She gave an account of Aunt Agna's last hours, and when I asked how her mother was coping, Prielle grew unusually evasive. Gently, gradually, I drew out the truth: The family's cloth trade had been badly damaged by the closing of routes through the north, and relations between her parents had grown as strained as their finances. I had long suspected that my cousin Damilla's husband was one of those men who consider wife beating a necessity rather than a choice, and I feared that a fall in the family's fortune would only shorten his temper. But what could I do? Prielle was only sixteen, still a ward of her parents, and I was hardly in a position to take over her care.

"You are so lucky, Elise."

I remembered hearing those same words from Rose, long ago, when she spoke of my marrying Dorian for love. "My father was a difficult man," I told Prielle now. "I know what it is to cower in a corner during a fight."

"No, I mean I envy your life here. Surrounded by such lovely things." Prielle's eyes gazed in wonder at the tapestries and the gilded furniture, sights I had long since taken for granted. "I would give anything to live as Princess Rose does."

And she would give anything for your freedom, I thought. At that moment it seemed a cruel trick of fate that these two young women should have been born in circumstances so contrary to their natures: Rose, with her quick mind and strong opinions, would have made a splendid merchant's daughter, while Prielle's gentle manner and appreciation of beauty would have been prized in any royal family.

"Her life is not as easy as you imagine," I said carefully. "We must all do what we can with the position we have been granted." These, too, were words I had once said to Rose, though Prielle was more likely to heed them. "I hope you will remember that I am here as your friend, should you need me."

Prielle squeezed my hand in gratitude, and I offered a tour of the

Great Hall and the castle garden to distract her from weightier topics. But I could not look at Prielle—that sweet, innocent girl—and not fear for her future. Without Aunt Agna's stern presence, her parents' enmity would be given free rein. I was helpless, however, to effect any change in Prielle's circumstances. My influence at court, such as it was, could not be wielded in her favor; she was of too humble a family to serve as a lady-in-waiting yet too educated and refined to be hired on as a servant.

I hugged her fiercely as we bade each other farewell, hoping the press of my fingers might instill some of my strength into her delicate body.

"We must not allow fear to quash our spirits," I said.

I said it as much for myself as for her. Concern for Prielle had now been added to my worry for Queen Lenore, and Dorian, and all the soldiers who served with him. Prielle smiled tentatively, an action that revealed a burgeoning loveliness. Her still-immature body had the angularity that comes with rapid growth, but once her face and figure filled out, she would be quite beautiful. Perhaps that would be enough to win her a good marriage, despite her family's precarious situation.

I attempted to greet each day with hope rather than dread, yet the same could not be said for Queen Lenore. Charged with ruling the kingdom in her husband's absence, she increasingly sought guidance through prayer with Father Gabriel rather than in conversation with the king's advisers. Sir Walthur muttered in frustration that the monk might as well be given a seat in the Council Chamber, and he stealthily managed most affairs himself, without the queen's knowledge. Hoping to effect a reconciliation between them, I urged Queen Lenore to attend a meeting of the council.

"The people look to you for leadership," I said. "It would be a great boost to their spirits if you were seen tending to state business."

"No, no," she protested. "Sir Walthur and the others care only for worldly matters. I must serve my subjects through prayer."

"A worthy mission," I said. "Yet a queen cannot remove herself from the world completely, can she?"

I said the words gently, with a smile, but she reacted as if I had slapped her.

"How can you not understand?" she asked, stricken. "We are steeped in sin, every one of us. Our very souls are in peril." For all her increasing interest in religious matters, I had never heard her speak of her beliefs in such stark terms.

"My lady, God shows mercy to those who repent, does he not? Whatever transgressions you may have committed have long since been forgiven."

She began to cry, crumpling into racking sobs that shook her frail shoulders. To see the woman I had so long admired undone by such misery was profoundly shocking, and for a moment I was at a loss as to what to do. Cautiously, I wrapped my arms around her and comforted her in the way I would a small child, with murmured assurances that all would be well. I do not know if she heard me, consumed as she was by grief. In time her cries softened into whimpers. She wiped her tears on the sleeve of her gown and looked up at me warily. Her dark, expressive eyes, still beautiful, still mesmerizing, stared at me with desperate intensity.

"Do you really believe I will be forgiven?"

"I do."

"To receive forgiveness one must offer it. That is what Father Gabriel says."

A burst of jealousy swelled within me, and I flashed back to my earliest days as Queen Lenore's attendant, to the envy I felt when she and Isla would laugh together in their native tongue. Once again I felt myself pushed aside in favor of another.

Or perhaps not, for I had a secret that could forge a new bond between us. Swallowing down my childish envy, I said, "I will defer to Father Gabriel in spiritual matters. But I must ask you to add someone new to your prayer list."

Her eyes widened in surprise, then delight, as I told her of the child growing within me. It was still early days—I had not yet felt the baby move—but I rightly suspected that it would distract the queen from her gloomy state. I asked her to tell no one else at present, even Rose, and she savored the secret as a precious gift, an offering of hope for the future.

As the heat mounted, our ambitions dwindled, and the summer days passed in a lethargic stupor. I walked in the garden, toiled over needlework with the other ladies-in-waiting, and attempted to plow my way through one of Sir Walthur's dry books of philosophy. I visited Flora most days, sometimes with Rose, whose vivaciousness sparked a long-lost twinkle of joy in the old woman's eyes. Most girls of Rose's age are unsettled by signs of the body's decline, but she never flinched at the sight of Flora's toothless gums or the touch of her gnarled fingers. She sat patiently through her great-aunt's rambling stories of times past, even as certain anecdotes were retold word for word from one day to the next. I waited anxiously for tales of Millicent to surface; Rose knew only that Flora's sister had left the castle in disgrace years before, and I dreaded facing her questions. Despite my fears, Flora never mentioned Millicent's name. It was as if she had never existed.

Most of our evenings passed quietly, with all the ladies retiring shortly after supper, but one night will forever stand out in my memories of that time. A group of traveling nuns took shelter at the castle, having heard of the queen's warm hospitality to religious pilgrims, and after we shared a meal, the eldest offered to play her harp. Music was a gift from the Lord, she told Queen Lenore, and playing for his glory was her form of prayer. I felt the presence of the divine as the woman coaxed notes from the strings, plucking with a delicacy and speed that could only have been the result of holy intervention. The peaceful spirit lingered even after I had returned to my room, and I went to sleep lulled by my memory of the music surrounding me.

I awoke in the middle of the night, troubled by a dream that I was drowning in a bath. I shifted back and forth, trying to shake the sensation, before I realized that the wetness against my legs was no illusion. By the faint, dying embers of the fire, I saw dark crimson staining the sheets. I cried out then, a desperate, horrified wail. I will never forget Sir Walthur's face when he stormed in, clutching a candle, disgust crumpling his features at the sight before him. He backed away, muttering that he would summon a maid.

"Mrs. Tewkes!" I begged. "Please, fetch Mrs. Tewkes!"

I lay there some minutes before she came. By the time she bustled in, her eyes weighted with sleep but concerned, I did not need her to tell me. I had lost the baby.

She had confronted such heartbreaking scenes before. With brisk ease she pulled the stained linens from the bed and eased my shift off my shoulders. As I shuddered, naked, she wiped the blood from my legs with water so cold it turned my skin to ice. She swaddled my legs in clean cloths before pulling a fresh nightdress over me.

"Anika will be here soon with blankets," she said. "I'll have her relight the fire."

I could not stop trembling. Mrs. Tewkes lay on the bed next to me and wrapped her arms around my shoulders.

"Shall I stay until you sleep?" she murmured.

I did not see how sleep could ever claim me again. Mrs. Tewkes held me in her embrace as I cried, my body heaving with such force that the howls threatened to break through my chest. Then my voice fell to an exhausted moan and my eyes, drained of tears, closed. Before I knew it, morning had come, and I awoke in my marriage bed, alone.

Fourteen

THE BURDENS OF LOSS

The sorrow was mine alone to carry. The servant girl Anika brought a bowl of broth soon after I woke, saying Mrs. Tewkes had told her I had fallen ill and would be spending the day resting in bed. I drifted in and out of sleep, rising once to change the blood-soaked cloth between my legs as my chest shuddered with withheld sobs. My dreams brought relief, but the knowledge of my loss struck with fresh force on each awakening. Awash in grief, I was thankful I had held my secret close. The sight of my own devastation reflected in others' eyes might have blinded me.

I kept to myself for two days. Sir Walthur must have guessed the nature of the incident that bloodied my sheets, but he did not impose upon my isolation, for which I was grateful. The unnerving silence of the room heightened my despair, and I might have plummeted still further into misery had Queen Lenore not paid me an unexpected visit. Throughout my years at the castle, I had taken pride in my self-reliance, but I clung to her like a child as the last barriers between us crumbled. She was no longer my ruler or mistress;

she was my friend, come to offer a lifeline of hope. My mother's face had grown indistinct over the years, but I could remember vividly how it felt to be held thus, to be comforted by someone who loved me.

The winter storms came early that year, and the ladies of the castle hovered before their hearths, the only place one could shake off the chill emanating from the stone walls. The unexpected cold dealt a more significant blow to the king's army, leaving them trapped on the far side of the avalanche-prone northern mountains. Denied a return to St. Elsip to wait out the winter, they dug in to shelters in remote villages as the rebels withdrew to their forts. A few valiant messengers braved the icy peaks to bring us news of our army's fate: The king's soldiers were forced to scavenge for food, these weary men told us, but their spirits were high and their taste for battle unquenched.

Given the uncertain times, Rose's seventeenth birthday was celebrated with little ceremony, yet she used the occasion to strike a blow for independence that shocked us all. From the time she was a baby, she had slept in a bedchamber adjoining her mother's sitting room; now she declared her intention to move to the North Tower. Queen Lenore, appalled, said she would hear of no such thing, but in the end she wearily succumbed to her daughter's tearful pleas.

When I expressed my surprise at her sudden change of heart, the queen said, "How can I deny my daughter some small measure of happiness? She has had precious little reason to smile in these bleak times. And Father Gabriel assures me that she may well benefit from a certain degree of independence."

The monk stood at her side, basking in his role as the queen's most trusted counselor. I did not think it at all wise to let Rose loose in an all-but-deserted section of the castle, out of earshot of the royal apartments, but I knew it was fruitless to go against his wishes. I nodded in a manner intended to be gracious, but Father Gabriel must have noted the grim set of my mouth, for his cold stare offered a silent challenge. I had been acknowledged as a rival, and I would be dealt with accordingly.

When Rose dragged me off to see the rooms she had chosen at the top of the tower, I could not help admitting to their charm. The main door opened into a semicircular receiving room, formed by the round turret walls, and the bedchamber lay through an arch embellished with engravings of twisted vines. Rose had brought in embroidered tapestries and covered the bed with purple velvet hangings to mark the place as her own. Despite the gray skies, the rooms felt bright and airy, with windows that were taller and wider than those elsewhere in the building.

Rose waved a hand toward the landscape outside. "Do you understand now, Elise?"

While most windows in the castle's upper levels looked out onto St. Elsip or the busy courtyards, Rose's view was of the open tournament field where her father and his knights so often competed, with grassy, rolling hills extending into the distance beyond. It was the countryside where she had learned to ride, where she had ventured with her mother on balmy summer days, stopping to enjoy a meal in the shade of an oak tree.

"Do you know how many times I dreamed of riding off toward that horizon? I thought I could keep going and going, until I arrived at a place where I was merely Rose, not a royal princess." Her voice sank to little more than a whisper. "A foolish fancy."

I could understand the lure of that vista, but for me the price to obtain it was too high. How could Rose tolerate the oppressive quiet of the North Tower, much less welcome it? I suspected that the change in quarters had been prompted by her impending marriage: a last chance to fashion a private retreat, where she could do as she pleased before submitting to the duties expected of a wife and ruler. But if claiming this section of the castle was a gesture of defiance, it was also an acknowledgment of her own isolation. She had no real friends, no one of her own age she could speak to freely. Rose and her maid, Besslin, did not share the trust that had bonded me to Queen Lenore, and the other young women who lived at the castle owed their living to the king; none would risk offending Rose's family by speaking their mind. It was, in many ways, a lonely existence.

Rose turned from the window, her expression solemn. "Elise, there is something I wish to ask you. I fear that my mother is sparing me the truth of the war's progress. Is it true the army has been greatly weakened by the winter?"

"You must not allow every little rumor to upset you," I admonished, smoothing the linens of her bed. Like many women who had spent their lives in service, I found the work done by anyone younger severely lacking, and Besslin appeared particularly lax in her duties.

"It upsets me if my father is close to defeat."

I turned and spoke in a sharp tone I would never have used with another of her station. "How can you say such a thing?"

"It's growing warmer. The snow in the mountains must be melting. Why have we heard nothing of our troops advancing?"

I had wondered the same thing. As it often did in times of trouble, my mind returned to Millicent's curse, her promise to take Rose at the height of her beauty. Was this the form Millicent's revenge would take, with Prince Bowen victorious and Rose dead at his hand, a sacrifice to his terrible lust for power? The very thought sickened me, but I feared he would not hold back from such atrocities.

"War is unpredictable by nature," I said. "Your father's men are the best-trained in the kingdom. They will prevail."

"They must." Rose stared at me with passionate intensity. She was not ready to rule, far from it, and I ached in that moment for all she had lost. Her mind should be taken up with thoughts of suitors and gowns, not the possible death of her father. "If all men had the strength of your husband, I would not doubt our chances of victory." She sat on the bed and ran her fingers along the curved embroidery of the bedspread. "Do you miss him?"

"Dorian? Yes, at times. But I cannot begrudge him a chance to serve in battle. He's longed for it his whole life."

Rose cast her eyes downward, suddenly shy. "Was it as you expected? Marriage?"

The wariness of her request, as if she were bracing herself for bad news, took me by surprise. I had never spoken of my true feelings for Dorian to anyone. And what were my feelings? They changed from day to day.

I considered my words carefully. "I had resigned myself to life as a spinster. Yet marriage suits me more than I expected."

"Ah, but you married for love," Rose said.

I smiled, amused. Love had played no part in Dorian's matrimonial plans, or mine. Whatever bond had formed between us had begun with sheer physical lust. Then I remembered the way Dorian had kissed me in the courtyard, in full view of the crowd. The promise he had made to be a better husband. Why do such things, if not for love?

"Affection can blossom with time," I assured her. "Sir Hugill is a good man, from all accounts." Those same accounts had also painted him as stern and humorless, hardly appealing qualities to one of Rose's temperament.

"I am sure he is worthy of my respect," Rose said dutifully. "It is only—" She looked away, hesitating over her next words. "I had hoped for more."

With the instant understanding that comes to faithful servants, I knew she was thinking of Joffrey. I remembered his dark eyes glinting with pleasure as Rose danced gracefully before him. It could never be more than a youthful diversion: Even if the king could extract Rose from the contract with Sir Hugill, she would never be allowed to marry someone who did not hail from a royal family. But what was the harm in mooning over a handsome young man? I welcomed any distraction from the dismal mood at court.

"I would not be surprised if a certain ambassador returned to dance with you as soon as the war is over," I said. "Mind you, he'll have to fight Sir Hugill for your favor. I imagine it will be quite a battle."

"Oh, really?" she asked playfully. "And who would be the victor?"

"Well, Joffrey has the advantage of youth. But we must not discount Sir Hugill's raging passion, which comes through so clearly in his letters."

Rose laughed and turned from the window. "Bless you, Elise. You know how to lighten my spirits."

"And you mine," I replied. Together we relived the night of Joffrey's visit, when Rose had first felt the stirrings of what could become love. He was the first man from outside the kingdom she had ever conversed with, and it was clear that she was taken by his tales of travel and exotic lands. She would not tell me what they had spoken of during their time in the Receiving Room; she took pleasure in keeping that one moment private, to be savored alone. Just as I savored my memories of Dorian as I lay in bed that night, imagining his homecoming and how we might celebrate.

The spring thaw on which our army had set its hopes was accompanied by torrential rains, creating impassable mud-soaked bogs. It was as if nature itself had taken the rebels' side. The weather dealt a further blow to the merchants of St. Elsip, whose businesses were already suffering due to the war, and my visits to Damilla and Prielle were overshadowed by a pervading sense of gloom. When I took Prielle aside and asked how she fared, she told me she suspected that her father was dipping into her dowry in order to pay the family's creditors.

"With no dowry what will become of me?" she asked.

I wanted to shake her parents out of their shortsighted selfishness. Could they not see that their daughter was their most precious possession, the thing they should cherish and protect above all? But Prielle begged me to say nothing, and I feared that her father would take his anger out on her if I spoke up.

"I'll see you married well," I promised. "Dorian has plenty of money. He will be happy to pay for your dowry if need be."

Prielle leaned into me as I wrapped my arms around her narrow shoulders. "Everything is changing, Elise," she said sadly. "I no longer know what my future holds."

"Nor can any of us," I said. "But you will not face it alone. I promise."

I hoped to present an image of strength to my frightened young cousin, but, in truth, recent events at the castle had shaken my own faith that all would be well once the war was over. The burden of leading without her husband's guidance for almost a year had devastated Queen Lenore's already precarious mental state, and I found it impossible to recapture the easy manner in which we once conversed. According to her maid, Heva, the queen rarely slept more than a few hours a night, rising well before dawn to begin her daily prayers. Even more worrisome, Heva had noted disturbing red marks on the queen's back, which she recognized as signs of the flagellation indulged in by the most fervent religious mystics. Sickened at the thought of such self-abuse, I marched off to confront Father Gabriel. Queen Lenore would never do such a thing without his encouragement.

To my surprise, he listened to my concerns with sympathy. However, he claimed himself powerless to control her actions.

"I am no more the queen's master than you are," he said, hands clasped before him. I noted the dirt ringing his fingernails, the stink of his grimy robe. How had the queen, known for her love of beauty, become entranced by such a character? "If she feels moved by the Holy Spirit to mortify her flesh, then she will do so."

There was only one event in Queen Lenore's otherwise blameless life that could bring on such self-loathing. Had she told Father Gabriel of the oath she had sworn at Millicent's urging? If so, then his hold over her was complete.

"How can the queen's disfigurement be pleasing to the Lord?" I asked.

"Do you presume to know the ways of our Father?" he retorted.

"The queen is following her own path to redemption, and I believe she will find it, sooner than you think."

And who will declare her redeemed? I came close to demanding. *You, when it serves your purpose?* For all his pious talk, Father Gabriel had revealed an all-too-human satisfaction in besting me. I wondered again, as I had before, what kept him among us. Genuine spiritual concern for the queen? Or the opportunity to sway a noblewoman of unsound mind? Despite my suspicions, Father Gabriel showed no signs of corruption; he had accumulated no possessions during his months at the castle, and Mrs. Tewkes told me he had received no payments from the household accounts. He even refused Queen Lenore's repeated offers of a bedroom, preferring to remain in his sleeping corner in the kitchen. Still, I vowed to keep a closer eye on his dealings with the queen. If she showed further signs of decline, I would put the blame firmly at Father Gabriel's feet, no matter what the consequences.

Sir Walthur's increasing dejection was another cause for concern. Our daily interactions were brief and formal; unlike other men of stature, he did not make conversation for the pleasure of hearing his own voice. He spent most evenings in front of the crackling fireplace in our sitting room, lost in thought, and I rarely disturbed his solitude. But one night he sat with his shoulders more hunched than usual, his face creased in worry, and my stomach lurched with a premonition of disaster.

I blurted out, "Has there been word from Dorian?"

Sir Walthur turned to me in surprise and shook his head. "No, none."

"I am sorry," I apologized. "I thought you might have received news."

Sir Walthur shot me a glare I took at first for irritation. Then I realized his eyes were fixed upon me intently, curious.

"What have you heard?" he asked urgently.

"Nothing," I protested. "I speak only as a wife who wishes to see her husband safely home."

Sir Walthur grunted. He put down his spoon and placed his hands flat on the table. "If it sets your mind at ease, I learned something that may turn the tide in our favor."

He watched as the meaning of his words settled across my face. "You know when to keep your mouth shut, unlike most other women. That is the only reason I speak of this. If I hear you have whispered of this to another person . . ."

"I would never betray a confidence," I countered smoothly.

"Very well." Sir Walthur pushed his empty bowl away and took a sip of his wine. He gripped the stem of the glass with his fist, an inelegant grasp that marked him instantly as a man of humble birth. Despite all his years at court, he had never mastered the manners of the aristocracy. Either he did not care or he took a perverse pride in flaunting his lack of pretension.

"I received word today that the Brithnians may be induced to join our cause," he said.

Given their fierce reputation, the Brithnians would be welcome partners on the battlefield. But did the need for such an alliance mean that our soldiers could not win the war on their own?

"Dorian told me our men could easily defeat the deRauleys," I said carefully.

"It appeared so. Even the king boasted they would return victorious in a matter of weeks. But nine months have passed and we have yet to fight a battle. Our adversaries appear intent on bringing us down with cunning. They attack at night, in secret, killing two here, three there, before disappearing into the darkness. Our losses are mounting, and we are no closer to rooting them out of their mountain hideaways."

The fragments of news passed around the castle had told otherwise, of frightened rebels on the run. Had such stories arisen from wishful thinking, or had they been purposely created to keep our hopes alive?

"Our men remain determined," Sir Walthur reassured me, "and they will prevail in the end. But our army has been weakened, much more than we expected. If the king returns with Marl deRauley's head but only half his knights, would it still be cause for celebration?"

Half his knights? It was not possible. The leaders of that army were Dorian's childhood friends, the husbands of women I spoke to every day. Such a bleak outlook meant Dorian was in greater danger than I imagined.

"And if the Brithnians take our side?" I asked.

"Victory would be ours," Sir Walthur said. "The Brithnians bring a certain ruthlessness our men lack. It comes of living in that miserable land, I suppose. Death is so common a feature of their lives that they do not fear it and they fight to the bitter end. Whether they can be trusted is another matter. Most likely Bowen is haggling for their services as well. In that, at least, we have the upper hand. Our treasury is far more persuasive than the meager fortune of the deRauleys."

"The Brithnian king would never take up arms against us!" I argued. "He has sworn himself a friend to King Ranolf."

Sir Walthur laughed, a bitter sound with no trace of amusement. "You have heard too many of the queen's sentimental tales. Money, not fellowship, is what forges alliances on the battlefield."

I knew that armies were often bought and sold for bags of gold. But Sir Walthur's offhand acceptance of such arrangements struck me as a betrayal of his own son's beliefs. Dorian enjoyed luxurious clothing and fine food, but he was not driven by the pursuit of riches. He fought because he had the soul of a soldier, proud to shed blood in the service of a greater good. Not all warriors seek battle as a way to line their pockets.

Sir Walthur pushed back his chair with an abrupt clatter and stood. "I must return to the Council Chamber," he said, reaching for one of the candles that lit our table. "We are sending an offer to the Brithnians in the morning. Only a few hours remain to calculate what we are willing to pay for victory."

He approached my side of the table and placed a hand on my shoulder. "You have served my son well," he said quietly. "I will do whatever I can to bring him home."

Sir Walthur was not one for emotional confidences, and I knew that this was the closest he would come to acknowledging that he had developed a certain affection for me. And if I had given Dorian an heir? How much would he value me then? An ache spread through my empty womb.

Sir Walthur's footsteps echoed down the hall, and I finished my supper alone by the dim light of the remaining candle. I had no knowledge of the kingdom's finances, but there must be gold enough to ensure the Brithnians' loyalty. Queen Lenore would empty the treasury if it meant the king's safe return.

Sir Walthur's pleas for discretion were well heeded, for I heard nothing of the Brithnians in the following days. It was only some weeks later that their appearance on the battlefield was announced, news hailed as if it were tidings of victory itself. Where the Brithnians had been scorned for years as dangerous, ill-kempt scoundrels, they were now praised as brave warriors, with much talk of the fond feelings between their king and ours. Whatever payments went to Brithnia were handed over in secret.

The news of the Brithnian reinforcements was the last we heard from the north for some time. I remember an endless succession of days, all spent waiting for word that never came. Additional guards were posted on the castle walls, each hoping to be the first to spot a messenger bearing the royal standard. In town the Easter festival passed with quiet prayers and reflection, the maypoles and dancing of past years eschewed. Queen Lenore froze whenever the door to her apartments opened, then slumped with disappointment when the visitor was revealed to be Lady Wintermale or a servant inquiring on a household matter. Rose sought distraction through literature, escaping to her room for hours at a time to write a poem in celebration of her father's victory. Thankful she had found a way to occupy herself during her ever-restless nights, I slipped her a few extra candles so her maid would not report to the queen how often Rose sat awake scribbling.

It was during those endless, expectant days that Flora entered her final decline. Though she lay unresponsive, barely conscious, I kept vigil by her bed, not wanting her to pass her final hours alone. At times I sat quietly, holding her hand; at other moments I was moved to pray. I do not know what provoked me to sing on that last night. Flora had told me Lorenz taught her the simple folk song during their brief courtship—perhaps I thought it would bring a final remembrance of past happiness.

"Mother."

I had to lean closer to make sure I had heard. Her eyes remained closed, as if she were dreaming.

"Mother. He is gone."

Flora's weak voice still had the inflections of a young woman shattered by heartbreak. I rubbed her hand, wishing I could find words to ease her anguish.

"Why? Why did he leave me?"

I could not bear to hear her relive Lorenz's suicide, his death casting a shadow over her own. Sometimes the truth is not ours to know, and her last moments should not be spent agonizing over events so long in the past. She deserved a peaceful end.

"He is waiting," I whispered. "Go to him."

Flora's breathing slowed. I watched the laborious intake and outgo of air. Then, hesitantly, she croaked, "Elise."

Caught by surprise, I leaned forward, until my face was almost pressed against hers.

"Yes, I am here."

"I am so sorry."

I shook my head, anxious to reassure her. "Hush. You have no amends to make with me."

Each sound was an effort, coming out through ragged breaths, as she summoned the will to utter a final warning.

"She is coming. I cannot stop her."

Fifteen

TILL DEATH DO US PART

We expected the end of the war to be announced with fanfare and rejoicing. Yet I have always found that the most life-altering events pounce without warning. As a girl I woke from a feverish dream to find most of my family dead. Years later I began one day a spinster, only to find myself betrothed by supper to a man I barely knew. And it was not so long ago that I had fallen asleep imagining the feel of a tiny baby's hand, then awakened to find my sheets awash in blood. So it was with the tidings that finally made their way to us from the north, mere hours after Flora had been laid to rest in the crypt of the royal chapel.

Later I learned that the confusion was the fault of the guards. Only the youngest and least skilled soldiers had remained to defend the castle, and those given the night watch had fallen asleep at their posts by dawn. The riders' presence was not noted until they arrived at the front gates and shouted to be admitted. The men were so ragged and their horses so ill used that the ancient gatekeeper, half addled and suddenly torn from sleep, thought them brigands and denied them entrance. Then a voice rang out, and the gatekeeper knew it for the king's.

Following the pattern set by years in service, it was my habit to rise early, and I had just finished dressing when I heard cries from beyond my window. I peered out and saw two grooms leading a pair of panting horses through the doors of the stables. It was an unusual time for visitors, but I gave it no further thought until I stepped into the front room and heard footsteps clattering through the hall outside.

I looked out the door and saw Anika racing toward me. She would have continued past had I not grabbed her by the elbow and demanded to know the cause of such commotion.

"The king has returned!" she cried, her eyes bright with panic. "I've been sent to the kitchens for hot water."

I released her sleeve, speechless with shock. The bread I had planned to eat for breakfast dropped from my hand as I rushed to the stairs. By the time I reached the royal apartments, I was running. I staggered through the door of the queen's sitting room only to stop so suddenly that I almost fell from the effort. There, before me, stood Queen Lenore, still in her sleeping gown, her hair falling in waves down her back. Before her, on his knees, was the king, clutching her body as a drowning man clings to a branch held out as salvation. Had it not been for his fur-trimmed tunic, embroidered with the royal seal, I would not have known him. His neat beard had grown out to a scraggly mass of tangles; his skin was red and weather-beaten, his eyes closed and sunken.

Queen Lenore stared at me, her own eyes wide with panic.

"I will fetch someone to tend to the king," I said calmly, my voice belying my fear. The king's attendants had ridden north with him; had any returned? And what of Dorian? I was about to ask for news of my husband, but Queen Lenore stopped me with a sharp glance, and rightly so. The king looked as if he could barely speak.

"I will tend to him." Queen Lenore reached out carefully with one hand and pressed it gently against the king's head. "Fetch clean clothes. He cannot be seen like this."

"Of course." I heard scuffling behind me, as servants and attendants gathered in the hall to await orders. "Shall I close the door?"

The queen nodded, her attention already returned to her husband. I slipped away and pushed back against the press of people outside. I caught sight of Lady Wintermale toward the rear, trying in vain to elbow her way through.

"What news?" she demanded. At her words the crowd around us hushed.

I shook my head. "I do not know." From King Ranolf's ravaged state, I feared there would be little cause for rejoicing. But I could tell no one what I had seen.

I reached out my arm and pulled Lady Wintermale forward. "The queen wishes to be alone with the king," I whispered in her ear. "Please see she is not disturbed."

When I returned with the king's clothing, I opened the door a crack, just enough to slide the folded bundle through the opening and into Heva's hands.

"The king wishes to address the court," she whispered. "Everyone is to gather in the Great Hall. But first the queen has asked for Rose."

I nodded. In all my imaginings of the king's return, I had pictured scenes of celebration, not the parade of long faces and worried grimaces that passed me in the halls. People moved quietly, carefully. Waiting.

Rose was still asleep when I arrived at her room. Her maid, Besslin, had taken advantage of her mistress's weariness to laze around herself, though she jumped quickly enough from her pallet when I came through the door.

"Fetch a gown," I ordered, then went to sit on Rose's bed. She was so beautiful as she slept, with her thick auburn hair swirled around her pillow and her skin flushed slightly pink. It was the most peaceful I had seen her in months.

I ran a finger along her cheek, and her eyes fluttered open. Seeing me, she jolted awake and sat up, alert with worry.

"Your father has returned," I said, smiling to reassure her. "He is safe."

"Lord be praised," Rose breathed. She pushed the covers off and slid from the bed. "Where is he?"

"I have just left him, in your mother's room."

Rose was in such a state it was all Besslin and I could do to arrange her dress suitably before she slid on her silk slippers and rushed for the door. She dashed along the corridors and down the stairs, so quickly that I was some distance away when she threw open the door to her mother's room. I heard her cry out as she entered, and then the door slammed shut, blocking the family's reunion from the curious eyes outside.

"We are called to the Great Hall," I urged the gathered courtiers. "Downstairs, everyone."

As I climbed down the main staircase to the Entrance Hall, I saw

Mrs. Tewkes waiting below. She swiftly maneuvered her way to my side.

"I saw Rengard, the footman who rode back with the king." She spoke quickly, with the cadence of one desperate to pack in more words than time allows. "His shoulder was cut so deeply it was a wonder he was able to stay on his horse. He said our men were victorious, but there was no joy in his words. What can it mean?"

My stomach churned with dread. I told her I did not know, that we must wait for the king, as we joined the stream of people entering the Great Hall. By the time King Ranolf arrived, the room was full. The nobles and favored families took their usual places in the front, facing the dais; servants lined the walls in the back. Personal maids stood behind their mistresses, while the farthest corners were filled with groomsmen and chambermaids, cooks and laundresses. I have never seen so many people gather in such silence.

The hush did not lift with the arrival of the king and his family. The broken man I had glimpsed earlier had vanished, replaced by a noble leader who walked proudly, his chin jutting forward and his bright eyes staring confidently ahead. To the maids and pages in the back, he would have appeared little altered by the trials of battle. Yet those whom he passed by directly must have noted the changes: the hair more gray than auburn, the slight hesitation with each step, the stiffness of his arms. Over the months of his absence, he had aged years.

The king took Queen Lenore's hand and bade her sit, then did the same for Rose. Both women were dressed in their formal finery, their somber expressions suitable to the occasion. Rose, her customary liveliness stifled, could have been a statue.

"I bring good tidings from the field of battle." The king's voice echoed against the stone walls. "The deRauleys are defeated. The kingdom is saved."

For a moment the words floated around us, above our understanding. Then a cheer rang out among the pages and stableboys, followed by shouts from the older men in the back. The sound rose as it passed among the maids, swelling as voice after voice joined in. I alone did not cry out, for I saw no jubilation in the king's eyes.

King Ranolf raised his hand, and a hush returned to the room.

"This is joyous news, and we will celebrate in good time. But our success has come at a great cost. Our adversaries fought hard and without mercy. We lost many fine men, among them, I am sorry to say, my daughter's intended husband, Sir Hugill."

I glanced at Rose, as did the whole court. True to her breeding, she maintained her poise, dropping her head in acknowledgment of his passing.

"Far too many others will return to us gravely injured," said the king. "You will have questions on the fate of loved ones, and I will answer them as best I can. But we will not know the full extent of our losses until our soldiers return home. Their progress will be slow, and I beg your patience."

A worried buzz began to spread through the knot of women surrounding me. They were the wives of knights, men who rode ahead of the foot soldiers, the first to engage the enemy. Men whose fine horses and expensive armor set them apart as especially worthy prizes. If there were heavy losses, our husbands would be among the victims. As the other women pushed their way toward the dais, addressing pleas to the king, I held back. If Dorian was dead, there would be no comfort in hearing the news first.

Most of the women received no answer to their questions. The king had been in the heat of battle himself, able to see only those who fell next to him, and had ridden from the battlefield with scarcely a moment to take in his victory. I watched one woman's face crumple as the king leaned down to speak, gently placing a hand on her shoulder. She staggered away, moaning with grief, and two of her cousins rushed to comfort her. Her husband was a friend of Dorian's, a hearty man whose voice carried a few lengths ahead of him. It was impossible to imagine him silenced forever.

As the crowd drifted apart and away from the room, Queen Lenore waved me over. I walked toward the dais, and she stepped before me.

"The king wishes to speak to you and Sir Walthur," she said, her hand touching my arm lightly.

Such a summons could only mean that the king wished to give us a personal account of Dorian's death. A peculiar calm settled over me, and I told myself I must honor my husband's memory by comporting myself well. I must not forget to thank the king, no matter how devastating the tale he told. I followed the king and queen across the hall to the Council Chamber, where Sir Walthur and the other advisers stood huddled in the doorway, talking in hushed tones. The king nodded to Sir Walthur. The other men, understanding the gesture as a dismissal, bowed quickly and turned away.

With Queen Lenore at my side, I followed the king and Sir Walthur inside. Though far smaller than the Great Hall, it was no less grand in its appointments. The walls were inlaid with carved panels depicting the kingdom's greatest wonders: the northern mountains, the cathedral of St. Elsip, the mighty river that coursed across the landscape. In the center of the room, an oval table made of dark wood had been polished until it gleamed. Gold candleholders taller than myself stood in the corners, their flickering light the only illumination in that tenebrous space.

"Dorian lives," the king said simply, and the intensity of my relief caught me by such surprise that I clutched the back of a chair, afraid I might crumple. Sir Walthur sucked in his breath, but his impassive expression did not change.

"Your son acquitted himself with great bravery," the king said, addressing Sir Walthur. "I intend to award him a title, for he saved my life."

The king clasped Sir Walthur's hand with his, and the gesture pierced my father-in-law's reserve. His mouth curved upward in the semblance of a smile, and his eyes welled with tears.

"My boy."

"Bowen would have killed me," the king said. "I did not think . . ." His voice drifted off, and I saw the weight of memory fall heavily upon him at the mention of his brother's name. He collected himself and continued.

"I never imagined he would come for me. I expected Marl and his thugs to relish the bloodshed, but I believed that Bowen would work his treachery out of sight. When I saw him riding toward me, I was so surprised I did not give a thought to defending myself. I sat and watched him come. His face . . . I did not know he hated me so."

I could picture Prince Bowen, enraged, brandishing his sword, riding at full power. Who would not quail at such a sight?

"Dorian was next to me. He had lost his helmet, and his armor was damaged. I ordered him to ride back and take a helmet from one of the men who had fallen. I was turned toward him, shouting my commands, when I heard a terrible cry to my left. I turned and saw Bowen. By the time I thought to raise my sword, Dorian had urged his horse between us and engaged with Bowen himself. The fight was short but fierce. I saw Dorian falter and fall from his horse. As he fell, he delivered a final thrust of his sword, piercing Bowen's stomach through a gap in his armor. He died there, before me."

"A bad end, but one he brought upon himself," Sir Walthur said bitterly.

"You said Dorian fell?" I asked anxiously. The men started at the sound of my voice, as if they had forgotten my presence, and I immediately regretted my forwardness.

"Yes"—the king nodded—"but he rose soon enough, and I rode off to share the news of Bowen's death with my men. By then Marl and his cousins had been killed as well and the few rebels remaining were running off in defeat."

The kingdom was saved, and my husband would return a hero. Humility was not among Dorian's virtues; a noble title would puff up his pride even more. But I would tend to him without complaint, for I had been given another chance at creating the family I longed for. Had I not heard tales of straying husbands who find their love for a loyal wife renewed after a brush with death? My relief at the king's news had proved vividly that my feelings for Dorian were more deeply rooted than I had allowed myself to believe.

I spent the following days preparing for my husband's return. As the troops began straggling back, I had hot water brought to the room and washed myself thoroughly, rubbing a few precious drops of perfume through my hair. I pulled on my finest dress and climbed the castle walls, prepared to give Dorian a suitable welcome.

One day passed, then another. Soldiers made their way down the road from the north, first a few on horseback, then waves on foot, filthy and hungry. Dorian was not among them. By the third day, I had begun to fret, for only the wounded had taken this long to return. The soldiers spoke of those yet to come with shaking heads and downcast eyes, and I began to fear the sight of the husband I so longed for.

As I ran my eyes over the trickle of slow-moving men, a familiar figure caught my eye. It was Dorian's manservant, Percel, one in a procession of hobbling men and carts strewn with those more gravely wounded. I rushed down the stairs from the top of the walls and ran to the castle gates, confronting Percel as soon as he walked inside. Much later I was grateful that this solemn young man had been the one tasked with such a heavy duty, for he did not waste time with flowery words or overblown sentiment. He simply told me my husband was dead.

"But how . . . ?" The words stumbled out, then caught in my throat. "The king told me he saw Dorian walk away from the battlefield."

Percel nodded, his face haggard. "I saw him at our camp after the king declared victory. He appeared as well as any of us. Tired and carrying the stench of battle, but otherwise unharmed. It wasn't until that evening, as we began making our way home, that he first spoke of the pain in his head. He said he had fallen from his horse, but he made it out to be no serious matter. As we traveled, he worsened. He began stumbling. His words slurred when he spoke. There were precious few horses left in good enough condition to ride, but given that my master was a favorite of the king, he was granted one. We tied him on and he drifted off to sleep. When we stopped for the night, he was dead."

I could not cry. I had feared Dorian dead, then been told he lived. Now he had died again. Which was the truth?

"They say he'll be taken to the chapel, with the other nobles," Percel said, pointing to the wrapped shrouds that were even then being carried through the castle doors. He watched the grim parade without emotion. "I shall have to tell his father, unless you would prefer to speak to him."

I could not face Sir Walthur. Could not bring him news I did not yet believe myself.

"He should hear the full story from you," I said. "I will go to the chapel."

I made my way through the Entrance Hall, down the corridors. The chapel had always been one of my favorite rooms in the castle, but now I dreaded entering. I paused in the passageway that led inside, my feet standing atop the stone that marked the royal family's burial crypt. I glanced at the most recent carving and knelt down to run my fingers over the letters of Flora's name. I missed her with a sudden, sharp ache. Not the feeble woman she had become in her last days but the Flora I had known years before, timid but kind, a force for good in a vicious world.

I walked inside, toward a group of weeping women, past motionless, bloodstained bodies laid on the floor. Most who had died on the battlefield would have been buried where they fell. Only these favored few were accorded the honor of returning home.

When two guards carried in Dorian's body, I recognized him immediately, even from across the room. I walked over slowly, my feet seemingly moving of their own accord. Dorian rested as if asleep, his beautiful face unscathed, his golden hair soiled by mud but unbloodied. I crumpled to my knees, certain that a mistake had been made and he would awaken at my touch. But my hand flinched back as soon as it felt his frozen cheek. The flesh had lost all vitality, its human warmth replaced by a waxy chill. Strapped to his thigh was the dagger he had so prized, and I pulled it free, my hands seeking the handle where his own had rested. Hesitantly, I cut a lock of his hair and slid it into my bodice. I considered speaking a few words, sending him to eternal rest with my blessing, but his rigid body mocked such sentiments. Dorian's soul had long since departed.

I stared at him long enough for my knees to grow numb against the stone floor. I did not stir until footsteps shuffled behind me. I turned to see Sir Walthur looking upon the body of his son, his face sunken with pain. He had never shown me affection. But the sight of this great man brought so low moved me to action. I stood and wrapped my arms around Sir Walthur's shoulders, and his face pressed against my neck as he gave in to his grief. Even murmured words of sympathy would have been a cruel invasion of such sorrow, so I remained silent. When he had collected himself, he leaned down and ran his fingers slowly over Dorian's face. He rose, avoiding my gaze, and walked away.

The men who brought my husband home were the final remains of what had once been a great army. After bidding my last farewell to Dorian, I left the castle and walked up the narrow stairs to the top of the walls. It was the place we had first kissed, on the day I'd agreed to marry him. Dorian had been gone from my side for months, yet I could still summon the press of his arms around me; I could feel his lips against mine. But when I tried to picture his face, all that came to mind was the grim death mask I had seen in the chapel. I sank against the wall, numb and lost. I did not know how to pass the rest of the day, or the following day. Or all the days to come. The life I had thought was mine, with a husband and children, was gone. My future had been slaughtered on a battlefield in the harsh northern mountains. Only I remained, unchanged. And yet changed completely.

Looking out, I watched a group of ragged camp followers along the road toward St. Elsip, the usual fallen women and peddlers who find war an opportunity for profit. They alone might regret the fighting's end. After the shuffling parade made its way across the bridge, one person broke off and turned onto the path leading to the castle. As the figure drew closer, I saw it was a woman, an ancient one, her back bent almost double. A persistent rain the day before had layered the ground with mud, and her steps were uncertain on the slippery uphill slope. I could not imagine what business she might have here, other than to beg.

The sunlight was low against the horizon; soon the trumpets would sound for supper. The thought of food brought a wave of nausea, but duty propelled me downward. By now Queen Lenore would have heard the news. She would wish to console me on my loss, and I must prepare myself to face the castle's sympathy. With a pang I remembered the obligations of a widow: the funeral that must be planned, the somber clothing I would have to order to declare my mourning. More than anything I longed to sink into my bed and burrow under the blankets, free to wallow in my misery unobserved.

I descended slowly, careful to lift my skirts so each footstep was unencumbered. As I walked past the gatehouse, I heard a commotion. The old woman was shouting at the gatekeeper, and something in her tone gave me pause. Her voice had the ring of authority, and her accent was that of an educated woman. I turned toward the gate and saw the woman pointing an accusing finger at the guards, promising that the queen would make them pay for their treatment of her.

It was Millicent.

I felt a rush of terror so unnerving I could not move. Her face, sunken and weathered, peered out at me from the hood of her cloak. She might have been a goblin from a fairy story, a crooked creature swathed in black who snatches children in the night. Her eyes fixed on me with malevolent glee. After so long a time, I would have thought myself impervious to her wiles. Yet I found myself drawn forward.

"Elise!" she crowed. "Come, take my hand."

"I'll take nothing." The vehemence of my rejection made the guards start. I addressed myself to the men, speaking firmly. "She's not to enter."

The youngest of them would have been children when Millicent was banished, but I could see by the nervous expression of the head gatekeeper, a man of some forty years, that he knew exactly who she was.

"She claims to have been summoned," he said to me uncertainly. "I've sent a page to inform the queen."

"This woman is not permitted to see the queen—or anyone else," I said in what I hoped was a firm voice.

"You've come up in the world, I see," Millicent said. "Tossing out orders as if you were a duchess! Am I the only one who remembers when you were fit for nothing more than carrying chamber pots?"

I turned my back and started for the rear courtyard. I could not drive Millicent off by myself, but a few returned soldiers would add force to my commands.

"How does our darling Rose?"

It was the "our" that enraged me, the sound of her raspy crone's voice laying claim to the person I most treasured. I whirled around in a fury. She must never see Rose. Ever.

"Begone!" I shrieked, my body aflame. The guards' mouths gaped in shock. I was playing into Millicent's hands, succumbing to the fear she thrived on, but I could not rein in my panic. "You are banished! Forever!"

"Forever?" Millicent said coolly. "Are you sure?"

Seen up close, she was no longer the proud woman who used to march through the castle with such authority. Her shoulders were curled in toward her body, and her lips sagged over empty gums. Yet my skin prickled and my throat tightened as if a cloud of evil swirled out from her, choking any who stood in her path.

Millicent lifted one twisted hand, and I flinched when I saw a flash of dark red. For a moment I thought she was reaching out with blood-spattered fingers, until I saw she wore crimson gloves. A piece of paper was crumpled in her fist, and as she pushed it toward me, the edge of her cloak fell back, revealing her forearm. The skin was a ravaged landscape of wrinkles and scars, pale and puckered with age. With a sickening lurch of recognition, I remembered the similar mark that still marred the queen's wrist. How often had Millicent cut into her own flesh in that hidden cave, calling upon dark powers to do her bidding?

She brandished the page in my face, close enough that I could discern the writing at the bottom. It was Queen Lenore's signature, one I had seen countless times on her letters. Taken aback, I paused, trying to sort through my tangled thoughts. Was the writing a clever simulation? It was not possible that the queen would summon the woman who had threatened her daughter with death.

Before I could work out the best course of action, the choice was taken from me. I heard footsteps approaching and turned to see Father Gabriel. He nodded humbly to the guards and said, "The queen gives her leave to enter. I will escort her to the Receiving Room."

Shocked, I watched in horror as Millicent smiled at me, enjoying her triumph. Her feet faltered in the mud as she took a step forward, and Father Gabriel reached out to offer the crook of his arm for support. As her decrepit, hunched body lurched toward his, their eyes met in a passing glance. It was so quick, so fleeting, and yet I saw it: the silent acknowledgment of two people who had met before.

Had Father Gabriel been doing her bidding all this time? Had he praised the virtues of forgiveness for the sole purpose of enabling Millicent's return?

"No!" I screamed. I stumbled forward, arms outstretched, frantic to halt their progress. I had just grabbed the back of Father Gabriel's robe when two guards took hold of my shoulders and pulled me back. The coarse brown cloth slipped through my fingers, and Father Gabriel turned in irritation, regarding me with disdain as I writhed against my captors. Millicent's face, slack with feigned bafflement, only enraged me more.

"I must speak to the king!" I begged the guards. "He will never permit her entrance!"

Others passing through the courtyard stopped to watch the commotion. In my panic I took in only flashes of my surroundings, but there were faces I recognized, servants and courtiers staring at me in amazement. In their eyes *I* was the madwoman, raving at a man of God and a seemingly harmless old woman.

The gatekeeper appeared at my side. He spoke in a low voice, his manner sympathetic. "You saw for yourself, she has a letter with the queen's mark. We cannot detain her."

"Please. I must warn the king."

He looked toward Millicent's hobbling figure, approaching the main entrance. Then he nodded to the guards, ordering my release. "Godspeed," he muttered.

I raced through the castle toward the king's room, only to be told that he had been summoned by the queen a few minutes before. Panting, heart hammering, I arrived at her sitting room to find the door closed, though King Ranolf's shouts came through clearly enough. A few ladies-in-waiting huddled together in the hallway, wide-eyed, their shock magnified when I cracked the door open and slid inside.

The king was pacing in front of the fireplace, face flushed red. He halted when he saw me, and for an instant I felt the terror of all those who had confronted him on a battlefield. Quivering with fury, he appeared capable of swatting me to the floor without a second thought. "Is it true?" he barked.

I nodded. "Millicent has been taken to the Receiving Room by Father Gabriel."

"She must leave at once!" he bellowed.

Queen Lenore spoke with a peculiar calm. "When you hear the full story, you will understand why I acted as I did."

"What story?"

"How Millicent helped us win the war."

King Ranolf looked as appalled as I felt.

"I have been in correspondence with her for some time," Queen Lenore explained. "I know it was wrong not to tell you, but I feared this very reaction."

Some time? My stomach knotted, and I stared at the queen in horrified wonder. How could she keep such a secret from us? And why?

King Ranolf glared down at his wife, body tensed like that of a cat preparing to pounce. "All these years spent searching for traitors," he murmured, his voice icy cold, "when the worst betrayal was here, before me, all along." Tossing aside his self-control, he roared with rage and kicked the chair next to his wife's, sending it careening across the room. Queen Lenore flinched as if the blow had been aimed her way, and I cowered against the wall.

"She begged my forgiveness," the queen said hesitantly, bracing herself for another blow. "She was near death, in fear of meeting her Maker. Does the Bible not tell us that every sinner deserves a chance at salvation?"

"It was Father Gabriel's doing," I interjected, etiquette be damned. "I believe he was sent by Millicent to act on her behalf."

Queen Lenore brushed off my suspicions with a quick shake of her head. "Of course not. He is driven only by his service to God."

She would never believe in their collusion without proof, and I had none.

"What lies did Millicent tell you?" King Ranolf asked.

"She said she would prove her loyalty. She has spent time among the Brithnians, as you know, and she is the one who persuaded them to take our side."

"Nonsense! We paid them well to fight with us. Sir Walthur was in contact with their ministers for weeks to make the arrangements."

"Do you think the deRauleys did not offer payment as well?

Millicent had the king of Brithnia's ear, ever since she cured his son of a wasting illness some years ago. Without her entreaties the Brithnians would have continued to play us against the deRauleys, taking gold from both sides while keeping their soldiers safely at home."

The king's thunderous expression did not soften, but he considered his wife's words without protest.

"I will never forget what Millicent has done to us or the threats she made to Rose," Queen Lenore said. "But can you not see? Without forgiveness there is no peace."

So this was the culmination of Father Gabriel's teachings: Queen Lenore was to gain her redemption by forgiving Millicent her sins. Already I could see the difference in her manner. Serenity had replaced the agitation that had tormented her for so long, and she spoke with the confidence of true belief. Her hands were clasped demurely in her lap, but my eyes were caught by the subtle movement of a thumb rubbing absently back and forth along the skin of the opposite wrist. Feeling the spot where Millicent's knife had dug into her flesh.

Seventeen years, nearly all of Rose's lifetime, had passed since the king banished Millicent from the castle, yet her hold over the queen had not lifted. I had long since discounted the notion that black magic had brought about Rose's birth. Yet what could explain Queen Lenore's continued allegiance to a woman who had vowed to see her family dead? It was as if a malevolent force had entered the open wound when her skin was cut open, a spirit whose commands she could not defy.

"Millicent has one dying wish: to spend her last days here, in the only home she has ever known."

The king came very close to refusing. But after so much loss, so much hurt, he no longer had the heart to battle his wife. Heva had told me, in confidence, that King Ranolf had slept in the queen's bed every night since his return, often waking with shouts from bloody dreams. Perhaps that is why he surrendered to her wishes in the end, to retain the comfort of her presence during those long hours before dawn.

"She will be confined to her room, under guard," the king said at last. "And Father Gabriel is to be sent on his way immediately."

Queen Lenore tried to defend the man in whom she had placed such trust, but the king halted her words with a stamp of his foot.

"He's had you in his clutches long enough! From now on you live by my counsel, and no one else's. That is the price I demand for Millicent's return."

Queen Lenore bowed her head, a saint accepting the terms of her martyrdom.

"Mrs. Tewkes can see to Millicent's care," King Ranolf muttered. "She is never to cross my path. Ever."

"As you wish. You will not know she is here."

The queen believed that such a promise could be kept. But it was not long before Millicent's presence would be felt throughout the castle. By opening the door to her, Queen Lenore had ushered in our doom.

Sixteen

EVIL UNLEASHED

The return of his nemesis did not dissuade the king from celebrating his victory over the rebels. If anything, Millicent's presence spurred him to make a public show of strength. The day after her arrival, he presided over a lavish feast, and once more the Great Hall echoed with music and the clamor of a hundred conversations. The celebration was more subdued than parties of the past, as the royal family was officially in mourning for Sir Hugill and the many other nobles lost, all of whom were spoken of movingly in toasts that extended well into the night. The king and queen handed out jewels and gold to knights who had distinguished themselves on the battlefield, a good number of them limping to the dais to receive their tokens. Queen Lenore put aside her usual drab clothing in favor of an elegant cream-colored gown, a sign, I hoped, that she was freeing herself at last from Father Gabriel's influence. According to Mrs. Tewkes, the monk had been escorted to the castle gates at first light and was last seen boarding a boat at the harbor, offering prayers of gratitude for his safe deliverance from the king's wrath.

Rose graced the younger knights with flirtatious smiles, flaunting the mischievousness she had suppressed since the war began. Lady Wintermale and others of her tradition-bound temperament looked on disapprovingly, but I saw no reason that Rose should shed false tears for an intended husband she had never met. Just as I could not condemn the recently widowed women who gulped down goblet after goblet of wine, losing themselves in frantic laughter or sobs. We all have our own ways of stumbling through grief.

And stumble I did. I moved through those days with a muddled mind, unsure how to complete the simplest tasks. Even my fear of Millicent barely broke through the fog; she was unseen and unacknowledged, a challenge to be confronted another day, when I had the strength. I lay for hours in the bedroom I still thought of as Dorian's, not my own, running my fingers over the jeweled handle of his dagger, crying myself to sleep while clutching a shirt that still retained a trace of his musky scent. I dined with Sir Walthur, making clumsy attempts at conversation, always aware what a poor substitute I made for his son. I wondered how much longer we could bear to share the same chambers without Dorian to bind us together.

Most of the nobles who fell in the north were laid to rest in their home parishes, but high-ranking men who resided at the castle were remembered with services in the Royal Chapel. The one exception was Dorian. As Sir Walthur's son and the knight who had saved King Ranolf's life, he was deemed worthy of a funeral in the cathedral of St. Elsip and buried with honor in a crypt near the altar. Sir Walthur and I had gratefully accepted Mrs. Tewkes's offer to make the arrangements, and the ritual was a fitting farewell to a beloved hero.

I could not cry. A few in the crowd might have admired my fortitude, but no doubt the rest felt cheated of a suitable display of mourning, distraught widows being essential to any proper funeral. I listened to Bible passages that compared Dorian to King David, and I watched my husband's casket, swathed in purple and green velvet, carried along the aisle. I placed one of my handkerchiefs inside the folds when the procession paused before me. It was the token I should have given him on the day he rode into battle. Instead it would accompany him on his final journey. I felt tears swell only once, when the herald who served under Dorian's command played a trumpet salute in his patron's honor.

The rest was empty spectacle. It was just the sort of formal affair that had tempted Dorian into irreverence when he was alive; I remembered sitting in the Royal Chapel the year before, at the funeral for an aged courtier, as Dorian whispered gossip about the old man's penchant for good-looking male servants. Had his wishes been taken into account, I knew that Dorian would have preferred to be buried amid drinking and dancing, with his friends competing to share the most outrageous accounts of his bad behavior. Instead his friends—those who lived—sat silent and stone-faced in their pews. Without their leader they were lost.

The funeral was followed by an equally somber midday meal in the Great Hall. When King Ranolf made a toast to Dorian, Sir Walthur blinked furiously, forbidding his tears to fall. Grand ladies who had once shunned me took my hand and murmured in sympathy; those who had been widowed welcomed me mournfully to our shared sisterhood of grief. At the end of the meal, I stood to take leave of the king and queen, and Rose leapt from her seat and rushed to my side. She threw her arms around my shoulders and clung to me, as if passing her youthful strength into my worn body.

"Is there anything I can do?" she asked. Her eyes and nose were reddened and raw; any stranger would have thought *her* the grieving widow.

"I do not know," I said, my mind blank. All I could think to do was lie in my bed, hoping to be overtaken by sleep's oblivion.

"You could come with me if you like. Mother has offered to have new gowns made up, and I would be grateful for your advice."

New gowns! It seemed a lifetime since anyone had given a thought to such frivolous things. But Queen Lenore was wise to provide her daughter such a distraction. For the first time since Dorian's death, I felt the urge to smile.

"I am no paragon of fashion," I said, "but I would be happy to have a look."

I realized as I said the words that they were true. Chattering about clothes would be an escape from the melancholy of Sir Walthur's apartments, an escape from my own misery. I could surrender to despair, forever mourning the family I had lost, or I could look forward, for Rose's sake. One glance at her sweet, concerned face and the choice was made.

She clutched my hands in hers, leaning in to speak in confidence. "I have been working on a new poem, celebrating Dorian's sacrifice. I hope to offer it as a gift to you one day."

Touched beyond words, I hugged her, hiding my tears in her hair. How delighted Dorian would have been, seeing himself immortalized in a heroic tale! There would be no end to his bragging. I could hear him speak as clearly as if he stood at my side, good-naturedly mocking my tears: *What now, wife? This is no way to celebrate a valiant soldier!*

I was forever grateful for that brief sound of his voice, for it acted as a strong shoulder pressed against my back, nudging me away from grief. Whenever I felt myself falter and weaken, I would remember Dorian's mocking smile, his impatience with those who wallowed in self-pity. If my husband were to live on as a hero, I must mold myself into a widow worthy of his reputation.

Rose's company was further balm to my spirit. Her laughter and blushes at the feast signaled an end to the brooding that had overtaken her during the war, and I encouraged her girlish fancies. However, she continued to retreat to her room for hours at a time, alone, and I felt uneasy at the thought of her walking those isolated halls unchaperoned. That protectiveness was the reason I snapped at Besslin, her maid, when I saw her giggling with a group of equally silly housemaids in the Lower Hall late one afternoon.

"Should you not be preparing your mistress for supper?" I demanded sharply.

She shrugged, unconcerned. "She told me she'd dress herself."

Rose preferred to wear her hair loose, cascading over her shoulders, and she favored simple gowns. I did not doubt she could make herself presentable without assistance, but I was irritated by Besslin's insolent manner.

"Never mind what she told you. Your place is upstairs, in case she has need of you."

"My mistress gave me the rest of the day off." Besslin grinned, delighted to prove me wrong.

Rose was no longer a girl. She was free to order her maid about as she pleased. Yet I hurried my steps toward her room. With the kingdom at peace and the king safe, I had thought she would no longer need to close herself off. If her mind remained troubled, perhaps she would confide in me.

I knocked lightly on Rose's door and stepped inside, but there was no response when I called out her name. Both the sitting room and the bedchamber were empty. I was about to leave and search for Rose elsewhere when something caught my eye along the wall behind her bed. A hanging tapestry had been pushed aside, revealing a previously hidden panel that had been pulled outward. I peered inside, breathing in the stale, clammy odor of a crypt, and saw a set of narrow, twisted steps. Hesitantly, I followed them downward into the darkness, fearing what I would find at the bottom.

I emerged into a room one flight below, a room I had not entered for years but remembered instantly. Before me was a tableau that froze me with dread: Beautiful, vibrant Rose sitting on Millicent's ornate bed, her eyes bright with excitement. Beside her a hunched, desiccated figure swathed in a threadbare green cape. And at their feet a spinning wheel.

"What are you doing here?" I demanded, staring at Rose.

"Elise," she said carefully, taken aback by my harsh tone, "surely you know my great-aunt Millicent?"

"Indeed she does." The words came garbled from Millicent's toothless mouth, but the imperiousness of her voice was immediately familiar.

"Aunt Millicent has been telling me of the olden days at court," Rose said. "She remembers when this tower was built."

"Rose's room was intended to be a nursery," Millicent said. Her skin was sallow and her red-rimmed eyes watery; whatever remnants of past beauty her face had once carried had long since vanished. "Wasn't it clever of my father to build that hidden staircase, so a mother could check on her child when she pleased?"

"It was quite a surprise when she knocked!" Rose exclaimed. "Mother told me Aunt Millicent was too ill to receive visitors, but clearly that's not the case. She has been showing me all sorts of wondrous things."

Smiling at me, eyes gleaming, Millicent waved one hand toward the spinning wheel. "Can you believe that Rose has never seen one?"

Sick at how easily Millicent had gained Rose's trust, I tried to suppress my rising panic.

"Guards!" I called out.

Rose stared at me, uncomprehending. Two men appeared in the doorway behind me, waiting for instructions. But what could I say? How could I explain that this seemingly harmless domestic scene terrified me?

"Why should an old woman not pass her days in useful labor?" Millicent asked with exaggerated innocence. "These guards made no objection when I asked a maid to bring me this wheel."

Of course not. They were too young to remember Millicent's hateful words at Rose's baptism. They had not seen the towering bonfire that lit up the sky that night.

"Isn't it the most curious thing?" Rose exclaimed, reaching out to feel the curved wood.

I leapt forward, shouting, "Don't touch it!"—but my sudden exclamation threw off her balance, and she slipped. Her hand flew forward, toward the wheel, and I saw blood burst from her fingertip as it collided with the sharp, pointed spindle. She pulled back with a whimper, and Millicent opened her arms to welcome her in.

Driven by a fear so visceral it banished all thought, I screamed and ran forward. I pushed Millicent away from Rose, and she fell back upon the bed. Rose leapt up, calling out my name, but I shut her out. My hands, moving as if by their own accord, gripped Millicent's bony upper arms to hold her in check.

"Is this how you would treat a poor old woman," she whined, "still grieving her sister's death? What a sad tale Rose recounted! Is it true the name of dear Flora's long-lost love was on her lips as she died?"

Anger surged through me at the sight of Millicent's triumphant face. I had told Rose the story of Flora's death in confidence, yet she had been quick enough to share it with this old crone. A woman who had driven her sister to the edge of madness.

"Flora told me all," I spat out, my voice rising with ever-increasing hysteria. "How you seduced the man she loved and drove him to his death. You could not have him for yourself, so you destroyed both of them. An innocent man and your own sister!"

"Elise!"

Rose tugged at my arm, trying to pull me away. I was dimly aware of the people gathering outside the door, drawn by the commotion, witnessing my madness. But I did not care. All that mattered was that I keep Rose safe.

"Go upstairs!" I ordered. "Now!"

Rose slunk off with a resentful pout. I abruptly dropped my grasp on Millicent's arms and watched as she slid in a jumble of limbs onto the floor before me.

"You are never to see Rose again!" I shouted. "Never!"

Millicent shot me a grimace that mixed pain and exultation. Her mouth moved, and I braced myself for a barrage of curses. Instead she laughed, a horrible taunt that echoed around me in that enclosed space. A sound that reminded me why she had once been called a witch.

I ordered one of the guards to keep watch over Millicent from inside the room and the other to fetch a mason to wall over the entrance to the hidden staircase. They looked at each other, unsure.

"Consult with the king if you wish!" I exclaimed. "Only do not delay! Hurry!"

Once it was clear that my demands would be heeded, I rushed upstairs to Rose's room. I nearly crashed into her at the top of the passage, where she had been perched, eavesdropping.

"Elise?" she demanded, wavering between anger and concern.

I grabbed Rose's hand and frantically scoured it for signs that the prick had allowed poison to enter her body. I found nothing. Her skin was as clear and smooth as ever, a single red dot the only evidence of what had transpired downstairs.

"You must never allow that woman into your presence again," I said firmly.

"Why not? She's old and sick. I felt sorry for her, left to rot alone."

"She does not deserve your kindness."

"Because she and my father quarreled years ago?" Rose scoffed. "Surely enough time has passed for them to put things to rights."

God help me, I came close to shaking her. How dare she speak of the break between Millicent and her father as a trivial disagreement! Then I realized: *She does not know.* I had thought Millicent's return to the castle would prompt her parents to recount the events of her baptism. Yet Rose remained coddled and ignorant, so oblivious to danger that she had willingly entered Millicent's room. What might have happened if I had not come along?

"Millicent was banished for cursing your family, shortly after you were born," I said quietly. "She wished for your death."

Seeing Rose's bewildered face, I feared I had been too blunt. One who grows up knowing only love could never understand such hatred.

"Why?" she asked.

Much as I wanted to help her, there were some stories better left untold. "Millicent thought your mother should heed her words over those of your father." It was hardly a satisfying explanation, but true enough. "She is a cruel, vindictive woman. And more dangerous than you know."

"Does she wish me dead still?" Rose's voice trembled.

It would be a kindness to quell her fears. Yet the truth would keep her safer.

"I do not know. I would not be surprised if she did. Your mother has chosen to show Millicent mercy, but I will not. Stay away from her, far away. I will have the entrance to this staircase bricked over, to keep you safe."

Rose nodded slowly.

"I doubt she will trouble you again," I offered as reassurance. "From the looks of her, she's not long for this world."

I remembered hearing those same words long ago, when the king brought news of Millicent's escape to Brithnia. It was said she had gone there to die, yet she lived on. Would she linger here as well, plotting a destruction we could not imagine?

The king would have to be informed of Millicent's intrusion, but I hoped to keep the news from Queen Lenore, whose mind was greatly troubled in those days over the fate of the war's wounded soldiers. While families of good standing had dispatched carriages to fetch their injured fathers and husbands, those of humble birth were sent to the stables, where they clutched their bloodstained bandages and groaned in agony. By the time the last stragglers arrived, close to a hundred men lay head to foot along the floor, almost covering the straw beneath them from view. A few servants were ordered to bring hot soup and tend to wounds as best they could, but otherwise the injured were left to suffer alone.

Over the king's objections, Queen Lenore had insisted on visiting the makeshift sickroom. The soldiers took great heart from the sight of her walking among them, asking after each man's family and offering words of cheer. She summoned Mr. Gungen and conferred with him on measures to improve the men's comfort: straw-filled pallets, hot water, clean blankets. From then on she requested daily reports of their progress and wrote personal letters of condolence to the families of the dead, a task that took up more time with each passing day.

"So many lost," she lamented. "I thought our care would hasten their recovery. Yet they die, one after another."

I could not summon suitably reassuring words, for I, too, had felt the same dejection. That very morning, hearing a commotion from the back courtyard, I had peered out from my room and seen the bodies of those who had died in the night being carried out from the stables, rigid statues wrapped in white linen. I counted twelve in all, loaded onto carts and pulled in a solemn procession through the courtyard. These dead farmers, tradesmen, and servants would be denied the ceremony granted Dorian; they would join their fellow fighters in a common grave, laid to rest with a few rushed prayers from the castle priest. As they passed, I saw groomsmen leading a pair of the king's stallions into the building. With such numbers dying, there would be space enough soon for the royal horses to resume their places.

The grim news from the stables was not spoken of openly, but I heard the whispers from servants and courtiers alike. More men died than recovered. The stench inside had become unbearable, and maids were refusing to touch the men's now-festering wounds. A few even balked at delivering their food until Mrs. Tewkes threatened to have them dismissed.

Even then I did not suspect what was to come. I did not see the suffering soldiers firsthand or think their fates in any way entwined with mine. There was no grand premonition of doom on the day I lingered in a Lower Hall storeroom, considering rolls of fabric for Rose's new dresses. Merely a gentle tug at my sleeve from a young maid.

"Excuse me, madam?"

I was still occasionally taken aback when servants treated me as a mistress rather than as one of their own. I turned to see a thin, pinch-faced girl who introduced herself as Liya.

"Mrs. Tewkes charged me with seeing to Lady Millicent's meals," she said. "Since yesterday she has refused to eat, and her room smells something awful. I think she's soiled her bedsheets, but she won't have me change them."

So Millicent's time had come at last. Here was a death I would not mourn.

"Speak to Mrs. Tewkes," I said dismissively. "She will tell you what to do."

The maid nodded. "I would not have troubled you, only she asked for Princess Rose by name. She said the time had come to make her final farewells."

The old witch was making trouble to the last. "She is not to see the princess under any circumstances," I said sternly. "Ignore her pleas."

"Yes, ma'am."

As I sorted through the bundles of cloth, fingering each piece to gauge its quality, I could not rid myself of the suspicion that Millicent planned some further deception. Was she using illness as a ruse to draw Rose to her bedside? I would not be at peace until I saw for myself what state she was in. I left the Lower Hall and took the main staircase to the North Tower, my steps echoing across the marble expanse. How many times had I followed this same route to Flora's room in happier days! Then I had hurried ahead in eager anticipation; now each pace was weighted with dread. The two guards at Millicent's door nodded and unlocked the latch at my request.

The large windows, which gave the North Tower rooms their expansive character, had been covered with dark curtains that shut out all light. Without a lamp it was difficult to see more than an arm's length before me. I could make out the shape of Millicent's bed, with a chamber pot on the floor beside it. What lay on top, unmoving, was unclear. I could be staring at a person, but it could just as well have been a jumble of linens. A nauseating stench assaulted me, inescapable even when I breathed through my mouth to spare my nose. Anyone who grows up on a farm cannot be dainty when it comes to earthy aromas, and I was never the sort to wave a perfumed handkerchief before my face every time I entered a stable. The smell of excrement mixed with blood was not enough to weaken me. There was something else, an underlying, tangy, bitterness.

The scent of decay.

Had anything less than Rose's life been at stake, I would have fled. Slowly, I made my way toward the bed, forcing each step, until the lump on the mattress revealed itself to be a human figure. The ridges of legs were visible underneath a thin blanket; skeletal hands clutched at the stained fabric. She lay on her back, her profile motionless, until I stood by her side. Her face turned, each movement an agony. As her features were gradually revealed, I found myself staring at a monster.

Millicent's weathered skin had been conquered by pus-filled sores that disfigured her once fine features, and sweat matted her white hair flat against her head. Her cheekbones and eye sockets protruded ghoulishly, showing the shape of the skull beneath, and her lips were pulled back in a grimace. Each breath in and out was labored, choked by the blood that trickled from her mouth. Her eyes, fixed upon me, were red and burning, a stare that held nothing but hatred.

She laughed, the taunt of a victor who has won a hard-fought battle. For Millicent saw from my face that I knew what disease had befallen her. She had taken her revenge on the king at last, bringing devastation to his very doorstep. She rejoiced in her suffering, knowing that her death would be the death of us all.

I had entered the room brimming with righteous anger, yet her cackle shattered my resolve. I turned and ran, desperate to distance myself from the creature she had become, my thoughts whirling. I had to find the king. I had to tell him what I had seen. I remembered the soldiers, dying despite Queen Lenore's concern for their care. I saw my mother's face, cruelly disfigured, in her final moments. My mind battled against these visions, the progression of logic leading me to one conclusion while I hoped desperately to be proved wrong.

When I arrived at the Council Chamber, I found only Sir Walthur and one of the court scribes inside. If Sir Walthur noted the frantic edge to my voice when I asked after the king, he did not acknowledge it, telling me to look in the queen's rooms before turning back to his papers. Sir Walthur had always been diligent in his duties, but now he rarely left the Council Chamber other than to take his meals. I thought his frequent absences from our family apartments a clear sign that he preferred not to share my company. Had I been wiser in the ways of grief, I would have understood that Sir Walthur was avoiding not me but memories of his dead son.

I found the king and queen seated near the windows of her sitting room. I could not remember the last time I had seen them together thus, engrossed in private conversation. With the weight of war thrown off, the king had regained a measure of health, and his face had lost the haunted look it carried on his return from battle. Though I could not hear his words, they had coaxed a smile from Queen Lenore, one that widened when she caught sight of me. The happiness of her welcome almost broke my heart.

"Elise," she said, waving me over. "You know how long Rose has begged to travel beyond the kingdom's borders. The king agrees that this might be a suitable time to undertake such an excursion. Can you imagine her face when we tell her?"

It had been so very long since I had seen the queen look toward the future with happy anticipation. It sickened me to cut her short with my dreadful news.

"I have come from Millicent's room. She is close to death."

"You bring good tidings, then," the king said with a smile, but Queen Lenore shook her head quickly.

Though I had planned to couch my suspicions in carefully chosen words, I found I could only speak the truth. In my heart I knew what had befallen Millicent. I had seen the same signs before.

"She has the pox."

Queen Lenore's eyes widened, but the king's expression remained unchanged.

"Nonsense. She's a sick old woman. It is her time."

"Sir, with my greatest respect, you have not seen her. Her skin is covered in boils, and she is bleeding from her mouth and nose. My mother died of the pox, and she had exactly these afflictions. I had it myself. I know."

I saw the shock of it in their faces, the fear that raced in the wake of my announcement.

"The soldiers," I said, turning to face Queen Lenore. "I fear they have been stricken as well."

"Impossible. I have been told that pox turns the skin black and swells up the body. I saw no such disfigurements."

"It can take different forms. The surest sign is the boils. When you visited, did you see eruptions on any of the men's skin?"

Worry began to cloud her eyes. "They had been sleeping outside, on the ground. Insect bites, I thought—"

The king interrupted, angry, as if by saying the words I had brought this affliction upon them. "We've had no pox in these parts for years!"

"Millicent came to us from Brithnia," I said. "Our soldiers have been struck after fighting at the Brithnians' side. Perhaps their men brought it with them into battle."

Faced with disaster on his doorstep, King Ranolf might well have crumbled with despair or raged against the cruelty of fate. Instead he rose abruptly, blazing with resolve, and announced there was no time to be lost. After kissing his wife's cheek and reassuring her all would be well, he marched from the room, shouting commands to his footmen and summoning his advisers to the Council Chamber.

Within an hour of my visit to Millicent, the castle was in tumult. The king ordered the wounded taken from the castle grounds to the convent of St. Lucia, escorted by the servants who had tended to them. Though sunset approached, carts and wagons were sent to St. Elsip to gather stores of ale, flour, and other provisions. Pages traveled to neighboring farms with bags of gold to buy livestock. None of the king's subjects knew the nature of the danger facing them, yet all did his bidding without hesitation.

It was not until that night, in the flickering candlelight of the Great Hall, that the king announced what some had already guessed. By then servants had returned from St. Elsip with tales of men in town whose wounds would not heal, who appeared frailer now than when they'd returned from battle. A sense of foreboding drifted through the castle like a damp mist, slowing our pace as we'd made our way to the king's assembly.

King Ranolf did not shy from speaking plainly. Our soldiers had been stricken with the pox, he said, to scattered gasps. St. Elsip—indeed the whole kingdom—might be swept by this pestilence, but he would not bow down before it. The sick men had been banished from the castle, and the next morning he would close the gates to protect us from any further threat of disease. Those who wished to join their families elsewhere were free to leave. For the weeks and months to come, the rest of us would remain sealed inside the walls, alone.

Seventeen

DESPERATE TIMES

Had the pox spread as quickly as our fears, we would have been dead by morning. Fires blazed in the Lower Hall fireplaces long past the hour they would usually have dimmed to ashes. Reluctant to face a morose Sir Walthur in my quarters, I chose to sit among the servants as I hastily wrote a letter to Prielle, urging her to remain in her home until the sickness had passed through town. Around me voices blended with the crackle of the flames, and I gazed into the heat even as it glazed my face with sweat.

A shadow loomed beside me, and I turned to see the young maid Liya staring at me with haunted eyes.

"Is it true? Lady Millicent has the pox?"

Though King Ranolf had not spoken her name during his address to the court, I had heard it whispered by others. I nodded.

"What shall I do?" she pleaded. "I cannot bear to go in there again."

When I had last seen her, Millicent was scarcely human. Food would be wasted on the decaying shell she had become.

"She's dead by now, or close enough," I said with firm authority. "Leave her to rot."

Liya, taken aback by my harsh tone, nodded quickly and scurried away. I did not care if she thought me cruel. Millicent deserved to lie on her deathbed unmourned and alone.

Exhausted from agonizing over their possible doom, the other servants began drifting off to their quarters, well aware that this crisis would not excuse them from performing their tasks the next morning. I took aside one of the boys who worked in the food storerooms and gave him a coin to deliver my letter that night. Having done my duty to what remained of my family, I returned to my room but spent the remainder of the night in a dazed stupor, denied the oblivion of sleep. When I heard sounds from the sitting room soon after dawn, I rose from the bed, relieved that Anika had brought breakfast, for I had barely eaten the day before. But when I walked out from the bedroom, I saw Sir Walthur pulling his prized collection of books from their perch on top of a chest and piling them inside a leather satchel. He stopped when he saw me.

"I am sorry I wakened you," he said.

"I could not sleep." I noticed two sacks lying at his feet. "Are you leaving?"

Sir Walthur nodded curtly. "I have decided to return to my estate in the country."

I had never imagined that the king's closest adviser would desert him during this desperate time. My face must have shown my shock, for Sir Walthur rushed to explain himself.

"'Twill be far safer there. Despite the king's assurances, I fear that the castle will not be spared the pox."

"I fear the same myself." It was the first time I had spoken my doubts aloud. Sir Walthur did not look surprised, only resigned.

"I confess, since Dorian's death I have felt drawn to what remains of my family. My older son has none of Dorian's charms, but he is loyal. His children are my heirs now, my legacy, and it is time I share what little wisdom I can with them. As Dorian's wife, you are entitled to a place with us."

I could not tell by the tone of his voice what he hoped my answer might be.

"Thank you," I said, "but I cannot desert my mistress or Princess Rose. They will have need of me."

"So they will." He turned back to his books, and I wondered if I had been dismissed. As I made my way toward the door, Sir Walthur stopped me.

"The king tells me you were the one who brought the pox to his attention."

"I saw the signs on Millicent. I wish with all my heart I had not."

"You have seen such signs before?"

I nodded. "The pox took my mother and three of my brothers."

Sir Walthur assessed me solemnly. "And you escaped unscathed?"

"It felled me for some days, but I returned to health."

"Then you should be spared this time," Sir Walthur observed. "You are indeed blessed."

No, I wanted to tell him, *I am cursed. What sin have I committed to have this scourge brought upon me again?*

"You do well to stay," Sir Walthur continued, closing the clasp on his satchel. "I fear that the castle ranks will be much diminished, and the king and queen will need your strength." He reached down and picked up his bags. "It's time I set off. If I start now, I might make the journey in two days."

"Have you called for a carriage?" I asked. "I will send Anika—"

Sir Walthur stopped me with a wave of his hand. "The carriages have long since been spoken for. Did you not hear the commotion last night? Lords and ladies arguing like children over who could make the quickest departure. No, I will travel as I once did, alone on horseback. My white mare will do well enough."

"Then allow me to help with your bags," I offered. "Unless you plan to have a word with the king first?"

"I said what I had to yesterday evening." A pained expression flickered across Sir Walthur's face, and I wondered what had passed between them. Sir Walthur was more than a counselor; he was one of the few men the king trusted completely. By the look on his face, the parting had been distressing for both men.

He allowed me to carry his satchel of books while he lifted the bags and flung them onto his back. Though his face had aged with grief since Dorian's death, he carried his twin burdens with shoulders firmly upright, aware that all eyes would be upon him. We walked downstairs and past the kitchens, stepping out of the doors opposite the stables. The scene before us in the back courtyard was one of disarray: Sheep and pigs brought in from neighboring farms wandered listlessly, while ladies in elegant traveling clothes haggled over horses and carriages, piles of possessions stacked beside them. In the mad rush to escape the castle, courtly manners had been replaced by greedy desperation.

It was a measure of how far standards already had fallen that no one ran up to assist the king's chief counselor. I noticed a young stableboy nearby, watching the proceedings with mouth agape. I grabbed him by the ear and pointed toward Sir Walthur.

"Fetch his horse and saddle, quickly!" I ordered.

The boy scuttled off, and within a few minutes Sir Walthur was on horseback, ready to depart. He leaned down toward me, raising his voice from its usual low rumble so as to be heard above the commotion.

"You will not reconsider my offer?"

I shook my head.

"Then I wish you continued health. And happiness. It's what Dorian would have wished for you as well."

My eyes filled up at the sound of his son's name. For that brief moment, I felt Dorian's presence, silently watching over us with his familiar amused smile.

Sir Walthur shook his reins, and his horse stepped gingerly through the press of people. Aimless amid the commotion, I could think of nothing else to do but follow him. Avoiding the horses and carriage wheels, I edged my way along the rough stone wall and passed through the arch into the front courtyard. The usually serene expanse of space had not been spared the tumult that had upended the rest of the fortress. The open space where children had once rolled their hoops and where knights had paraded for the admiration of Queen Lenore's ladies-in-waiting was overrun with pigs and chickens. Sacks of grain lay in haphazard piles, and knots of servants huddled together in unaccustomed idleness. A cacophony of voices almost drowned out the rattling carriages, but the people I saw in the courtyard were silent, wary observers to something I could not yet see. As Sir Walthur's horse approached the partially open gates, I took a few steps forward, then stopped in shock.

Through the narrow opening, I saw a swarm of people, pressed against one another, shouting for attention. My first thought was that they were angry at the king's decision to close off his court. Soon I saw that the truth was quite the opposite. These people, townsmen and country folk alike, were begging to join us. Forced shoulder to shoulder, they jostled and swayed against the guards' outstretched arms, a throbbing mass of bodies. Frantic mothers pushed their young children before them. One caught my eye and held her baby toward me.

"Take him!" she pleaded. "Keep him safe!"

I pulled back, horrified. I wanted to tell them the pox was already among us, that the castle might well become a tomb rather than a refuge. But such truths could not be said aloud. In any case I doubt that the hundreds gathered there would have believed me. They were desperate for salvation and thought the castle their only hope.

As Sir Walthur's horse and the last of the carriages approached the gates, the guards began to bellow, "Stand back! Stand back!" They heaved the heavy gates inward, widening the opening, and the crowd surged forward. A young boy of no more than five or six was the first to scamper inside. He gained but a few steps before a whip snapped and he fell with a piteous whimper. Another crack cut through the din, and I looked up at the carriage that had pulled alongside me. Elgar, now one of the groomsmen, stood on the driver's platform, reins in one hand and whip in the other. I caught a brief glimpse of the carriage's passengers through the window, two sisters who were distantly related to Lady Wintermale and had been at court for some years under her supervision; the older one swiftly yanked the curtain shut to hide their faces.

"Make way, you animals!" Elgar shouted.

Slowly, cautiously, the crowd parted, and Elgar's carriage clattered through the gates. It was followed by two others, then Sir Walthur. He did not look back. As soon as the last of the horses had passed, the guards returned to their defenses and the people outside resumed their pleading.

I turned back into the courtyard, narrowly missing a rooster being chased by a flustered boy. Such a sight may have diminished the castle's dignity, but I was grateful to the king for putting the needed thought into our provisions. It would take a considerable amount of livestock to keep the castle fed. Perhaps we would be forced to eat as men do under siege, allotted a small portion of porridge each morning to last us until sundown, the portions growing smaller as the days passed.

"Mistress Elise?"

I stopped at the sound of my name. Before me stood a young footman whose face I recognized, though I could not recall his name.

"There's a man out front who asked for you. The guards have orders to keep everyone out, no exceptions, but he tossed me a coin to do his bidding."

"A man? What man?" I asked.

The footman shrugged. "A townsman, nicely spoken. He wanted me to check that you were well, and so you are. Easiest money I've ever made."

He turned back toward the castle gates, and I followed, wary of approaching the frantic mass outside. The footman hovered just behind the line of guards, his eyes looking over the crowd, until he stopped and raised a hand. A figure pushed through the bodies, creating a steady ripple of movement on either side as he moved determinedly forward.

It was Marcus.

The changes wrought by age were easily noted: His hair was neatly trimmed rather than left to fall haphazardly across his forehead, and his figure had thickened into a healthy solidity. Yet I was struck by how much had not changed. We stared at each other, separated by a human shield of soldiers, and yet it was as if we found ourselves alone. Relief flooded across his face, and he spoke quickly, knowing that the times did not allow for pleasantries.

"Elise, thank God I've found you."

"What are you doing here?" I asked, disoriented by the unexpected sight of him amid the commotion.

"Hester's brother-in-law is ailing, and her sister asked if she could come and help. I drove her in this morning, but all the talk in town is of a strange illness. . . ."

"Take your wife home," I urged. "Immediately. You should be safe from contagion at the tannery."

"So it is true? It is the pox?"

"Yes."

The people pressed up against Marcus, suspicions confirmed, repeated my words to their neighbors, and the pleas for entrance took on a new urgency. Blindly, desperately, they believed their king could keep them safe. The captain of the guards, posted at the end of his line of men, frowned as he surveyed the tumult.

"Will you be safe here?" Marcus asked.

I almost laughed. Here I was, granted refuge with royalty, an honor the masses around us would think themselves blessed to share.

"Have no worries on my account." Even as the words were said, I realized the magnitude of what he had done. It was worry for me that had brought him here, through this crowd, despite the demands of his family. When disaster threatened, it was my safety that sprang to his mind.

"If you wish to leave," he offered, "you are welcome to stay with us, for as long as you like."

What would his wife make of my sudden appearance? I wondered. For I could see in his determined face the same man who had once told me that he did not love lightly. He could not hide his concern for my welfare, just as I could not disguise my own delight at seeing him again. Dangerous sentiments for a married man and a widow to reveal.

"You know I cannot leave," I said. Echoes of our long-ago parting resonated through the years. Once again Marcus offered escape, and I chose duty. This time he accepted my answer with resignation, as if he had expected no other.

"Elise, you must promise me—"

Whatever bargain he intended to strike was suddenly drowned out by a harsh bark from the guards' commander. The line of men tightened, and with a groan of wood and metal the gates began to move. Cries of dismay and anger erupted from outside. Marcus threw a hand toward me in a desperate parting gesture but was soon caught up in the press of bodies and pulled backward. A scrawny young man tried to push between two guards and was shoved away so roughly he fell sprawled in the mud. Marcus's stricken face disappeared among the mothers and babies and old men as the massive doors groaned shut. With a decisive clang, iron bars were slid across to hold the gates in place. Bewildered and heartsick, I looked around the courtyard, at the shepherds and pages and kitchen maids and stableboys. None appeared grateful to be locked away from the threat of illness. What I saw on every face was fear.

We might have removed ourselves from the world, but the castle was hardly serene. With the bleating of animals and the constant chatter in the halls, there was a flurry of activity to very little purpose. A good number of the nobles had chosen to leave, as I saw by the empty tables at supper that evening, but most of the servants had nowhere else to go. The king, the queen, and Rose sat in their usual places, more out of duty than hunger, for they only picked at their meals. Afterward Rose asked if I would accompany her to her room. She dismissed her maid and paced back and forth from the door to the window, anxious with nerves.

"The servants are saying Aunt Millicent is nearly dead of the pox. Is it true?"

"Yes." I shut my mind to the horrors of that foul room.

"Could she have passed the contagion to me?"

"She could not have done you harm in so short a visit," I said with a certainty I did not feel.

"I might as well be dead," she said mournfully. "My mother promised I would be allowed to travel once the war was over. I thought I would finally see something of the world. Instead I am doomed to rot behind these walls."

"It's hardly as bad as that." She must have a distraction, I thought, something else to set her mind to. "Have you made any more progress on your poem?"

"I have found it difficult to capture Dorian's vitality," she said, dispirited. Then she looked up at me, her eyes gleaming with an encouraging curiosity. "It would be a great help if you were to tell me more about him and his exploits."

I had to swallow a chuckle. Dorian's exploits were primarily of the lustful variety, hardly worthy of a young maiden's verse.

"I will think on it," I promised. "But I won't have you pining over fallen heroes. We must find other ways to occupy your time. Perhaps embroidery?"

Rose frowned. "Not much of a substitute for dancing."

"We shall make something pretty. Once the pox has passed, there will be talk of suitors again. We can't marry you off without suitably fine petticoats and nightdresses."

"Do you think I will be consulted on my next choice of husband?"

"Well, you are older now. No doubt you have certain preferences you wish to share with your father."

"Yes, I do."

"Hmm." I pretended to consider the matter. "Someone with dashing good looks, of course. Intelligent and well traveled. A man of the world, you might say. Who is as skilled at conversation as he is at dancing."

Rose laughed, her pink cheeks proof that my hints about Joffrey had hit their mark. She was now the same age I had been when thoughts of Marcus were all-consuming, when I could make my heart race by imagining his kisses. Perhaps Rose, too, found comfort in such fantasies. I hoped she did. I wanted to protect her against the pox above all else, but if I could preserve her spirit besides, I would consider my work well done.

When I remember those days, it is the watchfulness that I recall above all. Like many of the servants, I often climbed to the top of the castle walls to peer down at St. Elsip, but from so far away its fate was unclear. The most striking difference was the emptiness of the streets. Tiny figures could occasionally be seen scurrying in the distance, but the usual touchstones that marked the passage of time had disappeared: There were no market days, no calls to worship from the church bells, no children running in the fields along the riverbank. How was Prielle faring, I wondered, confined at home with her unhappy parents, fearful for her future? A girl of her sensitive temperament would feel the weight of such times more acutely than others, and I hoped desperately that the pox would pass her family by. Then my eyes would drift beyond St. Elsip, to the trees surrounding the tannery, and my thoughts would turn to Marcus. Was he safe? Would I ever see him again?

Within the walls we searched for signs of illness among us. Any stray cough was cause for whispers, and normal aches and pains were discussed as life-or-death matters. One kitchen maid became the object of frightened conjecture when she awoke feverish and was unable to rise from her bed; she was immediately shunned and sent to sleep in the stables. After that, no one dared show any weakness. But we were all unwell in mind, if not in body. From the youngest errand boys to Queen Lenore's remaining ladies-in-waiting, each carried the burden of fear. We soldiered on despite its weight, half-heartedly fulfilling our duties, silently marking off the days toward a time we might consider ourselves safe from danger.

Occasionally someone would ask permission to leave, and the gates would be opened a crack to allow that person to slip out. For the most part, those who left had family in the country and hoped their sister's or cousin's faraway farm might offer safety. Only one of these departures caused me any personal grief. One week into our seclusion, word spread through the Lower Hall that Mrs. Tewkes had gone. She had sent word to the queen and left under cover of night, without farewells to any of her charges. It was seen as a disturbing omen, for the woman had devoted her life to the king's service. We never imagined she would abandon us.

I had thought myself bound to Mrs. Tewkes by our shared love for my mother, and I was crushed that she had left without telling me. Perhaps she found a silent leave-taking easier to bear, but it exacted a heavy toll on those of us who remained. With her husband long dead and no children, I did not know who would take her in; she had never spoken to me of any family. But, as I was quickly learning, desperate times drive even the most levelheaded to uncharacteristic folly.

Still, with enough time, one's life adjusts to even the most surprising turns. I might never have given Mrs. Tewkes more than a passing thought again had it not been for Rose and her poem. Denied other pleasures, she devoted hours to writing her celebration of Dorian, occasionally reading passages aloud for my approval. I found the style greatly influenced by her mother's favorite works but admirable for one of her limited experience. Though the virtuous, self-effacing hero depicted in her work bore little resemblance to my husband, Rose had captured his looks and mannerisms well, and I thought it might be no bad thing if this image of Dorian one day supplanted memories of the man as he had been.

My only concern was the amount of time Rose dedicated to her scribbling. Little acquainted with the storytelling arts myself, I had thought a poem the work of one or two days; Rose's epic had now filled weeks, with no sign of an ending in sight. The skin beneath her eyes was smudged with gray, and every morning she requested fresh candles. When I asked gently whether she might turn her thoughts elsewhere, she brushed off my concern.

"I can't stop now," she said. "I have started the battle scene, where Dorian saves my father's life."

What could a coddled girl know of warfare? The images that came to my mind were dark and cruel: mud-caked horses driven to the limit of their endurance, sprays of blood spattering dull armor, sharpened swords tearing into human flesh. I did not wish Rose's mind troubled with such things; there was horror enough in our lives as they were.

"It's only . . ." Rose paused and straightened her papers, as if ordering her thoughts. "I do not know how to describe Prince Bowen. Marl deRauley is easy enough; he looked like a villain from all I've heard, with his black hair and giant dark horse. What was Prince Bowen like?"

She stopped and looked at me expectantly. He was her uncle, her father's brother, yet she had never met him. It was a wonder she had not asked about him before.

"I believe that in his youth he was very like your father," I said. "They both had the same red-gold hair, much like yours. I've been told he was quite handsome. By the time I met him, his looks had faded. The price of a dissolute life, I suppose."

I regretted the words as soon as I said them. Thankfully, Rose did not demand an accounting of his many sins.

"But how could he have felt such hatred? To murder his own brother?"

"Jealousy is a powerful force," I said. "Yet none of us thought Bowen capable of doing the deed by his own hand. It was the reason your father was caught off guard."

"Ah." Rose sighed and rubbed her eyes. "Yes, it will make a dramatic ending." She did not sound enthused at the prospect of writing it.

"I think you need a rest," I said, shaking my head when she began to protest. "You cannot write and write without pause. What if we read some other poems? Perhaps you might be inspired with ideas for your own."

"I don't see how that will do any good," Rose said. "I know Mother's books by heart."

Of course she did; books were a rare commodity at court. Suddenly I remembered the neat stack in Mrs. Tewkes's room and how astonished I had been to see it when I'd first arrived at the castle. Other than the queen and Sir Walthur, Mrs. Tewkes was the only person I knew who read anything other than Bible verses. Would she have taken her books when she left? Surely not all of them; a woman traveling alone would spare herself such a heavy burden. I decided to surprise Rose and excused myself to go downstairs and take a look.

The door to Mrs. Tewkes's room at the end of the Lower Hall

was closed, as it had been since she left. Like most doors at the castle, it had no lock, yet I hesitated before entering. Mrs. Tewkes had been such a powerful force to those of us who served under her; rifling through her things felt like a betrayal of the high standards she had always upheld. I told myself I was only doing this to help Rose, a goal Mrs. Tewkes would have praised, and then I pushed the door open. The room was shrouded in darkness; a heavy gray tapestry had been drawn over the window, blocking the sunlight. The stack of books sat in their usual place on the table, but deciphering their titles in such dim light was impossible. I walked toward the window to pull back the cover but stumbled over an obstacle between the desk and the bed. Distracted by the clatter, I reached down to right a stool that had fallen. From my lowered position, I found myself at eye level with the bed. Low enough and close enough to see that a human figure lay there.

The shock froze me in place. Who would show such disrespect to Mrs. Tewkes by sleeping in her bed? Could I back away unnoticed?

"Elise?"

The voice was little more than a croak. I crept to the head of the bed and stared down at Mrs. Tewkes, her face blistered and burning. The signs of pox were heartbreakingly clear.

"I was told you had left . . ." I began.

She stopped me with a shake of her head, wincing at the pain of the movement. "I did not wish to worry the queen." Her voice was weak, yet still tinged with its former authority.

"You cannot lie here alone! You'll need fresh water, food—"

"Who would tend to me in this state?"

Mrs. Tewkes, who once commanded an army of servants with little more than a glance, was now no better than a leper. Were it known she carried the pox, the king himself might push her out the gates. Watching carefully to make sure no one saw me leaving the room, I fetched water and a piece of bread, then emptied the waste from the chamber pot at the foot of the bed, my eyes watering at the stench.

"What else can I do?" I asked.

"My suffering will not continue much longer. I need nothing but your prayers." She turned her face from me. "You have already endangered yourself. Go."

"I will check on you again soon. Be assured, I will tell no one."

The sight of Mrs. Tewkes, resigned to her terrible fate, haunted me for the rest of the day. The following morning I returned to her room with a pitcher of water and more bread. I dampened a cloth and laid it over her forehead. The swollen spots looked close to bursting. Already I could see her eyes succumbing to the burning redness that came from hours of wakefulness. It was a mercy she had not seen the pox before, for she was spared the knowledge of what was to come.

This was Millicent's doing, I thought with a surge of anger. Though Mrs. Tewkes was too weak to respond to my questions, I knew she had been given charge of Millicent when the old witch returned to the castle. Millicent may have clutched her arm. Whispered in her ear. By cursing Mrs. Tewkes with this affliction, she had doomed all the servants as well, for few dodged the housekeeper's attentions. I felt the pox gathering like a mist around us, yet I could do nothing. Nothing but tend to Mrs. Tewkes as best I could, cooling her fever to offer a brief respite from pain.

She died two days later. She had not spoken a word since my first visit, and near the end, lost in a haze of eternal, blazing fever, she could hardly have been aware of my presence. Death, when it came, was a blessing, for it brought her the rest she had been so long denied. When her eyes closed at last and her body was released from its anguish, I pulled the bedclothes over her disfigured face and whispered a prayer for her soul. Every hour that I tended to her, I had known it was my duty to alert the king and queen to her fate. Yet I had not done so, hoping my care might be enough to save her. It was not. Mrs. Tewkes's death was a harsh reminder of the plague's grim resolve to claim both the wicked and the good. Yet my skin remained unblemished, my eyes clear.

As I left Mrs. Tewkes's room for the last time, closing the door behind me, a group of male and female servants walked past me in the Lower Hall, seemingly uninterested in my presence. They spoke in low tones, with none of the spirited banter that had always made this the liveliest part of the castle, but I saw no signs of fever or ill health. Had Mrs. Tewkes distanced herself early enough to halt the pox's spread? Was it possible the other servants might be spared? So intent was I on rooting out sickness among the maids and footmen that I did not look for it a few floors above, among those of higher rank.

Most ladies-in-waiting had deserted the castle, leaving Lady Wintermale as the queen's primary companion, a prominence she had not enjoyed for some years. She spent her days at Queen Lenore's side, disparaging the latest gossip even as she shared every morsel. I did not begrudge the woman her attentions to the queen; unlike so many who curry favor with flattery and lies, she prided herself on speaking the truth. Demanding and imperious though she might have been, all she did was for love of her mistress.

I first heard the sound as Lady Wintermale passed me in the hallway outside the royal apartments. She swept by with a brief nod in my direction, enough for me to see that her face was more flushed than usual, and then she cleared her throat with a brief, dry rasp. I stopped and turned. Lady Wintermale entered her room, pressing the door shut behind her. I followed, looking around to ensure I was not observed, and leaned my head against the wood. The cough came again, harsher this time. Then again. I had heard such sounds before, years before, on the farm. I had coughed in just the same way one morning, feeling flushed and out of sorts; the next day spots had erupted across my skin. Lady Wintermale might not know what such a cough portended. Or perhaps she was scouring her body even now for signs of those deadly blisters. My heart sank with misery. Such news could not be kept from the king and queen, yet I shrank at taking on such a duty. *I must be sure,* I told myself. *Not until I am sure.*

I waved toward a passing chambermaid. "Have you seen Lady Wintermale's maid?"

The girl shook her head. "Not today, ma'am. Nor yesterday, now I come to think of it."

I knocked on the door to Lady Wintermale's room. After a moment she opened it and glared at me suspiciously. Her cheeks were pink, her eyes bloodshot.

"Excuse me," I said, bowing my head respectfully. "If I might have a word with your maid?"

"She's taken ill," Lady Wintermale said. Then, seeing my face fall at her words, she hurried to explain. "A problem of digestion, she tells me. She has always had a weak stomach."

Mrs. Tewkes. A sick maid. A noble lady with a cough, staring at me with red-rimmed eyes. I saw it all in an instant, death progressing ever forward. Unyielding. Unstoppable.

But what could I say? Even as my world crumbled, I could not fling accusations at a woman who outranked me.

"Your own health is good, I hope?" I asked.

Lady Wintermale pulled her shoulders back, the very picture of righteous offense. "Excellent!" she pronounced. I did not understand then how a woman as direct as Lady Wintermale, so quick to point out fault in others, could blind herself to the truth of her own condition.

"If that's all," she sniffed before closing the door in my face. I waited a few moments, listening. The coughs did not resume. Would my suspicions alone convince the king to confine Lady Wintermale to her room? Who would be next?

A terrible vision struck me then, so clear that my stomach clenched in horror. I saw every inhabitant of the castle, servants and masters, stricken one by one with coughs and swellings, dying all around me in a surge of blood. Myself, alone in this vast castle, the only living person in a realm of corpses.

Eighteen

ENTOMBED

On my way to Queen Lenore's chambers, I was greeted by the king, who was arriving to accompany his wife to supper. With the court's drastic change in circumstances, many of the usual formalities had been abandoned, and the evening meal was now the only one served in the Great Hall. Multicourse feasts had been replaced by a few simple dishes, and the number of tables set was half what it had been before the war. Yet the royal family continued to sit on their dais, presiding over what remained of their court.

Queen Lenore greeted us with a smile.

"Allow me a moment, I must ready myself," she said, indicating her unadorned neck and arms. A woman of her position would never appear in public without jewels appropriate to her rank.

"Lady Wintermale . . ." I began, my heart pounding.

"Of course. She has the key to my jewel chest. Where has she gone?"

"I believe she has taken ill."

I spoke the words in a near whisper, but that did not lessen their effect. Queen Lenore caught her breath and took a step toward me.

"Ill?" she asked, clutching my arm. "What ails her?"

My somber face was answer enough, and she dropped her hold with a look of such despair that I ached for her.

"I am so sorry, but you should know that Mrs. Tewkes succumbed as well, though she took care to hide it from you. She died a short time ago."

"Mrs. Tewkes? Dead?" Queen Lenore's voice rose along with her panic. "If the pox has taken her, it will take us all. I thought us protected, but there can be no escape from such evil, I see it now. . . ."

I waited for the king to hush his wife. Instead he allowed her terrified ramblings to run forth unopposed. He sank into a chair and stared into the distance like one gone blind. It was the first time I had seen his gift for stirring words desert him, and his stillness chilled me more than the queen's prophecies of doom.

"We must leave this place." Queen Lenore's hands twitched in the folds of her skirt as she paced before her husband. "The king of Hirathion would give us refuge, would he not?"

King Ranolf did not respond.

"A boat!" she exclaimed. "Yes, yes, that is the way. We will keep to the river until we have sailed past the contagion. If we make it as far as the sea, there are many lands that would offer us shelter. I could send word to my father. He would take us in as long as need be, I am sure of it."

Even if the king had approved such a mad plan, I knew from my walks atop the walls that there were no vessels to be had. St. Elsip's harbor stood empty; anyone with a boat at his command had long since sailed away. There would be no escape by water.

"We are none of us spared." The king's hushed voice brought an instant stop to his wife's frantic movement. "I was a fool to think I could keep the pox at bay."

His voice was wistful, that of an old man recalling his youth. "If Lady Wintermale has fallen, there is nothing to be done. We must accept our fate."

Queen Lenore's legs crumpled underneath her skirts, and she fell at her husband's feet, burying her face in the hem of his tunic. Her trembling body erupted with desperate, tormented wails, distilling the very essence of human suffering. I could not help remembering the queen I had once known, long ago, who could lie in bed crying yet not utter a sound. Years of self-reproach had worn away that inner strength, and no defenses remained. King Ranolf sat motionless, making no attempt to ease his wife's anguish. Was this moment the death knell of their once passionate marriage? I could never have watched with such coldness as someone I loved suffered. Had it been Rose sobbing before me, I would have embraced her, stroked her hair, murmured words of encouragement—

"Rose!" I blurted out.

On hearing her daughter's name, Queen Lenore turned to me, her tear-stained face frantic with terror.

"She is well," I reassured her. "She has largely kept to her rooms since the gates were closed." I looked at the king, hoping he would understand where my thoughts were leading. "It may be her salvation."

"So there is still a chance for Rose," the king said with sudden urgency. "She must be distanced from anyone who might carry the pox, courtiers and servants alike. Elise, is it true that the illness cannot befall the same person twice?"

I nodded.

"Then you are the only one I trust as my daughter's companion."

I glanced from the king to the queen. She listened with her lips pressed tightly, stifling her objections. She would not oppose her husband's commands in my presence, but she would never agree to a separation from her daughter. That would be too high a price to pay.

"We would need food," I said quietly. "Firewood as well."

"See to it, then. Now. I'll send my man to assist you in the storerooms."

I nodded.

"Go about your tasks quietly. If word of this should spread, it might bring on panic. You and Rose must be locked away before anyone knows why."

Locked away. My heart sank at the prospect, but I forced my thoughts toward more practical matters. How long would we be shut off? What other supplies would we need? It would take more than a few days for the pox to make its way through the castle. Could we survive alone for weeks? Months?

"Go!" the king ordered.

Before I had time to understand what was happening, the process was set in motion. I rushed to my room and filled a sack with clothing and my few personal belongings; by the time I'd brought the bag to Rose's room at the top of the North Tower, barrels of wine were already being carried up the winding stairs behind me. I made my way down to the kitchens to help gather food. With Mrs. Tewkes and half the staff gone, the servants' quarters had sunk into disarray: Fires were no longer lit in the mornings, and meals for anyone outside the king's circle were prepared haphazardly, if at all. Yet the king's words still held sway there, and the kitchen maids assisted me quickly and without question. The castle had not fallen so low as to disregard the wishes of our master.

When I had satisfied myself that we had ample provisions, I dragged a final sack of dried apples to Rose's room. I bowed my head to the king as I passed him in the doorway, but he did not acknowledge my presence. Queen Lenore stood directly inside, her back pressed against the wall as if she might collapse to the floor without its support. When she caught sight of me, she beckoned me over with a quick flick of her eyes and thrust a small velvet bag into my hand. I caught a glimpse of gold through the opening and knew immediately what it was. I nodded, silently acknowledging her wishes, and placed the bag at the bottom of the trunk where Rose's dresses were stored.

Across the room Rose sat on her bed with her legs pulled up under her skirts. Her parents must have informed her of the king's plans while I was downstairs, for she asked no questions. Her lower lip drooped in a slight pout, an expression I was intimately familiar with, for it was the same expression of displeasure she had used ever since she was a child denied a sweet before supper.

King Ranolf's valet placed a final log atop a pile of firewood. He turned to the king and said, "That's all, my lord."

The king nodded and sent him out. I surveyed the confines of my new life. To my right was the large window overlooking the countryside, a landscape untouched by the contagion that had silenced St. Elsip. Stacks of food were arranged underneath, alongside tin buckets of water. To my left was the worktable where Rose did her writing and sewing; two chairs with tapestry seats and backs sat before the fireplace. Through an archway lay Rose's large bed, overhung with a purple velvet canopy. Underneath I glimpsed a corner of the straw pallet that would be my bed. I thought back to the hovel where my parents had raised six children in a space half this size. They would not have thought my imprisonment here a hardship.

"Elise, do you have what you require?" the king asked.

I nodded.

"Good." He did not move. I glanced at Queen Lenore and saw a woman crushed by grief. Her eyes were damp with tears as she gazed at Rose, gorging on the sight of her daughter.

"How long am I to be shut away?" Rose demanded imperiously. She began to rise from the bed, but the king raised his hand to stop her.

"I will leave that for Elise to determine." He signaled me to approach and whispered his orders out of his daughter's hearing. "Stay here as long as your supplies last. If the pox passes us by, I will notify you as soon as it is safe. Do you understand?"

"Yes, sir."

"Bolt the door, and do not open it for anyone."

Rose must have heard this, for she called out, "Am I not permitted visitors?"

"No," the king snapped, worry harshening his tone. "No one must come near you, don't you see? Any one of us might be carrying the sickness even now." He looked at me warily. "You have felt no signs?"

"No, sir."

"The future of the kingdom is in your hands."

Queen Lenore caught her breath in a choked sob, and Rose leapt off the bed. I extended an arm to stop her as the king cried out, "Stand back!" Rose's face fell as understanding washed over her.

"Mother?" she begged.

Tears streamed down the queen's face, and her voice emerged as a faint whisper. "We must keep you safe. It is the only way."

Rose's lips, so disdainful moments before, were now trembling. She looked from her mother to her father, desperate. "But you're not sick. Why must I be kept from you? I can't bear it. . . ."

The king turned his back on Rose, a gesture that would have appeared heartless to one who did not know him. I saw his dismissiveness for what it was: protection from his daughter's despair.

"Lenore!" he ordered briskly.

Wrenching sobs racked the queen's body as she sank against her husband's chest. Firmly, he wrapped an arm around her shoulders and led her toward the doorway, even as I caught Rose's wrists with my hands to prevent her from running across the room. The two women erupted in a cascade of sorrow: Queen Lenore's moans coming low and mournful, Rose's protests escalating into hysterical screams. The king pulled his wife outside without looking backward, her body crumpled against his. As soon as they were out of sight, I ran and bolted the door, just before Rose flung herself against it, pounding her fists frantically against the wood.

"Mama!" she shrieked. "Mama! Don't leave me!"

I kept my hands firmly on the bolt, ready to fight Rose off if necessary. But she released her anguish on the panels of the door, slamming her palms until they must have stung. When she finally fell to her knees, I wrapped her in my arms, as I used to do when she was a child sent screaming into wakefulness by nightmares. I knew that my embrace could not offer the same solace it once had, and my body ached with the misery of powerlessness.

"Elise," Rose pleaded, looking up at me with flushed cheeks and red eyes. "What if I do not see them again? What if they die?"

She had spoken my own fears aloud. But I took the king's orders to heart. My duty was to protect Rose, even at the cost of the truth.

"They'll be safe," I assured her. "The pox has made its way through the servants' quarters, far from your mother's rooms. They wish to spare you any chance of illness, that is all."

"How long must we wait?"

"Not long," I said. "A week, perhaps two. We'll pass the time well enough, you'll see."

Rose wiped her face with the back of her hand and took a deep breath, calming herself. "A week. We can manage."

"Of course we can," I said confidently, reaching out a hand to urge Rose to her feet. "Come, you must help me decide how best to arrange all these baskets of food."

Rose joined me in the task willingly enough. But the echo of Queen Lenore's sobs haunted the room. I tried to think of something to say, but it was no use. Nothing could drown out that heart-rending sound.

If I have shown some small talent in recounting the events of my life, it is thanks to those days confined with Rose, for they made me a storyteller. I ordered our days as precisely as Mrs. Tewkes once oversaw the household: breakfast upon rising at daylight; the morning spent reading or writing; a midday meal followed by an afternoon of needlework; a light supper, which Rose helped me prepare, marveling at my ability to cook over the flame in her fireplace; and, as the light outside faded, an evening of conversation, our voices drifting toward each other in the dark until we fell asleep.

The first few nights, I retold stories Rose had loved as a child, tales of fair princesses and noble knights slaying fire-spouting dragons. Legends in which spells were broken and love triumphed. When my store of such entertainment ran dry, I moved on to more truthful accounts. I tried to paint pictures of the place where I was born, describing how the mist rose from the ground at dawn when I walked to the barn to milk the cows. The way the oxen marched across the fields, laying out furrows behind them. The smell of simmering fruit filling us with hungry longing as my mother prepared provisions for the winter.

I did not tell it all: I spared Rose descriptions of the chilblains that plagued us during the winter or how it felt to huddle with my brothers under one threadbare blanket, shivering against one another in a bundle of bony limbs and rumbling stomachs. I did not speak of my father's beatings, my mother's blank-eyed despair. And nothing of the death that stole my family. I would not speak of the pox.

Instead I recounted my wonder when I saw the castle for the first time and my awe at her mother's kindness. I told of Queen Lenore's joy as her stomach grew round and the tender way the king laid his hand on her belly. How happy they had been on the day she was born. The remembrance of it brought pangs of loss, but such stories appeared to cheer Rose, for she often requested that I describe the same scene over and over. At times, as we lay there in the dark, the years melted away, and I could have been back in the maids' bedchamber with Petra, exchanging whispered confidences. How old and self-assured Petra had appeared to me in those days and how I had longed to mold myself in her image! With the passage of time, our disagreements had faded into insignificance; I was content to remember her as a loyal friend and mourn her departure from my life. Never having known such a friendship, Rose did not feel the lack, but I thought it the one richness she had never possessed.

The days wore on, each passing as the one before. When the room was bathed in daylight, we kept our spirits light. We went about our tasks as if it were perfectly reasonable for two women to live separate from the world, playing the parts of gracious ladies with no cares. But when night approached, our spirits grew darker along with the skies. With only dim views of each other's face by moonlight, we opened our souls. Rose began to demand that I fill in the gaps in my recollections.

"You have not spoken of my baptism," she said one night.

"What of it?" I asked warily.

"Millicent. The curse."

Her voice was weighted with sorrow. Even if by some miracle the king and queen were to emerge unscathed, Rose would carry the burden of these days forever. The girlishness that had lingered in her womanly body was gone, replaced by the knowledge that fate was capricious and cruel. That beauty and rank and wealth were no protection against loss.

After all that had passed, I thought it could do no further harm to hear the truth. Indeed the story came easily, for I remembered each moment with eerie clarity, from Millicent's appearance in the Great Hall to Flora's assurances that she would protect the baby. The only part I dared not speak of was Queen Lenore's account of her bewitchment in the cavern beneath the church of St. Agrelle. That tale, I determined, must remain as buried as the evil shrine itself.

"She had her revenge in the end," Rose murmured. "She brought death to my house."

I rushed to forestall such thoughts. "Millicent was a devious woman, but she had no magical powers. The pox spreads of its own accord, striking the godly and the wicked without distinction."

"Do you believe so?"

"Of course," I said firmly.

But I had no way of knowing whom it had struck beyond our door, for two weeks had passed since the terrible parting of mother and daughter. We had received no visitors, heard no footsteps pass along the hall outside. I had expected Queen Lenore to reach out to Rose in some way, through letters slipped under the door or whispers from outside. Had the king ordered her to stay away, or was it sickness that kept her from hovering outside her daughter's bedchamber? Rose's melancholy wafted over me, and there were no more stories that night, only silent remembrances.

Every morning Rose looked at me warily, her eyes asking an unspoken question. And every morning I left my bed and turned from her to wash my face, refusing to answer. To her credit, Rose did not moan complaints or beg to be set free; she followed my orders and went easily to the tasks I set her. When we had embroidered every one of her petticoats and mine, I declared we would start on her sheets; I could not allow our time to pass idly. As my stock of stories dwindled, I embellished insignificant court gossip into grand drama in an increasingly desperate attempt to fill the empty hours. One evening I told of a long-ago flirtation between a stout cook and her comically tiny beau, drawing out each incident of their romance in the hopes it would take us past sundown. Shadows gradually enveloped the room, and I began pulling out the laces of Rose's bodice in preparation for bed.

"You have told many tales of love," she said quietly, staring forward. "Do you not have one of your own?"

I blushed, though I knew she could not see me. I had not spoken Marcus's name in years. Could I tell our story with the detachment of age, or would my voice still carry a trace of girlish longing?

Rose's voice broke the silence as she stepped from her gown. "Forgive me. It must pain you to speak of the happiness you shared with your husband."

My husband. When Rose spoke of love, it was not Dorian's name that sprang to mind. I hesitated, remembering Marcus's face at the castle gates. The sight of him had released a tangle of emotions I thought long since buried, and I found myself yearning to recapture the selves we had once been, young and hopeful and churning with desire.

"There was another I lost my heart to, long before I married Dorian."

Rose turned, her eyes bright with expectation. She sat on her bed and curled her legs up under her shift. "Was it someone you knew when you were young? On the farm?"

I folded her dress and placed it gently in the storage chest at the foot of the bed. "No," I said. "I met him here, in town."

"Why did you not marry?" She had pulled her hair loose from its ribbons, and the auburn waves tumbled down her shoulders and arms. She looked like a child again, so free of cares that I felt myself hurtled back in time. If the tale of my heartbreak could divert Rose from her own, it was worth telling.

So I revealed what had passed between Marcus and me. With the wisdom of years, I was able to give us both a fair hearing, acknowledging our love for each other and the difficult choices we had been forced to make. Yet Rose was outraged on my behalf.

"There must have been some way you could have married Marcus and continued to serve at the castle," she said. "Cannot love and duty go hand in hand?"

"For a fortunate few," I said. "It did for your parents."

I knew as soon as I spoke the words aloud that I had made a mistake. Rose's face sank, and the room's darkness passed from soothing to oppressive. I jumped up quickly and lit a candle on the table beside the bed.

"All this talk of love has made me wonder," I said lightly, hoping to move Rose's thoughts elsewhere. "You never told me what passed between you and the handsome ambassador that night in the Receiving Room."

"You will think me so foolish." She stopped abruptly, with the sort of dramatic hesitation girls use when they wish to be urged on.

"Hardly. Have I not confessed my own tragic romance? I must have your story in return."

"You said something about your young man, Marcus. How you knew he had certain qualities, even though you'd barely spoken. It hardly seems possible, doesn't it, to feel you know a person you have just met?"

"Is that how it was with Joffrey?"

The words poured out of her in an unstoppable torrent. "If you could have heard him at the feast that night! He was charming, of course, as a man in his position must be. But it was not that. He spoke with proper deference, but also as an equal. I could have talked to him for hours and not once tired of the conversation. When he smiled, it felt as if my entire soul lightened. And then, when we danced and our hands touched . . . an understanding passed between us. Something beyond words. I know that it was wrong, but I led him to the Receiving Room without a second thought. I was desperate for a few moments alone."

She paused and looked down at her skirt, then continued in a hurried, nervous voice. "He kissed my hands and said I had stolen his heart. I know that courtiers make such declarations all the time, and I should have laughed in his face, but I did not. I believed him."

Her story had all the marks of youthful infatuation: love springing from a glance, two hearts coming together without words. I had read such stories a thousand times in the queen's poetry. Which did not make this tale any less true in Rose's eyes.

"Joffrey struck me as an honorable man," I said. "Not the sort to trifle with a woman's affections."

"I said I would visit Hirathion," Rose continued, cheered by my encouragement. "That I would not rest until I saw him again."

I remembered how it felt to be filled with that urgency, the surge of warmth flooding across the skin, the desperate need to see and touch your beloved, again and again.

"If the bond between you was as strong as you say, then your paths will cross once more," I assured her.

"They have, in a way."

Rose slipped a hand under her pillow and drew out a piece of paper folded into a tight square. She offered it to me silently, and I opened it near the candle that flickered at her bedside, gently spreading out the creases. It was well crafted, as one would expect from a man skilled in diplomacy. Joffrey sent congratulations on King Ranolf's victory and expressed his own sovereign's wish that their two realms remain united in friendship. He spoke of the warm welcome that would await her family should they choose to visit and the sights he hoped to show them. It was not a love letter, for any of the lines could have been read without suspicion by a curious parent or guardian; there was no such thing as private correspondence for a royal princess. Yet a tone of yearning pervaded every line, if one were disposed to see it.

"Is this the only letter he has sent?"

Rose shook her head. "There were others, before the war closed off the northern roads. This is the first I have received in months. I was so desperate to know if he still thought of me!"

"He did," I said. "He does."

"I know I cannot marry him," Rose said, looking at me with the intent stare that reminded me so much of her father. The look of a woman strengthening herself to take on the weight of leadership. "I will do my duty. I will marry a prince. But I want to feel what it is to love, just once."

King Ranolf would have thundered with rage to hear such a declaration from his sheltered Beauty. It nearly broke my heart.

"Then you will have it," I said. "Your parents have already agreed to such a journey. I will see to it that you and Joffrey are able to steal some time together, alone."

It was a reckless promise. Rose was brash enough to kiss him, perhaps more. I did not care. We passed the rest of that night in girlish chatter as she relived every moment of Joffrey's visit. Blocking out the darkness around us with memories of a time Rose shone with happiness.

That was the last lighthearted conversation I remember between us. A few days later, most of our buckets of water sat empty and the liquid in the final one covered no more than a finger's length. The stench of our chamber pots had long since overpowered the dried lilac and sage I had placed on the wooden box that enclosed them. By my reckoning we had been shut away for three weeks. Despite the king's admonitions to await his summons, I could no longer delay an expedition beyond our locked door.

"You must stay here," I urged Rose.

"Mother and Father . . ." Rose begged.

"You cannot leave this room until I tell you it is safe. I will find your parents, and I may venture into St. Elsip to see to my cousin, Prielle. I will be as quick as I can. Promise me you will wait."

Rose nodded her assent.

The bolt pulled back with a metallic screech. I opened the door and peered out into the hall. It was deserted. While the quiet of this remote wing had always unnerved me, I had never heard it so utterly silent. There were no distant footsteps, no clatter of horses or workmen from the front courtyard, no voices at all.

I dragged our foul pots to the privy around the corner and emptied them into the waste pit, then picked up a clean jug. Rose stood in the doorway, watching, her face blank. I handed her the new pot and took hold of our empty water bucket, nodding quickly to her before pulling the door closed. From the other side, I heard the bolt heave into place.

Before me snaked the gloomy corridor that led to the heart of the castle, interspersed with shadowy recesses marking the entries to the servants' passages. Finding my way to the royal apartments meant navigating these dark halls and stairs alone, and for a moment I lost the will to proceed. Fighting the urge to turn back, I tightened my grip on the bucket's handle and walked forcefully ahead. My steps echoed against the stone walls, and I quickened my pace until I reached the wide staircase that led directly to the public rooms on the main floor of the castle. I had never seen this stairway empty of people, and it was in that moment that I knew in my heart what I would find at the bottom.

The smell was what struck me first. Anyone who has slaughtered pigs or chickens on a farm recognizes the stench of death. I emerged from the stairs and walked hesitantly along the wide passageway that led past the castle's grand public rooms. And so I came to the chapel and a scene of carnage I wish I could banish from my nightmares.

It had begun in an orderly fashion. Ladies and gentlemen of noble birth had been laid in neat rows directly before the altar in preparation for burial, Lady Wintermale likely among them. But that careful respect had degenerated into sickening mayhem. As death stalked the castle, bodies had been tossed one upon the other in heaps throughout the room, the foot of one lying across the eyes of another. A few had been wrapped in white sheets, but the rest lay as they died, figures clothed in simple brown maids' smocks entwined with others clad in costly dyed velvet. I did not approach the scene close enough to recognize any of the faces; I doubt I could have done so, for the features were swollen and monstrous, the ravaged skin and blood-spattered lips giving all, no matter what their birth, the same death mask.

The nauseating odor made my head spin, and I dropped the

bucket, fearing I might faint. But I could not return to Rose's side without discovering the fate of her parents, even though I knew in my heart what that fate must be. Whatever turmoil the castle had suffered, the bodies of the king and queen would never have been added to this gruesome heap. They would have been left to lie in state, as their position demanded. Slowly, reluctantly, I quit the chapel and made my way up the grand staircase that cut through the center of the castle.

Queen Lenore's sitting room appeared unchanged: chairs arranged neatly before the fireplace, the harp in one corner awaiting a musician's entertainment. Only the withered flowers in a vase beneath the window showed any sign of neglect. Through the doorway of the bedchamber, I witnessed a scene that momentarily weakened me with relief. The king and queen lay peacefully together on the bed, their backs to me, asleep.

It took only one step to reveal the tableau as a tragic portrait. As I came close enough to see the king's face, I realized the pox had wreaked its devastation upon him. His handsome features had been conquered by oozing pustules, and his mouth, ringed with dried blood, had been forced open by his swollen, blackened tongue. To look upon him was to see death's agony made real.

Beside him the queen's face appeared remarkably untouched. Though red welts were scattered over her neck and chin, her cheeks remained smooth and her forehead clear. The pox, it seemed, had respected the remnants of her beauty even as it snatched her final breath.

The sight of them, together in death, nearly undid me. How could I tell Rose that both her beloved parents were dead? What comfort could I possibly offer after such a loss? Desperate to escape the rank air of the king and queen's death chamber, I raced from the room and down the stairs. I picked up the water bucket and hurried through the deserted kitchens, making my way to the well in the back courtyard. The horse stalls were empty, as were the pens that housed the sheep and hogs, and streaks of grain and flour traced the path where sacks had been pulled out from the storerooms. Discarded apple cores and gnawed bones were evidence that people had been here, not long ago, gorging themselves on the castle's provisions. But the clatter of my bucket and the squeak of rope as I pulled up fresh water brought no call, no response. Were Rose and I the only living creatures left inside this vast fortress?

I walked to the front courtyard and saw that the main gates stood open. Below me St. Elsip beckoned, and I was momentarily reassured by its sturdy houses and churches. I placed the water bucket in the castle's front doorway, awaiting my return, and ran down the hill toward town, my eyes hunting for any movement, any sign of life. The crowds of people who once would have jostled past me had vanished. I heard nothing but my own lonely footsteps as I walked through the eerily empty streets. Houses, shops, taverns—all sat silent behind bolted doors. Amid the quiet I felt the strange sensation of eyes upon me, watching. I myself was proof that the pox did not kill every person it touched. *I cannot be the only one,* I thought. *Others must have lived.* If so, they preferred to observe my progress from the shadows.

My aunt Agna's house had the same abandoned aspect as all the other buildings I had passed. Planks of wood had been nailed across the downstairs windows, and the door appeared to be bolted from the inside, for it did not budge or creak when I attempted to open it. I rapped a few times with my knuckles, then slammed the wood with a flat palm.

"Prielle!" I called out. "Is anyone there?"

I pressed my ear to the door but heard no movement inside. A weary sorrow settled over me, and I leaned against the doorway, unable to conjure up the will to move. I had thought my letter to Prielle would keep her safe from the contagion, but she had been taken all the same. Would there be no end to my losses?

A sudden clatter rang out through the silent street, and I perked up at the unexpected sound. More desperate for human companionship than wary of danger, I stepped out to see where it had come from. As my eyes roamed over the buildings, passing quickly across Aunt Agna's house, I thought I saw a flash of white at an upstairs window. Could it be a face, drawn by the commotion, just as I had been? Whatever it was quickly disappeared, and I put it down to a trick of the light.

A grubby, wild-eyed man emerged from a house at the corner, a bulging sack flung over one shoulder. He stared at me, then turned and ran. Had the pox so terrified him that he feared contact with any other living thing? I hurried to the house from which he had come and glanced inside. Silver goblets and painted dishes lay scattered across the floor. Only a well-off family could afford such fine things, and the man who ran out had been dressed in rags. I remembered the sack, his shifty expression. The man was stealing from the homes of the dead.

Fearing what other lawlessness I might stumble upon, I quickened my steps as I hurried back toward home. If thieves were ransacking St. Elsip, would they turn their sights to the undefended castle? How long would we be safe there? I felt so alone, so lost. So desperate for the sight of a familiar face.

I had arrived at the Bridge of Statues and, beyond it, the road that led to Marcus's tannery. The place where he had offered me shelter. A force beyond my body urged me forward, and I crossed the bridge, my steps picking up speed until I was running. I might have been a foolish young girl again, heart racing at the thought of seeing my beloved. Such was my desperate need for comfort that I did not pause to think what a sight I would present, appearing without warning, dirty and disheveled at his door. I did not consider the possibility that Marcus might be ill, or dead, his family perished around him. I stumbled along the muddy path through the trees, my thoughts fixed solely upon my destination.

Though I knew where the tannery lay, I had never visited it, so I was drawn up short when I arrived at a tall iron fence. The gate at the center was not locked, and I pushed it open carefully, taken aback by the size of the property. Before me stood a fine two-story brick house, with three chimneys. To the right was a large wooden barn, to the left a neatly planted kitchen garden. Behind the garden, some distance away, sprawled a spacious plaster-walled building that I took for the tannery, surrounded by modest cottages that most likely housed the workers. The stench I expected from such work was not evident, though perhaps that was due to the pox. All work must have come to a halt in the past few weeks. Perhaps forever.

I walked slowly through the gate. The garden appeared well tended, a promising sign. I took hold of the door knocker, a brass figure of a ram's head, and rapped twice. The door was opened by a young woman of fourteen or so, wearing a dress of fine-quality wool that indicated she was not a servant. She met my gaze directly, unnervingly so, for I found myself looking downward shyly as I asked for Mr. Yelling. She said nothing, simply turned her back to me and strode away, leaving the door open behind her.

Unsure whether or not to enter, I stepped into the doorway and peered around. The house was simple but well kept, though I caught only glimpses into the front rooms. The chairs and tables I saw were as fine as any pieces in my aunt's house. Scattered about were the usual odds and ends of family life: half-knit socks and a roll of yarn flung upon a chair, cloaks of various sizes hanging from hooks along the wall, an assortment of miniature carved wooden animal toys. I suddenly felt ashamed of my intrusion into Marcus's world. I had arrived on his doorstep uninvited and unexpected, taking his help for granted, as if he had no other worries or demands on his time. I had no right to expect anything from him.

I heard footsteps approaching from the back of the house, and there was no opportunity to do anything but stand at attention as Marcus walked toward me. The smile that brightened his features provoked an equally pleased grin on my face.

"Elise!" he exclaimed. "I am so glad you've come."

Faced with a welcome far warmer than I deserved, the confidence that had propelled me toward his door vanished. Wringing my hands nervously, I began mumbling apologetically.

"I am so sorry to disturb you. . . ."

"Nonsense!" he assured me, but I heard a hint of wariness as he glanced from my face to my hands, checking for signs of the pox. I had been adept at such studies myself in the days before all around me fell dead.

"Be assured, I am well," I said hastily.

"Please, come in."

He led me into the front room and insisted I sit down, taking a chair opposite. The girl followed, standing over his shoulder and watching me with an intensity that bordered on rudeness. A boy, a few years younger, peered around the edge of the doorframe, then pulled away when my eyes caught his.

Following my gaze, Marcus said, "My son, Lian. And this is my daughter, Evaline. Evaline, this is Elise. We've known each other since we were children." This was not strictly the truth, though close enough in spirit. Our bodies were grown when we'd first met, yet our thoughts and feelings had been childish, changeable. I still did not know what sort of man Marcus had proved to be.

Evaline continued to eye me warily. Uncomfortable with such scrutiny, I turned my attention back to Marcus. There was so much to say, but the words would not come. The ease of our initial greeting had stiffened into discomfort; the weary father before me had little in common with the love-struck young man I had carried so long in my memory. Had I made a terrible mistake?

"Have you come from town?" Evaline asked sharply. "Do you bring news of my mother?"

I remembered telling Marcus his wife was not safe in St. Elsip, that he must bring her home. Had he disregarded my warning? I looked at Marcus, my face silently asking the question, but he turned away.

"Elise has come from the castle, on a personal matter," he admonished his daughter. He rose from his seat and addressed me directly. "Come, I'll show you around the property, and we can speak in peace."

Evaline pouted with disapproval, but she said nothing else. Marcus led me outside and onto a pathway that led alongside the house. We passed the garden and stables, ending at a clearing that edged the forest. It was a tranquil spot, within sight of the house but secluded enough that two people could speak without being overheard.

"I must apologize for Evaline's behavior," he said, his face revealing the weariness that so often afflicts parents. "She has become quite unmanageable since Hester's departure."

"Your wife has been in town all this time?"

He paused, as if gathering strength to tell a story he wished forgotten. "I did as you told me. I went back to her sister's to fetch her, but by then, you see, she had already breathed the air of the sickroom. I thought of Evaline and Lian, their . . . health. . . ." He stumbled over the words, gripped by the hesitant stammer I remembered so well. I ached for him, to be faced with such a choice.

"So you put your children's safety above all else and returned home alone," I guessed.

"I told myself Hester would return of her own accord. I would not have barred her from the house, even if she were sick, I swear." It was clear he had not forgiven himself for turning back that day. For being afraid.

"Who is to say what passed? Your wife may be well, only afraid to travel."

Marcus looked at me intently. "Have many survived?"

I thought of the streets and houses of St. Elsip, seemingly empty of all but corpses. Tears began to stream down my cheeks, and my chest heaved with sobs.

Marcus put his arms around me, shoring up my body with the force of his embrace. The inappropriateness of such contact with a married man did not enter my thoughts; all I felt was an overpowering relief that the burden of bravery had finally been lifted. Here, at last, I could release my grief.

As my cries subsided, Marcus loosened his grip. I allowed myself a few heavy breaths to feel the weight of his arms a moment longer. When I fell silent, he pulled away. His face was tight with worry, and he avoided meeting my eyes as he ran his hands through his hair and took a step back. We had first spoken politely as strangers, then clung to each other as lovers. Lulled by the sunlight, the fresh air, the gentle chirping of crickets, I had imagined myself thrust back in time, to the days when Marcus had the power to lighten my cares. But the man who stood before me was in many ways a stranger, and this foolish dalliance had distracted me from a matter of life and death.

"I must go," I exclaimed. "I have left Rose too long."

"She lives?" he asked, his face brightening with hope. "Then the king's plan worked. The castle was saved."

"I wish it were so," I said, speaking quickly so I would not have time to conjure the image of the bodies piled in the chapel. "The king and queen are dead, and those who survived have fled. Rose and I are the only ones who remain."

"You cannot stay in that vast place alone!" Marcus exclaimed. "Is that why you sought me out? You are welcome to stay here, both of you. Under the circumstances no one would begrudge the princess taking shelter in such a humble home." His voice held the urgency of one who seeks peace through acts of penance. "There must be some way I can help you."

"You already have," I said.

"Elise . . ." Marcus looked into my eyes, a direct, unflinching gaze that caught me off guard. For a single tantalizing moment, he seemed about to confess to feelings I thought long repressed. Instead he glanced downward and rubbed his hands wearily across his cheeks and back around his head, a gesture that brought a pang of remembrance. I had seen him do the same years ago, clearing his thoughts.

"I'm hardly the person you should look to for comfort," he said sadly. "I'm barely managing as it is. We had to shut down the tannery, and with no work coming in I can no longer pay my men's wages. The pox may have destroyed my business for good. I've put up a brave front for the children, but they ask after their mother incessantly. I'm tired, so tired of lying to them."

"If the worst has befallen your wife, delaying the news will be no kindness. Best they know one way or the other."

I reached for his hand and brushed my fingers lightly against his. One last touch before facing what awaited me at the castle. "I must be off. I have been gone from Rose's side for too long."

"Wait." Marcus took hold of my arm. "It's long since time I went to St. Elsip. I will drive you."

I accepted the offer gratefully. After Marcus had bade farewell to his children, I took a seat beside him on the front bench of a worn-out cart.

"If there are thieves about, there's no sense in tempting them with my carriage," Marcus said, smiling wryly. "I am aware this is far from the royal transport you're accustomed to."

I burst into a laugh, a response far out of proportion to the joke. I laughed again as the cart started and my body lurched with the movement, hands reaching wildly for the plank of wood beneath me. Confined so long by my duties, I had forgotten how tightly they constricted. I shifted in my seat, trying in vain to take a position where I was not at risk of tumbling to the ground.

"I see that the soft living at court has spoiled you," Marcus teased.

"Indeed. I wouldn't dare be seen in a humble tannery cart."

"Imagine the disgrace," Marcus said, shaking his head in mock disapproval.

As I searched for a suitably witty retort, we passed an opening in the trees and the glint of sunlight on water caught my eye. It was the meadow where we had lain years before, the place where I had almost surrendered myself to him. Marcus's gaze followed mine, and I suspected that his thoughts did as well. We remembered the boy and girl we once were, delighting in each other and feeling happiness within our grasp. Then we looked upon the man and woman we had become: weary and frightened, wise in the ways that happiness can slip from the tightest clutches. We proceeded the rest of the distance to town in silence, unable to revive our lighthearted banter.

Marcus pulled up the cart at the bottom of the castle hill. "Please, consider my offer."

I saw the sadness in his eyes, the desperate need to salvage something of his self-respect. Suddenly, achingly, I wished he were coming with me, so I would not have to face the horrors of the castle alone. But Marcus was about to discover whether his wife was dead or alive; he must not be allowed to fret about me.

I thanked him, politely yet formally, and stepped down from the cart, taking care to walk away with a steady, determined stride. Ahead, the void of the empty courtyard beckoned, ushering me toward my final, dreaded duty. The weight of the water bucket slowed my already unwilling steps as I returned to the North Tower. No pretty phrase could soften the blow I was about to deliver. Rose's parents were dead, and I would be the sole witness to her terrible grief.

I rounded the corner nearest Rose's room and saw, to my surprise, that the door was open. My pace quickened. I walked briskly inside, laying down the water bucket and calling out Rose's name. There was no reply. The sitting room and bedchamber were empty.

Panicked with fear, I backed out into the hallway. I imagined Rose standing in the same spot, pondering her choices, and knew immediately where she had gone. And what she would see there.

I raced toward the king's apartments, my shoes clattering along the twisting passages.

"Rose!" I shouted out.

A sound from within, more a sniffle than a word, caught my ears, and I hurried inside. I found Rose hunched on the floor at her mother's bedside, clutching the queen's stiff, lifeless arm. Horrified, I dropped to my knees beside her.

"What are you doing here?" I admonished, instantly regretting my sharp tone. Rose was curled up in misery, a portrait of grief personified.

"I kissed her. I felt her breath," Rose mumbled.

Fear cut short my courtesy. "Your mother is dead, can you not see?"

"No, no, it cannot be!"

I leaned over and gently pressed my palm to Queen Lenore's cheek. Her skin felt cold, and her chest lay still. I knew the body capable of miracles. Could she have lain here for days, drifting in that hellish, sleepless state between life and death? Had the sight of her beloved daughter granted her the peace to die?

It was possible. It was also possible that Rose had imagined what she wished to be true. I would never know. All that mattered was that Queen Lenore's spirit was gone and Rose's life was in danger each minute she huddled against her mother's body.

"Get up," I ordered, grabbing Rose's hands.

She struggled to resist me, but I held firm.

"You cannot stay," I insisted, half pulling and half pushing her from the room.

Rose whimpered, but she stumbled along beside me through the sitting room and back out to the hall. I kept one arm around her shoulders, leading her forward, as she stared ahead dully. When we approached her chamber, she turned to me and asked softly, "Where is everyone?"

I hurried her inside, bolting the door behind me. Though I believed us alone, the thieves who ran loose in St. Elsip might be bold enough to venture into the castle before long.

"Elise, why did we pass no other ladies or servants?" Rose asked, her voice rising.

"Many fled," I said, not meeting her eyes.

"Or they're dead." Saying the words aloud brought their full meaning to her attention. "Are they?"

"Not all." Once the pox had passed, those who had survived would return. Rose and I would not be abandoned here, alone, forever. . . .

"You're lying! They're dead! All dead!"

The cries sprang from her body like an evil spirit. I enveloped Rose in my arms, but she collapsed to the floor. I crouched down next to her, pressing my hands to her back and trying to cradle her head in my lap, but she would not be comforted. Like a hysterical child, she wrested herself from me and curled her body in despair, screams hurtling out from the depths of her being. I feared that the sight of her parents had driven her mad.

Suddenly there was silence. Rose lay with her hands wrapped

around her legs, hugging them close to her chest, her tangled hair cascading around her. Her eyes were pressed shut, her breathing heavy.

"Come," I murmured carefully, "you must rest."

She did not protest as I lifted her to the bed, nor when I loosened the laces on her gown and stripped her to her shift. I pulled back the covers and tucked her underneath. The last rays of daylight were gleaming through the window, an hour when I would customarily be preparing dinner and planning my stories for the night. I asked Rose if she would like something to drink, and she shook her head. I lay down beside her and stroked her hair, a gesture meant to soothe, but she was already calm. Eerily so. As I watched her through that night, lighting one candle and then another, she lay peacefully but not at peace. Tears trickled silently down her cheeks, but she made no sound. The abnormal quiet unsettled me more than her earlier hysteria.

"Others have survived the pox, just as I did," I told her. "We are not the only ones spared."

"Spared," Rose whispered. "To what purpose?"

I watched her blank eyes stare upward. Those were the last words she uttered that night, and the following day and night. I was afraid to leave her side as she lay in a daze, ignoring my questions, refusing more than a few sips of water. I told myself that such grief was to be expected in one of her emotional nature. In time she would come around.

Then the spots appeared.

Nineteen

THE FINAL BATTLE

I saw them first on her hands, lying flat atop the blanket. Four pink eruptions, each no wider than a mole. Hardly cause for alarm to one who did not know what they portended.

Had Rose noticed? Given her lethargy, I did not think so. But her stupor and disinterest in food took on an ominous weight. I had thought her distressed more in mind than body. I had missed the signs of the illness overtaking her, draining her strength in preparation for its onslaught.

For a moment I sank against the bed and grieved her fate. All the king's precautions, all my care, had been for nothing. Helpless and overcome, I could barely keep myself from sobbing in anguish that the person I loved most in the world was to be taken from me. Then, suddenly, my mind recoiled from the thought. With the same stubborn determination that had led me away from the farm, I vowed that Rose would not die. I would cling to her and cling to life. The pox had taken my mother and my brothers. Mrs. Tewkes. Queen Lenore. I would not relinquish Rose.

I reached into the bag of supplies I had brought from my room and pulled out a small wooden box from the bottom. Opening it, I surveyed Flora's arsenal of herbs and tonics. There was no cure for the pox, but I refused to fall back in helpless surrender. I would weaken my deadly foe by attacking the disease on all fronts. Already Rose's skin was heating up from fever, so I must start by cooling her down. I grabbed a clean cloth from a table and soaked it in water, then laid the wet fabric over Rose's brow.

"You're flushed," I said. "This will make you more comfortable."

Taking one action, no matter how inconsequential, was enough to raise my spirits. I scooped up a bowlful of oats and boiled them in a pot over the fire; when they had softened into mush, I insisted Rose have a few spoonfuls for nourishment. I brought her a clean shift and told her it was time to wash the one she was wearing. Watching her strip off her gown would allow me a glimpse of how far the pox had progressed.

Rising slowly from the bed, Rose loosened the ties in front, and the garment slid down off her shoulders. I wanted to weep at what I saw: an army of pink pustules invading her tender, helpless skin, migrating from her shoulders and forearms down the small of her back and stomach. Even in her dazed state, Rose must know what such a sight signified.

"Are these the signs?" she asked, her voice devoid of curiosity.

"It's early to say. . . ." I fumbled.

"It is the pox," Rose said simply. Was she so dulled by grief that she did not care whether she lived or died?

I knelt before her and clutched her wrists, twisting them slightly to draw her attention toward me. My hands pressed against her skin, as if my strength could pass into her very bones. "It began this way with me, and I lived. As will you."

Rose wrenched herself from my clutches and reached for the clean shift I had laid out on the bed. She pulled it over her head, turning from me, avoiding my eyes, and climbed back into the bed.

"Go, Elise," she said softly. "Save yourself."

"I am not the one who needs saving." I felt unreasonably furious, so much so that I had to walk to the other side of the room and busy myself with cleaning out the soup pot. Did my feelings mean so little to her that she would disregard them completely? How could a young, beautiful girl go so easily to her death? No. I would not allow the thought to linger in my mind. If it could not be imagined, it would not happen.

Through the rest of that endless day and the one that followed, I tried to summon Flora's voice in my mind, guiding me toward the ways I could ease Rose's suffering. When the spots turned an angry red and bulged up from Rose's arms and chest, I soaked strips of cloth in boiling water and pressed them against the pustules until they burst. I rubbed a salve over the resulting sores to lessen their sting and dabbed essence of mint across her chest to ease her breathing. When Rose's cheeks burned with fever, I brought a bucket of cold water sprinkled with dried lilac to her bedside and bathed her from brow to feet. As soon as I had finished, I pulled off her sweat-dampened sheet and covered her gently with my own.

"Elise." Rose's fingers reached out to clutch my hand.

"Yes, my darling?" Her voice was little more than a croak, but I rejoiced to hear it. She had not spoken for close to two days.

"Do you remember my dreams? The witch?"

I remembered them well, those nightmares that had shaken Rose from sleep with desperate screams. On those nights so long ago, I had cradled her in my arms until she stopped crying, feeling her body slowly go limp as she drifted off. If only it were as simple to console her now. If only the pox would release her from its clutches long enough to grant her an evening—an hour!—of sleep.

Rose's lips parted slightly in a weak attempt at a smile. "You were the only one who could calm me. You made me feel safe."

"You are safe with me, Rose. Always."

"Mother. Father."

What heartbreak can be conveyed with two simple words! I ached for her loss as if it were my own.

"If they are dead, I am queen."

I told her to shush, that such matters could wait, but the thought had troubled me as well. Rose was now the ruler of this ruined land, the person St. Elsip's survivors would look to as they struggled to remake their lives and their town. How could Rose take on such a burden, even in the best of health? Who was left to help her? Would our enfeebled kingdom fall to invaders who knew we could not fend them off?

"I never told you . . ." Rose's voice trailed off, and I urged her not to tire herself, but she gathered her strength and continued. "I used to imagine you were my older sister, watching over me."

I remembered leaning down to grab her tiny body by the waist, swinging her around in a flurry of skirts and giggles. Rubbing my nose against her pudgy cheeks as Queen Lenore's other attendants looked on with narrowed, disapproving eyes.

"I have always loved you as if you were my own flesh and blood," I said.

I knelt by the bed and gently ran my fingers over her forehead. The heat from her fever brought a flush to my own skin.

"There is something I must tell you."

I had never intended to confess the truth of my parentage to Rose, and perhaps it was wrong to trouble her mind with such revelations in her weakened state. The only defense for my actions is the truth. In that moment I told Rose what I thought she needed to hear: that her parents might be dead but her family was not destroyed. There was still one person at the castle who would be forever bound to her by blood.

"The man who raised me was not my father," I said. "My mother was seduced before she was married. By Prince Bowen."

Rose had strength for only a slight gasp. "Why did you not tell me?"

"I did not wish to dishonor my mother's memory. The only reason I speak of it now is to tell you we are truly family. I will not leave you."

Rose slipped her hand over mine; her palms were sticky with sweat.

"We are cousins, then," she whispered.

I nodded. "Yes, my darling. And sisters in spirit."

"I am so glad." Rose's voice was barely louder than a breath. Her hand fell away from mine, but her eyes remained open, staring upward, burning with exhaustion. My own memories of the pox were faint and jumbled, but I could recall all too well the torment of wakefulness. Without sleep Rose would have no escape from her anguish. She would suffer through a never-ending twilight of pain.

With relentless determination the illness advanced through Rose's body. By the following day, her breathing was ragged, her skin inflamed. The only sound she made was an occasional moan, and I winced with every cry, feeling her suffering as my own. When her tongue began to swell and she choked, panicked, on the food I offered, I poured water drop by drop into the corner of her mouth. Like the mother birds I had seen feed their young, I chewed tiny morsels of bread to soften them before gently nudging the pieces past her lips.

That afternoon, when the fading sunlight reflected my inner foreboding, I wondered how much longer Rose could endure such suffering. My own experience of the pox was no guide: I did not know how many days I had been sick or how my symptoms varied from hers. Rose's face had been spared the worst of the swelling, and I considered her resilient beauty a beacon of hope until I remembered her mother's similarly smooth face, unaltered yet dead nonetheless. If my ministrations were prolonging Rose's pain, all my efforts amounted to nothing more than cruelty.

If she could but rest. The thought haunted me, for I knew it was in my power to grant her the relief, if I would but dare. Among the many formulas listed in Flora's ledgers was one for a sleeping potion, one I had never made and that she herself had cautioned me against. I remembered Flora's voice, warning me that every body accepted its properties in different measure; the same amount that lulled one person into slumber might kill another. Rose's debilitated condition would put her at even greater risk. If I had sensed any improvement, any slight lessening of her agony, I would not have taken such a terrible risk. But she had grown worse by the day, by the hour, until she was clinging to life solely by chains of pain. If she were to die—and I could barely acknowledge the thought—would it not be the ultimate act of love to grant her peace in her final moments?

I knelt beside her and whispered her name. "If it has become too much to bear . . ."

I could not finish. In any case Rose showed no sign that she had heard me. Her eyes stared into mine blankly, unseeing, so inflamed that it hurt to look upon them. I hunched by her bedside, fearing that each shuddering breath might be her last. Time slowed. My knees grew numb against the stone floor, and my back ached; still I kept vigil over her. Rose had not slept for days, and I had dozed no more than a few hours in all that time. My thoughts had become frantic, feverish. I got up from the floor and peered out the window. Night was approaching, a time when only the wicked are about.

My mind whirled with tangled thoughts, each memory leading to another. The sunlight in Marcus's garden, cleaning my skin of death's stench. The same bright light in my face many years before, as I sat with Marcus along the riverbank, watching ships sail into the harbor. Marcus and Rose in the castle courtyard, their faces pink with cold, reaching up to catch snowflakes in their hands. Rose as a swaddled baby, clutched in her mother's arms while Millicent vowed to see her dead. Flora's voice telling us that no harm would come to Rose under her care. Was the potion I feared most the one that might save her?

I grabbed Flora's ledger from the wooden box where I kept the collection of herbs and powders. Frantically, my fingers flipped the pages, until I found the list of ingredients. I had all but one: lavender blossoms. A memory pulled at me, elusive yet insistent. I closed my eyes and pictured myself following Flora through the castle garden. I could see her gauzy skirt graze the pathway as we passed the lavender bush. I could remember its sweet, fragrant scent. My smile of pleasure. Flora's girlish voice: *You feel it, don't you? Lavender's power to soothe the soul.*

In that moment the decision was made. If I sat in this room any longer, waiting for Rose to die, I would go mad. I pulled a shawl from my trunk, then paused, staring at the gleam of red and green that beckoned from the bottom. I had saved Dorian's dagger as a remembrance of my husband, never expecting to have a use for such a lethal object. But now, with bandits about, such a companion might strengthen my courage for what lay ahead. I strapped on a leather belt and slid the dagger in along my waist, gripping the handle to harden my resolve.

I picked up a candle and opened the door. The weak flicker of candlelight was hardly enough to see by, but I could have found my way in utter darkness, so familiar was the route. My footsteps clattered through the vast, silent space as I navigated the twists and turns of the fortress-turned-tomb, the place where I had lived through unimaginable happiness and crushing sorrow. I moved swiftly past the Great Hall, the scene of so many grand banquets, and into the Receiving Room, once my beloved queen's domain, now simply another desolate, empty shell. No voice called out at the sound of my approach, yet I could not escape a pervasive feeling of watchfulness. As if the shadows of all those lost were watching me pass, waiting to see what I might do.

I pushed open the small door on the far side of the room and stepped out into the garden. The last rays of sunlight bathed the plants in an amber glow. Weeds had overtaken the beds, and the gardeners—had any remained—would have been harshly reprimanded for the unruliness before my eyes. But I rejoiced to see it, overgrown and untended as it was. An echo of past happiness still lingered there, along the paths I had wandered with the queen and Flora and Rose. Death might surround me, yet here I witnessed rebirth. The rosebushes were sprouting buds, and the herbs were bursting with new growth. If any hope remained, it was here.

I brushed my hands against the tender petals and breathed in the mingled scents, restocking my heart with happy memories. Though thoughts of Queen Lenore brought a pang of loss, I allowed myself to picture her sun-flushed and smiling, following Rose through the vine-covered archways. For all the kindnesses she had done me, I owed her the honor of remembrance. Not as she'd died, but as she had lived.

Finding myself in the heart of the rose garden, a place as holy to me as any church, I sank to my knees. Clutching my hands together, I closed my eyes and prayed for guidance, whether to Flora or to God I could not tell, for they became intermingled in my mind. I prayed for Rose's salvation and my own, for the strength to carry on living if she did not. Slowly, the fear that had weighted my body began to lift and my breathing eased. Whatever happened next, I would know I had done all I could.

I stood and made my way to the lavender bush, where the first flowers had burst from their buds. Pulling off a handful, I slipped them into my sleeve and braced myself for the return journey to the North Tower. It took my eyes some minutes to adjust from the outdoor twilight to the indoor gloom, and the flickering shadows seemed to mock me as I waved my candle in a pitiful attempt to banish them. Intent on my destination, I did not notice the faint glow emanating from the Great Hall. Indeed I might have passed by it altogether had a sound not immobilized me with terror. It was a voice, calling my name.

Slowly, I crept toward the open archway and peered inside. My gaze passed over the marble floors, the lofty walls, the priceless tapestries. Across the room a beacon of light pulled me forward, toward the royal thrones, where a darkened figure sat in wait.

Millicent.

The woman I had last seen as a near-skeleton had not lost her air of decay. Her mottled, scarred skin was stretched tight across her face, and white hair hung in thin wisps across her forehead and cheeks. But she had draped her hunched frame in the lush green cloak I remembered so well, and a glittering crown was perched atop her head. What a fool I had been to think the pox could fell such a woman! Her sunken eyes gleamed with the reflected light of the lantern at her feet. She watched me approach, step by step, savoring the moment. For what satisfaction is there in victory without an audience to applaud it?

So this is how it ends, I thought, *with Millicent triumphant.*

"Have you come to pay me homage at last?"

Her shrill voice catapulted through the room, coming back at me in a horrifying echo. I could only stare at her in mute dismay. I was tired, so very tired, and utterly drained of the will to fight.

"Elise." The word was a hiss, a desecration of my name. "Bow down before me as the rightful ruler of this land."

"Rose is the rightful ruler," I said, not nearly as forcefully as I'd intended.

"Not for long."

The terrible finality of her words chilled me. How could she know that Rose was close to death? Then I remembered the secret passageway that connected her bedchamber to Rose's. Was it possible that she had been able to hear us from her sickbed? That while I thought her dead, Millicent had been listening to Rose's moans and my desperate prayers?

"I am the last of my family's line," Millicent proclaimed, "and with Rose's death the throne passes to me. As it should have, long ago."

She had the look and bearing of a madwoman, yet I could not deny that her words held a certain truth. Had she not been born a woman, what a ruler she might have been! Freed of the bitterness that had so corrupted her soul, she would have been capable of greatness.

"Even Flora agreed, did she not?" Millicent looked at me with wide-eyed innocence, knowing that the name of her deceased sister would play upon my sympathies. "She knew that my brother was a fool. Yet he took the reins of leadership, and I was left with no greater task than to find a husband. Imagine, Elise! Would that have been enough for you?"

I had always spoken in favor of Rose's inheriting the throne. How could I not feel a pang of sympathy for Millicent as she once was, a woman whose talents had been crushed by custom and expectations?

"The kingdom must have a strong leader in these troubled times," Millicent continued. "I will be your savior!"

Did she know how closely her cry of victory mimicked a lunatic's cackle? Or did she simply not care? There was something magnificent about her still, sitting in self-righteous glory upon the throne that had eluded her for so long. I stood at the edge of the dais, looking upward, an obsequious position that brought a twisted smile to her face.

"You have done your best for Rose, but it is too late. Come—we shall celebrate the dawning of a new era. I assure you, Elise, it will be unlike anything you have ever experienced."

She pulled herself up to stand, clutching the throne with one hand and reaching forward with the other. I caught a flash of burnished gold and saw she was wearing King Ranolf's signet ring. The ring that had been handed down from father to son for generations as a symbol of their rule. The thought of Millicent pulling it from the king's lifeless finger filled me with an overpowering rage. Her lust for power had destroyed the royal family and transformed a glorious castle into a graveyard, yet she had emerged from the ashes, gloating at her victory.

Millicent flourished the ring before my face, demanding the ultimate gesture of supplication. As her twisted knuckles came to within an inch of my face, I felt the belt cut into my waist. The press of the dagger against my side. With a swift, sudden movement, I took hold of her hand and tugged with all my strength. The jerk knocked her off balance, and she toppled from the dais, landing on the floor with a dull thump. For all her menacing air, Millicent was still an old woman, and her frail body was no match for my ferocity. Her cloak and skirts had fallen back to reveal her skeletal legs and arms, a pathetic sight that might have evoked sympathy in any other circumstances. But I had no shred of compassion left for Millicent. I would never allow the kingdom, no matter how weakened, to be ruled by such a creature.

I drew the dagger out from my belt and brandished it before me. My body retained the memory of Dorian's lessons; I could still feel his arms pressed against mine, guiding my strokes. My hand seemed to move of its own accord, following the steps laid out by my husband years before: Twist the blade sideways so it slides between the ribs, then thrust upward with a sudden, brute force. Show no hesitation. No mercy. Millicent's screams and mine blended together as I took aim at her heart, plunging the dagger into her flesh until the handle—and my hand upon it—jammed against her chest. Blood gushed from the wound, spattering my fingers and sleeves. I pulled the blade free and stared, appalled, as the crimson liquid poured from her bodice.

Millicent's mouth gaped in silent agony as she struggled to breathe. I took a step back, then another, distancing myself from the pool of blood that was gathering at my feet. Her knobby hands grasped at the air, and her body writhed as her life force gradually seeped away. She looked, for once, like a harmless, helpless old woman, and I was momentarily aghast at what I had done. Then I saw her eyes, blazing with a hatred that banished any doubts. I would never be safe until she was dead.

Millicent had fooled me once before, when I thought the pox had taken her. I would not make the same mistake again. I watched as her twitching movements slowed, as her eyes closed and her gasps faded into silence. Gingerly, I stepped forward to check for signs of life. Millicent's arms and legs lay motionless, and her chest was still. Her mouth hung open, frozen in an eternal, futile cry.

How, then, could her tormented screams still assault my ears?

I turned to look behind me. There, in the doorway, stood my cousin Prielle, eyes wide with shock, shrieking loud enough to wake the dead.

As if such a thing were possible.

The sight of me rushing toward her, bloodied and still clutching my murderous weapon, did nothing to ease her distress, for she shrank away from my embrace, trembling. I wiped the dagger flat across my skirt to clean it as best I could; I knew I would never wear the dress again.

"Prielle, thank God you are safe," I said. "Please, do not be afraid. I can explain."

"I thought . . ." Prielle struggled to keep her voice steady. "I thought I would be safe here. When you came to my house that day . . ."

"You were inside? Was it your face I saw at the window?"

Prielle nodded. "When I received your letter, I did exactly as you said. I stayed indoors and waited for my parents. They left as soon as the fighting ended, to reestablish trade with their partners in the north."

Prielle's parents had followed the same roads used by the returning soldiers, walking through a cloud of contagion. I could already guess how her story would end.

"They said they would be gone only a few days, and I waited and waited, but they did not return. As soon as word got out about the pox, the servants fled—said they'd take their chances in the country. But I remembered your warnings, and I stayed. Alone!"

I put a hand on her shoulder to calm her, for tears were now coursing down her cheeks.

"I guessed my parents were dead. They would never leave me so long otherwise, without sending word. But I did not know what to do! And then one day I heard a knocking on the door, but I was too frightened to answer. I peered out the window, and when I saw your face, I was so happy, for I thought myself rescued at last, and I rushed down the stairs, but by the time I came out, you had already gone."

"I am so sorry," I said. "So very sorry."

"I didn't know what to do. But today I decided I would rather take my chances with the pox than stay another hour in that house by myself."

The shadows had deepened; the candle I had brought and Millicent's lantern had both been extinguished during our scuffle. Soon Prielle and I would be left in complete darkness, and who knew what further perils might lurk there?

"I am so glad you have come. But we cannot stay here."

I glanced back at Millicent's body, a jumble of twisted limbs that bore little relation to the imposing figure that had once held such power over me. She was dead. Why, then, did I feel so empty?

Suddenly I remembered Rose, lying alone all this time. Without my cajoling had she given up the fight for her life?

"Come," I urged Prielle. "We must go to the princess's room."

My heart dropped when we first entered the bedchamber, for Rose lay so still she might have been an effigy carved atop a tomb. Then, hesitantly, she turned at the sound of my footsteps. Her cheeks were pink, but not the blazing scarlet that had so frightened me in the days before. Her eyes were bloodshot and her skin slick with sweat, but my dear Beauty was awake and alert. The fever had broken. Rose had survived.

I had imagined myself falling to my knees in grateful prayer should Rose be spared. And I did sink to the floor, but it was not to give thanks to God. I collapsed because I no longer had the strength to stand. Relief mingled with a suffocating grief, and with wretched moans I wept for the king and the queen, for all those souls who lay forgotten and unmourned in the chapel below. I wept for Prielle's family and my own, for my poor dead brothers who had known only drudgery and hunger in their short lives. And I cried for my younger, innocent self, who had died along with all the rest.

The sheets rustled. I raised the hem of my gown to wipe aside my tears and runny nose, and brushed back the hair that had come loose from its holders and hung ragged about my face. Leaning against the side of the bed, I rested my head on the pillow next to Rose's. She stared at me in confusion, her mind still muddled.

"Elise." Her voice was as faint as an echo heard from a far-off corridor.

"I am here, my darling."

Rose looked over my shoulder, trying to make sense of the unfamiliar face that had entered her room.

"We have a new companion," I told her. "My cousin, Prielle. I know you will become great friends."

Prielle hovered behind me, unsure of her place. I waved her forward, and she joined me at the bedside, her pinched expression loosening as she looked down at the princess she had so long envied. Then, in a gesture that touched my heart, she dipped in a curtsy. Rose watched, motionless as a figure on St. Elsip's Bridge of Statues, then looked back at me.

"Is it true?" she whispered. "My mother?"

Before I could formulate the right words, she understood what my hesitation portended. I watched as the full force of it hit her anew: the fate of her parents, the castle, her life. She closed her eyes in a vain attempt to blot out the vision, and I was overcome by hopelessness. The anguish I had seen wash across her face was beyond my power to heal.

Prielle stared at me with questioning eyes, and I saw her for the first time as she must have appeared to Rose: a thin, terrified girl, clad in a filthy dress more suited to a beggar woman than to a successful merchant's daughter. Great blotches of red marred her bodice and skirt, and I realized to my horror that the stains were

Millicent's blood, pressed onto Prielle's gown from my own. I glanced down at my reddened, sticky hands and felt my stomach twist with revulsion. Frantically, I pulled off the dress. I tossed aside the lavender twigs I had picked in the garden and scrubbed my hands and arms until the skin stung. Once I had changed, I told Prielle to do the same, insisting she take one of Rose's gowns. Our old clothes I burned in the fireplace, destroying all evidence of my murderous deed.

I watched the flames catch at the fabric and tried to formulate a plan for the coming days. I now had two young women in my care, looking to me for guidance. When Rose was well enough to travel, we would go to Marcus—a thought I clung to as a beacon, lighting my way forward. But that would be merely a temporary respite. Rose was now the ruler of this land; she could not hide from her duties forever. Who would serve as her advisers, her courtiers, her ladies-in-waiting? Who would clear the bodies from the castle? Restock the stables with horses and the storerooms with food?

And how could Rose ever sit upon her father's throne, now that it was sprayed with Millicent's blood?

When nothing remained in the fireplace but ashes, I urged Prielle to lie on my pallet. I could hear Rose's down-filled mattress rustle as she shifted position, and I wondered if her thoughts were mirroring my own. The pox may have passed, but I feared for her nonetheless. Would her agitated mind deny her the rest she so desperately needed? Could her fragile body withstand such strain? Consulting Flora's ledger once again, I mixed up the sleeping potion, forcing my attention to remain on the task at hand rather than on the risk I was about to take. Gently, I urged a spoonful into Rose's mouth, then watched as her eyes fluttered shut and her hands fell slack against her bedcovering. I continued to watch as her chest lifted and sank in a peaceful, unchanging rhythm.

At long last my Beauty slept.

Yet I could not. I watched her throughout that night, attentive to every breath and whimper. When the sun came up, I cooked a mix of oats and nuts in the fireplace and devised a list of activities to fill the day, just as I had done when Rose and I were first locked away. I took out my sewing basket and asked Prielle to join me in embroidering handkerchiefs. I found the poem that Rose had written to honor Dorian and read it aloud, trying my best to add dramatic flourishes. Prielle listened, wide-eyed, and gushed in admiration at the end. But Rose made no response. She would not speak or eat. She refused even to look at me.

As the hours passed, I became increasingly desperate. In the evening I exhausted myself baking a cake in a skillet over the fire, using up the last of our sugar on a dish I hoped would tempt her. The cake itself emerged sunken and half burned, and though Prielle accepted a piece gratefully and gobbled it down in a flurry of crumbs, Rose turned away from my offering without a word. In a fit of frustration, I threw the pan to the floor. Even that clatter failed to rouse her interest. Her face remained toward the wall, resolutely blank. As the shadows overtook the bedchamber once again, her empty eyes seemed to gleam, a point of harsh clarity when all else was dim.

Prielle sat huddled on the floor in front of the dying fire, her thoughts as much a mystery to me as Rose's. She had told me once she hoped for nothing more than a good marriage and a home filled with beautiful things. Was that simple wish to be denied her as well? I felt a wave of love for that frightened yet good-hearted girl, even as my patience with Rose's willfulness dwindled.

"Tomorrow you will rise from this bed," I told her. "You must eat, else you will never get well."

"And what then, Elise?" The words were clipped, cold. "Prepare for my coronation? Push aside my mother's body that I might sleep in the bed where she died?"

"Of course not," I snapped. And yet what else had I imagined? This was the seat of the kingdom's rulers. If she were to take up the crown, it would be from here. "We will leave the castle for a time, until it has been put back to rights."

"To rights?" she asked mockingly. "As if I could ever forget what I have seen here!"

"You will not. Yet this is your home."

"No longer. Not without Mother and Father. I never wanted the throne, or the jewels, or the adulation. My parents are dead, and I wish myself dead alongside them. Better that than condemned to a lifetime as queen!"

She had not yet regained the strength to shout, so her final words came as a rasp. Yet I saw the fire blaze once again in her cheeks. If she was set against the life laid out before her, she would not fight to regain it.

Before I could protest further, she had pulled the cover over her face, hiding from my judgment. I turned to look at Prielle, who sat with her knees drawn up toward her face and her arms wrapped around her legs. She looked like a cowering child, and for once I had no words of reassurance to offer. Darkness overcame us, and

I did not rise to light a candle or move from the chair in which I collapsed. I simply sat through those endless dark hours, my mind tormented with the twists and turns of a puzzle that had no solution.

I must have dozed at some point, for I awoke with a renewed understanding of why it is wise to retire to bed come nightfall. For evil thoughts take strength from the dark, while hope thrives in the light. With the coming of day, my circumstances did not seem as dire as they had at midnight. Rose and Prielle remained listless yet unfevered, and I gave thanks for their continued health. It would not be long before I could seek out Marcus—my heart fluttered at the thought—and he would help us decide our next steps. For a time, at least, we would be free of the castle's misery.

Despite her lethargy I insisted that Rose get out of bed and wash. I changed her covers and took off her sweat-stained nightdress, insisting she choose a clean gown from her trunk. Pouting, she pulled out the first that came to hand, a simple dress, free of adornment, that seemed in keeping with her dreary mood. The bodice hung loosely at her waist, and I was dismayed by the proof of how much weight she had lost. Yet her face showed none of the hollowness that illness often brings. Her once expressive eyes no longer sparkled, and her pale cheeks had lost their healthy pink glow, but she was still beautiful. When I attempted to brush her hair, she pushed my hand aside, and I used the ribbons I had picked out to arrange Prielle's wavy tresses instead.

Rose sank into the chair before the window, overlooking the country view that had first drawn her to this room. Silently, she watched the unchanging hills and fields, and I tried not to be discouraged by her languid manner as the day progressed. I convinced her to take a few sips of soup at midday, but she did not join Prielle and me in hushed conversation. Noting Prielle's weary expression, I urged her to lie down for a rest in Rose's bed, and she soon drifted off, the worry easing from her face. How very peaceful she looked, free of all cares, and I wished I could be granted the same respite. Minutes dragged as if they were hours. How many times had I warmed water over the fire, tried in vain to ply Rose with food, stared at these four walls? I felt I had been trapped in that tower for years, watching over a princess whose loveliness remained unchanged, even as the last of my own youth melted away.

It was the rumbling I heard first, faint yet steady. Hoofbeats.

"Rose? Do you hear that?"

I might as well have addressed an empty room. Rose sat as she had all day, ignoring me. I leapt to my feet, straightening my gown and smoothing loose curls off my face. Though I could not see the front courtyard from the tower windows, I heard the clatter of horseshoes on the paving stones, a familiar sound from the days when the castle bustled with life. I had thought our visitor must be Marcus, but surely the pounding was louder than what a single carriage would make?

"I will see who it is," I told Rose.

My spirits lifted as I fled the room. I rushed down the stairs to the entrance hall and out the front doors, pulling up short when I saw what awaited outside. A contingent of proud, muscular horses stamped and whinnied along the drive. Their riders had the stiff bearing of soldiers, but the finest sort, dressed in velvet tunics and tall leather boots. A few held swords with elaborately carved handles. As I walked warily toward them, they gathered in a ring around me, staring with the wonder of people confronted by a mythical creature. At the center was a slim man who led his white horse forward to stop next to me. He held himself with the stillness of authority, and every aspect of his appearance signaled noble birth, from the soft leather of his riding gloves to the way he gazed at my face and clothes, assessing my importance.

I bowed my head. "I am Elise Tilleth, lady-in-waiting to Princess Rose."

"She lives?"

The voice rang out to my left, and I turned to see a man slide down from his saddle, doffing the slouched hat that had partially obscured his face. It was Joffrey, the ambassador from Hirathion, staring at me with a desperate intensity.

"She fell ill, but the worst is past."

"Ah . . ." The gentle exhalation was a poor expression of the relief that washed across his face.

"I regret to report that the pox did not spare her parents," I continued. How easily the polite words came, neatly glossing over the horrors that lingered in the building behind me. "Our losses have been terrible indeed."

Joffrey was silent a moment, allowing the effect of my words to settle among his companions. Then, collecting himself, he indicated the imperious man on the white horse and said formally, "May I present His Majesty Prince Owin of Hirathion."

"We heard tales from travelers who fled your kingdom," the prince said. "Tales of a royal princess locked away, awaiting rescue. Joffrey was most insistent we come and discover the truth of the matter."

The prince was still quite young, I noted. The age when a man is most likely to be tempted into a quest to save a beautiful maiden. He dismounted and glanced about. "Where are the groomsmen?"

"Gone, or dead. Along with the guards and the cooks and everyone else."

"You and the princess are here alone?" Joffrey asked me, horrified.

"That will not do," said Prince Owin. "Take me to her."

The demand brought a restless movement from one of the soldiers. Moving forward, he revealed himself as a burly man of middle age, the sort of loyal fighter entrusted with the safety of an heir to the throne. "If she's been sick, it would be better to stay away," he urged.

Joffrey looked at me searchingly, his eyes silently begging for approval. "You say she is recovered?"

I thought of Rose, sitting in mute despair. Could this man's face help lure her back to the world?

"She is weak, but the pox is no longer with her," I said. "I am sure of it."

Prince Owin pulled off his gloves and tossed them to one of his men with the carelessness of someone whose needs have always been tended to by others. "Gilbart, take the men and search the grounds for other survivors. Joffrey and I will see to the princess."

I had been granted time by then to accept the state of the castle as it was, but its air of eerie foreboding struck me anew as I led the two men inside. They flinched at the stench that filtered out from the chapel, and the silence of the halls settled upon us as we walked. There were no questions, there was no conversation. Just the sound of our footsteps climbing higher and higher, to the tower at the top of the castle.

I tapped lightly on the door to alert the girls to my arrival, then pushed it open. For a moment an image was framed before us: Prielle, lying asleep on the bed, her golden-brown hair tumbling onto the pillow, skin burnished by the sunlight. Her delicate pink gown—a princess's garment—enhanced the blush of her cheeks. One hand lay demurely across her stomach; the other was flung sideways across the bed, as if in a gesture of welcome.

Ignoring all propriety, Prince Owin strode into the room and fell to one knee beside the bed. "Princess Rose," he murmured.

Directly behind me Joffrey caught his breath, and I whirled around to see if he would be the one to correct his master's error. But Joffrey was not looking at me, or the prince, or Prielle. He was looking at Rose, sitting in the chair by the window, in a position initially hidden by the open door. Her lower lip had dropped in surprise, and she stared at Joffrey in astonished silence. Joffrey was at her side in an instant, reaching for her hands, clutching them to his heart as her expression softened from bewilderment to joy. Here, at last, was the girl I had thought forever lost. A girl who might yet be capable of happiness.

"Elise?"

Prielle's perplexed voice carried from the bed, and I saw that the prince's voice had roused her from sleep. He reached out a hand to clasp hers, then pulled it toward his lips for a kiss. It was a reckless gesture, to touch one he thought recently felled by the pox, but the prince was flush with the bravado of youth.

I had every intention of clearing up his confusion. But then I heard something that made my heart leap. Rose's laugh. And I knew immediately that I might never hear that sound again if I told the prince the truth. To those who would judge me harshly, I can only say that the idea came to me fully formed, as if delivered by a higher power. With a simple switch of names, Prielle could live the pampered life she had longed for and my dear, darling Beauty would be free.

For so great a deception, it was easily accomplished. Prielle was dressed in a manner befitting royalty, while Rose, her striking looks muted by illness and clad in a plain gown, was easy to dismiss as a mere attendant. Joffrey's thoughts were quick to follow my own. He was the only member of the long-ago delegation from Hirathion who had seen Rose up close, the only one who could have pointed out the prince's mistake. It was treason for him to go along with such a ruse, yet he did it willingly, risking death to secure Rose's happiness—and his own.

With a few whispers and glances and nods, it was done. It was Prielle whom Prince Owin carried down from the tower, Prielle whom he insisted be swathed in a blanket and cradled in his arms on his white horse. Rose took a place on Joffrey's mount, clutching her arms around his waist and pressing her face against his back, until they seemed to form a single figure. Prince Owin's man Gilbart tied my satchel of possessions to his saddle and lifted me onto his horse behind him.

We rode off, and I did not look back.

Those who tell the tale of Sleeping Beauty end it here, with the princess saved by a prince's kiss. Is it the truth? A princess was locked in a tower, and she was discovered by a prince. But she did not sleep, and it was not his kiss that brought her back to life. Though a royal wedding was celebrated—completing the requisite happy ending—

the princess was not the woman who said her vows that day. She disappeared into a new name, a new life. One she had finally been able to choose for herself.

Attendants make for poor heroines, and I do not care if my role in Rose's story is forgotten. But I do not wish the lesson of her life to be obscured in myth. What saved Rose was love. Not the infatuation an impressionable youth may feel on seeing a pretty, helpless girl asleep on a bed. No, the love I speak of is far more powerful. It is the love between those who have grown from girls to women together, exchanging laughter and tears, sharing a bond no one can break. The love that kept me at my dearest companion's bedside, hour after hour, willing her to survive. The love of a mother and father who deafened themselves to their daughter's cries in order to keep her safe. The love of a man who risked everything to give his beloved a fresh start.

A love strong enough to beat back death.

EPILOGUE

Does Raimy believe me? I have watched my great-granddaughter's eyes widen in both wonder and dismay as I recount my story. But she may think it no more than another fairy tale, the embellished ramblings of a dotty old woman.

I tell her that Rose and Joffrey lived happily ever after. And they did, or near enough. For can a young woman who has seen her family home turned into a tomb ever be truly happy? Blessed though she may be with wealth and honor, she will forever suspect that death lurks in the shadows. On those first nights away from the castle, which we passed in the home of an elderly kinswoman of Prince Owin, Rose would burst from sleep with screams, tormented by the same nightmares that stalked my own rest. I held her tightly, fearing that her poor, weakened body would give way under the onslaught of such sobs. Joffrey, too, was watchful and tender. He tried to tempt her appetite at table each evening, and I saw him gently trace a finger along her cheek and whisper endearments when he thought them unobserved.

Prielle rose to her new role as if born to it, relishing each curtsy and bow directed her way. If she was occasionally unsure on a matter of precedence or etiquette, her hesitation was seen as an effect of her illness, not cause for suspicion. And Prielle was a quick study. Whether or not she set her sights on Prince Owin from the start, an understanding had soon formed between them, and I knew he would ask for her hand. For a young prince enamored of dramatic gestures, it would be the ultimate rescue.

Prielle and Rose were to be granted a fresh start, but for me the journey to Hirathion brought nothing but dread. I would be living among strangers, a knight's widow who would be looked down on by ladies of noble rank. Rose had need of me now, but for how long? She would have a loving husband and, God willing, children. She could begin a new life. I could not. I had no heart for it.

After all I had lost, all I had seen, I longed for a home of my own. A place I would be welcome as I was. Much as I loved Rose, I yearned for Marcus.

I berated myself for harboring such thoughts, based on little more than a few moments spent in his presence. His wife could have survived the pox, in which case I had no claim to him. Even if he was a widower, he might not wish to wed again. But I had felt something spark between us on that day in his garden. And that feeling was enough to fuel my resolve. For too long my fate had been in the hands of others. This time I vowed to make my own way.

I wrote Marcus a letter. How I agonized over those lines! Surely no poet ever measured his words as carefully. I asked after his family, adding in an offhand manner that perhaps I could visit at some time in the future. In all it was a respectable effort, sociable but not overly familiar. I only hoped he would divine the wishes entwined among the polite sentiments.

The same messenger who took my letter at first light returned with a reply by dusk. Marcus was indeed mourning the loss of his wife, who had died at the home of her sister. The pox appeared to have run its course in St. Elsip, and a few ships had even brought supplies to the harbor. All this was heartening news, but not as much as the letter's final line:

"You are most welcome to visit at the earliest opportunity." Followed by a scribble added in haste at the edge of the page: *"Please come."*

Had I the soul of a poet, I would tell Raimy that Marcus swept me into his arms as I swore undying love. In truth we were cautious when we met again and all too aware of the children's eyes upon us. I was a woman of thirty-two, not a headstrong girl, and we spoke as long-parted acquaintances, exchanging news in measured tones, careful that our voices not carry the weight of our expectations. Afraid to speak our hopes aloud.

It was only in darkness that we revealed the truth of our feelings, in actions more than words. After the children had been sent to bed, we sat before the dying embers of the fire. He reached for my hand and I for his. His lips brushed against my cheek, my hands along his shoulders. We explored the shape of each other cautiously, the curves and warm skin familiar and yet not, for we were older and time had changed us both. It was during those moonlit hours that we became pledged to each other once again, whispering endearments as his hands cupped my cheeks. My love for him, I was delighted to discover, was like those crackling embers: Time and distance had dampened its heat, but the gentle coaxing of Marcus's tender kisses brought it roaring back to life.

I stayed two days. Enough to know that Marcus's home would one day be my own, that the bond between us was strong enough to build a future on. Though we had waited so long to live as one, our vows were delayed still further, for Marcus had to observe the mourning period for his wife, and I refused to leave Rose and Prielle until I had seen them settled.

Rose's wedding was a modest affair, but it was suffused with a joy that larger ceremonies often lack. Joffrey watched his new bride with delight throughout the celebratory dinner, marveling that such a creature could be his. She in turn seemed to drink in her husband's admiration as if it were an elixir, charming everyone from the courtiers to the servants with her bright smile and witty conversation. Though Joffrey called her Prielle in public and furthered the story that she was a cloth merchant's daughter, he addressed her in private as Beauty, and I knew that their shared secret would forever bind them together.

On the morning of the wedding, I carried out my final duty to Queen Lenore, presenting Rose with the necklace of golden flowers her mother had entrusted to me when she saw her daughter for the last time. Rose caressed the fragile blooms lovingly, tracing the same ridges that her mother's fingers had once followed. Then she gathered the strands together, slipped the necklace back into its velvet bag, and pressed it into my hands.

"You will be married soon yourself, Elise. This is my gift to you."

I said I could not possibly accept, but Rose quickly silenced me. "I know you have always admired it. She would want you to have it, in gratitude for all you have done."

She silenced my further protests by reminding me that such a piece was far too extravagant for a merchant's daughter. "I could never wear it without raising questions," she said. "You are a knight's wife. It should go to you."

And so I wore jewelry fit for a queen at the wedding of Prince Owin, which was celebrated in suitably lavish fashion. Prielle carried herself regally through it all, noble in poise yet gracious in her manner. Hailed as Princess Rose, she displayed a genuine affection for her new husband that boded well for their future partnership. But their marriage marked not only the coming together of a man and woman. With those vows Rose's kingdom and Owin's were joined together, and King Ranolf's line came to an end. His castle, seat of a realm that no longer existed, was left to crumble.

Rose sobbed on the day I left her, as did I. But, to her credit, she never begged me to stay. Given her taste for romantic tales, she would not deny me a second chance with the man she dubbed my true love. Prince Owin had granted Joffrey a title and an estate upon his marriage, in recognition of his loyal service, and Rose and her husband would be moving to a manor house at the foot of the Trillian Mountains, overlooking the sea. Rose told me the sight of the water calmed her spirit, and I remembered her furtive outings to St. Elsip's harbor, when she had stared longingly at the open water. I suppose it was a touch of her mother's blood, for Queen Lenore came from a seafaring people.

Our parting was filled with vows of friendship and exclamations of devotion, though I feared that our differing circumstances would ultimately form a barrier between us. Rose's home became renowned for its elegant taste, the liveliness of its entertainments, and the culture of its mistress, with poets, musicians, and artists welcomed as honored guests. But I did not share in such diversions. As Rose supervised the hanging of tapestries and the placement of furniture, I was back on the outskirts of St. Elsip, plunged into a new life. Sleeping and waking with a husband who was both business partner and lover, old friend and new acquaintance, caring for children who were not mine by blood yet mine to raise. I was not accustomed to running a household; indeed I knew little of cooking and nothing of tanning. Yet I did what needed doing to hold my makeshift family together.

I visited Rose when I could, and I am glad to say I was at her side during the birth of her first child. To me alone she confided the visions that haunted her still, the tears that came unbidden and were beyond her power to stop. I did what I could to ease her pain. But Rose's home was a journey of some days from mine. When I in turn was blessed with a child, my darling Merissa, it became even harder to pull myself away. That is the way of it when friends are parted for too long, no matter what the affection between them. Bonds stretched over too far a distance cannot help but weaken with time.

When Rose had asked me if my marriage to Dorian was a happy one, I had not known how to respond. With Marcus the answer was clear. Some days, ground down by Merissa's cries or Evaline's spiteful tongue, I lost myself in bitterness and thought on the life I might have had with Rose. But the feel of Marcus's arms around my shoulders restored my balance, and his joy in our chaotic, cobbled-together family inspired me to give thanks for my many blessings. I even cried to see Evaline married. Never would I have imagined that it would be her grandchild, Raimy, who would prove the greatest joy of my final years.

As for Rose, she brought three beautiful children into the world, two boys and a girl. I always think of the youngest with a pang, for it was she who took Rose's life. It was a difficult birth, undertaken in Rose's fortieth year, when she thought herself past childbearing. She greeted her daughter with happy tears, I was told, before succumbing to the bleeding that has taken so many a mother. Sir Joffrey was kind enough to send me a letter in his own hand, though it did little to assuage my grief.

St. Elsip never fully recovered from the pox's onslaught, though houses that were abandoned for years are slowly welcoming new inhabitants and we hear whispers that an ambitious nobleman wishes to take up residence in the still-imposing castle. The time will soon come when none remember the pox. The shadow that hung over the stone tower will lift, and the building will once again host tournaments and feasts.

Raimy certainly wishes it so. If the castle springs back to life, she will find a place there, I am sure of it. Courts are always open to young women of charm and beauty.

As for myself, I have no desire to walk those halls ever again. In my waning years, I am content to sit before a warm fire with a full stomach. Though the aches in my legs and teeth grow more grievous with age, the pain of the past has subsided. I can think of Queen Lenore and Rose as they were, strolling in the garden, sunlight burnishing Rose's auburn hair and making her mother's dark eyes sparkle. I can remember their laughter, and the smell of leaves and petals I crushed between my fingers. I can remember myself behind them, content to play a supporting role in their story.

Once I chose to hide the keepsakes of my previous life rather than acknowledge all I had lost. Now I find comfort in such memories. The leather bracelet Marcus crafted for me so long ago, when we were little more than children, is once more wrapped about my wrist, a testament to a love that endured past youthful infatuation. Queen Lenore's golden necklace would look foolish adorning my scraggly neck, but I often sit with it laid out in my lap, admiring the delicate workmanship, recalling the nights when I gently pulled aside the queen's dark hair to fasten the clasp.

I am soothed by the thought that Sleeping Beauty's story will live on beyond us all, a tale of evil defeated and love triumphant that will resonate through the ages. And that is as it should be. For the truth is no fairy tale.

Acknowledgments

Writing may be a solitary pursuit, but the right support system can make all the difference in the years between first draft and publication. Since the early days of this project, I have kept a mental acknowledgments list of all the family and friends who encouraged me along the way. Now I can finally make it official.

First, I would like to thank my parents, Mike and Judy Canning, and my sister, Rachel, for being my first and most loyal cheerleaders. You kept my spirits up when the going got toughest, and I feel incredibly lucky to have grown up with such an amazing family. An extra shout-out to Rachel for her ability to make me laugh until I can barely breathe.

To my husband, Bob, thank you for stepping up to keep the Blackwell household running whenever I got into "crazy writing" mode. I could not have done this without you. (Extra bonus points for regularly fixing breakfast for three children so I could sleep in after a late night of writing—the greatest gift a night-owl mother can get.) A special thanks to my daughter, Clara, whose many viewings of Disney's *Sleeping Beauty* led to the inspiration for this book.

To my fellow writers Jennifer Szostak, Mary Jean Babic, Mike Austin,

Adam Beechen, and Peter Gianopulos: Each of you gave me a crucial pep talk when my confidence was faltering, and somehow you knew just the right thing to say (clearly, you all have a way with words). This roller-coaster writer's life is a lot more fun with you along.

To my friends and fellow book lovers Sarah Lyke, Gayle Starr, Helen Widlansky, Laura Pryzby, and Barbara Kirchheimer: Your friendship and encouragement have enriched my life. I'm grateful I can call on you for a laugh, a sympathetic ear, or a good reading recommendation.

To my agent, Danielle Egan-Miller: Thank you for believing in this book—and me—from the very beginning. You are not only a passionate advocate and talented editor, but also great company (with fantastic taste in 1980s schlock fiction). Thanks also to Joanna MacKenzie for incisive editing and plot suggestions. Shelbey Campbell, you have my eternal gratitude for pulling me out of the slush pile.

To my editor, Amy Einhorn: Thank you for your encouragement, your passion for excellence, and the perfect title. I am a better writer for having worked with you. Thanks also to Liz Stein for her helpful guidance through the world of publishing.

Finally, I owe a debt to the musicians who inspired me through the many, many revisions of this story. Keane's *Under the Iron Sea*, Mumford & Sons' *Sigh No More*, and *Clarity* by Jimmy Eat World may have no obvious connection to Sleeping Beauty, but I think of those albums as the unofficial sound track of my book—music that created an atmosphere that felt true to Elise and Rose's world.

About the Author

A graduate of Northwestern University and Columbia University's Graduate School of Journalism, Elizabeth Blackwell has worked as a magazine editor and freelance writer. She lives in the Chicago suburbs with her husband, three children, and an ever-growing stack of bedside-table books.